FIRE WITCHES OF SALEM

COLLECTION ONE

THE CHAOS AND ASH TRILOGY

CARRIE PULKINEN

Fire Witches of Salem Collection One
Chaos and Ash
Commanding Chaos
Claiming Chaos

ISBN: 978-1-957253-21-3

CHAOS  AND ASH

FIRE WITCHES OF SALEM
BOOK ONE

CARRIE PULKINEN

CHAPTER

ONE

People loved to claim they were descendants of the witches they couldn't burn. We actually were. Our ancestors literally could not be set on fire. Neither could we. My sisters and I were elemental witches, and fire was ours to command. The veil between worlds was thin in Salem, and we belonged to the order of witches duty-bound to keep the monsters at bay.

We were the Veil Keepers.

Yep, the witches were the ones that kept Salem safe. Ironic, right? It had always been that way too. Good thing my ancestors couldn't burn, or this town—and everything around it—would've been screwed six ways to Sunday a long, long time ago.

Of course, they didn't burn witches in Salem. Everyone knew that. They hanged them here, pressed one of them to death, but my family originated in England. Back in the sixteen hundreds, my great-great-who-knows-how-many-greats-grandma was tied to a stake and set on fire. Well, the wood around her was set ablaze. The flames incinerated her clothes, and when the inferno extinguished, Granny stood there naked and unscathed, laughing at the astonished looks on their faces.

Man, I would've loved to have seen that. She might or might not have set the village on fire to make her escape. The details didn't matter. The important thing was that we were here in our little shop on the edge of downtown, preparing to take out yet another horde of monsters to keep safe the very people who would have murdered us four hundred years ago.

Fun times.

My sister Ember laid her forearm across the table, and I dipped my needle into the enchanted ink. Closing my eyes, I focused my energy, drawing from the goddess and infusing the sigil I was about to create with my vim.

"You're raiding a vampire nest, right? So, speed and strength?" With my fingers wrapped firmly around the grip, I pressed the tip of the needle against her skin and drew the first line.

"Vampire ghouls, but yeah."

Ick. There were two different levels of vamps in the world. First, the so-called normal kind, who could pass as humans. They still fried in the sunlight, but at night, a mundane wouldn't know them from one of their own. The other kind, ghouls, were disgusting. Imagine if a zombie and a vampire had a baby and the zombie traits were the dominant ones. Mind-less, bloodsucking monsters. My lip curled at the thought.

"Throw in a bit of protection, and I'll be set." Ember smiled, but her eyes were tight.

I pressed a little harder, clenching my teeth. "You know I don't do those."

She winced. "You could."

"I can't."

"I wish you had more self-confidence. You broke the family curse for Hecate's sake."

That much was true. Another witch cursed our bloodline centuries ago. The third daughter of every Holland mother would die in infancy. Once birth control became a thing, our ancestors stopped after two kids rather than risk losing a little girl. Well, they tried to anyway. My mom's pill failed, and I was the result. Somehow, she managed to keep me alive into adulthood, breaking the curse, but that didn't mean I was some kind of prophet or whatever. I got lucky. Nothing more.

I turned off the machine and sat back in my chair. "The last thing I need is you going into a vampire nest thinking you've got protection when you don't. I never mastered that sigil, and Cinder paid the price. I can't lose you too."

A shadow crossed her features, her gaze shifting downward before meeting mine. "We're going to find her."

"Are we? She searched for Mom and Dad for months, insisting they were alive, and now she's gone too. Who's next? You or me? We won't find her."

Her jaw tightened. I couldn't tell you how many times we'd had this conversation, yet no matter where we looked or what we tried, our sister had vanished, and I was to blame.

"Okay. Speed and strength will do." She pressed her lips

together, giving me what she probably thought was an expression of sympathy.

It looked like pity to me, and I was not having it. I picked up the machine and returned to her sigil, losing myself in the rhythmic pulse of the needles. I'd be lying if I said I didn't take a tiny bit of pleasure in knowing these things hurt like a bitch. It was "no pain, no gain" in the most literal sense.

Black ink penetrated her skin, the faint blue glow indicating my magic was infusing her with the desired properties. Okay, it wasn't all my magic. Mostly, I channeled the goddess and the power of the universe, the energy traveling into me and out through the enchanted ink. But my vim went into every sigil I tattooed, and it took a while to recharge when I'd done a lot, like tonight.

Ember was my last canvas out of five in the past hour. With a hunting party that big, they must've been expecting a slew of bloodsuckers to come out of that nest.

The fatigue was worth it to do my part. Goddess knew I couldn't fight a monster to save my life. That was why I was the coven librarian and Ember was the badass butt kicker.

"If you're not covered in vampire goo when you're done, do you want to have a drink at the Twisted Thistle?" I shook the tension from my hand before putting the finishing touch on her sigil, bringing the bottom loop down and around like the tail of a cursive G, ending it with a fine point, exactly how my dad had taught me.

She scrunched her nose. "I made plans with Shade and Chrys. Sorry."

"Oh." I tried to hide the disappointment in my voice, but I failed miserably. "That's okay. I should head to bed early, anyway. I'm re-cataloging the grimoires tomorrow. Dad's organizational skills were lacking at best. He never reshelved anything in the right place."

The back door opened, and Shade poked his head in. "Hurry it up in there. The sun's about to set, and I do not want to miss prime hunting time."

"Speak of the devil," I muttered as I wiped the excess ink from Ember's arm. Shade had been the earliest and most vocal witch in the coven to point out my inadequate fire magic. Not that he had any room to talk. He relied on incantations and enchanted artifacts—which he checked out from *my* library—to do his job. I might've been the lamest pyrokinetic in town, but he was the lamest witch all around. I fought the urge to stick my tongue out at him.

Ember pursed her lips, cutting her gaze toward the door he disappeared through before looking at me. "You know what? Why don't you come with us? If we are covered in ghoul guts, it'll be nice for someone else to drive. Congealing innards get sticky fast."

I tugged my dad's Zippo from my pocket and popped open the top. An orange flame grew from the center, flickering in response to my magic. "You want me to go monster hunting with you? I think you've forgotten what happened last time."

Her nostrils flared. There was a reason Ember knew all about ghoul guts, and that reason was me. "You can wait in the car. Be our getaway driver."

"I've been banned from hunting." I touched the flame to the new sigil on her arm, activating it, and the design glowed bright red before fading to a cool blue. The magic would last at least six hours. Once it dissipated, the tattoo would disappear along with her enhanced powers.

She arched a brow, admiring my work. "You're getting really good at this." She tugged her sleeve down. "And you won't be hunting. Just driving."

I laughed dryly. "I don't think the rest of the crew will go for it."

"They won't have a choice. I've made up my mind. You're coming." She rose to her feet and tossed me the keys. "Let's go."

"If you say so." I locked the shop and followed her out the back door. Our black van, complete with magically tinted windows and a hidden arsenal in the floor, sat in the alley behind the eighteenth-century building that had been in my family from the beginning.

The reason Ember was so sure the other witches wouldn't object to my tagging along was that they couldn't. Our parents were the High Priest and Priestess of the Salem order, as were my maternal grandparents and great-grandparents. Being in charge was our birthright, and when Mom and Dad died, the power passed to us.

Well, it passed to our older sister, Cinder. When she went MIA, Ember inherited the torch. And me? I was the introverted librarian tagging along for the ride on my family's coattails.

Actually, that's not fair. I wasn't an introvert. I just hated people.

A gust of wind whipped through the alley, blowing my hair

into my face. Blue strands stuck to my lip gloss, and as I peeled them off and pulled my locks out of my eyes, I found Shade glowering at me.

"Ember...?" His teeth didn't part as he spoke.

My sister smirked and smacked the hood of the van. "Load up. We're burning daylight."

Shade's mouth dropped open. "She's..."

Sis cut him a look that could have melted a glacier in one hot flash. She might have once threatened to roast his chestnuts on an open fire if he ever insulted my magic again, and she probably would have done it. Or at least singed them a bit.

His Adam's apple bobbed, and his right eye twitched. "She's not dressed for hunting."

I crossed my arms over my black corset and shifted my weight to my left leg. Shade wore black spandex pants with a matching shirt. His blond hair was slicked back into a man bun, and a pair of what looked like seatbelt straps crisscrossed his chest, holding a set of wooden stakes.

Chrys, the friendliest witch on the team, wore a similar outfit, though the leggings looked much better on her petite frame. Her chin-length jet-black bob shone in the fading sunlight, and she rolled her eyes, fighting a grin behind his back. Ember and the others wore the same kind of clothes. Take the weapons away, and they all could've been on their way to goth yoga.

"She might snag her tights." Shade crossed his arms to mimic me, so I parked my hands on my hips.

"Fishnets are replaceable. My boot up your ass might be permanent."

"Load. Up." Ember opened the passenger door and cocked her head at me.

"As you wish." This time, I did stick out my tongue.

If Shade glowered any harder, his skull might crack, but he did as he was told and climbed into the van with the others.

I slid into the driver's seat and started the engine. "Where are we headed?"

"The old cemetery outside town. Chrys spotted a few near the mausoleum just before sunrise this morning."

I nodded and reversed out of the alley before hanging a left on Washington. "Let's go kick some vampire butt."

Shade blew a hard breath through his nose, but I ignored him. He was still miffed because I wouldn't go on a second date with him last year. One night with an arrogant prick was more than enough, thank you very much.

The orange sun sank toward the horizon ahead, painting the sky in rich reds and purples. As we approached the top of the hill, the cemetery came into view. Most of the graves had simple headstones, many sinking at awkward angles due to years of neglect, but our target stood near the back fence. The decrepit mausoleum where who knew how many ghouls rested inside.

I pulled as close to the gates as possible, parking sideways so we could make a quick getaway if things got out of hand. Tension built inside the van, making my skin prick. With the sun so low in the sky, the tree's bare branches looked like black bones silhouetted against a watercolor canvas. Spindly fingers stretched across the canopy, their long shadows crisscrossing on the ground like an intricate web.

Leaving the engine running, I turned in my seat to look past the headrest. The witches behind me sat utterly still. Chrys pressed her palms together in prayer to the goddess, while Shade rested the tips of his middle fingers against his thumbs, his lips moving as he silently recited an incantation. Miles and Ginger in the way back seat closed their eyes, either in meditation or prayer. It was hard to tell with those two.

Ember took a deep breath and blew it out, ending her prayer to the goddess. "Everybody ready?"

"Almost," Ginger said.

I pursed my lips, a question forming in my mind. "If vampires fry in the sunlight, why do you wait until dusk to take them out? Seems like you could go in at noon, leave the door open, and stake them all in their sleep."

"Where's the fun in that?" Ember winked before sliding out of the van, and I rolled my eyes. Her life was in peril on a daily basis, and she wouldn't have it any other way. The threat of a mile-high stack of grimoires falling on me was the extent of danger in my life, but someone had to hold down the fort while the big kids played. Lucky me.

Chrys opened the side door, and the rest of the witches filed out of the van. She popped open the secret hatch in the floorboard and pulled out a utility belt with a few knives attached at the hip. The rest of her tools belonged in a garden. She had a spade, a hand-held hoe, and one of those thingamajigs with three claws at the end that was normally used for breaking up dirt. How her gear would help her fight vamps was a mystery to me. Earth witches were weird.

Ember grabbed her enchanted sword, a three-foot-long,

solid silver blade with a fireproof rosewood handle and skull pommel. She swiped it through the air as if testing its balance, which was totally unnecessary. She'd had the thing for five years, so she was probably showing off. After twirling it at her side, she gripped it in both hands, blade pointing to the sky. Fire erupted at the hilt, cascading upward until flames engulfed the entire blade.

Yep, definitely showing off.

The rest of the witches pounded pavement toward the gate, but Ember hung back, giving me that supposed-sympathy-but-looked-like-pity expression. "You'll be okay waiting in the van?"

I held up my phone. "I've got three ereader apps and a million books in my TBR. I'll be fine. I might even take a nap."

She nodded and slid the door shut before joining the rest of the crew. They hopped over the waist-high brick fence, not bothering with the gate, and prowled through the cemetery. I could practically hear the dry leaves crunching beneath their boots as they shrank into the darkness and disappeared. Shade's shadow magic came in handy sometimes. I had no problem admitting that, despite his sour demeanor.

While the big kids went off to play with monsters, I clicked my favorite reading app and opened the next installment of the romance series I was addicted to. My goal was to read one hundred novels this year. I still had forty to go and only three months to do it. If these damn monsters would stay on their side of the veil, it would be easy-peasy. With the way things were going lately, I might not make it.

I rolled down the window, stuck my feet through the

opening, and sank into my seat, losing myself in the story. Reading had a way of making time stand still and move at warp speed all at once. I wasn't sure how long I'd been sitting there when the shouts echoed from the mausoleum, but it couldn't have been that long. I'd only devoured three chapters.

I snapped my head toward the cemetery, squinting as I peered into the trees. Shade and his damn shadow magic. I couldn't see a thing. I mean, sure, we had to hide ourselves from the humans. If they knew what monsters lurked in the darkness of their quaint little town, all hell would break loose. They'd destroy each other faster than the monsters ever could, so secrecy mattered.

But it didn't stop the irritation bubbling in my gut. I wasn't part of the hunting party, so I was as blind as a human out here in the van.

"Ember!" Chrys screamed, and a flash of firelight illuminated the mausoleum for half a second.

My pulse thrummed, and I sat upright, shoving my phone into the cupholder. Shouting was normal, right? They loved it when the monsters fought back. Danger was wired into their DNA.

The shadows flickered, Shade's magic faltering. That was also normal. Using magic drained us. Even a master witch couldn't hold on to a spell forever.

Another shout. A smack like a body hitting concrete. A pained grunt.

It was the vamps getting their undead asses kicked. Ember was the toughest witch in Salem. She might've been a little reckless, but so were most adrenaline junkies. It was fine. Everything was fine.

Until it wasn't.

The magical shadows rolled toward the mausoleum, billowing at the base of the door before dissipating into the ground. Actually, no. Not the ground. Into Shade. He lay flat on his back, a bloodsucker pinning his shoulders down.

Crap. Where was everyone? Shade was a pain in my rear end, but I didn't want to see him become dinner for the undead.

I opened the door, and my boots thudded on the pavement as I hopped out of the van. My chest burned, my fire magic concentrating in the center of my being. Ember described the sensation as a raging inferno, but to me, it felt like heartburn. The warming sensation spread down my arms until my fingers tingled. My leg muscles tightened, and my stomach clenched as I prepared to sprint into the fray.

But before I could take a step, Ember emerged from the mausoleum, her flame-licked sword swinging through the air and slicing the vampire's head clean off. She kicked the corpse, and it rolled to the ground before melting into goo. After giving Shade a hand up, they both raced back inside.

The final rays of sun disappeared behind the horizon, and I was about to return to the safety of the van and the comfort of my book when movement around the side of the structure caught my eye. A shirtless vampire crept toward a five-foot marble cross, its pale skin gleaming in the moonlight. Dark red blood rimmed its mouth, making my stomach sour. Hopefully the vamp had made a mess of his meal last night, and it wasn't my friend's life force smeared across his face. I held my breath, waiting for a witch to dart out after him, but he kept creeping, and no one noticed.

Well, crapity crap. I couldn't let the monster leave the cemetery. I might have been banned from hunting, but I was still a Veil Keeper, and it was my responsibility to keep the city safe. I chewed my bottom lip, scrunching my nose as the vamp made it halfway to the gate.

I should alert the others, call for Ember or Chrys to come out and nab the bloodsucker. They had the tools and the skills to take it out easily. I had neither. Swallowing the lump in my throat, I forced a scream, "Vamp overboard!"

The commotion inside the mausoleum continued as if I'd only whispered. The vampire, however, heard me just fine. He stopped, tilting his head and looking at me like I was the most delicious slice of blueberry blood pie he'd ever seen. Baring his fangs, he hissed and bolted toward me.

Great plan, Ash. Shouting was definitely the way to go.

My palms tingled, sparks dancing around my fingertips as I bounced on my toes three times. Then I ran. My boots gripped the pavement, propelling me forward, and thank the goddess, I reached the stone wall before the vamp. I planted one hand on top of the fence, kicking up my legs and clearing it easily. I'd have to send my high school track coach my thanks when this was done.

There were four ways to kill a vampire: sunlight, fire, beheading, and a stake through the heart. Since I didn't have a sword or a UV lamp, my inborn gift of flames would have to do. That and a swift kick to the gut.

I planted my boot in the vamp's stomach, and he stumbled backward into a pile of dead leaves. Rubbing my hands together, I willed the heat to gather in my palms. My fingertips crackled, and as I curled them inward, the sparks ignited.

"Hey, Drac. I've got a kiss for you." I held up my hand and blew on the tiny flame growing from my palm. Fire rolled across my fingers and dropped to the ground a foot shy of my fangy foe. Whoops. I'd been aiming for his pants, but the leaves made perfect fodder for burning him alive...umm...undead.

It hadn't rained in weeks, and the dried shrubbery lit up like a bonfire, taking the vampire with it. He wailed as the flames consumed him, leaving behind nothing of his body but goo and ashes. Enemy number one vanquished. Why was I banned from monster hunting again?

I walked into the fire, being careful not to ruin my boots in the sludge that was once a vampire, and stomped out the flames. Well, my plan was to stomp out the flames. The problem was, they'd already spread out in a four-foot circle and licked upward into a thick spruce. Uh oh.

This was magical fire, though. I should have been able to pull it back inside. To extinguish the flames with my power, just like I'd lit them to begin with. With a deep inhale, I focused again, imagining a cool fog rolling over the flames, putting them out.

The fire grew hotter. The flames jumped from the burning spruce to a maple. You'd think bare branches would take a while to ignite, but no. Magical fire, remember? The inferno jumped from tree to tree, thick gray smoke billowing into the sky.

"Ember…" I backed away from the chaos I'd created before turning on my heel and darting toward the mausoleum. "Ember, I screwed up again!"

My boot caught on an exposed root, and I tumbled toward the entrance, scraping my knees on the concrete. I shot to my feet and launched myself through the door, straight into the path of the last vampire attempting to flee. It smacked into me, our skulls knocking together with a crack before I careened back and it landed on top of me, fangs bared.

I struggled beneath its weight, but it reared back, ready to strike like a viper.

Shade appeared above my head, his face pinched like he'd sucked on a lemon and whiffed a foul fart at the same time. He jabbed a blade into the vamp's back and twisted it before yanking it out. He'd saved my life.

He had not bothered to remove the corpse from atop my body, however. His sour expression turned to one of smugness as the vampire's form melted into a gelatinous mess right on top of me. Cool, sticky goo rolled over me, soaking my corset and making my skin crawl. It smelled of rotten fish and sulfur, and a bit of the nastiness dripped from my cheek backward to my ear.

Covered in ghoul guts. That was what I got for trying to help them.

Ember offered her hand, so I accepted the gesture and let her tug me to my feet. She pointed a finger at the goo on the ground, and a flame shot out, incinerating it. If I wanted to keep my clothes, I'd have to wait until I got home to wash the mess off myself.

"Ash..." Chrys called from the doorway, her voice incredulous. "What did you do?"

"I stopped a vampire from escaping." I followed her out the door to find the entire cemetery engulfed in flames. Heat permeated the threshold like when you first opened an oven door, and the blaze crackled, tree branches snapping and falling to the ground.

"You lit the place on fire." Chrys kneeled, digging her hands into the dirt. She whispered an incantation, and a shockwave extended out in a circle, dirt rising and falling on top of the fire.

Her attempt helped. She extinguished the flames on the ground, but she couldn't do anything about the trees. "Where's a water witch when we need one?" she said as she rose to her feet.

"Can't you call the fire back?" Miles asked.

I held in a dry laugh. He hadn't been in the coven long, but he should have known better. *Everybody* knew better.

"Her magic doesn't work like that," Ember said in my defense.

"It should," I muttered under my breath.

Sirens blasted in the distance, growing louder as they approached, and Ginger jerked her head toward the van. "The humans will handle it. Let's jet."

"Agreed." Ember nodded. "Cloak us, Shade."

The air thickened as the shadow magic activated. Everything took on a grayish tinge, meaning we could see the world but the world couldn't see us. If only I could unsee the vampire guts dripping from my corset.

We ran to the van, Ember heading to the driver's side. I

tossed her the keys and opened the passenger door. As I climbed inside, Shade stopped beside me and eyed my bloodied knees.

"I told you you'd snag your tights." He smirked and crawled into the back seat.

I hated it when he was right.

"Good morning, sunshine." Ember gave me a tentative smile and gestured to the wad of black plastic in my hand. "What's in the bag?"

"What's left of my corset. I didn't get the ghoul guts off in time, and it ate a hole through the lining." I clutched the bag and brushed past her in the narrow hallway. Damn vampires needed to stay in the spirit realm where they belonged. There were plenty of reasons ghosts, ghouls, and faeries lived in another dimension, and toxic innards were near the top of the list.

"I'll get you a new one on my way home from work." She followed behind me, matching my pace as I went down the stairs and out the back door.

"No need. I've got plenty." I tossed the bag into the dumpster and gestured to the corset I had on. They really weren't as uncomfortable as people made them out to be. Plus, I had a tendency to slump, and the snug fit reminded me to stand up straight and be the proud elemental witch I was. Ha.

Ember twirled her keys around her finger before clutching them in her hand. "Yeah, but it's my fault you were at the cemetery last night."

"And it's my fault for trying to use my defective fire magic and burning the place to the ground."

A familiar look of pity pinched her features, so I shook my head and said, "I'm a librarian and sigil artist. I should know better by now."

She shifted her weight to her right leg. "You were tired. Five sigils in a row would have taken a toll on Dad too. I bet if you'd had time to recover properly, you would have—"

"I wouldn't."

"You might have…"

I sighed and tilted my head. I knew my place, and I should have stayed in it.

She glanced at her phone and held the screen toward me. "The humans put out the fire. At least now they might do some upkeep on the place, take care of the graves."

"Mm-hmm." I stood in the doorway, leaning my shoulder against the jamb.

Ember returned her phone to her pocket. "I'm heading to work. Want to grab dinner at Rockafellas when I get home?"

"Sure." I waved as she climbed into her black Jeep and drove away.

Ember worked at Spellbound Axe, which was perfect for

her. She got paid to teach people how to throw sharp objects. Being the coven librarian was a full-time job—the perfect job for me—so membership dues paid my salary. With my home upstairs and the library and shop downstairs, I rarely left the building. Last night was a reminder why.

Before I could spin the disco ball at my pity party for one, I locked the back door and headed for the library. My Mary Janes thudded on the hardwood as I stepped into my sanctuary and took a deep breath. The musty smell of old books filled my senses, relaxing the tension in my shoulders. I rolled my neck and inhaled again.

Ahhh... This was where I belonged.

To the right lay the arsenal. Dozens upon dozens of magical artifacts sat on the wooden shelves, each one labeled with its purpose, instructions, and remedy. I had created the laminated cards for the items because a couple of inexperienced witches botched the spells a while ago.

People weren't supposed to check out items unless they'd done their research and knew how to use them, but when a seventeen-year-old, who was trying to cure his genital warts with magic, came running in with boils covering his entire body, I had to drop everything and look up a spell to reverse the hex he'd cast on himself. I wasn't a healer by any means, but research was my department, so I helped him.

Of course, I told him to see a real doctor for his problem. Magic couldn't fix everything, and a warty wiener was better than puss-filled boils any day of the week.

So, every artifact now came with instructions, thanks to

me. That project was complete, so it was time to organize the grimoires.

I hit the switch on the wall, and the overhead lights hummed to life, casting a dim, warm glow on the tomes. Wooden cabinets lined the other three walls, while six rows of shelves stood in the center of the room. Ancient texts stood next to new editions, and stacks of books that needed to be reshelved sat in the aisles, making it nearly impossible to find anything.

When my dad ran the library, he'd locate the books by sense. If he closed his eyes and said a location spell, his magic would lead him to the volume he needed. I could do that too, but it would be a helluva lot easier if they were organized. The Dewey Decimal System was still in use for a reason.

It worked.

I started with the sigil books, since those were the most familiar. I'd studied them from cover to cover when I was training to be Ink Master, and though I rarely needed to crack one open anymore, they were my favorite. Embossed sigils adorned the deep burgundy covers, and as I ran my fingers over the first volume, magic tingled on my skin.

I set it on the shelf nearest my desk and picked up the next one on the stack, volume three. Where was two? The books left in the pile were volumes six, four, eight, seven, and nine, in that order. I couldn't very well organize them if I didn't have all the books, so I scanned the cabinets along the wall, looking for the burgundy cover. Nothing.

Creeping down the aisle between the piles of books, I searched and searched. A thick layer of dust coated the shelves and everything on them. It looked like I'd be getting after the entire room with a feather duster soon.

The next aisle of books was even worse. Volumes thrown haphazardly on the shelves created a chaos that made my muscles crawl beneath my skin. It would take weeks to organize this mayhem, and if I didn't find sigil book two, I'd never sleep at night. Looked like it was time to use magic.

Straightening my shoulders, I tipped my head toward the sky...I mean ceiling...and called on my magic. "What was lost will be found. Near or far, show me where you are."

The vibrating energy in the room stilled, leaving only a faint tickle above my head. That was weird. If the book were in the library, I would have been pulled right to it. Instead, the weak vibration came from far away...as in upstairs. What was it doing up there? I hadn't cracked open a sigil book in ages, so it couldn't be in my room.

I ground my teeth. "Ember..."

Why on earth would she be studying sigils? Wasn't it enough that she was good at *everything* else? Sigils were supposed to be my thing.

I stomped out of the library, up the stairs, and through the kitchen. She'd left her cereal bowl in the sink again, which made my irritation with her double. When I reached the hallway, I expected the vibration to pull me into the first bedroom, Ember's. Instead, it led me farther down, past my room, and toward Cinder's.

Okay, that was weird. Cinder always made a big deal out of me and my ink, so I couldn't fathom why she'd be studying them. Leave it to the oldest to coddle the youngest, right?

Honestly, I appreciated her encouragement more than she knew.

I hesitated in the doorway. I hadn't set foot inside her room since she disappeared. Ember had gone in, looking for clues as to where she might have gone, but she'd found nothing. No notes scribbled on scraps of paper. No maps to her location. Nada.

With a deep inhale, I crossed the threshold. The moment I stepped inside, the sigil book's vibration stilled. I whispered the location spell again, but nothing happened.

"Huh." I took a giant step backward, into the hallway, and poof. The magic took hold, pulling me back into Cinder's room. "Strange."

Poof again. The book's vibration stopped the second I crossed the threshold.

"What have you been up to, big sister?" I straightened my shoulders. Time to find out exactly what she'd done. "Confess, expose my magic sleuth. I call on you to reveal your truth."

Golden sparkles gathered in the air, revealing a thick gray cloud billowing from the ceiling, stretching down and engulfing the entire space. She'd cast a cloaking spell to hide something, and unless I removed it, my location magic would be useless in her room.

I stepped out and ran to the kitchen to mix up a quick potion. Solomon's seal, star anise, and a pinch of basil formed the base of my spell. I mixed everything together, and as I added a drop of lavender oil, pink smoke rose from the bowl, the mixture turning into a fine powder.

Back in Cinder's room, I blew the dust into the air and said, "Magic cloak, I now revoke."

The moment the final word crossed my lips, Cinder's spell fought back, slapping me across the face like a scorned lover. The gray cloud thickened, swirling around me and making my skin sting. I made the mistake of breathing it in. My nostrils burned as if my dear, sweet oldest sister had shot a stream of fire from her fingertips straight up my nose.

I coughed and stumbled back into the hall. "What the actual eff, Cin?"

Why would she need a spell that strong in her bedroom? All I wanted was to find sigil book volume two, but apparently, even in her absence...or her death—I wasn't ruling it out yet—Cinder thought that was too much to ask.

Shaking off the essence of her uber-mega-ridiculously-too-strong-spell—what was she hiding?—I crossed the threshold for the fourth, and hopefully final, time. I'd have to find the book the mortal way.

A quick scan of her bookcase revealed nothing of use. A high school yearbook, a few horror novels, a figurine of a black cat dressed like a reaper. Her nightstand stood empty on top. I was afraid of what I might find in the drawer, but I had to look.

My lip curled. Great. Now I'd seen my sister's vibrator, a hot pink number with a little tail sticking out the front...or maybe it was for the back? Either way, it was a sight I couldn't unsee.

"Why are you making this so hard, Cinder?"

I went for the underwear drawer next. I'd already seen what she put inside her hoo-ha, so I might as well rummage through what she covered it with. Black lace and pink satin.

Nothing kinky, thank the goddess. Also, no book. I didn't find it any of her drawers, so I moved on to the closet.

Shoving her shirts aside, I fumbled through the small space. Every pair of shoes, minus the ones she had on when she went MIA, sat in an orderly fashion along the wall. She had a few boxes on the shelf above the hangers, but none were big enough to hold the tome I was searching for.

I dropped to the floor, my knees thudding on the wood. I didn't have a clue why she had felt the need to hide my book, but my irritation tipped to frustration. Next would come anger, and I refused to be mad at a dead woman. *Possibly dead*, I corrected myself.

"Seriously, Cin. What else are you hiding?" I felt along the baseboards, searching for a secret panel in the wall or the floor. Yes, Ember rummaged through her room when she first went missing, but my middle sister wasn't the greatest at attention to detail. She'd told me she checked for hidey holes, and I'd taken her word for it so I wouldn't have to come into this room and deal with the emotions it might dredge up.

I missed the heck out of Cinder. My parents too. But I refused to get all blubbery over it again. Tears wouldn't bring them back. Actions might, but so far, none of our attempts had done a lick of good.

We'd tried scrying, location spells, talking to everyone who knew her, even in passing. Nothing. It was like she'd dropped off the face of the earth. We'd even filed a missing person report with the human police. She either didn't want to be found or she really had disintegrated into the ether. That or she somehow got sucked through to the other side of the veil, and if that were the case, she was as good as gone forever.

Anyway, I'd managed to keep the feels in check thus far. No need to go slogging down memory lane now.

I followed the floorboards around the entire room and didn't find any panels. Ember had done a good job after all. A sweep of my phone's flashlight beneath the bed revealed nothing but a few dust bunnies. No latches. No disturbances in the wood. That left one place Ember might have missed.

Rising to my feet, I tugged on the mattress, but it didn't budge. Weird. It wasn't some ultra-thick support mattress. I should have been able to at least slide it to the side, but it was stuck. Magically stuck.

"Cinder, Cinder. I've found your secret stash, haven't I?" I hovered my hands above the sheets, and sure enough, magic tingled on my palms. A simple weight spell held the mattress in place, or so I assumed. The cloaking spell masked the true magic, so she must've counted on that to do all the work. This weight spell was Witchy 101 stuff. I didn't even need a potion to cancel it, as long as she hadn't amplified it to fight back. Surely she wouldn't do that to me twice.

"Light as a feather, soft as down, I turn this spell right around." The air thickened and then popped, releasing the pressure as the charm disintegrated.

My stomach tightened as my fingers slid beneath the mattress. Lifting it was a breeze without the spell in place, and lo and behold, there on the boxed springs sat volume two of my sigil collection. Next to it lay a leather-bound book with the

Tree of Life debossed on the cover. A piece of brown twine wrapped around it, securing the pages closed.

I grabbed them both before letting the mattress fall back into place. Why in the goddess's name would she hide this volume? Or better yet, *who* was she hiding it from?

Not me. I'd memorized every sigil in this book years ago, and Ember couldn't be bothered to learn them. I pursed my lips, my gaze shifting from my book to the leather one.

"Ugh. Whatever." I had it back, and that was what mattered. Now I could get on with the cataloging I should have done a month ago.

I pulled the door shut behind me and made my way downstairs to the library, where I dropped into my chair and laid the books on the desk. The leather one I had never seen before, so I untied the twine and opened it to what should have been the title page. But this wasn't a book. It was a diary.

Cinder's diary.

I slammed it shut and fumbled with the twine. Once I secured it, I slid it into the drawer and rested my elbows on the desk, pressing my fingers to my temples. I didn't keep a diary myself. My innermost thoughts were best left deep in the recesses of my mind, and my sister's needed to remain in hers.

Eyeing the journal in the open drawer, I chewed my bottom lip. It was tempting, I'd give it that, and if I were ten years younger, I would have dived right in. At twenty-four, I could control my urges now...most of the time.

I shoved it closed and picked up the sigil volume, fanning through the pages. As I rose to place it on the shelf, a thick piece of yellowing parchment drifted to the floor. Huh. This book was old, but not *that* old. The pages had just begun to turn around the edges. The loose one could've been printed a few hundred years ago.

I snatched it up and sank into my chair before turning on the desk lamp. My pulse sprinted as I unfolded it and found a set of three sigils I had never seen before. Centered down the middle of the page, the symbols appeared hand drawn. The patterns of the ink indicated the artist had used a quill rather than a pen. Intricate arrays of curved and straight lines criss-crossed and coiled into elaborate designs no amateur could accomplish with a tattoo machine. These were graduate-level sigils, if I'd ever seen any.

The only other writing on the page was a single word beneath each design:

Chaos.

Mayhem.

Discord.

"What the ever-loving...?" I traced my finger over the top design. The coarseness of the paper felt rough against my skin. "Where did you get this, Cin?"

The back of the page was blank. No header or footer or even a page number to give a clue as to where it came from. A black magic tome, possibly? Maybe, but no sinister vibrations emanated from the page. I couldn't feel any magic at all. Could Cinder have neutralized it?

I wasn't sure, but curiosity had me itching to try one out. Power over chaos? Yes, please. With a snap of my fingers, I could have the library organized and cataloged in an instant. Maybe then I could catch up on my reading goal.

Long strides carried me out of the library toward the front of the building. My tattoo machine sat on its stand, a fresh supply of ink on the shelf above it. I set the parchment on the table, but I hesitated to set up the device.

My dad had warned me never to try a new sigil alone, and he was talking about the ones from our collection. Without knowing where this one came from, I had no clue how my body would react if I did it wrong.

But when was the last time I'd messed up a sigil—besides protection, which was the trickiest one? Years ago, at least. I was well on my way to becoming an Ink Master if I still had a master to train under.

I crossed my arms, tapping my foot as I stared at the page. Ember would be gone for hours. My inbox was empty, which meant no one had leads on any new disturbances in the veil. The coven wouldn't need me for a while, and if anyone botched a spell, they could see our resident healer, Patrice.

The front door was still locked. I had an hour before the tourist shop was supposed to open. A smile tugged at my lips. "Let's do this."

Was it reckless? Probably, but Ember didn't own the market on heedless decisions. Bookish girls could be rebellious too.

Besides, our lives had been total chaos for six months, first with my parents' deaths and then with Cinder's disappearance. A little control over the uncontrollable would be welcomed by us all.

I practiced first with pen and paper, gently tracing the design to get a feel for the dips and curves. Sigil tattoos had to be drawn freehand for the magic to work, so I drew it on another sheet and compared the two. It was as perfect a match as could be. Easy peasy. I had this.

With my mind made up, I poured the magical ink into my favorite well and rolled up my sleeve. If this sigil lasted the full six hours, imagine what I could get done. Excitement bubbled in my stomach as I attached the needle and turned on the machine.

The first curve of the design hurt like a bitch. The skin on the inside of the wrist was thin, which made it a painful place for tattoos. Chaos's symbol was long, though, so I needed my entire forearm to make sure I got the proportions right.

I winced with the next line. I'd forgotten just how painful these could be. The third line extended up my arm, almost to my elbow, before bending down and swirling a bit like a treble clef. Deep breath in. Long exhale. The needle pulsed in and out of my skin so rapidly that the noise sounded like a vibration.

Sharp pain in my temple told me I was clenching my teeth, so I relaxed my jaw and put the final swoop on the design. My entire body tingled. Both channeling magic and receiving it felt like the kind of adrenaline rush you'd get before skydiving. Or so I imagined. You'd never see me jumping out of a perfectly good airplane on purpose.

With the machine back on its rack, I held up my arm to admire my work. It looked exactly like the original. Time to light this baby up.

I reached into my pocket for the Zippo, but my hand met an empty pouch of fabric. I patted down my jeans, but the familiar metal rectangle didn't protrude from any of my pockets. Crappity crap. I must've left it in my room.

Call me lazy, but I did not feel like traipsing all the way back upstairs to get it. Ember would tell me to use my fire magic. A little spark was all I needed to activate the sigil. If I had drawn this on anyone else, I wouldn't dare. One little flash from me would likely go haywire and singe someone's eyebrows.

A new sigil on myself, though... Why the hell not?

I rubbed the tips of my fingers against my thumb, charging up my magic. My palm pricked with energy, and I focused it into my index finger before pointing it at my arm. Heat rolled from my chest outward until a tiny flame shot out, lighting the design on fire.

It glowed bright crimson like it was supposed to, but as the flames subsided, it didn't fade to cool blue. The sigil remained red, undulating like hot magma flowing through a tunnel.

Uh oh. That didn't look good.

Nausea churned in my stomach, and my breakfast threatened to make a reappearance. My head spun. I squeezed my eyes shut and waited for the dizzying sensation to pass. A garbled roar sounded from somewhere outside, but I couldn't be bothered to look out the window. I was too busy trying to keep from passing out.

"Ouch. Son of a bitch." I clutched my head, applying pressure to counter the skull-splitting sensation.

The garbled roar grew louder. *"Who dares summon Chaos?"*

Seriously? Was another tour guide going off-script? Our city was so rich in history and horror, yet some tour companies always felt the need to embellish the truth for better ratings.

Wait. Did he say...chaos? The sigil on my arm pulsed. Nah, that would be too much of a coincidence. Still...

I stumbled to the window to get a look at the culprit, but the street lay empty. Not a soul in sight. The roar filled my head, nearly bursting my eardrums. *"Answer me!"*

My stomach lurched. I barely made it to the trash can in time to stop the partially digested fruity cereal from spilling all over the floor. I heaved again, and again the voice roared.

Holy mother of the devil himself. That raspy, roaring voice hadn't come from outside. It had come from inside.

Inside *me*.

CHAPTER

THREE

I swear my brain rattled in my skull; the voice shook me so hard. My stomach was finally empty, though, so that was a plus. Pressing the heels of my hands against my temples, I stumbled to my feet. A growl rumbled between my ears. What the hell had I just done?

The page of sigils lay on the counter, so I grabbed it and paced to the library. This headache was bad enough to unalive me. Hopefully it wouldn't hinder my magic before I found a cure. I had to find the book of healing spells before I passed out from the pain. If the library was organized like it was supposed to be, I could open a drawer, find the little card for the book I needed, and know exactly where it was. Or, if it was organized like the plans I had for it, I could type *spell to relieve headaches* into the computer, and I'd get a list of possibilities with their locations in the stacks.

Instead, I had to use a location spell. A spell to find a freaking spell.

"Release me, witch," the rumbling voice demanded.

"Believe me, buddy. As soon as I figure out how, I will." I closed my eyes and took a deep breath, preparing for the incantation.

"Release me now! Where is my skull?" he screamed and then roared so loud my entire body shook.

"I don't have your skull, but you're about to crack mine." I clutched my head, my nostrils flaring as I blew out a breath. "Listen, man...or monster. Whatever you are, if you don't quiet down, I'm going to black out. Then I won't be able to help either of us. I have to fix me before I can figure out how to fix you, so shut the eff up for a minute, okay?"

He growled at a tolerable level this time.

"What was lost will be found. Near or far, show me where you are." I'd done this spell so many times I didn't need a potion to activate it. The book tugged me toward it, and relief flooded my veins. I grabbed the volume from the shelf and returned to my desk to find headaches in the index. The pages rustled as I flipped to the spell.

"Thank the goddess." It was a simple one. No potion required for this one, either. "May the light of the goddess lift my pain. My headache will ease like a cleansing rain."

The splitting agony reduced to a dull ache, and I could finally think. Holy mother of magic. I had a voice inside my head, and it wasn't the running dialog I constantly had with myself. My forearm throbbed, and I laid it on the table to find the sigil pulsing red.

"That is my mark."

The pain in my head intensified, making me wince. "I need you to use your inside voice. You know...since you're *inside* my head."

"Why is my mark on your person?"

My person? Who talked like that? Better question... "Who are you?"

"I am Chaos—" he started to boom.

I clutched my head again. "If that's your inside voice, then you need to whisper. Seriously."

A soft growl rumbled between my ears. *"I am Chaos, Prince of Hell. Why did you summon me?"*

"Prince of..." A maniacal giggle bubbled from my throat. No way. I had not done what I thought I'd just done. "You're..." I bit my lip. "You're saying you're a demon?"

"A Prince of Hell."

"Which is a demon." I picked up the page of sigils. *Demonic* sigils. Oof.

"I am no simple fiend. I am of the highest level in Hell, a commander of armies, a destroyer of all who vex me."

"Right, but you're still a demon. I mean, all the creatures of Hell are some sort of demon, princes included. Is that correct?"

He grunted, clearly displeased with my assessment. *"Yes."*

"Great. Now we're getting somewhere. You're a demon prince, and you're inside my head. Want to tell me how you got there?" Because the only sigil I had ever flubbed was Cinder's protection tattoo.

I laid my arm next to the design on the paper. It was a perfect match, so there had to be another reason why, instead of harnessing power over chaos, I'd invited *Chaos* to take up space in my head.

"How did you summon me from my imprisonment?"

Fantabulous. Not only had I possessed myself with a demon prince, but I'd nabbed one straight from his prison cell. He must've been a bad, bad boy. "Who threw you in the brig? Lucifer himself, Hades, or do you report to someone in the middle?"

"How did you summon me, witch?"

I blew out an exasperated breath. "We aren't getting anywhere ignoring each other's questions. First off, I have a name. It's Ash, and I want you to use it. You say witch like it's a bad thing to be."

"It's an abominable thing to be!"

"You think so, eh? And demons are soooo nice to be around." Frakity frak. This guy had to go. Rather than sitting around and arguing with the voice in my head, I should be finding a spell to kick him to the curb. What volume would have the steps to perform an exorcism?

My own growl rumbled in my throat as I slammed the healing book shut and focused my energy. "What was lost will be found. Near or far, show me where you are. Exorcisms."

"What are you doing, wi...Ash? You cannot exorcise a Prince of Hell. Not without my skull."

"Watch me." I rummaged through the stack of books where I felt the magic pull me, but the one the spell had led me to was for exiling fae back across the veil. Still, I flipped through the pages in hopes it had a chapter on demons. The most useful thing I found was a healing salve to spread over a faery bite.

Those nasty little suckers had mouths full of razors. Tinkerbells they were not.

I cast the location spell again, this time making sure to focus on demon exorcisms. A crooked stack of books stood in front of me, threatening to tumble to the floor, but I couldn't be bothered with it. I tiptoed around it, swinging my hips away from the pile to avoid giving it any incentive, and made my way to the back of the room.

The overhead lights barely illuminated this part of the library, so I relied on the magic to guide me to the right book. Covered with black leather, the tome vibrated in my hands as I picked it up and carried it back to my desk. An embossed pentagram took up most of the front cover, and the spine creaked when I opened it.

Fabulous. It was written entirely in Latin.

I whipped out my trusty cell phone and opened the translate app. Hovering the camera over the first page, I let it do its thing. You'd think, with how advanced AI was and all, that someone would have invented a spell-casting app by now. Just tell the software what you wanted to do, and it would scan all the documents on the witchy web and find you the perfect incantation.

Maybe I'd work on that after I organized the coven library. One thing at a time, Ash, and right now, I needed to get Chaos out of my head.

"Your attempts will be futile." At least he'd learned to modulate his volume. *"No simple witch can banish me."*

"I'm no simple witch." Now it was my turn to boast. "I'm Ash Holland, as in the Holland witches of Salem. Direct descendent of the first High Priestess on this continent. The women in my family are so important, the men take *our* last name." Not that I was all that important myself, but our lineage sure as hell was.

"*A Holland witch,*" he grumbled.

"Damn straight. Now that you know who you're dealing with, zip it so I can send you on your way, mm-kay?"

He responded with silence. Halleluiah.

With the help of the translation app, I found an incantation for banishing a demon across the veil. It wasn't *exactly* an exorcism, but it was close enough. I hoped. The translator was far from perfect, but I knew enough Latin to get the gist of what this spell would do. Honestly, I didn't care where it sent Chaos, as long as he vacated my head.

Closing my eyes, I centered myself. "Goddess, please assist me in banishing this demon. As I will it, so mote it be."

Magic tingled in my stomach, working its way up to my chest. I lit the appropriately colored candles and smudged the four corners of the room with white sage.

"*That scent is atrocious.*"

"Of course it is to you, *demon.*" I dripped as much disdain from the last word as my current state of focus would allow. "Now shut it."

Tracing my finger along the words, I recited the incantation, doing my absolute best to pronounce the syllables right. A long E spoken with a short sound could be the difference between banishing this creature and turning my beautiful blue locks into swamp moss.

Yes, I knew that from experience.

When I'd uttered the final word, I closed my eyes, inhaling deeply and bracing myself for whatever it felt like to have a demon forcibly removed from your body. I'd seen plenty of movies about it, but I highly doubted it would be as painful as if a Catholic priest were in charge. Witches did everything with more finesse.

So much more finesse, in fact, that I didn't even feel the creature leave my body. "Huh. That didn't hurt at all."

"That is because I'm still here."

"Well, crap."

"I told you it wouldn't work. You cannot remove me from your person without my skull in your possession. You should not have been able to summon me without it."

I dropped into my seat, the chair creaking as it absorbed my weight. Looked like a squirt of WD-40 was in order for this thing. Hey, witches didn't use magic for everything. We'd exhaust ourselves with menial tasks and have nothing left for the important stuff like monster hunting...and book cataloging.

Flipping through the pages of this ancient text, I scanned the Latin with my phone, hoping to find a more specific exorcism spell. No luck.

"Why is my mark on your person?" Chaos asked, his voice dripping with annoyance.

I was the one with a demon knocking around inside my skull. If anyone should be annoyed, it was me. Then again, he didn't possess me on purpose. Maybe a little communication with the beast wouldn't hurt.

"Most draw a demon's mark on the ground inside a sacred circle before summoning him."

"Yeah, well, I didn't know these were demon-summoning symbols. We're a light coven; dark magic is forbidden. I thought I was going to harness power over chaos and organize my library."

A deep chuckle reverberated in my chest, but it didn't come from me. *"You summoned a Prince of Hell for organizational reasons?"*

"You don't listen very well. I just said I didn't know these were demon marks." Wait. Was he listening to my actual voice, or could he read my thoughts? Maybe I was wasting my breath. *"Can you hear me now? Can you read my mind?"*

"You are an Ink Master. That explains your ability to draw me from my prison."

"I'm not an Ink Master." I waited for a response, giving him more than a beat or two to reply to my argument. When he didn't, I figured he couldn't actually read my mind. "My dad was the Ink Master. I'm just the apprentice."

"Self-deprecation is rarely a quality in a witch with your level of power. You are an Ink Master. You would not have been able to summon me into your person otherwise. Or did your father summon me, using you as a vessel?"

My nose scrunched involuntarily. "Will you stop calling my body my 'person'? It's weird. And I am not a vessel. My dad is dead. I did this. I will fix it."

"You are the Ink Master and a fire witch. The most powerful Veil Keeper in Salem."

I snorted. "Hardly."

"It's the truth."

"Sure." I couldn't stop the laugh rolling up from my belly if I tried. "You're a funny little demon."

"You have no concept of my size. I am a mighty warrior." His voice increased a few decibels with each word.

"What did I tell you about inside voices? Anyway, like I said, I'm just the apprentice."

"An apprentice operates under the supervision of a master. Is there another of that level besides your father?"

I shrugged. "Nope. It's just me now."

"Are there other ink witches in your coven?"

"I'm the only one."

"Then you are the master."

"Okay. Fine." I threw up my hands. "You can call me the Ink Master if that will make you happy."

"The only thing that would make me happy would be for you to remove me from your person."

"And to do that, I need your skull, right?"

"Correct."

"Perfect. So I'll fetch your severed head, perform another banishing spell, and then you can be on your way. Where can I find your skull?"

His growl rumbled in my chest. *"I do not know."*

FOUR

"What do you mean, you don't know?" I shot to my feet and paced to the front of the shop. In my excitement about harnessing power over chaos and then the detriment of my possessing myself with *Chaos*, I never opened the store.

"I am not aware of my skull's current location." Chaos grunted like he was annoyed again.

"I understood what you said, doofus. I mean, *why* don't you know?"

"That is not what you asked."

"Well, it's what I meant." I turned the Closed sign over to Open and disengaged the lock. Since our building was on the edge of downtown, we had to keep up appearances. Our mom had converted the front quarter of the downstairs into a witchy shop—one of the bajillion already in Salem. We offered smudge sticks, candles, spell kits, and other souvenirs for the tourists and local people who practiced witchcraft but didn't possess any real magic.

"I have been trapped in darkness across the veil since the witch who vanquished my brothers and me bound us. I have no knowledge of where she placed our skulls. Without them, we cannot resurrect."

"No wonder you don't like witches. I mean, the realm across the veil is nasty enough, but to be imprisoned in darkness there? Yuck."

The bell above the door chimed, and a pair of women in black jackets and witch hats—one purple, one green—scurried in. The quickest way to stand out as a tourist in Salem was to wear a witch hat, but I wasn't about to tell them that. Tourism made up a huge chunk of the city's revenue, and the money we made from our little storefront paid the taxes on the building.

"Welcome to the Holland Witchery." I plastered on my salesperson's smile and gave a little wave.

"Hi." Purple Hat returned the gesture, but Green had already picked up a love spell kit in one hand and a heart-mending spell in the other. An interesting decision was about to be made.

"How long have I been imprisoned that witches can walk freely amongst mortals?"

I let out a huff of laughter. "Those aren't witches."

Green's head snapped toward me. "What?"

"Umm... Oh, I said 'Those aren't the right stitches.' I was talking to myself. I used the wrong stitches on this corset." Running my finger along the seam, I drew her attention toward the fabric and away from my rude comment. The last thing I needed to do was insult the customers.

"Are you a real witch?" Purple approached the counter with a smudge stick in her hand. "Do these really work?"

"Witches who cannot recognize their brethren?"

I cleared my throat. "It depends on what you're using it for, but yes. Sage helps to cleanse negative energy from a space."

She grabbed three more sticks from the bin and laid them on the counter.

Green Hat put the heart-mending spell back on the rack and brought the love spell to the register. I held in a chuckle. If she planned to make whoever hurt her fall in love, she would be sorely disappointed. Our magic never interfered with free will, and the spell kits we sold didn't do much more than help the mundane focus their intentions.

"What century is this?"

"It's the twenty-first."

"What is?" Purple tilted her head, looking at me quizzically.

Crap. If I kept talking to Chaos like everyone else could hear him, I'd be on the fast track to the looney bin. I grabbed the spell kit and scanned the barcode. "This is the twenty-first love spell we've sold this week. Must be in the air." I waved my hands, wiggling my fingers to indicate magic.

"Must be." Purple cut a sideways glance at Green, clearly disapproving of her choice. The women turned to leave, and the bell chimed again as Ember strode through the door.

"We've got a case..." She froze and flicked her gaze toward the customers. "...of smudge sticks in the back. Can you help me?"

Purple and Green scurried on to the next shop while Em locked the door behind them.

"Nice save." I strode to the entrance and flipped the Open sign to Closed. "What's up?"

"You are supposed to be retrieving my skull, not selling trinkets to humans playing at magic."

I gritted my teeth. No way in all the Underworld could I let my sister know how badly I'd screwed up this time, which meant *not* answering the disembodied voice. Light witches were forbidden from summoning demons, and especially from trapping them inside their own bodies.

"I demand you release me."

I raised a finger toward my sister. "Hold that thought. I need to pee, and then you can tell me all about it."

Ember huffed. "Hurry. I took off work for this. The police chief is waiting for us."

"'Kay." I scurried around the counter.

She followed me into the back, through the sigil area, and into the library, where I was planning to have a pointed conversation with the demon in my head.

"Actually, I think it might be number two. I'm going to head upstairs for some privacy, if you don't mind. That breakfast burrito I had this morning isn't agreeing with me."

"I thought you had cereal." She plopped into the squeaky chair at my desk, making a face as it groaned.

"I had the burrito after you left. Be right back." I darted up the stairs before she could say anything else. Rounding the corner, I paced down the hall and ducked into the bathroom. After turning on the extraction fan and running the water, I fisted my hands.

"Listen, Chaos. Since you can't release yourself, I don't

think you're in any position to be demanding stuff from me. My coven and I are the supernatural police of Salem. A select few humans in high positions of authority know about us, and if they ask for our help, it's because something bad happened and they suspect magic was involved. The veil is thinner here in Salem than anywhere else."

He had the nerve to growl after my speech. *"I am aware of the magical nature of this town. I was summoned here long before you came into existence."*

"Good. Then you understand the kind of shit that can go down here. We just took out a nest of vamp ghouls who'd somehow made it to this side, so there is no telling what's going on now."

"Locating my skull is the first step to solving your problems."

I scoffed. "You have no idea the scope of my problems right now. My sister is the acting High Priestess. She absolutely cannot find out I summoned you."

"Perhaps she could be of assistance."

"Nope. No way. I made this mess; I'll clean it up. But first I have to deal with the humans' problem. Once that's done, I'll find your skull. I need you to keep quiet while I'm around Ember. We could be looking at mutiny if the coven found out I was consorting with a demon."

Ember rapped her knuckles on the door. "You okay in there?"

I flushed and whispered, "Please be quiet."

His growl reverberated through my entire body. *"Very well."*

After shutting off the water and the extraction fan, I sprayed some air freshener to cover up the fact I had not stunk up the place and plastered on a smile as I opened the door. "All better." I linked my arm around Ember's and guided her away from the bathroom. "What's going on?"

Her boots clunked on the wood as we descended the narrow staircase. "A group of teens has gone missing from the woods. One made it out and swears a monster took his friends."

Chaos rumbled inside me, so I cleared my throat, stopping him from speaking. "A monster, eh? Did he get a good look at it?"

Ember stopped at the bottom of the stairs, resting one hand on her hip. "Cracked skin the color of partially burned charcoal."

The skin around my eyes scrunched as I tried to imagine the description. "So like black and gray?"

She nodded. "With curly horns coming out of its forehead."

"That's a demon. Lower-mid-level. Still not capable of maintaining a human form."

My mouth pinched, and I cleared my throat, but Chaos didn't take the hint.

"The skin looks like charcoal because it is burnt. It will flake and rain down around it as it moves, scorching the earth."

"Whoa." I pinched the bridge of my nose and squeezed my eyes shut. That was not good.

"Are you okay?" Ember rested a hand on my shoulder.

"Yeah. Just a lingering headache from yesterday. It sounds like someone summoned a demon. You don't think they were coven members, do you?"

"They'd better not be. With all the shit that's gone down in the past few months, a power grab wouldn't surprise me, though. I've heard rumblings about my lack of leadership skills."

My empty stomach suddenly felt like a brick dropped into it. Why hadn't the idea crossed my mind before? "Wait. Do you think Mom, Dad, and Cinder... Do you think someone's picking us off one by one? Do we have a traitor in the coven?"

"No. No way. They might submit a vote of no confidence to the Higher Power, but they wouldn't use violence or kidnapping." Her words may have said that, but the tightness around her eyes and mouth said she wasn't so sure.

"Mutiny is already abound."

"No, it's not." I stomped toward my tattoo machine.

"What's not?" Ember followed.

Crap. Can it, Chaos. "It's not a coven member. They wouldn't dare. So, what do you want then? If I could figure out a way to make speed and strength permanent on you, it would save us a ton of time."

"I need you to come with me and check it out."

I laughed. "You've got a short memory, don't you?"

"It's not an active scene. Whatever took those kids...*if* anything took them at all...is long gone. Hell, the boy could have been tripping on acid and imagined the whole thing."

"Let's hope." I crossed my arms and worried my lower lip between my teeth. It sure would have been handy if Chaos could read my thoughts. I had so many questions. "I'm still not sure I should go. What if something is still there? I could burn the forest down if I had to fight."

"Nothing is there. The humans have been there for two

hours already. If a demon wanted to take someone else, he'd grab a mundane before he'd mess with a witch."

"Unless he had a vendetta against witches."

I scoffed. "Like you?"

"Or like you," Ember replied, though my comment was directed at Chaos. "You're the best at reading spells. I need you to figure out what, if any, magic was used so we can locate the missing kids."

"If they're really missing."

"Exactly."

"All right. I can handle that, but if a hungry beastie pops up, that's all you."

She grinned. "Deal."

"I don't like this." I slid out of the van and slammed the door before pacing around to the driver's side. Ember wasn't packing her sword, nor did she let me arm her with sigils. "What if something happens? What if it's a trap?"

Her brows shot toward her hairline before she recovered. "It's fine. Look, Chief Higgins is right over there, and his gun is holstered. If there was a threat, he wouldn't be chewing on a toothpick with his hands on his hips."

I crossed my arms. "He'd be blind to a magical threat."

She waved a hand dismissively. "It'll be fine. Here." She slid open the side door and retrieved her sword from the secret compartment in the floorboard before laying it across the back seat. "It's ready if I need it. I'll take care of you, little sister."

It wasn't me I was worried about. I had no problem turning tail and running if things went south. Ember, on the other hand, would fight a demon with her bare hands bound behind her back before she'd retreat.

"*Move toward the law enforcer,*" Chaos said. "*I sense a rift.*"

"A rift?" I clamped my mouth shut. I seriously had to stop talking to the voice in my head.

"What?" Ember closed the door. "Did you say a rift?"

"*A tear in the fabric of the veil. A hole.*"

"Yes, I know what a rift is." I rolled my eyes.

Ember narrowed hers. "What's wrong with you? You're not making sense."

I ground my teeth. "Sorry, I misunderstood you. I think I sense a rift in the veil. Like a hole or something."

She cocked her head. "How? What does it feel like?"

"Umm... Different?"

Chaos grunted. "*The other realm has a lower vibration. I sense it bleeding through.*"

Think, Ash. What spell could I cast to sense the change in vibration? Ember knew I couldn't just *feel* something like that. An unmasking incantation like the one I used in Cinder's room wouldn't work. That would just show magic, not the difference in energies between worlds.

"Different how?" She jerked her head toward Chief Higgins to indicate I should follow.

"I don't know. It's just a feeling. Give me a second to figure it out." Dry leaves crunched beneath my shoes, and I racked my brain to think of a spell to pick up on what Chaos could naturally sense. Of course! I'd found a boundary-locating spell in one of the older tomes that could identify the perimeter of a hex keeping someone or something in one place. That could work, but I'd need to head back to the van for the potion kit.

Wariness drew Higgins' face into a scowl, making him look either nauseated or constipated. I didn't know him well enough to determine which. He had a thick black book tucked under his arm, and when we approached, he shoved it toward me. "This look familiar?"

The second my skin touched the leather cover, foreboding magic seeped into my fingers, chilling me to the marrow. I shoved it against his chest and jerked my hands back, rubbing my palms together. "Next time, warn me when you're sending dark magic my way so I can protect myself."

I focused on the tiny flame burning in my soul, imagining the light filling my body before creating a protective bubble around me. It wouldn't stop an attack if the book was hexed, but it would keep the sticky, icky magic from seeping into my skin.

I held out my hands, and he gave it back to me. "This isn't ours, if that's what you're implying."

"Where did you get it?" Ember peered over my shoulder and visibly shivered. As far as we knew, our coven had one dark magic book that our great-great-great grandmother had confiscated from a bad witch way back when. She'd locked it in a vault in the cellar, and no one had seen it since.

"Jason Monroe had it." Higgins used his tongue to move the toothpick from one side of his mouth to the other while he looked us up and down. "Said he and his friends got it from the thrift shop in town and used it for a séance but they contacted more than a ghost."

I cracked open the book and flipped through a couple of pages. Drawings of demons, dark spells, and demonic sigils filled it from margin to margin. Someone had scribbled notes in the white space as well. The librarian in me wanted to gasp and clutch my pearls, but I highly doubted a dark magic practitioner cared much for book etiquette.

"A witch could easily summon a shedim demon with that book."

Maybe so, but a human couldn't unless the rift in the veil existed before they started the incantation. "I'm going to put this in the van. We'll have to lock it in our vault."

Higgins nodded. "Whatever it takes to keep your wicked spells out of the kids' hands."

"I told you it isn't ours." I gave Higgins the stink eye before turning on my heel and marching away.

"Is there a rift here?" I whispered.

"Just past the spruce tree in the clearing. You must close it, or others may escape."

I hit the key fob to unlock the van and slid open the side door. In the bottom of the secret compartment lay another even more secret hidey-hole that only Ember and I knew about. Two taps of my index finger, my ring finger, index again, and then my pinkie unlocked the hatch. I slipped the book inside, tapped out the key backward to lock it, and grabbed the brown satchel containing our travel spell kit.

"Why do you care if others escape? You're Chaos. Wouldn't it please you to see our world fall under demon control?"

"Nothing would please me less. We must have balance. Order and chaos must be matched, or both our worlds would implode."

"Well, when you put it that way." I locked the van and jogged toward the clearing.

Ember parked her hands on her hips and squared off with the chief. "Did you call us here for help or to accuse us? You said yourself the missing kids are human."

"I said they aren't on the coven roster you gave me. They could be new recruits." He took the toothpick out of his mouth and tucked it behind his ear.

It was a good thing Ember didn't have her sword because the look on her face said she was ready to draw it and take his head clean off.

"We don't recruit." I stood next to her, resting my hand on her arm to calm her. "People are either born with magic or they aren't. If they are, they find us. I promise you, our coven had nothing to do with this, but we will find out what happened."

His gaze cut from Ember to me, his posture relaxing marginally. "Do you think it could be related to the fire in the old cemetery?"

I did my best to keep a neutral expression. "I thought they decided a discarded cigarette started it."

He shrugged. "Seems odd the ground fire had been extinguished while the trees were ablaze. I'll leave you to it." He grabbed the toothpick and put it back in his mouth.

Ew. "Heat rises." I returned his shrug and headed for the rift before he could ask any more questions.

"Can you believe that guy?" Ember fumed beside me. "After all the help we've given him... The safety we provide to the people of Salem." Her hands curled into fists, her energy shifting, vibrating more intensely like she was about to summon her fire.

"Cool it, Em. We don't need you setting the forest alight. That's my job."

"Right here," Chaos said.

"No kidding." I stopped in my tracks. Three feet in front of me lay a summoning ring the size of my bedroom. A thick line of salt encircled the space, and half-melted black candles sat on the inside where the five points of the pentagram would have been if they'd bothered to finish the spell. "We're lucky the *kids* didn't burn down the forest. Jeez."

Ember let out a long breath. "Is this what you felt? But they couldn't have summoned anything like what the kid described unless they had help."

"You think we've got a rogue witch in town?" I set the bag at my feet and rummaged through it for my supplies. A bit of horehound, some heather, and dandelion ought to do the trick.

She shook her head. "How? We would know. We have the Witch Watcher in place. It would have sounded the bell if a new witch stayed in the city limits for more than twenty-four hours."

I crushed the herbs in a small copper bowl and poured in the lavender oil. "Have you been reinforcing it? The spell has to be invigorated every two weeks."

"Cinder always did that." Her voice sounded tiny, her gaze drifting to the grass.

"And Mom before her," I said. "It's the duty of the High Priestess."

"Well, shit." She plopped cross-legged on the ground next

to me. "What about that book? Aren't you supposed to scan the resale and tourist shops to confiscate all the real magic before kids like Jason Monroe and his buddies can get their hands on them?"

I blew out a hard breath. "We've both gotten behind in our duties."

"Maybe a power grab by one of the older witches wouldn't be such a bad thing." She bumped her shoulder against mine.

"Don't say that. Leading this coven is our birthright. We can't help it if we weren't prepared for all hell to break loose. A little fire, please?" I held the bowl up, and she pointed her finger, shooting out a controlled flame as if it were the easiest thing in the world to do. For her, it probably was. I rose to my feet and brushed the leaves from my jeans.

"Don't step inside the circle."

"Thanks, genius."

Ember clambered up next to me. "What's that supposed to mean?"

Crap. Recover! "Gorgeous? It means you're beautiful, silly."

"Oh."

Holding the bowl in front of my face, I whispered the incantation and blew the smoke into the circle. It spiraled upward, coating the inner rim in a translucent haze. Near the opposite side, not quite in the center, the smoke gathered, darkening into a thick mass before disappearing through the rift. "Found it."

Ember's mouth dropped open. "How in the hell...?"

"Back up," Chaos demanded. When I didn't follow his order,

he boomed, nearly splitting my skull, *"He is drawn to my power. Back up now!"*

"Who?" My gaze snapped to the smoky tear in the veil, where a charcoal arm with thick talons protruding from each finger jutted through. "Oh, crap! The demon!"

I backpedaled, grabbing Ember's arm and dragging her away from the summoning ring. A muscular shoulder appeared next. Then the side of a thick neck, and finally the fiend's head. He had a wide face with a flat nose like a pug. A set of four-inch spiraling horns grew from his forehead, and as he snarled and pulled the rest of his body through the rift, black drool dribbled down his chin.

Ember yanked from my grasp and stalked toward it—typical Em—while my heart lodged in my throat and my feet froze to the ground—typical me. "Ember, you're unarmed!" I shouted, and then I whispered, "What should we do?"

"Don't move."

"I couldn't if I tried." Ice flushed my veins, and my knees wobbled. I had never come face to face with a demon before, and let me tell you, I was not reacting the way a witch should. I should have been casting spells and kicking butt. Instead, my knees nearly buckled, and every spell I'd ever memorized evaporated from my mind as if I'd set a pot of my memories to boil on the stove and forgotten about it.

The demon growled, stepping one clawed foot back and shifting his weight, preparing to lunge at my sister. Em stood literally two feet away from the monster. It would take three seconds for him to fillet her. I couldn't let that happen.

"Hey, ugly," I shouted, my feet still glued to the ground. "When was the last time you brushed your teeth?"

The demon's eyes snapped toward me, and his lips peeled back over jagged fangs, showing me no one had ever introduced him to a toothbrush.

"Careful, Ash. I cannot protect you without my corporeal form."

"Holland witches don't need protection." I don't know why Chaos's statement rubbed me the wrong way, but it did. I must've been channeling Ember's ego because I stomped forward, rubbing my palms together, ready to burn this bastard to the ground.

My fingers sparked, and I curled them toward my palms, lighting flames in both hands. Ember held a fireball the size of a cantaloupe.

"Fire won't harm a demon."

"This is magical fire." I wound up like a baseball pitcher and hurled the biggest flames I could create at the demon. They bounced off the circle and landed in the dried leaves.

The demon roared and lunged. His horns smacked the perimeter, jarring him, and he careened back, falling on his butt. Don't you know that pissed him off? He shot to his feet and rammed into the magic again. A shockwave pulsed from the circle.

"The cage holds."

"Not for long. Ember, go get your sword. We've got to banish this sucker before he breaks free." Grabbing my bag, I stomped out the flames, backed away from the circle, and dropped the kit on the ground. I wiped the copper bowl with an enchanted tissue to neutralize the magical residue and assembled the ingredients for a binding spell. I added the final component—a single drop of peppermint oil—and the concoction released a puff of purple smoke before turning to a fine powder.

I held up my hand and whispered a prayer to the goddess before casting my spell. "Standing tall or on your knees, in the name of the goddess, I force you to freeze."

I blew the powder toward the demon as Ember bounded back with her sword clasped in both hands. But the spell hit the circle's perimeter and shot back toward me. "Son of a bison!"

The enchantment wrapped around me like a magical boa constrictor, squeezing just tight enough that I couldn't move my arms and rooting my feet to the ground.

"Interesting." Ember reached for the circle, and her fingertips pressed against the invisible barrier. "Nothing can get in or out. I've never seen a ring like this cast before."

"That is because the magic used was meant to trap a demon. Only those who practice the dark arts use it."

"It's a demon cage. Of course you haven't." I struggled against the spell, which was pointless. I'd cast the strongest one I knew, and no, I could not unbind myself. What would be the point if it were that easy to escape? Another witch would have to release me, but my sister was preoccupied.

Ember pretended to lunge at the demon, laughing as she feinted right, then left. The fiend was not amused in the slightest. He roared and rammed against the magic. A sound like cracking glass reverberated through the clearing.

"Would you mind unbinding me before that creature kills us both?"

My sister winked at the demon, getting in one last taunt before she recited the unbinding incantation. Lucky for me, Ember had that one ingrained in her vim and didn't require a potion. The hold on me disintegrated, and I stumbled, dropping to my knees.

"We'll have to break the circle before we can banish him." I dumped the contents of my bag on the ground, scrambling to find the right ingredients—again—to make the potion. "I'll bind him; you stab him."

"The shedim has two hearts. Both must be pierced to vanquish him."

Well, wasn't that hunky dory? "Where? Side by side?" I whispered under my breath.

"In the center of his chest, one above the other."

I crushed the herbs with a pestle and looked at Ember. "I've been learning about demons. If this is the kind I think it is, he'll have two hearts in the center of his chest." I pointed to the two spots on my body where I imagined they would be. "You have to pierce both to vanquish him."

"I am so glad you're a bookworm." She spun her sword at her side. "I'd have just taken off his head."

I unscrewed the cap on the peppermint oil and tipped it toward the bowl. Nothing came out. "Crapity crap. I used the last drop in the spell that bounced off the circle."

"Can you improvise?" Ember's eyes grew wide, and I followed her gaze toward the circle.

The demon crouched at the far side and took off like a sprinter, ramming the perimeter and shattering the spell. He was free, and we were screwed.

The shedim ran straight at me. My heart didn't just leap into my throat; it tried to escape through my nose. Ember jumped in front of the beast and swung her sword, giving me a chance to scoop up an armful of ingredients and get the hell away. I ducked behind a tree trunk and laid out what I'd nabbed, hoping to Hades I'd packed an extra bottle of peppermint oil...or at least stashed a York patty or something. Peppermint was essential for this spell to hold.

"Improvise faster!" Ember called above the racket of demon snarls and sword slashes. She grunted like she had the wind knocked out of her. Then the demon wailed. Payback was a bitch.

"Why would your sister taunt such a demon? He will shred her once he is finished playing with her."

"If you both would can it for a minute, I might be able to stop that from happening." I tossed aside a bottle of lavender oil. It might slow the beast down, but I needed something sharp and quick if I wanted to bind him. "In answer to your question, that's Ember for you. Hot-headed, quick-tempered badass, who's the most loyal witch you'll ever meet."

He scoffed. *"Witches are only loyal to themselves."*

"Says the demon who's helping me vanquish another demon." Lemon grass, chamomile, bee balm. If I wanted to give this guy the best nap of his life, I'd be set. Wait... That wasn't a bad idea. A relaxation spell combined with what I had of a binding potion could slow him down enough for Ember to do her thing.

"Does the shedim have any immunity to magic that I should know of? I mean, aside from being impervious to fire?" I uncorked the lavender and chamomile when my gaze locked on the bottle of spearmint by my right foot. This just might work.

"Sadly, none of us do, or I wouldn't be in this predicament."

"Good to hear." I put a drop of each oil into the bowl. Nothing happened. "Shitake mushrooms. Come on!" I stirred the contents and peeked from my hiding spot behind the tree.

Ember grasped her sword in both hands and swung it over her head, spinning in a circle as her right leg swept out and connected with the demon's ankle. The demon flailed backward, but he caught himself before his ass could meet dirt. My sister was so good at pissing off her foe. The shedim swiped a taloned claw forward, catching her t-shirt and tearing it nearly in two.

"That was my favorite top, you sorry sack of incubus jizz." She slashed again, ripping into his thigh. His pained screech nearly tore my head in half.

"He's angry. She will not last much longer."

"Whatever gave you that idea?" I whispered the incantations: first the binding spell in hopes that the spearmint would be strong enough, and then the relaxation invocation. The potion simmered. Then it sizzled. Then it popped, and a green flame shot out six inches from the bowl. "Huh. That's new."

"Have you tried this spell before?" I didn't appreciate the wariness in his voice.

"Apparently, this is my day to step out of my comfort zone." The potion turned to black granules, like fresh ground pepper, rather than the powder I expected.

"Will it work?"

"Only one way to find out." I poured the grains into my palm and fisted my hand. Pushing to my feet, I peered around the tree to gauge the demon's location. At least one of the Holland sisters had to look before she leaped.

Ember stabbed the fiend in the gut. It wailed and jerked away, wrenching the sword from her grasp. Black goo oozed from the wound as it yanked the sword from its belly and tossed it aside.

"Any day now, Ash." Ember grabbed a set of daggers from her ankle holster.

With the demon's back toward me, I whispered a silencing spell so I could attack in stealth mode. My feet pounded the ground, but I made no sound as I darted toward it.

Ember jabbed her dagger into its shoulder. It swung its arm, claws raking my sister's stomach. A pained shout ripped from her throat, and she doubled over.

I hurled the enchanted granules at the beast's backside.

They stuck to him like ticks on a dog before absorbing into his ashy skin. He lifted his arm again, his movements slow and heavy.

"That's the best I could do. Are you okay?" I grabbed Ember's sword and ran toward her, ready to stab the fiend through both his hearts. She couldn't hear me, thanks to my silencing spell.

"Oh no." Ember made a grabby motion with her hands. "This is personal. He's mine."

Who was I to steal her chance at retribution? I handed her the sword.

"Never mess with a Holland witch." She jabbed the sword into the center of his chest and twisted. The razor edge sliced up and then down, creating a foot-long gash.

The demon stumbled back and let out a skull-splitting screech that would have the whole town wondering what kind of animal died in the woods. I guess I should've cast the silencing spell on all of us.

Ember doubled over again, her sword and daggers toppling to the ground. I clutched her shoulders, bracing her as the demon wailed again before crumbling to bits and being sucked back into the rift.

"Show me where he got you." I tried to lower her to the ground, but she shrugged me off. "Ember…"

Oh, right. The silencing spell. "What I've done is now undone. As I will it, so mote it be."

"The shedim's claws are tipped with poison. If he broke skin, she will need a healer to draw out the toxins."

"Show me." I peeled her hands away from the wound.

Three bloody slashes stretched diagonally from her rib cage to her hip. "We need to get you to Patrice. You need a healer."

She spoke through gritted teeth. "You have to close the rift. More demons can come through, and there's no circle to contain them."

The adrenaline in my veins chose this moment to dissipate, allowing a wave of fatigue to wash over me. I must've cast at least six spells in the last twenty minutes. My vim was waning hardcore, taking my thoughts with it.

"How? What spell will seal it?" I asked.

She laughed and then winced. "You're the smart one. I thought you had the entire library memorized."

If only. "A patch, maybe? A little help, please?" My question was intended for Chaos since he seemed to be an expert in the matter.

Ember replied, "Yeah. We'll need to get closer." She reached for me, and I helped her walk to the rift.

"The fibers of the veil are thin like strands of silk. They'll need to be woven back together for a permanent hold."

Weaving the fabric of reality. With this level of fatigue and Ember's injuries? Yeah, right. "We'd need a few more witches to have the power to seal it for good. I can make a glue, though. It'll hold long enough for us to call in reinforcements."

"Yeah. Do that." Ember leaned forward, bracing her hands on her knees. "Fast."

I grabbed my bag and dumped the contents back inside before racing around the tree where I'd left the rest of the supplies and stuffing those in too.

Back at the rift, Ember's complexion had taken on a grayish

hue. We didn't have much time. My hands trembled as I mixed the ingredients for the magical glue. Angelica, basil, and heather turned to green liquid when I poured in the wormwood oil.

"The poison will solidify her innards before turning her skin to ash."

"I'm working as fast as I can." The potion popped and sizzled. I grabbed Ember's hand to channel her magic, which I felt really, *really* bad about. She needed all her strength to fight the poison, but I couldn't do this alone.

"A simple patch to close this hatch. As I say, keep the demons at bay." I tossed the potion at the hole in the veil, and the torn sides moved toward each other, sticking together. A thick scar ran down the length of it, but as soon as the perimeter spell wore off, no one would be able to see it.

Ember sagged, my stubborn sister refusing to give in. After grabbing my bag and her weapons, I wrapped her arm over my shoulders, and we stumbled to the van together. I buckled her into the passenger seat and tossed our gear into the back before texting Patrice to let her know we needed her.

The drive took ten excruciating minutes. I fought to keep my eyes open and on the road while Ember rested her head against the window, her eyes closed, mouth open. Ghostly white rimmed her lips, and her shallow breathing seemed forced.

"We've got time, right? She can come back from this?" I didn't bother whispering. Even if Ember were awake, I doubted she'd remember me talking to "myself."

Chaos grunted. *"I've never seen someone survive a shedim attack. You are strong witches, but the poison is spreading quickly."*

"Fabulous." I came to a screeching halt in front of Patrice's house and laid on the horn.

She scurried out, wearing a long, flowy brown skirt and a light pink top. She'd piled her curly red hair on top of her hair in a messy bun, and a pair of reading glasses hung from a chain around her neck.

I slammed the door and ran around to Ember's side before pulling her out. Her eyes rolled back and her head lolled to the left as we dragged her inside and laid her on an exam table.

"What happened?" Patrice cut Ember's shirt the rest of the way open. The skin around the wounds looked like partially burnt charcoal...just like the demon's.

"It's demon poison. A shedim got in one good swipe before she vanquished him. Can you draw it out?"

"I'll do my best." She dumped jars of herbs and liquids into a bowl. Normally, I'd watch her intently, trying to learn as much as I could about her spells, but this time, I kept my gaze trained on my sister's paling face.

"Patrice will fix you, Em." I gripped her hand in mine. Her finger twitched, but she didn't have the strength to hold me. "I'm so sorry I didn't get the demon under control faster."

"Not...your fault," she whispered.

"Yes, it is. I take full responsibility. I should have checked the perimeter to see if the binding spell would penetrate it before I wasted the powder." And if I'd kept the kit stocked properly, I would've had enough peppermint oil to make a second proper binding spell.

"You are not to blame. If she hadn't taunted the beast, he would not have been so strong. His anger increased his power."

"If I'd kept up with the thrift shops, I could have nabbed that book before it got into the wrong hands. I can list a million reasons why this is my fault." A sob bubbled from my chest to my throat. "I can't lose you too, Em. You have to be okay."

Ember groaned, and I snapped my gaze to Patrice. She chanted the incantation and returned to my sister's side.

"The blame lies with those who summoned the shedim."

"Shut up." I could appreciate what Chaos was trying to do, but damn. If I wanted to wallow in self-pity, he needed to let me.

"I didn't say anything." Patrice narrowed her eyes at me.

"Sorry. Talking to the voice in my head. It's been a day." I laughed dryly.

"So it seems." She spooned the mixture over Ember's wounds, and it disappeared beneath her skin.

Em gasped, her bloodshot eyes flying open as she clawed at the table. She thrashed, and a gurgling sound emanated from her throat.

"What's happening? This isn't helping; it's hurting her!" I tightened my grip on her hand, trying to hold her steady.

Patrice grabbed her other arm. "The potion is traveling through her body, collecting the poison."

Ember's legs flailed. Her knee drew upward and crashed into my shoulder before her boot thudded on the table. Ouch. That would leave a bruise, for sure. She went utterly still. Her chest didn't rise and fall with her breath. Her hand fell limp in mine.

"Is she...?" My voice trembled.

"Wait for it..." Patrice snatched an oversized Mason jar from a shelf and twisted off the lid.

Ember's wounds bubbled. Black sludge pooled in the gashes.

"Take this." Patrice shoved a ginormous syringe into my hand. "Draw out the poison and put it in the jar."

I did as I was told, sticking the tip of the device into my sister's stomach and pulling on the plunger. Thick liquid slowly filled the vial, and I squirted it into the jar. When I returned to the wound, it had already refilled with more sludge. I sucked out the poison again while Patrice worked on the other side.

We filled six vials a piece, the liquid reaching the jar's rim before Ember's own flesh and blood were visible in the gashes. Patrice hovered her hands above the wounds and whispered another incantation.

Ember gasped, her hands flying to her face as she looked around wildly. "What...?"

"Shh...shh..." I took her hand again, and this time, she held me back. "The demon poisoned you, but we get it all out. You're going to be okay." I looked at Patrice for confirmation, and she nodded.

"These gashes require sutures. Give me a minute to gather my supplies." She patted Ember on the leg before turning and leaving the room. Patrice wasn't just a witchy healer. She was also a nurse practitioner. Lucky us.

"Your healer is talented."

"We've got the best of the best in our coven."

Ember lifted herself onto her elbows. "We sure do. What

kind of spell did you throw on him? He looked like he was moving through molasses."

I shrugged. "I had to combine two spells since I didn't have enough oil for another binding."

"Well, it worked." She winced and laid her head down. "Good job."

I scoffed. "Hardly."

"You don't take compliments well."

Not when I didn't deserve them.

"Here we are. This will sting a little." Patrice held up a syringe of what I assumed to be numbing medicine.

Ember laughed. "I've been through worse."

"What happened out there, anyway? How did a shedim get through the veil?" She injected the wounds and threaded a hooked needle.

"Apparently, some wannabe witches got ahold of an actual dark magic grimoire." I shook my head. "They never should have gotten their hands on it."

Patrice pursed her lips as she sewed. "A mundane wouldn't be able to summon a demon. Someone had to have witch ancestry, at least."

"They could if the veil was already open," Ember said. "We found a rift in the center of their summoning circle."

"How did it get there?" she asked.

"Good question." My brow furrowed. "And how would they know where to find it in the first palce? We had to cast a spell to locate it."

"Maybe the demon drew them there," Ember said. "A beast that powerful can't slip through the veil, even with how thin it is here. Ghouls and fae, sure. That's what our job is for, but something with that much magical power would need to be summoned."

The veil was good about that...keeping the baddest of the bad on the side where they belonged. The more magic an entity possessed, the harder it was to cross into our world.

"That is precisely what happened. The shedim sensed the people in the forest and drew them to the rift. Once they performed the summoning, he was free to pass through in both directions."

"That's got to be it," I said. I bet they really did want to have a fun little séance. Poor kids. I couldn't imagine what the demon did to them after he pulled them through the rift. If they were lucky, moving from our world to the other killed them instantly. The mundane couldn't exist in their physical form in the spirit realm.

"What about the circle?" Ember asked. "Someone had to be a witch to put it up."

"We'll have to talk to Jason and see what he knows about his friends. I bet Patrice is right about the ancestry. If not for that circle, the shedim would be running rampant in Salem."

Patrice tied the last stitch and cut the thread. "But that leads us back to the question of how the rift got there in the first place. If it wasn't just a thin spot, someone created it. Purposely or not. Could there be an uprising on the other side?"

"There is no uprising." A low growl rumbled between my ears. *"Summoning a Prince of Hell can fracture the veil. The threads weaken and tear. It has happened before."*

Fantastic. It was my fault after all.

CHAPTER

SEVEN

"How are you still awake? I feel like I'm about to keel over, and all I did was cast a few spells." I unlocked the back door and held it open for Ember.

She trudged through and grabbed the handrail to haul herself up the stairs. "Casting spells can be more taxing than fighting, and you performed what? Five? How are *you* still awake?"

Eight if you counted the location and exorcism spells I tried before she got to the shop, but she didn't need to know about those. I helped her onto the couch and took off her boots before turning on the television. A reporter with a solemn expression told the story of the kids. The police would be holding a press conference in an hour.

Ember's phone chimed, and she groaned, wincing as she

dug it out of her pocket. "It's the chief wanting an update. I better call him."

"'Kay. I'll make dinner." I kicked off my Mary Janes and padded to the kitchen while she dialed the chief.

"Your body requires rest."

"No shit, Captain Obvious. It also requires food." I rummaged through the fridge and found a bag of fresh mushrooms, some spinach, and half a rotisserie chicken. The pantry offered dried pasta and a jar of spaghetti sauce. A trip to the grocery store was in order, but I had enough for tonight.

"Chicken spaghetti it is." I poured some olive oil into a pan and dumped in the spinach and mushrooms to sauté them. "Now that I've got you alone, I need answers." The mushrooms sizzled in the oil, the spinach wilting as I pushed it around the pan. "Since I caused this trouble, how do I fix it? Will sending you back heal the veil?"

He didn't answer.

I set a big pot of water to boil and opened the jar of sauce. "Hello, Chaos? Are you still there?"

He waited a full thirty seconds before he said, *"I was not the first Prince to be released."*

"Whoa. Wait... What?" Spaghetti sauce splashed onto the stove as I dumped it in the pot. I didn't bother to clean it up. Yeah, it would be stuck on good from the heat of cooking, but...

"You're telling me someone else summoned one of your brothers?"

"Discord either escaped or was released a time ago. I haven't sensed him in this realm, but my power is limited while in your human form."

"Can you elaborate on 'a time ago,' please? How long ago?" I swirled a wooden spoon in the sauce.

"Time runs differently across the veil. I don't know."

"And why would someone want to summon one of you?"

"To harness our power."

"But you're Princes of Hell. Couldn't you just swipe your claws and poison them? You said yourself you've never seen anyone survive a fight with the shedim, and he was a mid-level demon. Surely no one could contain you."

His growl tickled my chest. I hated to admit it, but I kinda like it when he did that. *"Only a witch with immense power could contain a Prince. Like you, for example."*

I laughed. "Only a screwup like me could *accidentally* contain you."

"You have no concept of your power."

"Anyway..." My cheeks heated. We'd already established I didn't take compliments well, so why did he keep dishing them out? And why was I blushing over a *demon's* opinion of me? *Get it together, Ash.*

"We are also known to make deals. Demons of any level will do a witch's bidding for a price."

"Let me guess. The price is usually their soul." I dumped the pasta into the boiling water.

"Precisely."

"So, it's possible there's a rogue witch in Salem who summoned Discord, a Prince of Hell, to do their bidding, and they sold their soul to do whatever it is they want to do. And said witch also cast the summoning circle the kids used in the forest this morning."

"The witch would not have to be rogue. Desperation makes people act out of character. Demons prey on that weakness."

"Well, crappity crap." It could be a coven member, or it could not. I chopped the chicken and added it into the sauce along with the mushrooms and spinach. "On the bright side, at least I'm not the cause of it this time."

"Summoning me weakened the veil even more. I doubt that was the only rift that will need to be sealed."

"But you said no one could summon you without your skull. Is that not the case for your brothers? I'm the only thing remotely close to an Ink Master for hundreds of miles."

"You are *an Ink Master, but yes, it is the case. If Discord was summoned, the witch used his skull. He will be searching for Mayhem and me so that we may collect our price from the witch who trapped us."*

"Uh-huh. And what happens if he finds you...trapped inside me?"

"He will kill you."

"Holy frak." The timer buzzed, so I drained the water and dished up the food. "And what happens if I can't find your skull? Will you be a voice inside my head forever? I mean, if your brother doesn't find us?"

He went silent again, and that made an emptiness form in the pit of my stomach. "Let me guess. I'm not going to like your answer."

"How did you know?"

"You got quiet. That's your tell. When it's bad news, you'd rather say nothing."

"A demon cannot coexist with his host indefinitely."

I waited for him to elaborate, but he didn't. My insides twisted into a knot, the food suddenly not smelling nearly as enticing as it had a moment ago. "Chaos, what will happen to me?"

"I will take over, and you will simply be a voice in my head. Then you will cease to exist."

The knot in my stomach rose to my throat. I swallowed hard. "How?"

"My soul will bind with your body. Your current form will erode, and mine will be born from it."

That sounded like a goddess-damned horror movie. I imagined my flesh falling off in chunks as a monstrous face ripped from my abdomen, tearing me in half. A shiver ran up my spine.

"Why would you do that?" My voice was barely a whisper.

"I would have no choice in the matter. The process has already begun. Hence, the importance of finding my skull."

Hellhounds and hand grenades. What the actual eff had I done? This couldn't be happening. I was... And he... And the rifts... My hands trembled, so I set the plates on the counter. "What are we going to do?"

"What's taking so long?" Ember shouted from the living room. "I'm so hungry I could eat a donkey's ass."

"First, you will take care of your physical bodies. You'll be useless otherwise. Then you will locate my skull and return me to my corporeal form. Once I am free, you will find the witch who summoned Discord and put an end to her madness. Only then will your city find peace."

"Ash?" Ember called.

"Coming..." I picked up the plates and slowly made my way to the living room.

Caring for our physical bodies, I could handle. Finding Chaos's skull might be an issue, but I could go it alone. Freeing him should be as easy as trapping him was. Battling a witch who had a Prince of Hell in her pocket...that was Ember's department.

Well, shit. "I can't do all this alone."

"You must tell Ember what you've done. Her skills may be required to retrieve my skull. I doubt it was left unguarded."

"But you're a demon," I whispered right before I entered the room.

"She is your sister. She will understand your mishap."

Would she? I wasn't so sure. "Here's dinner." I set our plates on the coffee table and darted back into the kitchen to grab two bottles of beer. After today, we needed something stronger, but beer would have to do.

Ember twisted off the cap and downed half the contents. "Thanks. The Chief was none too pleased when I told him what happened."

"I bet." I shoved a forkful of spaghetti into my mouth. "He still blames us?"

"I think I've convinced him we aren't involved, but he's suspicious. He agreed to let us talk to Jason tomorrow, though, so that's a plus. Hopefully he can give us enough info to piece all this together."

"What about the rift? The patch I put on it won't hold forever."

She finished chewing before she answered, "I already sent Shade and Chrys to take care of it."

Great. Yet another excuse for him to gloat over me. He had the energy to repair the rift correctly when I didn't. Forget the fact I'd done a huge amount of spell casting and helped battle a demon. That wouldn't matter to Shade. Him fixing something I couldn't do properly would be all he needed.

My thoughts must've been clear on my face because Ember patted my knee. "Since it's been on the news, curious humans will be swarming the place. They'll need to hide what they're doing, and Shade is the best at shadow magic."

"I know that." I shoved another forkful into my mouth, but I wasn't hungry. Chaos was right. I needed to tell Ember what I'd done. I had pertinent information that she, as acting High Priestess, needed to know.

Telling her the truth was the right thing to do, but that didn't mean it would be easy. My screwup had almost gotten her killed today, and now I was about to inform her that her baby sister had a demon inside her who would take over completely if she didn't vanquish him ASAP.

"What a day, huh?" Ember took a swig from her beer. "I'm sure glad it's over."

My mouth went dry, and I felt like I'd swallowed a wad of cotton. "It's not quite done yet. I need to talk to you about something."

She spoke around a mouthful of food. "If it has to do with the library or the shop, it can wait. I'm beat."

"It doesn't. I..." Deep breath in. Let it out slowly. *You can do this, Ash.* "I accidentally summoned a demon. Not the shedim. A different one." I clamped my mouth shut, my shoulders drawing toward my ears.

Ember laughed. "Tell me, dear sister. How did you *accidentally* summon a demon?"

She didn't believe me. If Chaos hadn't been talking to me all day...helping me solve this mystery...I wouldn't believe it myself. I made mistakes all the time, but not like this.

"Show her my mark."

"You're right. I'll start with the worst and move backward from there."

Ember's brow furrowed. "What?"

I shoved my sleeve up to my elbow and held out my arm. Chaos's sigil glowed deep red. "I found this page of sigils in Cinder's room. This one is for power over chaos...or so I thought."

I ran my finger over the mark, and Chaos's growl vibrated in my chest. If I didn't know any better, I'd have said he was purring. That sounded way too content to be a growl.

"It's beautiful. You definitely got all the artistic talent in the family." She ate another bite.

"Yeah, well, it turns out this sigil belongs to a demon called Chaos."

"A Prince of—"

"A Prince of Hell to be precise. He's one of the highest-ranking demons in the realm, and I somehow called him over and trapped him inside my head."

She laughed again. "You're joking."

"I wish I were."

"You…" She took a giant bite of food, her right cheek protruding as she chewed.

I turned toward her, folding one leg beneath me. "I know it sounds nuts, but it's true. He's been talking to me all day. How do you think I knew so much about the shedim?"

"You read tons of books. You know just about everything."

"Chaos told me what we had to do. Pierce the two hearts. He also told me about the poison claws, so I knew to get you to Patrice to draw out the toxin."

She set her plate on the coffee table and chugged the rest of her beer. "If there were a demon inside you, you'd have vanquished him by now."

"I tried, believe me. The only way I can get him out of *my* head is to find *his*. A witch vanquished him way back when, but she kept his skull so he would be imprisoned in darkness across the veil. I have to find his skull in order to set him free."

That was enough for her to swallow right now. I'd save the part about him taking me over for another time.

She eyed me skeptically. "You're not playing some kind of prank, are you? Because I am in no mood for…"

I drew an X over my chest. "Cross my heart. I'm as serious as can be."

She stared at me, waiting for me to crack a smile. When I didn't, she widened her eyes. "Holy shit, Ash. A demon?"

"I know. On the plus side, he's given me some insight into the rift ordeal. Though that's not good news either."

She squeezed her eyes shut and shook her head, no doubt biting back all the profanities she wanted to sling at me.

Holland witches never dabbled in dark magic. Not even by accident.

I set my mostly full plate next to hers. "Do you need time to process, or should I continue?"

She made a circle motion with her hand. "Keep going. Get it all out now before I lose my ever-loving..." She drew in a deep breath.

I cleared my throat. "The veil has been weakened, and there will be more rifts. The fibers are deteriorating because someone summoned a demon prince. Or so Chaos thinks, right?"

"Correct."

I nodded. "He says yes."

She looked sideways at me. "Is that what he says? And I suppose *he* is the demon prince whose summoning caused this mess?"

I shook my head adamantly and held up my hands. "For once, this is not my fault. His brother Discord, who was also in the dark prison, got out a while ago. Chaos thinks that must be what weakened the veil. My summoning him made things worse, but I was not the catalyst."

She raked her fingers through her hair. "So someone else summoned a demon prince...Discord?"

"Right."

"Who? Why?"

I explained the conversation I'd had with Chaos in the kitchen and how it could be a rogue witch or someone from the coven. "Maybe John will reveal the culprit when we talk to him tomorrow."

She picked up her empty beer, shook it, and set the bottle

back on the table. "What on earth would someone in our coven want with Discord? I can't wrap my mind around it."

I sighed. "I don't know. We don't even know how long ago he was summoned. Time is different across the veil, but..."

Ember arched a brow, silently urging me to continue, but I pulled a Chaos and kept my mouth shut. I had an idea of who... and why...and it wasn't good news.

"Talk to me, Ash. What are you thinking?"

"Activity has picked up tremendously over the past month, right? You've had more beasties to hunt than ever."

"Yeah. We're getting close to Halloween, though. The veil is at its thinnest in October."

That was true, but this seemed like too much of a coincidence. "Wouldn't you say the activity started picking up right after Cinder disappeared?"

She froze, her mouth half open, whatever words she'd planned not making it across her lips.

I tapped the tattoo on my arm. "I found the page of sigils in Cinder's room, under a powerful spell. She was hiding them from me. From us."

"No way. Cinder would never summon a demon. She was High Priestess. She had all the power she needed. She..."

"She was desperate to find Mom and Dad. She insisted they were alive out there somewhere."

Ember kept shaking her head. "She wouldn't, Ash. A Holland witch would never summon a demon. Never."

"I did."

"By mistake. Cinder doesn't make mistakes."

"She ran off to find our parents. Her protection sigil didn't work. What if she found out what happened to Mom and Dad and summoned Discord to make a deal to find them? What if he killed her? What if she sold her soul to him to protect us? What if…?"

My mind reeled. There were too many what-ifs to consider. "Would he kill her, Chaos? If she released him from his prison, wouldn't he owe her? Or would he need to feed and kill the first person he saw?"

"Demons do not feed like ghouls," his voice rumbled in my head. *"He would be in debt to whomever freed him."*

I blew out a breath. "Oh, good."

"However…" Silence stretched inside my head. Crap. Whatever he said next would be bad news. Again. *"If their request was not in proportion to their favor, he would require a price be paid for his assistance."*

"Oh, shit."

"What's he saying?" Ember asked.

"That any what-if scenario could be what happened."

She drummed her fingers on her knee. "We don't know Cinder is the one who started this."

"I found the page of sigils in her room. The evidence is pretty damning."

Her head still shook. "Where did you find it? I searched it and found nothing."

"You didn't look under her mattress."

"I… Wait." She pursed her lips. "Are you okay? This demon you're hosting sounds like he's been a helpful guy so far, but… You're not going to lose control and try to kill me in my sleep? He's not going to kill you?"

"I have no reason to kill your sister. I require your assistance to locate my skull, so I promise I will not take over until I have no choice."

"That's reassuring."

"It's the best I can do."

"I'm fine."

"Good." The look on Ember's face said she was shutting this conversation down. She idolized Cinder and didn't want to hear anything about our beloved big sis dipping her toes into the dark arts.

I stood and picked up the plates. "Chaos promises to be a good boy if you'll help me find his skull."

She grabbed the empty bottles and followed me to the kitchen. "First thing in the morning. If we don't recharge, we'll be useless."

"I know." I rinsed the dishes and added them to the dishwasher before scrubbing the spilled sauce from the stove.

"Seriously, Ash. The mess will be here tomorrow." She dropped the bottles into the recycle bin. "You can clean it then."

"I'm almost done."

"Your sister is right. Your body requires rest."

I rubbed a disinfecting wipe over the counter and tossed it in the trash. "Okay. Let's get some sleep. Demon's orders."

CHAPTER

EIGHT

Steam rose from the water's surface, and the scent of lavender oil wafted to my nose as I poured Epsom salt into my favorite potion. A hot bath would do wonders for my aching muscles. I slipped into the tub and sighed as the warmth engulfed me.

The sigil on my arm turned a deeper shade of crimson, and it pulsed as I ran my finger over it. Chaos rumbled inside me, the contented sensation rolling from my chest downward to my toes.

"Why do you react like that?" I traced the design.

"That mark is the closest thing to a corporeal form I have...and I haven't been touched since I was imprisoned."

"Oh." I jerked my hand away. *Good going, Ash. You were petting a demon.* I didn't want to ask exactly which part of him I was stroking.

I sucked in a breath and slid under the water, holding it as long as I could before I was forced to come up for air. Rule number one of possession: Don't get intimate with your demon.

That probably wasn't a rule, but it should have been. I had a lot of research to do.

"Do you have any tips for finding your skull? Tell me about the witch who cursed you. How did it happen?"

Silence answered, and I imagined him glowering, which was no easy feat since I didn't have a clue what he looked like. "Are you as nasty looking as the shedim? Do you have horns?"

"The witch who cursed me was immensely powerful. Her magic was stronger than any I'd seen."

"Was she your lover?" I clamped my mouth shut. Why the hell would I ask him that? I was exhausted. Borderline delirious. I needed to wash and haul my ass to bed before I talked myself into a pickle.

Thankfully, he ignored my last question. *"Your missing sister might not be the one who summoned Discord, but I believe she knows who did."*

"She must, right? Why else would she have your sigils?"

"Exactly. In my demonic form, I do have horns. I also have a human form, and I believe the saying 'beauty is in the eye of the beholder' applies. What is nasty to you could be beautiful across the veil."

"Is the shedim beautiful?"

He chuckled. *"No, he is considered one of the vilest in appearance."*

"Good to know. You don't have to answer that other question I threw out there. It's none of my business."

"I didn't plan to, and you are correct."

"Right. Good." I finished washing and pulled the plug before grabbing a fluffy blue towel and drying off. Standing in front of the mirror, I squeezed the water from my hair and wrapped the towel turban-style around my head.

"Why is your hair blue?"

I shrugged. "Why not? I like to play around with colors. It was hot pink a few months ago."

"It is a nice shade."

"Thanks." I dipped my fingers into the jar of moisturizer and spread the cool cream across my face. "I'm glad you approve."

"You're beautiful." His voice grew deeper and even more rumbly. *"Your body is exquisite."*

A warm shiver ran up my spine, a pleasant sensation right before my stomach dropped so hard it nearly splattered on the bathroom floor. "Wait. What? You can see me?"

"Mm. The view is spectacular."

I yanked the towel from my head and covered my lady bits. "You can see through my eyes?" I nearly shrieked.

"Of course. And feel with your skin. We are bound."

"Holy Hecate." I shut off the light and darted into my room. I grabbed some underwear from my unmentionables drawer and squeezed my eyes shut before putting them on, which was no easy feat. My right leg went through the hole just fine, but my left big toe got hung up on the crotch and I did this little jumping dance across the room before falling backward onto my bed.

"Close your eyes so I can get dressed!" I unhooked my toe and shoved my leg through.

His deep chuckle rumbled all the way down to my stomach. *"I don't have eyes of my own."*

"Ugh!" I grabbed a shirt from my closet, tossed the towel into the bathroom, and spun around. Facing my full-length mirror. "Crap!"

I turned back around and pulled on the shirt. "You could have told me you see what I see."

"I assumed it was obvious."

My jaw clenched. It was obvious now that I thought about it. He'd seen the summoning circle and the demon inside it. He'd also seen me completely naked. So much for not getting intimate with my demon.

"Listen here, mister. We need some ground rules. No more peeking when I'm not wearing clothes, and no comments about my body. Got it?"

"If I refuse to comply?"

"Then I'll sage the shit out of every room in the house. I'll make sage perfume and cook with so much sage, you'll choke." Yet another reason I should have realized he had access to my senses. He'd commented on how bad the sage smelled when I'd tried to evict him. *Use your brain, Ash.*

"I can tolerate the foul odor."

I looked in the mirror, slamming my brows over my eyes for emphasis. "For someone who claims to hate witches, you seem awfully hot and bothered."

"What can I say? It's been ages since I've seen a woman as beautiful as you."

"Since you've seen *any* woman." I turned off the lights and climbed into bed, sliding my feet beneath the sheets. "I'm done. No talking while I'm trying to sleep."

"Your body is stressed. You should pleasure yourself to relieve the tension."

"You'd like that, wouldn't you? Perve."

"What man wouldn't? Give it a try." He made that purring noise again that filled my whole body with warm fuzzies.

"Stop that. I mean it. I'm going to sleep, and when I wake up, I expect an apology for these unwanted advances." Leave it to me to possess myself with not only a Prince of Hell, but a horny one at that.

He chuckled. *"Understood."*

I lay back and was out the moment my head hit the pillow.

FIRM HANDS SLID down my sides before agile fingers toyed with the band of my panties. Lips grazed my stomach, and I reached out to grasp muscular shoulders. His breath, hot against my skin, raised goosebumps on my flesh. I gazed down, and he looked at me with eyes as green as emeralds. He grinned wickedly, and the black of his pupils bled outward, filling his irises before consuming the whites. My pulse thrummed, though not from fear. He pressed his lips to my naval before gliding his tongue downward and sliding my underwear from my hips. Gripping my thighs, he blew a warm breath across my center, and my entire body tingled with need.

. . .

"Asн!" My sister's voice cut through the room, and I bolted upright, awakened from my dream. "Why are you still in bed? We have to talk to Jason in half an hour. Let's go." She turned on her heel and left my bedroom door open as she marched down the hall.

My pulse still sprinting, I swallowed the dryness from my mouth and threw off the covers. "What the hell, Chaos?"

"I'm sorry."

"You better be. How dare you put those images into my mind? I wanted to sleep, not have sexy dreams about the demon in my head."

"You..." Surprise laced his voice, and I imagined a quizzical expression in those emerald eyes of his.

"You really are a perve, you know that?" I stomped to the bathroom to brush my teeth.

"I'm sorry about the things I said last night. As I mentioned, I have been imprisoned for ages. I should not have spoken like that to you, but I didn't put images into your head. Whatever dreams you had, sexy or not, they were your own."

I spit and rinsed. "Yeah, right."

"I promise I didn't violate you in your sleep, but I notice you woke up quite aroused." A smile played in his voice. I could practically see the amusement in his eyes.

"It was just a dream," I grumbled as I brushed my hair. "You didn't experience it too, did you? Where do you go when I sleep?"

"My consciousness goes dormant too, and I had my own dreams, which weren't nearly as pleasurable as yours."

Fantastic. He came on to me, yet *I* had the inappropriate dreams. Figured.

I got dressed, doing my best to avoid looking in the mirror or at any part of my body. After getting ready for the day, I found Ember standing in the kitchen, her arms crossed.

"Finally." She tossed me a granola bar and motioned to the tumbler of coffee on the counter. "We're late."

"He's being held for psychiatric evaluation. It's not like he's going anywhere." I shoved half the bar into my mouth and carried the coffee downstairs. It was hot as hellfire, but I sucked down as much as I could on the drive to the hospital and popped a mint into my mouth before we headed inside.

Frigid air blasted my skin as the doors slid open, and the sterile scents of bleach and antiseptic made my nose tingle. We hung a left and paced down the hall toward the psychiatric ward. Fluorescent lights hummed from above, tinting the white walls and floor in a greenish-yellow hue.

"What is this place?" Chaos asked.

"It's a hospital. I guess a demon wouldn't have much need for medical professionals."

"It's not like any hospital I've seen."

"It's exactly like every hospital I've seen." I jogged to catch up with Ember.

"You look like you belong in this ward when you talk to him like that. Put in an ear bud so you can pretend to be on the phone." She stopped outside a door. "What's he saying?"

"He's never seen a hospital like this."

"What did they look like in his time?" she asked.

"Dark. Rancid stench. The candles had exposed flames rather than being held behind glass in the ceiling."

"Whoa." I tugged my ear buds from my pocket and put one in my ear. "He's from before hospitals had electric lights."

"I hate to break it to you, buddy." Ember knocked on the door and peered through the little square window. "If your skull was stolen before Salem had electricity, it might not exist anymore. We're looking at your vanquishing happening at least one hundred fifty years ago. Maybe longer."

"It must exist. Discord was freed."

"So were you, kinda," I said. "You're trapped in me now, but you're not in prison. Maybe another Ink Master made the same mistake as me."

"Let's hope not. Otherwise, your life will end soon."

I flinched at his words. "Thanks for the reminder."

"What did he say?" Ember asked.

Chief Higgins opened the door, and thankfully, I didn't have to answer. My sister had enough on her plate right now without worrying about my impending doom.

"His story hasn't changed since yesterday," Higgins said as he stepped into the hall. "He's sedated, so I don't know how much help he's going to be."

"Any details he can provide will help us get to the bottom of it." Ember caught the door before it could close and stepped inside. I followed without making eye contact. I was still miffed at the chief for blaming us.

Jason Monroe lay in the bed by the window. The curtains

were open, and he squinted against the sunlight. Ember walked around the bed and pulled them halfway closed.

"Better?" she asked.

He nodded and stared blankly ahead.

"I'm Ember, and this is my sister, Ash. We'd like you to tell us about what happened yesterday. Can you do that?"

"I already told Higgins and three of his officers. I'm not talking to any more police." He slurred his words, an effect of the drugs they pumped into him.

I stood at the foot of the bed and rested my fingers on the plastic. Jason's hair was a mess, his eyes rimmed with red. Otherwise, he looked completely unscathed. "We aren't police."

"What then? Reporters?" He crossed his arms. "I'm not crazy."

"We know," Ember said.

"How did you escape the monster?" I asked, and his gaze flicked to mine. "You said it pulled your friends through an invisible hole. How did you get away?"

"I shouldn't have." He clasped his hands in his lap and lowered his eyes.

"But you did." Ember touched her fingertips to his shoulder. "And we need to know how."

He laughed dryly. "I wasn't inside the circle."

"And the other kids were?" Why on earth would they be inside a summoning circle?

"Amanda said it would protect us. That we should stay inside it while we held the séance, and no spirits could harm us. She, Andrew, and Caitlyn did what she told them. I was showing off, trying to impress Caitlyn by being the tough guy. But the circle didn't protect them. It trapped them." He choked on a sob.

My heart ached for the poor guy. This Amanda chick either didn't know what she was doing, or she meant to sacrifice her friends. Or both. "I know it's hard to relive this, but tell us about Amanda. Is she the one who brought the book? Did she claim to be a witch?"

He toyed with the edge of the blanket and shook his head. "The book was Caitlyn's. She collects old stuff, found it at a thrift store forever ago. She's used it before and nothing happened, so I don't know how..." A tear slid down his cheek. He didn't bother to wipe it away.

"And Amanda?" Ember asked.

"Andrew met her last week. We were hanging out in Caitlyn's basement, drinking, when Amanda told us she was descended from witches. She'd turned eighteen and found out the names of her birth parents. She traced her ancestry to Salem, so she came here to find her roots."

A witch who grew up human. That explained why she might not know the difference between a summoning ring and a protection circle. "Why that particular spot in the woods? Why not do it in the basement?"

He shrugged. "Amanda said witches worked in nature. The rest of us went along with it."

Ember fisted her hands, impatience carving lines in her forehead. "Why that spot? Who chose it?"

"We all did, I guess."

"Why?" I asked.

His shoulders drew toward his ears and stayed there. "You'll think I'm crazy if I tell you."

"We don't so far." Ember's teeth didn't part as she spoke, and I couldn't blame her. Getting information out of this guy was like squeezing wine from a raisin.

"We won't think you're crazy. We're trying to help figure this out." I walked around to the side of the bed, ready to strangle it out of him if he didn't hurry up.

Okay, no, I would never actually strangle someone. But Ember might.

"It felt different there. We walked into the woods and headed straight for that spot like it *wanted* us to do the séance there."

"That makes sense." I looked at Ember, who nodded.

"It's as we suspected."

"You believe me?" Jason clutched my wrist, startling me. "Tell me you believe me."

My gaze flicked to his hand, and Chaos growled in my head. *"He shouldn't be touching you."*

Jason's eyes widened in a look of sheer terror. His grip tightened, his breath coming in short pants as if something...or someone...had reversed the effects of the sedatives.

"Down, boy," I said to Chaos as I pried Jason's grip from my arm and stepped away. His expression immediately returned to a vacant stare. "Thank you for talking to us."

Ember followed me to the door, her face solemn. "You were right," she said as she pulled the door shut. "The demon drew them there. A witch who didn't understand magic was in the wrong place at the wrong time, and three people are dead because of it."

I nodded. "And I highly doubt she had the power to summon Discord."

"Which means we're back to square one, with no clue who started this mess."

"Cinder had a clue."

Ember looked at me sideways as we paced down the hall.

"She had the sigils in her room," I said. "It can't be a coincidence." We exited the building and climbed into the van.

"I hear you." Ember started the engine and backed out of her parking space. "But whatever clue she had; she took it with her."

"Maybe not." I rubbed my palms on my jeans. "I found her diary under the mattress with the sigils."

She slammed on the brakes. "And you're just now telling me about this?"

"I tried to talk to you about it last night, but you shut me down. The page of demon symbols was inside one of my sigil books, and that book was lying next to her diary."

She looked at me like I'd grown horns. "What did it say?"

I ran my fingers through my hair to make sure I hadn't. Whew. No horns. "I didn't read it."

"Why not? It could have clues to what happened to her. To Mom and Dad."

I held up my hands. "First off, it has her private thoughts. There might be stuff in there we don't want to know, and I'm not in the habit of snooping. Second, I was a little distracted by the demon in my head and then the one in the woods. It's in my desk drawer."

"If she did summon my brother with his skull, she might have known where mine is."

I hated to admit it, but it was in everyone's best interest for us to peruse Cinder's private thoughts. I sighed. "We'll read it when we get home."

NINE

"Oh, hell." Ember rolled to a stop on South Washington Square, bordering Salem Common, an eight-acre park in the heart of downtown. "Can we not make it from point A to point B without a fiasco?"

She grabbed her phone and pressed it to her ear while I peered out the window at the commotion. People screamed, throwing their arms over their heads and running for cover. A black mass followed a man who darted toward the gazebo, a stray blob freeing itself from the herd to latch onto his neck. He swatted it away, and it hit the ground before rising and rejoining the mass.

"Is that a swarm of fae?" I crawled over the console, into the backseat to retrieve my spell kit. Crap. I never had time to restock it.

"Sure looks like it. Shade is on his way. Can you slow the critters down until they get here?" She pulled off the road and parked in a no-parking zone. Chief Higgins would make the ticket disappear if need be. He owed us that much.

"There is a rift here. I can sense it."

"No shit, Sherlock." I balanced the bowl on the back seat and dumped in the ingredients for my newly concocted spell. "Stray fae get through here and there year-round, but I've never encountered a swarm that big."

"I despise the fae."

"Don't we all?" Their high-pitched laughs were enough to drive anyone mad, but those teeth... Tiny, razor-sharp daggers filled their mouths, and they loved the taste of human blood. They were the mosquitos of my nightmares.

Ember exited the driver's side and opened the back door. "No talking to Chaos when the other witches are around. The demon business is between you and me for now. If no one has a hostile takeover planned yet, they will when they find out you performed dark magic."

Way to blame it all on me, sis. Then again, she wasn't wrong.

"It was an accident, but I get it. I was afraid to even tell you." I made twice as much potion as last time. I might need to slow the onlookers down too, so they didn't get too close to the faeries.

"I'm glad you did." She strapped her sword to her back and attached two daggers to her thighs before gripping my arm. "Hey. You know you can tell me anything, right?"

"I know." I forced a smile, and she let me go. I'd always been closer to Cinder. Ember and I got along just fine, but when I had a secret to share, I went to Cinder. Em was trying to fill that void for me. The least I could do was give back a little.

"You know what's weird? I'm not scared of Chaos. You'd think being possessed would be the most frightening thing ever, but it's not. I think he kinda likes me."

His deep chuckle reverberated through me. *"I can think of worse witches to be trapped inside."*

She scrunched her nose. "You're right. That is weird."

See why I always confided in Cinder? I dropped the spearmint oil into the mixture, activating it, and poured the granules into my hand. "I hope Shade is close. I don't know how long this spell lasts."

"He was ten minutes out."

I nodded and climbed out of the van. My boots crunched on the fallen leaves as I marched toward the faeries and shouted, "Hey! Your main course is here."

Did I mention they loved witch blood even more than human?

The swarm flew toward me, and the onlookers gasped. One of the little suckers broke free from the brood and nipped at my neck, taking a chunk of skin with it. That was a lucky shot; it wouldn't happen again. Did I also mention how much I hated faeries?

I bent down, pretending to scoop a handful of dirt, and threw it into the fray. Their velocity slowed until they appeared to be flying through invisible mud, their little brown wings flapping in slow motion.

"What in the world?" a man asked, and people gathered

around, a new swarm, just as dangerous as the first, descending on me.

Glad I made a double spell. I whispered the incantation, putting as much of my vim into it as I dared before tossing the granules in a circular motion, making a ring around the area. It didn't fill all eight acres—how could it?—but hopefully it slowed their thoughts down too or the humans would have a slew of conspiracy theories when this was through.

Now if Shade would get his ass here, we could hide this from the rest of the town, I could locate the rift and close it, and we could be on our way. I dropped my spell bag on the ground and squatted next to it before preparing the perimeter location potion. Thankfully, I still had all the ingredients for this one. Restocking would be at the top of my to-do list as soon as we got home.

Along with reading Cinder's journal, finding Chaos's skull, exorcizing him, finding Cinder... I was giving myself anxiety just thinking about the length of that list.

I crushed the herbs in the bowl, and the energy around me shifted. Everything took on a grayish tinge, like I was looking through fog.

"It's about damn time." I glanced up at Shade before continuing my potion. He'd brought Ginger and Miles along too. "They're just a few fae. You didn't have to bring the calvary." I dropped in the final ingredient, and the mixture smoked before turning to fine powder.

Shade stepped toward the swarm and poked a faery. Its mouth opened slowly as if it were trying to snap at his finger.

"What the hell kind of magic is this? I've never seen this spell before."

"It's experimental. I made it on the fly when we fought the demon, and it worked for that." I stood and poured the powdered spell into my palm.

He curled his lip. "Would have been more efficient to freeze them."

I fisted my hand around the powder, fighting the urge to test the hardness of his jaw with my knuckles. "I didn't have the right ingredients, or I would have."

He clicked his tongue. "Some girl scout you are, running into a fight unprepared. If I were you, I'd have premixed binding and perimeter locators on hand." He swept his gaze across the Common. "Where's the rift? I suppose you need me to seal it too?"

Who was worse? The fae or Shade? I wasn't sure. Would it be awful of me to shove him through the rift once I found it? Maybe a little.

"The only reason I couldn't close it before was because I had fought a *demon*. When was the last time you battled a creature from Hell?" I brushed past him, said the incantation, and blew the powder into the air. Like last time, it turned to fog and rolled through the grounds until it met the rift.

Ember stood next to me, facing the others. "Round up the little buggers and shove them through. Ash and I will seal it."

Chaos growled in my head. *"I don't like the way he talks to you."*

I turned and walked with her toward the rift. "Shade is an ass."

"I heard that!" He plucked a faery from the bunch and examined it.

"Good," I shouted back without turning around.

"Your High Priestess should protect you from him."

I laughed and lowered my voice. "I don't need protection from Shade. He's all bark and no bite."

Ember shot me a warning look. "Where's your earbud?"

"Sorry. I'll be quiet." I slipped my bag off my shoulder and rummaged through it while Ginger shoved an armful of fae through the rift.

"Here." Miles held a vial toward me, his gray eyes shifting as he spoke. "Shade asked me to make a few to keep on hand in case it happened again."

I pressed my lips together, wanting ever so badly to refuse his offer for the simple fact that Shade had commissioned the potion. I was loath to use my vim with his intentions, but it would speed things along.

"Thanks." I accepted it, but I want it noted how reluctant I was. Also, Miles was the new guy. Sure, he was great at spells, but why would Shade have commissioned them from him? Probably to turn him against me. The dipshit.

"How do these creatures survive in a realm infested with demons and ghouls?" Shade asked as he sent an armful through the tear. "Seems like they'd be easy pickings."

"The other realm has multiple layers, like this one. Much like spirits can linger here undetected in a separate plane, the fae exist in their own level of the realm. Demons have their own space, but they can freely cross the layers."

I paraphrased what he said.

"That makes sense." Ember gave me the look again, reminding me not to reveal the voice in my head.

Shade narrowed his eyes. "Why do you know so much about demons?"

"Because I read." I crossed my arms. "You should try cracking a book sometime."

With the last of the fae on the correct side of the veil, I popped the top on the brew and took Ember's hand. "Fabric torn will be reborn. Seal these treads so we don't end up dead."

Shade scoffed behind me, no doubt expecting my incantation to fail, but I ignored him like the adult I was supposed to be.

I poured the mixture over the rip, and the treads shone gold as they stitched themselves back together. "Thanks for that," I whispered before giving Ember's hand a squeeze and letting go.

"Anytime." She turned toward the others. "Great work today. Thanks for getting here on such short notice."

"Are you going to call a meeting to talk about why this keeps happening?" Ginger asked.

Ember shook her head. "Not yet. I have some more research to do."

"A group brainstorming session would be beneficial," Shade said. "The more ideas we have, the faster we'll find the problem and fix it."

"I bet it's something on the other side," Miles said. "Maybe the fae are organizing. They aren't all mindless bloodsuckers like these."

Ember cut her gaze to me before speaking. "We're working on it. Give us some time."

"But..." Shade started to argue, but Ember lifted her hand.

"Go home before the humans get unstuck," she said. "Bottle some spells for freezing monsters and sealing the veil. If you can, bottle some of your shadow work for us to carry when you aren't around. I know it won't be as powerful, but it'll help in cases like this."

He nodded. "Okay. Keep us informed."

"Will do," Ember said, and we headed for the van.

When we got home, I carried in my travel spell kit to restock it. No way was I using someone else's spell again. Especially one from Shade. I needed to soak in a tub of hand sanitizer and hyssop in a bathroom full of sage and drink a gallon of basil and patchouli tea to clear his ick from my body and soul. I shuddered and set the bag on the kitchen counter.

Ember gripped my shoulder. "Are you okay? Is the demon...?"

"I'm fine. Chaos has been quiet since we left the Common. I just..." I lined the empty bottles next to the bag and opened the pantry. "Why did you tell Shade to make the freezing and sealing spells? You know I can make them. It's literally *my job* to supply you with whatever you need to hunt monsters."

She slid onto a stool across the counter. "I'm sorry. I was trying to get him off our backs so we could figure things out."

I dumped an armful of herbs next to the bottles. "Shadow magic, okay. He's the only one in the coven with that kind of power, so sure. Ask him to bottle that, but don't take away one of the few ways I can contribute to solving the problem."

A growl rumbled in my head. *"You shouldn't let such an insignificant little man affect your emotions like this. You are a Holland witch. He is nothing."*

"I know." I sighed heavily and refilled the peppermint oil. "I'm working on it."

"When you find my skull and free me, I'll see to it that he never bothers you again."

I laughed. "Thanks. Wait... What do you mean by that?"

"What would you like? I can drive him mad with a touch, or if you prefer, I can tear him limb from limb before dragging him to Hell. I haven't decided which would be a better punishment for the way he treats you."

"Absolutely not!" It was tempting, but no. I grabbed a big copper bowl and my mortar and pestle from the cabinet.

"What's he saying?" Ember asked.

"He's telling me all the things he could do to Shade once he's free."

Her brows crept toward her hairline.

"He won't. Will you, Chaos?"

"I make no promises."

I fisted my hands on my hips. "Well, you better start. You will not harm a coven member. Understood?"

"Understood. I won't...unless you ask me to."

I fought a grin and looked at Ember. "He's a demon. He's got to learn the way we do things around here."

She rolled her eyes. "You mean passive-aggressive jabs and pissing contests as often as possible?"

"Exactly." I set the rest of my supplies on the counter. "Where's the journal?"

"In my desk drawer downstairs."

"You could've grabbed it before we came up," she grumbled as she headed to the library.

"Yeah, well..." I dumped the ingredients for the sealing spell into the bowl. This whole ordeal was a giant shit show. I'd summoned a friggin' demon, for Hecate's sake, and there was a good chance Cinder...our former acting High Priestess...had summoned one too. Salem was turning into total chaos with all these tears in the veil...that the Holland witches were apparently responsible for, and Shade just had to one-up me every chance he got.

Oh, and now the asshat was in the process of turning Miles against me. And with Miles would go Ginger too. She was super nice to me now, but she and Miles were dating, so...

"Whoa," Ember said as she froze in the kitchen entrance. "What's gotten into you? It looks like a tornado tore through the place."

"What?" I snapped before glancing around the room. Holy mother of magic. Loose herbs littered the countertop, and my orderly line of bottles was now scattered across the room. Some lay on the floor while others rolled across the opposite counter. A box of baking soda had fallen open on the tile, and footprints —my footprints—tracked from the pantry to the sink to the place I currently stood.

"What the hell?" Ground sage coated my hands, so I paced to the sink and rinsed it off. I didn't remember doing any of this. That could only mean one thing... "Chaos?"

A full three seconds passed before he answered. *"Yes."*

"Yes? That's all you have to say?" I picked up the strewn

bottles and lined them up again before getting a dustpan after the rest of the mess. Ember returned to her stool and laid the journal in front of her.

"I'm trying not to take over, but our souls are melding. You're the epitome of order. That's the only reason you've been able to resist my nature for so long."

"For so long? A day and a half is long?"

Ember pinned me with a steely gaze. "What's going on? Did Chaos make you do this?"

"You need to tell her."

"The hell I do." I scrubbed the counter with a disinfecting wipe.

"Stop!" Ember slapped her hand on top of mine, stilling me. "I want to help get this demon out of your head, but I need to know what's going on. I'm only hearing one side of your dialogue, so you need to explain it to me."

I sucked in a deep breath and tried to slide my hand out from under hers. She tightened her grip. "It's not important. Let's just read the journal and see if Cinder mentioned anything about finding a skull."

"It is important. I have never seen you make a mess in your entire life. Even as a toddler, you were organizing your toys more than playing with them."

"Tell her."

"Okay. Fine." I pulled my hand again, but she didn't let go. Cocking my head, I gave her a hard look, and she finally released me. "You've got so much shit on your plate right now; I didn't want to worry you."

She folded her hands on top of the journal. "Worry me, Ash. Please."

"It's..." I drummed my nails on the counter twice. "Chaos can't stay in my head forever."

"Obviously."

"His consciousness is kinda melding with mine, and if I don't send him packing soon, he'll sorta take over." I shrugged and returned to my cleaning.

Her mouth formed a straight line. "Say that again without the qualifiers."

I huffed. "His consciousness is melding with mine, and if I don't get him out soon, he'll take over."

She leaned on her forearms. "This is serious, Ash."

"I know it is. That's why I didn't want to tell you." I dumped the contents of the mixing bowl into the trash. Who knew what I'd thrown in there during my chaotic blackout?

"How long do you have?"

"I don't know. Chaos?"

"With your immense power, no more than two weeks."

I looked at Ember. "Two weeks, tops. Read the journal while I restock the kit. It's our best bet for fixing all this."

My sister scanned the pages while I made another batch of sealing potion. Thankfully, Chaos stayed quiet and didn't turn me into Hurricane Ash again. Ember gasped a few times, and I tried to ignore the growing expression of alarm widening her eyes as she absorbed whatever Cinder had written.

She swallowed audibly and looked up from the pages. "Holy Hecate. The curse, Ash. You didn't break the curse by surviving. You *are* the curse."

The blood in my head plummeted to my feet. I held onto the counter and slowly made my way around to Ember. "What do you mean, I *am* the curse? What does it say?"

"She knew you would find it. Cinder knew you'd detect the spell."

I clenched my teeth. "What does it say?"

She let out a slow breath and opened the journal to the first page. "'Dear Ash. If you're reading this, I never made it back.'" She pushed the book toward me. "Do you want to read it?"

I shook my head and sank onto the stool next to her, a sense of dread tightening my stomach, making me feel like I'd swallowed a brick.

Ember nodded and continued reading aloud. "'I know you planned to organize the library in Dad's absence, so I hid your favorite sigil book next to this journal in hopes that you'd find it should I go missing too. I really did leave in search of our parents. I didn't lie about that, but there are other things you need to know. You and Ember.' Hold on. I need a drink. Want one?"

I swallowed the dryness from my mouth. "Sure."

Ember grabbed two beers from the fridge and popped the tops before returning to her seat. She took a long pull from her bottle and slid mine toward me. The icy bubbles loosened the thickness in my throat, but they did nothing to quell the sense of impending doom churning in my gut. Chaos hadn't said a word, which was a very, very bad sign.

"'Our parents lied to you about the curse. They lied to us all. Every High Priestess that came before Mom lied too. You aren't the miracle baby she made you out to be. There's a reason why you're the only third daughter to survive. Mom didn't have the heart to kill you.'"

My eyes blinked rapidly of their own accord. I took another swig of beer, but it barely made it past my throat.

Ember continued, "'The curse wasn't that every third daughter of the High Priestess would die in infancy. It was that she would go insane and murder everyone in the coven.'"

"Wait. What?" No way would I murder the coven. I loved our coven and most of the people in it. "That can't be right."

Ember gave me a sympathetic look and read some more. "'I know it's hard to believe, but mom showed me the curse. It was in the dark grimoire in the safe.'"

I shot to my feet. "This can't be happening. I need to see it for myself."

"Hold on." Ember grabbed my wrist and tugged me back

into my seat. "You need to hear the rest of this first. 'The dirty secret of our coven is that if the High Priestess has a third daughter, she murders her. It has happened several times over the centuries, and the knowledge about the real curse is passed orally from the High Priestess to her oldest daughter. That's why I now know.'"

Holy mother of magic and mayhem. What the actual eff? "I've got a demon inside me. Chaos, are you the reason I'm supposedly going to murder my coven? Are you going to force me to do it?"

Five seconds passed before he responded. *"You have my word that I will not force you to murder your coven. The only person in danger from this possession is you."*

"What about after? When you take over completely?"

"I thought the plan was to find my skull so that won't happen."

"But if we don't?" My voice trembled, hysteria edging my words.

"If we don't, no more harm will come to your coven. I promise."

That should have relieved me a little, but it didn't. "He says it won't be because of him. What else did Cinder say?"

"'Mom has been searching for a way to break the curse since you were born. She was certain she'd figured out how to end it for good without harming you. The witch who hexed us harnessed the power of three demons, and only three demons can break the curse.

'Mom and Dad went into the woods to summon one. They cut a deal with him. I overheard them talking about it. They promised their souls in exchange for him delivering the fiends responsible.

The demon required the grimoire, so they took it back to the woods, but the one they bargained with was a trickster. He took the book and our parents, but not before I tore out the page identifying the only demons who could break the curse. The ones who created it.'"

I opened my mouth to speak, but whatever words I thought I had to say got stuck in my throat. The page of sigils that had fallen out of my book. I had possessed myself with the same demon who cursed my bloodline.

"Chaos..." I said, my jaw clenched.

Silence answered me.

"There's more," Ember said. "'The one who cursed us moved to Boston and joined the Magic Society there. I broke into their library, and that's where I discovered what she had done. She had promised her own soul and her firstborn's in exchange for the power, but she never planned to hold up her end of the deal.

'She vanquished the three demon brothers but hid their skulls. Without their bodies intact, they can't reform in Hell. They're trapped in a dark prison, and never got to collect her soul. The only way to break the curse is for us to release them. They are the only ones who can help.'"

"Chaos!" I shouted, and Ember jumped. "Is this true? Did you curse my family?"

One second. Two seconds. Three seconds. *My brothers and I let the witch use our power, yes.*

"But you said if I went insane, it wouldn't be because of you. Liar." My hands curled into tight fists, and my heart rate kicked into a sprint.

"No, you said it wouldn't be because of me. I said I wouldn't murder your coven or make you do it while in possession."

I crossed my arms. "Lying by omission is still lying."

"I'm a demon." I could almost see his nonchalant shrug.

"That's no excuse, mister." I jabbed my finger forward as if he were in front of me. "You have to fix this. I can't murder my entire coven."

My sister arched a brow. "Are you done?"

"Not yet. Did you know about this all along, demon boy?" I fumed. How could he betray me like this?

"I have known since you told me you were a Holland and the youngest of three."

I sucked in a breath to berate him more, but he continued, *"If you want to save your coven, you have two options. Find our skulls and release us. We will be in your debt, and I will try to convince my brothers to release you from the curse in exchange for our freedom."*

Sure. That sounded like an easy task. Not. "And option two?"

"Allow me to take over. Give your life to me, cease to exist. Without you, your coven is safe...until the next third-born daughter arises."

I told Ember what he said.

"Let me guess," she scoffed. "He suggests the second option."

"While that would be the easier of the two, my brother would still be imprisoned, and you would no longer exist. The world is a better place with you in it."

"Is that so?" I rolled my eyes. "He votes for option one.

Release him and his brothers, break the curse, and we can all be done with each other for good."

"I didn't say…"

"What?" I snapped.

"Nothing. Does Cinder mention if she found Discord's skull?"

I looked at Ember. "Did she write anything else?"

"I wondered if you were ever going to let me finish. 'I've located Discord's skull, and I'm going to release him. I'll convince him to take me into Hell so I can find Mom and Dad. I hope to bring them back right away, so you never have to read this, but if I don't return, you have to release the other two. We can end this. I know we can.'"

"Does she say where she found the skull?"

"Anything else? A treasure map with X marks the spot for the other skulls?"

Ember shook her head. "Nothing. The rest of the pages are blank."

"Well, crappity crap." My shoulders slumped. "What now?"

Ember drummed her fingers on the counter. "Cinder got the intel about the skulls from the Boston Magic Society's library. Sounds to me like another break-in is in order."

I choked on my beer. "You want to break into a dark witch coven's library? Are you insane? Do you know how many boobytraps they'll have set? I wouldn't be surprised if they have magical acid to burn our faces off Indiana Jones-style."

She lifted one shoulder dismissively. "Cinder pulled it off. Why can't we?"

"Because she's *Cinder,* the most powerful witch in our coven, if not in all of Massachusetts."

"Actually—"

"Oh no." I held up a finger. "Don't you 'actually' me, mister. You're in no position to demonsplain. I'm putting you in a timeout."

"But—"

"Nope."

"If you'll—"

"Zip it."

He growled, but he didn't say any more. Good boy. Once I got him out of my head, I'd have to teach him to sit.

Ember tossed her empty bottle into the recycle bin. "I'll humor you. Cinder may be the most powerful witch in the coven on her own, but you and I together are a force to be reckoned with. We've already vanquished a demon and a swarm of fae. We've got this."

"Do we?" I got nauseated even considering this suggestion, but... "Maybe if we had Shade, we could pull it off, but you and me alone...?" My body shuddered in revulsion. I despised that man way more than necessary, but I couldn't help it.

"We can't involve him."

Thank the goddess. "I agree one hundred percent."

"We can't let anyone know about this. A light witch consorting with demons is grounds for banishment. A family member of the High Priestess doing it could mean our family losing control of the coven. Add to that the fact they've been lied to about the curse for centuries, and... Cinder will bring our parents back. We owe it to them to keep the coven under control."

I scrunched my nose. "We do have a very good reason for

consorting with these particular demons. Maybe we could enlist one other monster hunter. Someone who can fight... Just in case."

"You can fight, Ash."

I laughed dryly. "I can also accidentally set their headquarters on fire."

"Spells, sis. Sigils and spells are your weapons. Forget about the fire."

My teeth clicked together. *Forget about the fire*, she said to the freaking fire witch. I knew she meant well, but I couldn't lie. That comment stung.

"You can do this. Your coven and your life depend on it."

Ember clasped her hands beneath her chin and flashed a fake smile. "What do you say, dear sister?"

My nostrils flared as I blew out a long, slow breath. I was supposed to be the voice of reason. Ember was the impulsive one. I tried to talk her out of her worst decisions. But at this point, I didn't see any other way. I mean, aside from letting Chaos take over my body, burn it up, and turn it into his own.

Hecate help me. "I say we're breaking into the Boston coven library."

ELEVEN

A chill that had nothing to do with the weather crept up my spine as Ember and I silently slid out of the van and gathered our gear. Thick clouds blanketed the sky, too high to be rain clouds but ominous enough to add to the foreboding feeling tying my insides into knots.

We'd parked in an alley four blocks from the Boston Magic Society's headquarters, and thank the goddess it wasn't raining. Wet leather chafed like a mother effer. I needed to work on a spell to fix that. Fireproofing had been my initial goal—Ember relied on it so her clothes didn't char and fall off every time she fought a monster—but an end to the chafing was next on my list.

Ember strapped her sword onto her back and secured daggers on her thighs and ankles. She looked like a total badass, as usual. I slung the magic kit crossways on my shoulder and checked to be sure my boots were tied.

"Here. Take this, just in case." My sister shoved a six-inch, sheathed dagger toward me, complete with leather straps to wrap around my thigh.

"You said no one would be there." I accepted the weapon and attached the scabbard to my leg. Better safe than sorry.

"It's the Hunter's Moon tonight. They'll be in the Boston Common performing their annual ritual. Dark magic practitioners hold this full moon above all others."

I narrowed my eyes. "And you don't think they'll leave anyone behind as guard? They can't even trust their own people."

"Mm-mm. Remember those boobytraps you were worried about? It's your job to nullify them without setting off the alarm. I'll do the rest."

"Fabulous."

Headlights approached from the cross street, and Ember flattened herself against the van. "You've got Shade's spells?"

My lip curled. "Yeah."

"Good. Activate one to get us from here to there. Be ready for the second one when it wears off."

I stuck my finger into my mouth, pretending to gag.

Ember rolled her eyes. "Real mature, Ash."

"His intentions just don't mix well with my vim. We're like oil and water. Colors that clash. Eating a greasy burrito on a transatlantic flight."

The car passed, and she slid the door shut. "Then why did you sleep with him?"

"I..." My mouth hung open as I tried to find the words to defend myself.

"You had sex with the man you despise?" Chaos sounded incredulous, and I couldn't say I blamed him. I sometimes had trouble believing it myself.

"There was alcohol involved. Alcohol leads to bad decisions. I know it was wrong." In my defense, I had just finished a fabulous enemies-to-lovers romance novel, and I was still caught up in the magic of my favorite trope. A lower-level demon had slipped through the veil, as they did in Salem from time to time, and the team had vanquished it. No ghoul guts or cemetery fires involved.

Tequila shots in the kitchen to celebrate. Ember went to bed; everyone else went home. Shade stayed. You can figure out the rest. I woke up with regrets; he woke with goo-goo eyes. Cocky asshats didn't handle rejection well. We went from mildly annoying each other to mortal enemies in one night flat.

"Did he force you? I'll tear off his limbs and shove them into every orifice on his body."

Now that would be a sight to see. "Down, boy. Nobody forced anybody. It was a mutual mistake."

"You set?" Ember's voice pulled me to the present.

"Ready as I'll ever be to sneak into a boobytrapped, dark magic HQ." Which was not at all.

"Activate the first shadow spell."

I really did gag a little this time, but I tried my best to hide it as I popped the cork on Shade's bottled essence—double gag—and poured the black powder into my hand. Then I read the slip of paper he'd included with the vials. "Hide from sight our magical plight. With the power of Shade, my intent is conveyed."

Seriously? Who wrote themselves into a spell? I was certain he rhymed it that way just to grate on my nerves. Whatever.

I blew the power into the air, and it billowed into a thick gray cloud before falling around us, cloaking us. The world turned unsaturated, nearly grayscale, and we hoofed it toward the entrance.

Okay, that wasn't so bad. Maybe I had been a bit overly dramatic about using shadow magic. Note to self: act like an effing grownup. Especially when he was poking me. Metaphorically, of course, because his poker would never get close enough to poke me again.

Two blocks from our target, a homeless man sat huddled against a building. A little brown terrier lay beside him, snuggled in a green blanket while the man used a piece of a cardboard box to block the wind. My heart ached for the pair, so I dug in my pocket and pulled out a ten.

He didn't react as I approached, and when I laid the money on the ground next to him, he sucked in a ragged breath, his hooded eyes growing wide like saucers. "A blessing from the goddess," he mumbled.

I smiled. "Something like that."

"Ash!" Ember shouted. "No time for bleeding hearts. Let's keep moving."

The man tucked the money into his shirt, completely oblivious to our presence.

"The spell mutes sound too?" I followed my sister across the intersection. The building stood one block away.

"I told him to put everything he had into them. He'll probably sleep fifteen hours tonight. He looked like shit when I picked them up."

"Well, color me impressed."

"Me too. Maybe I won't kill him. He seems useful to you."

I laughed. "I suppose he can be."

Ember lifted her brows, silently telling me to fill her in.

"He says Shade might be useful, so he won't kill him."

"Probably won't."

She crossed her arms, widening her stance. "If he so much as pretends he's going to harm one of our coven members, I'll send him right back to his dark prison and turn his skull into powder so he can never resurrect."

"I would like to see her try."

I held up my hands. "Stop, both of you. Let's focus on the mission, mm-kay? My heart is beating like a racehorse trampling through my chest, and I would like to get this over with before they get done with their ritual."

"Hmph," he grumbled.

"Right back at ya, dude," I said.

Ember parked a hand on her hip. "I'm not kidding."

"He already promised not to hurt anyone in the coven." I pulled another shadow spell from my satchel and popped it open...without cringing, I might add.

With our cover reinforced, we crept toward the three-story brick building. The racehorse in my chest kicked into overdrive, and I sucked in a deep breath, hoping to slow it before I hyperventilated.

"This is as close as I'm willing to get until we know what

kind of magic is protecting the place. Do your thing, sis." Ember motioned toward the front door.

"Here we go." I kept the kit stocked with individual ingredients so the hunters could make whatever spells they needed on the fly. This time, I had an idea of what we'd be up against, so I'd packed a slew of ready-made potions.

This spell, however, was a specialty of mine. I'd practiced it so much I didn't need the help of a potion. Being the youngest, I'd used it plenty of times to snoop in my sisters' rooms, finding all the charms they'd put up to hide things. "Confess, expose my magic sleuth. I call on you to reveal your truth."

I directed my intention toward the door and the nearby windows. Gold sparkled in the air, looking for signs of magic, but it fell to the ground, dissipating. Huh. That was odd.

"No magic on the entrance?" Ember asked.

"Doesn't appear that way." I crept up the stairs and tried the handle. "Just a lock."

Chaos growled in my head.

"What?" I asked.

"There's magic inside. Dark magic obtained from my realm."

"Of course there is. They're a dark magic coven. It's kinda their thing." I dug a lock-picking kit from my satchel and kneeled in front of the door.

"It's too dangerous. You should wait until I'm free so I can take out the coven. Then you can access all their knowledge without risking your life."

"There's a problem with your plan. Two, actually." I slid the tension wrench into the bottom of the keyhole and applied a little pressure. "We don't *take out* other covens. They're not a group of serial killers. They're a bunch of self-serving witches who like to stir up trouble in their own town. Not our problem. They don't mess with us, and we don't report them to the Higher Power."

"Is he trying to convince you to kill them all?" Concern creased Ember's forehead.

"He's afraid we're going to get hurt." I slid the rake in above the wrench and scrubbed it in a circular motion, disengaging the pins one by one.

"Better them than you."

"Problem two: I can't free you without *accessing their knowledge*, so zip it and let me get us inside before the shadow spell wears off." I fought a grin. I hated to admit it, but it was kinda sweet that this big, growly demon was concerned for my safety.

Wait a minute. Demons weren't sweet.

"Why do you even care? If I do nothing, you get to take over in a couple of weeks. You'll be free whether I live or not."

He missed several beats as he formulated his reply. For a demon named Chaos, he sure had a lot of control. *"I am in your debt, and..."* Another beat. Make that two. *"You deserve life."*

The lock disengaged, and I shoved the tools into my satchel. "We're in." I tapped the door with my finger, making sure it wasn't going to blow off the hinges at the first creak. It swung freely, so I stepped back and directed another magic-revealing spell into the opening. Again, no enchantments protected the entrance.

"This doesn't feel right." I rose to my feet, but my stomach didn't go up with the rest of me. It continued sinking into my boots. "A human could have picked this lock. I know the BMS isn't an ethical coven, but they'd protect their assets from the mundane if only to cover their asses with the Higher Power."

"The shadow spell is wearing off, so make a decision. I'm going in." Ember strode past me with the confidence of a gazelle walking into a pride of lions. Sure, she could outmaneuver them, but she was oblivious to their strength. Typical Ember.

I slung the satchel over my shoulder and followed her inside, closing the door behind me. Ember lit a fireball in her hand, and I shined a flashlight around the room. Ah. This made sense. The front of their HQ was a witchy shop like ours. If a mundane wanted to rob it, they couldn't have them bursting into flames the second they stepped inside.

I blew out the breath I was well aware I'd been holding. Temptation to see if they sold any actual spells in their shop had me itching to check the place out, but Ember's impatient glare as she stood by the door leading deeper into their lair kept my curiosity in check.

"What lies beyond that threshold can kill you."

"I figured as much." A quick test with my trusty gold sparkles revealed an electrification spell. I tilted my head and watched the glitter cling to the fabric of the enchantment. "This layer of protection has been here a long time. See how it's rooted to the floor and door frame?"

I gestured to show Ember how the fibers thickened where the layer of magic connected to the building. "They must all have tokens that allow them to pass through unharmed."

She unsheathed her sword. "Can you unravel it gently, or do I get to tear it apart?"

"I've got this." The last thing I needed was for Ember to get electrocuted and leave me alone with whatever beastie they might have guarding the place.

I snatched two black tourmaline pendants from the rack and rubbed them with horehound leaves. After a quick incantation, they glowed blue before fading back to their normal hue. We slipped the cords around our necks and eyed the deadly door.

I took a step back. "If this doesn't work, we'll be Kentucky fried and dead on the floor."

"Do you think it'll work?" She flicked her gaze to me before focusing on the electric field blocking our way.

"It should. Unless…"

"Good enough for me." Ember stepped through the door without even an arm hair standing on end.

My stomach clenched along with my jaw, my hands fisting instinctively. One of these days, her gall would get her killed. Hopefully this would not be that day.

"This was genius, Ash," Ember whispered. "We can get in and out without them knowing we were here."

"That's the plan." I stepped in behind her.

"Good luck with that."

"Thanks for the vote of confidence."

Chaos grunted. *"Can you not feel the demonic magic in the air?"*

"Nope." I shined my flashlight around the room. A long rectangular table took up the center of the space, with chairs crammed around all the sides. At the head of the table loomed an ornate...I could only call it a throne, with gilded edges and intricate dark magic carvings.

"Stop and try. It's unmistakable."

Ember curled her lip. "A little pretentious, isn't it? Their archives must be farther back." She gestured at the door, waiting for me to check it for magic.

"Hold on." I took a deep breath and focused on the energy in the air. It felt sticky, like the magic performed there wasn't always done with good intentions. Obviously, or they wouldn't be a dark magic coven. "What am I looking for?"

"The lowest vibration you've ever felt. It will penetrate your flesh and hum in your bones. Concentrate."

"Let's go, Ash." Ember jerked her head toward the door.

"Wait. He's teaching me how to sense demon magic. It could come in handy." I closed my eyes and let all the energy in the room wash over me. I'd need an insanely hot shower when this was through. Sticky, icky remnants of dark magic clung to my skin, but something *other* engulfed me too.

Like Chaos described, the vibration was lower, slower than anything I'd felt before and it did indeed penetrate all the way to my bones, giving me the same pins and needles sensation as when your foot falls asleep, but much, *much* deeper.

"Holy Hecate. Is this what your presence will feel like once you're out of my head?"

"Mine and every demon you encounter. Proceed with caution."

"Always." I joined my sister at the next doorway and activated the magic-revealing spell. "This one isn't protected."

"Probably because of what's waiting for us inside." Ember clutched her sword in both hands and crept down the staircase.

My flashlight penetrated the darkness, revealing a long corridor that slanted even farther downward. We were headed deep into the basement, and I could guarantee the door leading to the surface outside would be protected with something even more potent than the electricity spell cloaking the inside door. I had no idea if our crystals would shield us from it, which meant we had one way of escape if things went south. Back the way we came.

I said a quick prayer to the goddess that things would stay above the equator.

The corridor spilled out into a massive, stone-lined room, and silence engulfed us. The musty scent of old books, which usually brought me a sense of peace, smelled more like rot and clay. Not a single window lined the wall near the ceiling to let in an ounce of light. We must've been too deep.

I swept the beam along the wall, illuminating a switch attached to a silver plate. Metal tubing ran up the surface and across the ceiling toward a massive chandelier. I flipped the switch.

Lights from sconces added to the brilliant chandelier bulbs, revealing a library so massive I couldn't hide my envy. My mouth dropped open as I took in rows and rows of shelving units so tall they had wheeled ladders attached to each one. "Whoa."

"Wow." Even Ember was in awe. "They have twice as many books as us. How are we going to find anything?"

I chuckled. "I'll tell you how." A card catalog stood right in front of us, gleaming in the warm light, dark cherry wood housing columns of five-inch drawers with golden handles.

One day, my library would be this organized. Maybe not as flashy and big, but it would be awesome.

"*Ash?*"

"Mm-hmm?" I slid out a drawer and ran my fingers over the cards, a smile tugging at my lips.

"*Have you forgotten about the demon guarding this place?*"

Honestly? Yeah, I had forgotten. The library was nothing short of magnificent.

"Oh shit." Ember backed into me, ramming me into the catalog. The drawer slammed shut on my finger, and I yanked it out, sticking it in my mouth as if that would ease the smashing pain.

"Find the info fast," she said over her shoulder. "I'll take care of the beastie."

I spun around and nearly peed my pants. An eight-foot creature with a massive jaw and fangs that belonged on a sabertooth tiger prowled toward her, and it was entirely made of clay.

So that was what I smelled.

CHAPTER

TWELVE

"Here, demon, demon." Ember made a come get me motion with her hand and crept off to the right. The fiend grunted at me, looked at her, and lunged. Smart move for the demon; bad news for me. He planned to take out the most dangerous threat first so he could toy with the weaker one. Yay.

She stabbed her sword right into his gut and twisted before yanking it out. He stumbled, but the clay reformed, filling in the gash within seconds. "Does this library have advice on how to kill a golem?" she asked.

Chaos growled. *"Being trapped in a golem is almost as bad as the prison you rescued me from. He is their slave and will do their bidding until he is released."*

"And I guess their bidding is to protect their secrets at all costs. How do we release him?"

"Only the one who trapped him can."

"Fabulous. Hey, Em? He can't be killed, so just keep him busy while I find the book."

"Challenge accepted." She spun in a circle and swiped her sword, taking his arm off at the elbow. I was about to say one point for Ember, but a new arm formed where she'd cut him, and the one on the floor turned to goo, rolled across the concrete, and attached itself to his leg.

"That's not fair." Ember backed up, drawing the golem farther away from me. I had a feeling she'd never fought one of these before, so she'd either have the time of her life or end up dead. The faster I could find the book, the more likely it would be the former.

I yanked open the drawer with the letter D and flipped to the cards about demons. "Frickity frak. There must be a hundred entries." A quick glance at the drawers below confirmed it. There were three D drawers.

"How about curses?" The C drawer wasn't much better. At least fifty volumes held information about curses. "I would appreciate any advice you could give me, Chaos." Because I was getting nowhere, which meant bad news for my sister.

She grunted, and I looked up in time to see her fly backward and smack into a bookcase. Really bad news.

"The witch who cursed your bloodline was named Smith."

"You could have told me that five minutes ago," I grumbled as I opened the S drawer. Not that it would help, with Smith being such a common name.

I flipped past sage, salt, and slime (ew). "Smith!" Flip, flip, flip. "Huh. There are only three, and they're all Isabel."

"That is her." Chaos's voice was full of menace.

I yanked the cards from the drawer and ducked between shelves as a fireball whizzed past. It smacked into a case of ancient-looking texts, but instead of setting the entire basement ablaze, it bounced off and returned to Ember's hand.

That was how fire magic was supposed to work.

Finding the books was easy-peasy, thanks to their librarian's organizational skills. I tugged them from the shelf and plopped onto the floor. The first one I opened was filled with healing spells, cleansing rituals, and other light magic stuff. I supposed even dark witches needed to lighten their loads from time to time. Playing with evil could take a toll.

"Isabel belonged to your coven before the curse."

That much I knew, but her name had been struck from the record books. Magically erased so she would never be spoken of again. "What turned her bad?"

"No rush, Ash. I'm having a blast." I couldn't tell if she said that with sarcasm or not. You never knew with Ember.

"I found the books," I called from the safety of the stacks.

"Let's take them all." Her sword met clay. The golem grunted.

"Then they'll know we've been here. They could locate them and cause us a mess of trouble." I flipped the pages.

"Good point." Slash, stab, grunt. "Continue."

"A love triangle," Chaos answered. *"Isabel was betrothed to your great-great-great—"*

"Who knows how many greats? Got it."

"Hester, your ancestor, arrived from England, and he fell in love with her, betraying Isabel."

"Oof. Hell hath no fury." The second book had tons of potions and spells of the unsavory variety, but nothing about the curse or where the skulls might be hidden. I put it back and opened the next one. "Bingo. This must be the one Cinder used to find Discord."

I ran my finger along the first page, a journal entry describing Isabel's pain and her intention. I only skimmed it, but let me just say... She was pissed.

The next page laid out the curse, how she did it, and the ramifications. Like Chaos said, she was supposed to pay with her soul.

Should my plan not work, their wrath will be exerted on my descendants. Return their skulls to them and beg for forgiveness, lest my entire lineage be doomed to hell.

CINDER CAME HERE ALONE. She had to find the book while fighting off the golem and get out undetected. How in Hell did she do it?

I flipped the page. "Good goddess, look at this." A map. A freaking map!

"Ugh!" Ember grunted before her head smacked the concrete floor at the end of the aisle. The golem dragged her out of my view.

"Shit! I'm coming, Em!" I ripped the map from the book, slammed it into its space on the shelf, and ran toward them. I skidded to a stop when I saw my sister dangling upside down from the creature's massive fist.

"Let her go!" I yanked the dagger from my thigh scabbard and hurled it at the golem. It hit him in the gut, but it disappeared inside him, his clay absorbing the weapon like a black hole. I grabbed a binding spell from my satchel, said the incantation, and threw it at him. Powder exploded in his face, and he dropped Ember—on her head—to wipe his eyes. He didn't freeze.

But my sister did.

The creature roared and started toward me. He swung his meaty arm, and I ducked. He clipped the top of my head, but my momentum carried me forward, and I slid toward Ember.

"Time to go." I hooked my arms beneath her shoulders and dragged her backward into the corridor.

"*Use another spell.*" That Chaos. Ever helpful.

"If the binding spell didn't work, I doubt anything else will." I groaned and dragged her toward the stairs. It was all uphill from here. Literally.

"*Let me help.*"

"How?" My foot met the first step as the golem prowled toward me. Yep, toying with the weaker one now that the threat was incapacitated. Demons were so predictable.

Chaos took my question as permission. My head spun, and I squeezed my eyes shut. When I opened them, the golem lay beneath one of seven toppled bookshelves. The library had been torn apart...in a state of complete...*chaos.*

"*It won't hold him long. Run.*"

One foot behind the other, I got my sister up the stairs and through the meeting slash ritual room. I was about to drag her through the electrified door when Chaos yelled, "Stop!"

I froze. "What?"

"Her pendant is gone."

"Crappity crap. It must've fallen off when he held her upside down." I slipped mine off and put it around her neck along with my satchel.

"What's your plan?"

"Well, I have a whole other life inside me. A Prince of Hell. You can keep me safe, right? I doubt a little electricity would hurt you."

"I..."

"I'll let you take over like you did down there and in the kitchen. Get me through the spell and then give me back control." And then we'd have a long talk about consent.

"That's a horrible plan."

The sound of wood crashing echoed from below before feet pounded the stairs.

"Unless you have something better, do it now."

The golem roared, reached the top of the stairs, and lunged.

I blacked out, meaning Chaos took complete control. Yay. My plan worked.

Until it didn't. My demon got Ember through the spell no problem, but even without control of my body, I felt every magical jolt of electricity as it ripped through me, tearing my insides to shreds.

Then...nothing.

CHAPTER
THIRTEEN

Every muscle in my body ached. My skin was raw, and the scent of burnt flesh assaulted my nose. I blinked my eyes open and squinted against the daylight streaming in through the windows. It felt like daggers through my pupils. I recoiled.

"There she is." Ember sat on the mattress next to me, and my blurry vision finally came into focus. To my right, a family photo taken in the library and a twelve-inch phoenix statue sat atop a wooden dresser. The closet door on the adjacent wall stood halfway ajar, and a stack of books lay on the nightstand next to me. We were in my bedroom.

"How the hell?" I tried to sit up, but my skin felt like it was tearing with every move I made. My head fell back on the pillow.

"Shh..." Ember gently touched my shoulder, sending pain

slicing down my arm. "Don't move. Patrice is working on a spell to heal your burns."

"Burns?" How could I possibly have burns? I was a fire witch, and *that* part of my magic actually worked.

Ember nodded. "Electrical. How do you feel?"

"Extra crispy." The words rasped through my aching throat, and I winced.

"What were you thinking?" She brushed a strand of hair out of my face. "Why did you take your crystal off?"

"To put it on you. You lost yours in the fight." I cringed, the pinching motion of my face intensifying the pain.

"Here. Drink this. It'll help numb the pain until Patrice gets back." She held a straw to my lips, and I sipped the bitter liquid. Hints of amaranth, chamomile, and dandelion flooded my tastebuds.

"Can she pour it over your entire body? This pain is excruciating."

I laughed and winced again. "Hey, at least my plan worked."

Ember gave me another sip. "Chaos?"

I nodded. "He can't handle the pain."

"Typical man." She laughed. "Though he's probably the only reason we made it out."

"We wouldn't be in this pain if your plan had worked."

"We wouldn't be alive if it hadn't. How are we alive? How did we get here?"

Ember cut her gaze to the open door before getting up and closing it. "I told Patrice to let herself up when she had the potion." She lowered her voice. "After you froze me... Who knew magic wouldn't work on a golem, right?"

"Sorry about that."

She shrugged. "You didn't know. Anyway, after you froze me, and I realized no spells would work, I was sure we were done. But you, little sis, are stronger than you think. How did you get me up the stairs so quickly and away from the golem? Your spell wiped my memory for the time I was frozen."

"I dragged you. Chaos stalled the beast." The tea had eased the rawness in my throat a little. It did nothing for the rest of the pain.

"How?"

"I let him take over like he did in the kitchen. The golem went haywire and tore the library apart. While he was busy, I got you up the stairs. Then Chaos took over again to get us through the electricity spell. I blacked out after that."

"That makes sense. I can imagine the pain you must have felt, and if he felt it too... His power leaked out and gave me the biggest adrenaline spike I've ever felt. I busted through the freezing spell in time to watch the golem stop at the exit and fall back. He must be bound to the library. Anyway, I scooped you up and got the hell out."

"So much for getting in and out undetected. Do you think they'll retaliate?"

"Only if they figure out it was us. Tell me you know where the skulls are."

A knock sounded on the door before I could answer. "Everybody decent?" Patrice called from the other side.

Ember winked and pressed a finger to her lips in a *shh*

gesture before opening the door. I could *shh* all she wanted. My throat felt like I'd swallowed the Sahara.

Sympathy crumpled Patrice's brow the moment her gaze locked on me. "Wow. You weren't kidding, Ember."

How bad did I look? I was tempted to ask for a mirror but thought better of it. I didn't want to know, and I certainly didn't want Chaos to see me looking like a blistered tomato. My status as the most beautiful witch he'd ever seen would be knocked down to zero.

Not that it mattered what he thought about my looks. It didn't, but he'd surely use my scorched skin as proof my plan didn't work, which it *did*.

Patrice swirled a bundle of straw in a mug and flicked the liquid over me. "How did you get electrical burns over your entire body?"

I looked at Ember, who luckily had already devised a story that didn't involve us breaking laws and harboring a demon. "We had water in the basement. A breaker had flipped, so the power was out. Ash tried a spell to get the circuit running again, but it bounced off the reflective cover and hit the water. She was standing in it, and zap. She's lucky I heard the thud when she flew back onto the stairs."

Gee, thanks, Em. Way to make me look like an idiot.

"Only a fool would cast electricity while standing in water."

"No kidding." Whoops. No talking to Chaos in front of others. Why was that so hard to remember?

"This will make you feel so much better." Patrice finished sprinkling me with her potion. "Drink the rest of it." She offered me the mug.

I lifted my arm, and the searing pain of movement caused a garbled yelp to erupt from my throat. Ember took the container and pressed it to my lips, pouring it into my mouth slowly as I drank.

Patrice recited the incantation, and a glorious cooling sensation swept through my body, dulling the pain. The tension in my muscles eased, and I no longer felt like I'd been breaded and dropped into a vat of oil.

I lifted my arm. My skin felt like it was stretched too tightly over my frame, but I could move without sounding like an injured animal, so that was a plus. I pressed my fingertips to my cheek. Though the skin was smooth, it felt raw, like I'd stood on the windy beach too long in winter.

"Ahh. Sweet relief."

"You'll be tender for a bit." Patrice dropped the straw bundle into the mug and clutched it with both hands. "Take a cool bath tonight, and you'll be back to normal soon. No corsets until you are. They'll chafe."

"Thank you." I pushed to sitting, and my corset stayed on the bed where I'd lain.

Ember tossed me a t-shirt. "Sorry. Had to free the girls. You were burned beneath your clothes."

"Take care." Patrice flashed a sympathetic smile and slipped out the door.

I put on the shirt. The fabric felt like sandpaper against my skin. Could she not have picked something softer? "Do you have my bag?"

Ember gestured to the floor near the nightstand before tossing a pair of flannel pajama pants my way. I put them on and stood to look in the full-length mirror. Pink tinged my skin, but I was blister-free.

"The fabric rubbing your body is irritating. You should stay naked until you're healed."

"And look in every mirror I pass? You'd like that, wouldn't you?" I grabbed the satchel and set it on the bed before sinking onto the mattress.

"Very much."

Ember looked at me quizzically.

"Demons are perves." I grabbed the page I'd torn from the book.

"I merely suggested a way for us to heal faster."

"There is no 'us,' mister. This is my body, and you're about to vacate it." I peered at the map as Ember sat next to me. "It's not quite as detailed as I remember."

A lopsided pentagram took up most of the page while a few squiggly lines here and there could have indicated topography. A cross sat near the bottom right point of the star, and an arched line sat below the left side.

Ember pointed at a set of three wavy lines. "That could mean water. Do you think it's the ocean?"

"I don't know. There's water over here too." I pointed to the top left. "I bet the skulls are hidden at the points of the pentagram."

"Except there are five points and only three skulls. What's at the other two?"

"Traps."

I repeated Chaos's answer.

"Fabulous." Sarcasm laced my sister's voice.

"That's probably a church." I pointed at the cross. "If we can figure out which one, we can line it up with a modern map."

"This map is nearly four hundred years old. Whatever church it was, it's not there anymore."

"Good point. Most of the buildings from that time don't exist anymore."

"How did Cinder figure this out?" She took the paper and flipped it over. The back was blank. "What else did the book say?"

"Just a warning to her descendants that if her plan didn't work, they'd need to find the skulls and beg the demons for forgiveness."

She scoffed. "Like demons can forgive."

"If forgiveness is warranted, we can and do."

I couldn't tell you why Ember's assessment of demons irked me so much, but I snapped back, "They aren't all mindless monsters like the ones you've fought. They can be intelligent and even nice sometimes."

"I wouldn't go as far as nice."

Ember blinked twice before she replied. "I don't know what lines he's been feeding you, but he is a *demon*. A creature from Hell."

I narrowed my eyes. "A prince."

"Even worse."

My nostrils flared. "Chaos has done nothing but help us. If not for him, we'd still have no idea about the curse or what happened to Cinder."

She bristled. "If you'd read her journal first instead of tattooing yourself with a demonic sigil, we sure would."

"We'd still need him. We can't break the curse without him." I crossed my arms and inclined my chin.

Ember laughed dryly. "You sound like you're glad you possessed yourself."

"Maybe I am. Getting to know him has opened my mind. Not all demons are bad."

"By your standards, yes, we are."

She shook her head. "I'm going to write this off as shock from your burns. Get your head straight and figure out this map. I'm going to work."

Ember turned on her heel and marched out the door, and I fought the urge to crumple the map in my hands. She didn't know Chaos like I did. Once I got him out of my head and into his physical form, she'd see.

"I think our bond is affecting you. I'm going to pull inward and go quiet for a while."

"Oh? You're not going to offer to destroy her like you did with Shade?"

"She's your blood. Family is sacred."

"Whatever." I slid the map into my satchel and carried it downstairs.

FOURTEEN

A giant mug of coffee sat steaming on my desk as I scowled over the cryptic map. Ginger womaned the front of the shop today, so I had hours to focus until Ember came home. Plenty of time to figure this out, yet I couldn't concentrate.

After seeing the Boston coven's incredible library, I couldn't stand to look at mine. I wanted to fix it. To organize it and make it grand. But I had much more pressing matters to deal with.

I sipped my coffee and fired up my laptop. The public library had an entire room filled with books and articles on Salem's history. Sadly, none of it was digitized, so I'd have to take a trip to the town archives. Maybe getting away from my own would help me focus.

"You're frustrated." Chaos's voice startled me, and I nearly spilled my coffee on the map.

"That's a word for it." I set my mug aside and pressed my

fingers to my temples. "I can't focus. The secrets are stacking up, and I'm horrible at keeping them. I feel bad for snapping at Ember... Why did I snap at her? I can't even remember what set me off."

"She made a generalization about my kind, and you felt it as an insult. You defended me."

I slid down in my chair and leaned my head back. "She doesn't know you."

"Neither do you. Have you forgotten why your sister and parents are missing? Why you're cursed? My brothers and I felt no remorse for making the deal with the witch Isabel. It's what we do."

He had a point. Whatever fondness I was beginning to feel for him, I needed to squash it like a cockroach. He was the reason for all this trouble. For everything. My forearm heated, and I pulled up my sleeve to see his sigil glowing red.

"It's our bond. As long as it exists, you'll feel a kinship with me, as I feel with you."

Well, that was good news. All I had to do was get him out of my head, and then I'd be able to think straight. Step one: go to the library and find a map of sixteen hundreds Salem.

"What's this?" Shade grabbed the map and squinted at it. I'd been so caught up in my head, I hadn't heard him or Miles come in.

"Is that a map?" Miles peered over his shoulder. "That's the old church in Hingham, isn't it?" He pointed to the cross.

"How do you know that?" If only I could ask him for help. I jerked my sleeve down. "Is it still there?"

He shrugged. "I'm interested in cartography. Yeah, it's still there. It's the oldest in Massachusetts. Where did you get this?"

I yanked the map from Shade's hands and shoved it into my bag. "From a friend. It's a history project I'm working on. What do you want?"

"Ember didn't text you?" Shade picked up my coffee and took a sip. "This tastes like tar."

I ground my teeth and pulled out my phone. No messages, but that was no surprise. She was pissed at me, as she should have been. I was out of line defending a demon. "What do you want?" I asked again.

"Wow." He set my mug down and clicked his tongue. "The sister of the acting High Priestess doesn't even know what's going on. How sad."

"My offer with him still stands."

I fought a grin. If only.

"We need sigils," Miles said. "We've located a small rift in the veil, and a couple of gnomes got through. They're digging up someone's garden."

I snorted. "Gnomes? Why do you need sigils for gnomes? They're two feet tall."

Shade squared his shoulders at me, fisting his hands to make his muscles flex. "They're also hungry and venomous. Are you going to do your job, or should I contact the Higher Power and ask them to send us a real Ink Master?"

Chaos's growl reverberated through my entire body, but if it was audible, the guys didn't react. I straightened my spine, staring at Shade as I chose my words. The string of profanities I wanted to throw at him would only drag me down to his level.

"This is ridiculous." Shade's nostrils flared, and a wildness filled his eyes. "I can't believe someone like you has such a high rank in the coven." He swiped his arm across my desk, sending my coffee, lamp, and laptop crashing to the floor. As he stomped toward the closest bookcase, he jabbed his fingers into his hair and pulled at the roots.

"This setup is shit." He knocked over a stack of books and kicked one across the room. "This coven doesn't work." He grabbed the bookcase and rocked it, trying to pull it down. It was too big, weighted more heavily at the bottom so it stayed upright.

"Ahhrrgh!" He went for the books, grabbing them two at a time and hurling them to the floor. He'd gone crazy. He was acting like total...

"Chaos..." I said through clenched teeth.

He growled in answer.

"Stop it right now," I said to both the demon in my head and the man tearing apart my library. Neither obeyed.

I shot to my feet and screamed, "I said stop!"

Chaos grunted, and Shade froze, looking at the mess he'd made with confusion in his eyes.

"Are you finished with your temper tantrum?" Again, I spoke to them both.

"I..." Shade looked at his hands, his eyes widening as his gaze locked on my laptop covered in coffee.

"He deserved worse."

I pressed my lips into a hard line. Chaos would get a reaming later, for sure. Right now, I needed to get these guys set and out of my building.

"Is everything okay?" Ginger stood in the doorway, alarm tightening her features. "What happened?"

Chaos happened, but I couldn't let them know that. "Shade threw a hissy fit when his words didn't cut me deep enough."

He looked at his hands again. "I didn't. I don't..."

"The evidence suggests otherwise." I put my things back on my desk and threw a stack of napkins onto the puddle of coffee.

"Are you okay?" Miles asked him, and he nodded. Of course Shade's new little pet would only be concerned about his owner and not about the disaster he just caused.

"Come on." I brushed past them. "Let's get those sigils done before the gnomes eat all the cats in Salem."

They followed me into the studio, and Ginger returned to the front of the shop. I put on my professional face and gifted the boys with thicker skin and resistance to venom. As I put the finishing touch on Miles's tattoo, my sleeve slipped up, revealing a bit of Chaos's symbol.

"What do you need a sigil for?" he asked.

I yanked my sleeve down and returned the tattoo machine to its stand. "Protection from bullshit." I cut my gaze over to Shade, who still looked confused as hell. I knew the feeling.

Did he apologize for the mess he made? No. Did I expect him to? Not really, but it would've been nice. At any rate, he owed me a new laptop if the one he knocked off the desk was broken. Actually, Chaos owed me a new laptop.

"Thanks for your help," Miles said. "Sorry about the mess."

"Yeah. Thanks," Shade muttered before shuffling out the door.

"Have fun fighting gnomes," I called as they walked away.

With the guys out of my hair, I returned to the library to grab my bag. My jaw tightened at the disorder, but I would have to deal with it later. I locked up the stacks and the entrance to our apartment and slipped out the back door.

Brisk wind stung my still tender cheeks, and as I hung a right on Essex Street, I pressed my phone to my ear so I could gripe out Chaos without looking like a total whack job. "What the hell was that? I told you not to mess with him."

"He disrespected you."

"Shade always disrespects me. It's nothing new."

"He needs to learn his place."

I rolled my eyes. "He knows his place. That's why he acts the way he does. I bruised his fragile ego."

"And he is determined to bruise yours."

We passed a witchy shop and a monster museum. Dozens of tourists milled about, looking into store windows and chatting. The sun shone high in a cloudless sky, its heat helping tame the bitter wind.

"You can't go around making people crazy, especially when I have explicitly told you to leave someone alone." I stopped in front of a resale shop and sighed. Who knew what magical artifacts or books occupied the shelves in there, and it was my job to root them out. Yet another task that kept moving farther down on my to-do list.

"I won't allow anyone to harm you."

"He's not harming me." I continued on my way to the town archives. "I'd tell you to get it through your thick skull, but since you don't have one at the moment..."

"Funny."

"Seriously, though. Don't do that again."

"I make no promises."

"Of course you don't. You're a demon."

"Exactly."

My face pinched, no doubt making me look like a sour kangaroo, but whatever. I had two annoying men battling for my last nerve and a daunting quest that seemed damn near impossible to complete. A nap and a stiff drink would do me good, but I didn't have time for either.

A sense of calm washed over me as I approached the three-story brown brick building. I ascended the stone steps toward the entrance, a set of wooden double doors with columns on both sides holding up a small portico, and rested my hand against the textured concrete pillar.

"No matter what we find, who we see, or what happens in here, you are not, under any circumstances, to take over and make me or anyone else tear this place apart."

"Again, I make no promises."

Not good enough. I curled my hand into a fist. "I mean it, Chaos. Libraries are sacred spaces that deserve our respect. They're the only public buildings you can go to and just be. No one expects you to buy anything. You don't have to have a reason to be there. I need you to promise me you won't cause trouble in here. You've damaged enough libraries."

He grunted. *"I won't apologize for stopping the golem from killing you, but I do regret making Shade damage your belongings."*

"Promise me."

A mother and her small daughter exited the building, the girl's arms full of picture books, a smile brightening her face. The mom looked at me quizzically as she passed. Crap. I'd absently returned the phone to my pocket, so I looked like I was talking to myself.

"Chaos..." I fished my earbuds from my bag and put one in before tucking my hair behind my ear so it would show.

Silence for one beat. Two. *"I promise I will try."*

That would have to suffice. "Okay. Let's do this." I stepped over the threshold and took a deep breath. Ahhh... Books.

A curved staircase led up to the third floor, and I had to force myself not to climb it two steps at a time. On the top floor, the city archives room stood in the back of the building. I passed row after row of reference books, all shelved in their proper places, and a smile tugged at the corners of my mouth.

"You enjoy this place?"

"I'm a librarian," I whispered. "Of course I do." Especially the reference section. Books were my jam.

Lucky for me, no one else needed to look up Salem's history today. I had the room to myself. Dropping my bag on the table, I strode to the computer kiosk on the far wall. At least their card catalog went digital. A quick search pointed me to a volume detailing the layout of sixteen hundreds Salem and the surrounding area.

"See how easy it is to locate things when they're organized?" I found the book on the third shelf, right where it was supposed to be, and set it on the table.

"Some thrive in chaotic environments."

I opened it to the table of contents. "Do they really, though? I mean, you're a demon called 'Chaos,' and your brothers are 'Discord' and 'Mayhem.' Are there any princes of Hell called

'Order' or 'Organization?' If so, I don't see how they could possibly be scary."

"Not all demons are meant to instill fear. Some gain trust before unleashing their wrath."

"Uh-huh. But are there any demons whose power is organization?"

"No."

"That's what I thought." The table of contents wasn't nearly detailed enough for a five-inch-thick book, so I flipped to the index to find the right page. "Here we go. The oldest map of Salem."

I tugged the pentagram map from my bag to compare the two. Sure enough, the squiggly lines did indicate water, which helped me line it up. The cross was the church Miles thought it was. Damn. If I could get him away from Shade for long enough, he might be able to help figure out exactly where the points on the pentagram indicated. I doubted these were drawn to precise scale considering their age.

I snapped a picture of the map with my phone. I'd have to blow it up to make it the same size as Isabel's. As I shoved my phone into my pocket, the energy in the room shifted and Chaos growled.

"Do you sense it?"

I focused on the sensation, a faint disturbance in the vibration, so low I would have never detected it if Chaos hadn't taught me what to look for.

"Demon," I whispered and snapped my head from side to side. The room appeared empty, but there was no mistaking the low vibration in my bones. "Where?"

"Another rift has opened. It senses me."

"A rift *inside* the library?" Oh no. I could not allow a demon to wreak havoc on this archive. I grabbed a bottled perimeter location spell, closed the door for privacy, and blew the dust into the air.

The cloud billowed, collecting around a teeny tiny tear in the veil, no bigger than the palm of my hand. I could seal that before the beastie even made it through. Uncorking the bottle of veil-mending magic, I prepared to toss it on the opening, but a set of spindly fingers with suction cups on the ends like a frog grabbed the sides of the tear and ripped it open.

A one-foot-tall troll-looking creature hopped through, sneered at me, and headed straight for the marble bust of the city's founder, Roger Conant, standing on a dais in the corner. It climbed the statue, bared its pointy teeth, and bit into old Conant's head.

"What the hell is that?"

"An imp. A low-level demon incapable of speech or rational thought."

"Great." I set the veil healing spell on the table. "How do I vanquish it?"

"Pierce its heart. Only one, in the center of its chest."

The imp gnawed on the statue, making an *om nom nom* sound until one of its teeth snapped. It hissed at the bust, its hand covering its mouth as it darted to the floor and backed away. Its nostrils flared, and it crawled across the tile, using its long arms to propel it like a monkey.

"That would be easy-peasy if I had a weapon on me." I

moved around the table, putting distance between the little monster and myself.

The imp reached for a book on the bottom shelf, and I shouted, "Hey! Hands off."

It hissed and grabbed the volume, anyway. Then it took a giant bite out of the spine.

"Son of a serpent. That is not the way to devour a book. Drop it." I clapped and stomped my feet, trying to scare it. I was rewarded with another hiss.

"Perhaps a freezing spell?"

"You think?" I grabbed the potion from my bag, which would now have to be restocked *again*, and threw it on the little fiend while I recited the incantation. The half-eaten book dropped to the floor, and the imp froze with an *oh shit* expression on its hideous face.

Okay, now what? I had nothing to stab it with. "Can I shove it back through like we did the faeries?"

I didn't wait for an answer. Gripping it by the slimy shoulders, I hoisted it from the ground and pushed it into the rift. It wouldn't pass through. I shoved again, really putting my weight into it, but all I managed to do was get imp slime all over my shirt.

"What am I doing wrong?" I set it on the floor. That little guy was heavier than he looked.

"The imp wasn't summoned from Hell. He escaped, drawn to my energy. As long as I'm here, he can't be forced through."

"But the faeries could?" I wiped my hands on my pants.

"They aren't demons."

"Great, and as long as I'm here, you're here. But if I leave, he'll eat the rest of the books."

"The only option is to vanquish him."

"Which requires a weapon." I scanned the shelves. "I could knock him on the head with a big book."

"You must pierce his heart."

"Fabulous." If only I wore stilettos, I could stomp him like a grape and make him go splat. I blew out a hard breath. The door rattled, someone trying to come in.

"Huh," a voice sounded from outside. "It's locked. Let me get the key. Be right back."

"Well, crap." Someone wanted in the archives, and a visible rift floated in the air while a demon lay on the floor. I had about two minutes to clean up this mess before all hell broke loose.

Well, technically, I guess a little hell had already broken loose.

I spun in a circle, taking in the room. Books, books, more books, computer kiosk, more books. Crap on a cracker. Nothing even remotely close to a weapon called this space home. I wrung my hands, my mind scrambling to come up with a plan.

"A little help, Chaos?"

"I can stall the people outside by—"

"No. No, you can't." I wrung my hands again, and a jagged fingernail scratched my palm. I was way overdue for a manicure, but that was so far down my list it had fallen off the bottom.

The imp let out a muffled screech, its arm twitching as the spell began losing its hold. I chewed on my broken nail. I was screwed.

Wait... I looked at my finger and sucked in a breath. Of course! I had a metal nail file in my bag. I rummaged through and found my mini manicure set. I grabbed the file and held it up. "Do you think this will work?"

"I think it's our only shot."

The imp's lips peeled back over its tiny fangs, and it hissed as I approached. I couldn't think about what I was doing, or I'd talk myself out of it, so I gritted my teeth and jabbed the file into the slimy creature's chest.

It wailed once, turned into a puff of smoke, and the rift sucked it back through. Whew.

"Here we go," the librarian's voice came from right outside the door.

"Not yet," I whispered and darted toward it. I still had to seal the rift and clean up the mess.

Holding my hands over the lock, I whispered another incantation I'd used frequently growing up—a locking spell. That should hold them. I wasn't sure why I didn't think of doing that earlier. I would blame it on stress. The door rattled, the knob turning back and forth, but it wouldn't budge.

I allowed myself one deep breath before I sealed the rift. Fatigue made my head spin, and I stumbled as I returned the half-eaten book to the shelf. Hopefully it wasn't the only copy available. I reshelved the volume I'd been reading and gathered my things before releasing the lock.

Swinging the door inward, I gasped, pretending to be startled by the people across the threshold. "Oh, excuse me." I tried to shuffle past them.

"This door is supposed to remain open," the librarian scolded.

"Sorry. Someone was on their phone out there, and it was distracting. I won't do it again." I hurried to the staircase and darted down the steps, hoping they didn't notice the imp slime covering my shirt.

I made it outside without any more issues, and I stopped by a tree a block away. My pulse thrummed, and it took a minute to catch my breath, but it was done. "Well, that was fun."

"Indeed. You handled that like the powerful witch you are. I'm impressed."

"Please." I strode across the intersection and headed home. "I vanquished him with a nail file. I'd hardly call that the actions of a powerful witch."

"You improvised, and you prevailed."

"I am good at that, apparently." Two more blocks, and I could peel these slimy clothes off. Yuck. "You said the imp sensed you, and that's why the rift formed? How does that work?"

"The veil was already thin in the library. The imp was drawn to my energy when we stepped inside, and it was able to tear the veil as it was compelled to be near me."

Fabulous. Lower-level creatures could already slip through thin spots without any help. "Can't you turn your bat signal off while we take care of this? I don't need imps breaking through everywhere I go."

"If had had a corporeal form, I would have more control. With you as my host, I'm afraid my energy bleeds through your skin, creating a beacon for all demons."

"Great. So the rifts are going to follow us wherever we go?"

"And it will only get worse. Our bond is solidifying faster than I thought it would. My power permeates your form, and your human flesh can't hold it in."

"Wait." I stopped in my tracks and pressed my hand to my chest. "What are you saying? I thought we had two weeks before you took over completely. You said I was the order to your madness."

"At the rate we're bonding, it's more like two days."

"We're not bonding any faster than we were before. What changed since yesterday?" A pendant in the thrift shop window caught my gaze, and I stopped to look at it. An upside-down pentagram embossed on what looked like bone hung from a black cord.

"You allowed me to control your form twice."

"So? What makes you think that sped things along?"

"You lashed out at your sister for making a generalization about my kind. You're growing fond of me."

I laughed dryly. "Believe me, buddy, I am not growing fond of you. Getting you out of my head is my number one priority." Right after I checked this artifact for magic. I glanced left and right to be sure no one was watching before I whispered my magic-revealing spell.

"Really? Because I'm growing fond of you. Before you summoned me, I would rather have plucked my eyes out with a pitchfork than have relations with a witch."

My gold sparkles passed through the glass, hovered over the items in the window, and then dissipated. No magic, thank the goddess.

"You've been in a dark prison for hundreds of years. You're fond of anything with boobs." I turned away from the window and froze. A group of people on a history tour formed a circle around a man with a wild look in his eyes. He jabbed his fingers into his hair and ran toward another man in the group.

His target didn't move. The man bounced off his chest and careened into a woman. She shoved him, and all hell broke loose. They shouted and pushed each other, grabbed each other's bags, and dumped the contents on the ground. It was total...

Yep, you guessed it. Chaos.

"We need to get inside."

"No kidding." I turned on my heel and booked it the last block to our building.

FIFTEEN

"Two days?" Ember shouted through the phone. "Why didn't you call me sooner?"

"I literally just found out. I called you as soon as I washed the imp slime off and changed clothes." I set an enchanted crystal in the corner of my bedroom and activated the ward.

"Where are you?"

"In my bedroom. I set up a shield to hold in magic, so he won't bleed out past my door." I'd also sent Ginger home and locked up the shop. With all the magic I'd used in a short amount of time, to say I was spent was an understatement.

"Stay there. I'm coming home." She ended the call, and I dropped onto the bed, exhausted.

The second my lids closed, an image of the man with dark hair and green eyes played through my mind. He stood six-foot-four and had a broad, muscular chest and abs I could do laundry on. Fire flashed in his eyes as he prowled toward me, and his low vibration wrapped around me, sinking all the way to my bones.

Whether I was dreaming or not, a normal person would have shit their pants if a big, predatory Prince of Hell looked at them like he wanted to consume them. Not me. Every nerve in my body tingled, and I smiled.

He inhaled deeply, his brows drawing down like he wasn't sure if he should devour me in a fun way or a literal way. My pulse thrummed, and I rested my hands against the smooth skin on his chest. Heat permeated my fingertips to pool in my core.

"Ash, wake up." Ember poked my shoulder, drawing me from my dream. "I gave you an hour to recharge, but we've got to get moving."

I sat up and rubbed my arms as if I could chase away the sensation of my hormones flaring to life over a demon. My mind sure had fabricated a sexy one. *Oof.*

"Mmm... Another good dream?" Chaos teased.

I ignored him. "Sorry. Too much spellwork." I swung my legs over the side of the bed and grabbed my boots.

"Tell me about the imp. What happened? Did you find a map? Why did you set up a ward?" She paced at the foot of my bed, her hands curling into fists before splaying and curling again.

I laced up my boots. "I'm sorry for snapping at you earlier. It's the bond. As soon as I get him out of my head, I'll be normal again."

"I figured as much." She stopped pacing and rested a hand on her hip. "What happened?"

I relayed the events in the library, vanquishing the imp, and the effect I...Chaos...had on the tourists. "So I set up the ward to keep his magic contained while I rested."

"Your fatigue weakened my ability to keep my magic in check. I'm better now."

She arched a brow. "A nail file?"

"It was all I had."

"Not bad, little sis." She nodded her approval. "Did you find a map?"

I showed her the photo. "When Miles came in for a sigil, he recognized the cross as the old church in Hingham. He says it's still there." I pulled Isabel's map out of my bag. "He studies cartography. If he wasn't so far up Shade's ass, I'd suggest we pick his brain for the other locations."

"Absolutely not. We will handle this on our own." Ember laid the paper map on my mattress and compared the image on my phone. "We need to print this." She tapped the screen a few times, and the printer hummed to life down the hall. She handed me the phone and strode out of the room.

"Any guess as to where your skull might be?" I peered at the pentagram. "Did she give you any clues when she vanquished you?"

"None. She imprisoned us before she hid our skulls."

"Fabulous. I wonder, though." I grabbed my crystal pendulum and held it over the map. The metal chain felt cool in my grip, and as I swung it in circles over the pentagram, I focused my intent on finding Chaos's skull.

My chest heated, my magic humming to life. I stilled my hand, letting the crystal's momentum guide it to one of the points on the star. The motion slowed until the pendulum hung still, right in the middle of the map.

"Well, that sucks. I was hoping a little divination would show us where to go." I returned the pendulum to the shelf.

"Isabel would not make our skulls so easy to find."

I shrugged. "It was worth a shot."

Ember returned with a printed version of the pic I snapped. "We know for sure this is the church?" She angled the printout so the two maps lined up.

"It looks that way. See the water here and here?" I pointed to Isabel's squiggly lines and then at the library's map.

"And these other points? What are they? Did Miles say anything else?"

"I don't know. I snatched it out of Shade's hands before they could examine it more closely. We'll have to go to each point and see if Chaos can sense anything."

"I'm certain she hid them behind a spell. Your magic-revealing incantation will help before I could possibly sense anything...unless she has demons guarding the locations."

"Ugh. Please, no more golems." I pointed to the church on the map. "I say we start there. At least we know exactly what place we're looking for."

Ember nodded. "Agreed. Let's go."

"I need to restock my kit. Give me twenty minutes." I followed her out of my room.

"You also need food. Keeping up your strength will help you keep me in check."

"I'll grab a few energy bars, and then I'll have no problem putting you in a time-out."

He did that growly purr again, and I shivered in a good way. Yeah, this bond needed to be broken ASAP.

After I threw together a few premade spells and stocked my kit, we climbed into the van and headed to Hingham. It took an hour by car, so I could only imagine what the trek must've been like way back when. Did Isabel walk? Go on horseback? Arrive by boat? A woman scorned and cursed to spend eternity in Hell was capable of anything, I supposed.

"She did not want these skulls found, did she?" Ember hung a left on Main Street and rolled to a stop in front of the church. "Why so far away?"

"She and her entire bloodline are cursed. I bet she'd have gone farther if she had the means." I slid out of the van and slipped my satchel onto my shoulder. The church was a two-story beige wooden structure with a steeple. It sat atop a little hill, and a black fence surrounded it.

"Does Chaos sense anything demonic?" Ember asked as she strode toward the front door.

"Nothing, but it will be masked by magic."

"He doesn't. Let me check the area for spells before we barge inside. She probably hid the skull in a crypt or basement. That's what I would do."

I stood at the gate and recited my favorite incantation, casting my magic wide to cover most of the front lawn. Gold sparkled in the air and dissipated as it fell to the ground. "Nothing out here."

I moved closer and cast the spell on the building. I expected to see at least a little magic around the doorway, but the glitter dissolved like it had on the lawn. The sun sank into the horizon, turning the sky shades of purple and red, and an early-riser owl hooted from the tree to our right.

"Inside or around back?" Ember asked.

"Back." I turned and headed around the building. I couldn't say why I felt drawn that way, but I did. Maybe it was a hunch. Maybe I'd cast my spell so many times I didn't need it anymore. Who knew?

As we rounded the back of the building, I headed straight for the cellar door. The energy here felt different. Like it used to spark with magic, but it had now gone stale. "Am I sensing demonic energy?"

Ember drew her sword. "I don't know. Are you?"

"I sense nothing."

"No. It must be something else." I heaved the door open and descended the steps, still feeling drawn to something by who knew what.

The basement looked typical of old homes that were built before electricity and indoor plumbing became the norm. Metal tubing ran along the walls, enclosing the wiring that had been added later, and exposed ductwork stretched across the ceiling. Some shelves stood against the far wall, but I wasn't interested in those. A staircase next to them led up to the ground floor, but I hung a left, the stale magic sensation pulling me to a waist-high door with a broken padlock.

I started to tug the door open, but I paused, letting the energy wash over me. I didn't feel the low vibration in my bones, but I waited for Chaos to chime in before I continued. "Anything?" I asked him.

"There is no demonic energy in this basement, but I sense a rift forming outside. Another lower-level demon has sensed my magic."

"Crap. Okay. Em?"

"Yeah?" She turned from the bookcase she'd been examining.

"I've got this. Can you head up and vanquish the demon that's about to crossover?"

She grinned. "With pleasure."

Ember bounded up the stairs, and I opened the small door. A tunnel stretched out before me, the stale magic culminating at the end. I crawled inside. Crazy, I know. I was usually much more cautious, but somehow I *knew* whatever hex was used to seal this corridor had been broken.

I reached the end and cast my spell. Glitter clung to the walls, revealing the smoky cloaking spell that used to hide this space. No active magic remained. "There was a skull here."

Chaos growled. *"Discord. I sense his energy."*

"Look at this," I said, as if he had a choice. He saw everything I saw, including the two-foot wooden cube sitting in the back corner. Its hinged lid stood open, revealing emptiness inside. "You're right. It was sealed with magic."

"My brother's skull was in there."

"Well, it's gone now."

"Obviously."

I shined my phone's flashlight around the space and gasped. There, pinned to the dirt wall with an array of daggers, hung the rotting corpse of a five-foot-long hairless dog. Broken capillaries created a reddish web over its ashy skin, and its yellow eyes bulged from their sockets. Curling my lip, I backed out of the tunnel and dusted off my pants.

"Cinder found this place, broke the spell, and killed the beastie guarding it."

"She defeated a hellhound. Your sister is powerful."

"No kidding."

"It runs in the family."

"Most of the time." I swept the basement to be sure we didn't leave any signs of magic behind before heading up the steps. The evening had bled into full dark by the time I reached the surface, and I looked across the yard in time to see my sister do her famous spin and swing, lopping off the head of the demon who'd crawled through the rift.

One of its horns stuck in the dirt, keeping it from rolling down the hill, and as she reached down to grab it, the whole thing crumbled to ash before getting sucked through the tear in reality.

"Why could that one be killed by beheading, but the others had to be stabbed through the heart?" I strode toward the rift, searching my bag for the sealing spell along the way.

"Because that kind has no heart. It was an immature incubus."

"Yikes." I found the right bottled spell, and Ember and I joined forces to seal the rift. It was bigger than the last one, and we all saw what happened when I got too tired and Chaos bled out. Well, Ember didn't see, but I'd given her a pretty good description.

She wiped her sword with a handkerchief and slid it into her back scabbard. "What did you find in there?"

I jerked my head toward the van. We'd gotten lucky so far, and no one had shown up to question us. Best not to press it. "Cinder was there. It's where she found Discord's skull."

She started toward the parking lot. "Are you sure?"

I nodded. "Chaos sensed his brother's energy, and I sensed..." What did I sense? I was still trying to wrap my mind around it. "I recognized her handiwork." I climbed into the van.

Ember stowed her weapons before getting into the driver's seat and starting the engine. "How are you feeling? Do you have it in you to hit another one tonight?"

"I don't have a choice, do I? There are four more possible hidey-holes, and I have about thirty-six hours left to live."

"We must find my skull before then."

"That's the plan." I laid the maps on my lap. "How do we want to tackle this? Go clockwise and hit them all in order?"

"Works for me." Ember located the general area on the GPS and pulled up the directions. "It's an hour away too. Counter-clockwise would be faster."

I was about to agree with her when a nagging sensation pulled in my gut. "Hold on. We know Discord's skull was here. Would she really hide another in the next closest spot?"

"You think she did every other point on the star?"

"And set traps at the other two." I tapped the map.

"You're overthinking this. If she skipped the next point clockwise, the last skull would still be located at the point next to Discord's."

"You're right. That doesn't make sense." I chewed my lower lip. Overthinking was my specialty.

Ember pulled to the side of the road. "Tell me where we're going."

"You felt a pull in your gut. That is your magic speaking to you. Listen."

I laughed. "My magic doesn't work like that."

"Most of your magic is yet untapped. You found the hiding place in the church without a spell. Trust yourself."

"I used spells." I rolled my eyes. "He's telling me to trust my gut because I kinda knew where the first skull was hidden. But I used spells to confirm it. I could have just as easily been wrong."

Ember arched a brow. "But you were right."

I shrugged one shoulder.

She screwed her mouth to one side like she wasn't sure she wanted to say what she was about to say. "Dad can do that, you know. It's why the mess in the library never bothered him."

I shook my head. "He used location spells to find things."

She grabbed my hand, stilling my drumming fingers. "He taught *you* the location spell to find things. He just *knew* where to look, and he was trying to help you realize that magic in yourself. It's a rare power, Ash, and he was sure you had it. I'm sure too."

Wait. What? *That* was why he kept the library in a shambles? He was naturally drawn to whatever he needed to find, so the mess didn't matter to him. It mattered to me, though. It drove...it still drives...me crazy, but there was a method to his madness.

I gazed at the map, and tears gathered on my lower lids. All this time, I thought my dad was wasting his energy casting location spells to find books that could be easily organized, when he could simply sense them with his inborn power.

Could he have been trying to bring out the same power in me? Could I...?

I swallowed the thickness from my throat. "We don't know that I inherited it."

Ember squeezed my hand, and I sniffled. If he had just told me what was going on, our relationship would have been so much smoother.

"I got into so many arguments with him over the mess. Why didn't he tell me what he was doing?"

"Honestly?" She released my hand and gripped the steering wheel. "Your self-esteem was already so low because your fire magic isn't as prevalent as mine and Cinder's. If he told you he wanted you to develop another power, and you couldn't, you might've never recovered."

I laughed dryly and wiped my tears. That sounded about right. "Well, if I have that power—and I'm not saying I do—I have no idea how I tapped into it at the church. And dad's not here to guide me."

"I can guide you."

"You're a demon. Why do you think you can guide me?"

"Because I feel the power too. The tugging in your gut is your magic speaking to you. I can help you listen."

Great. The parasite inside me was more familiar with my magic than I was. Figured. "Why the hell not? I'll be dead in a day otherwise, so what have I got to lose?"

Ember grinned. "That's the spirit, sis."

I stared at the map, willing the gut tug to take hold, but nothing happened. I breathed deeply, relaxing my muscles and letting my vision blur. No tug.

Another deep breath. I rolled my neck, loosening the tension and allowing the energy around me to guide my thoughts.

Nothing happened.

Of course nothing happened. I knew it wouldn't. "Well, what now?" I asked no one in particular.

"Give it time to build. Clear your mind of everything but the map."

"Right. Sure." With my elbow on the armrest, I pressed my fingers to my temple. "Let me not think about my impending death that's looming closer by the second."

Ember clasped my shoulder. "You can do this."

I nodded and stared at the map again. "I can do this." My life depended on it.

"Focus."

I fixed my gaze on the pentagram, letting everything around it go fuzzy. Cinder was counting on me. Mom and Dad could still be saved. Maybe.

"Focus..." Chaos reminded me. *"There. Do you feel it?"*

The fact he felt it before me was a bad sign in the *how much time does Ash have left before a demon takes over her body?* department, but yeah. I felt it. I sensed a gentle tugging in my stomach, trying to tell me where to look.

"Think specifically about my skull. Mayhem's can wait."

Four possible destinations and only one of them could save my life. "It makes sense to go to the closest one."

"You won't find it by logic. Use your gift."

He was right. I knew he was right, but my brain was battling for control. I always used logic. Wasn't that my gift?

Thinking rationally. Keeping things in order. Planning. Organizing.

"Ash..."

Grrr... I had to let go of my thoughts. Which one felt right?

My muscles tensed, my nails digging into my palms as I squeezed my fists. My first thought was clockwise. But counterclockwise would get us to a destination faster. Or maybe we should try the top point.

"What is your gut telling you?"

Without another thought, I dropped my finger onto the map. "Counterclockwise."

"Are you sure?" Ember asked.

"Yes." It was the closest point. It made sense to go there next.

She nodded once and put the van in gear. "Here we go."

Chaos stayed silent. Whether he agreed with my choice or not, he didn't say. I took the quiet as an opportunity to recharge my vim and leaned my head against the window. The glass felt cold against my skin, and the gentle vibration of the wheels on the road lulled me to sleep.

I woke as Ember shut off the engine in a mall parking lot. The good news: it had closed at eight p.m. Few cars dotted the lot, which meant the employees closing shop were the only ones inside.

The bad news: shopping malls didn't exist in the sixteen hundreds, so finding the next hidey hole would be impossible.

I straightened in my seat and compared the two maps. "Are we sure this is the place?"

Ember turned her hand palms up. "No. I drove around to

see if an old building still stood, but this town is as modern as can be. Whatever structure she hid it in is long gone now. Maybe you can sense it."

My cheeks puffed as I blew out a breath. "I can try."

Ember holstered her weapons, and I grabbed my satchel before we crept through the parking lot toward the mall entrance. Lights attached to towering poles cast circles of illumination on the asphalt, and a paper fast food bag tumbled by in the wind.

A man wearing jeans and a red flannel exited the mall, snapping his gaze in our direction. Ember yanked me down behind a pickup truck. "Do we have any more of Shade's spells?"

I checked the bag and did not curl my lip in disgust. Yay me. "One. Should I activate it?"

"I can't walk around with all these weapons without garnering unwanted attention, so yeah. We don't have a choice."

I uncorked the bottle and activated the spell, cloaking us in a shadow that would follow for at least five minutes. Ten if we were lucky. Ember straightened, and I followed her toward the entrance. She goosed the man in the side as we passed, and he squealed, rubbing his ribs like something bit him before darting to the Mazda in the back of the lot. My sister snickered. I rolled my eyes.

"Ember likes to antagonize."

"You should've seen her when we were kids." I stopped in front of the left side door while Ember tried them all, beginning at the right.

"They're locked," she said. "Got your picking kit?"

I reached for the handle in front of me and tugged the door open, gesturing for her to enter.

"See?" She strode inside. "You do have dad's power. You knew exactly which door was unlocked."

"I paid attention to which one the guy left through." I followed her in and tugged the door shut behind me.

"Attention to detail is a powerful tool too." She rested a hand on her hip. "Where to now?"

"I feel the tug. Do you? It's behind your navel."

I focused on the sensation in my belly, and sure enough, it was there, just like at the church. I couldn't see the location in my mind, but an invisible force guided me down the corridor. The path split, and I followed it to the right without hesitation. A single door, painted beige to match the wall, stood between a shoe store and a candy factory.

"This way." I motioned for Ember to follow and stepped through the door.

She lit a fireball to light the darkened hallway, and we made our way down, taking a sharp left turn at the end before descending a steep staircase into the basement. The massive furnace and metal ductwork gave off Freddy Krueger vibes, but my target was a piece of plywood nailed to the wall and blocked with an empty shelving unit.

"Help me move this." I grabbed one side, my sister got the other, and a screech pierced my eardrums as we dragged it across the floor.

I scanned the area for a crowbar or anything we could use to pry the wood from the wall. Ember had her own idea. She slammed her boot into the wood, knocking a jagged hole in the center. She kicked again and one more time before grabbing the splintered pieces and tearing them out, making a hole big enough for us to pass through.

"You should have let me check it for magic before you busted it down," I said.

"Oops." She gestured to the opening, and I cast my spell, sending golden sparkles on the hunt for magic.

A few stuck, revealing a faint disturbance in the air, like a magical heatwave. "It's old, but there's a ward here. Not on the wood; it was cast long before the space was covered."

Ember nodded. "Give people the heebie jeebies so they won't want to continue into the tunnel."

"It must've worked. They sealed it off."

Ember climbed into the forbidden space, and I followed. The deeper in we went, the more unfinished the space became. The wood floor gave way to dirt, the walls going from studs and support beams to plain old earth.

The tunnel stretched on for another fifty yards before spilling out into a small chamber about the size of my bedroom. A sickening feeling joined the pull in my gut, and I grabbed Ember's arm, stopping her from entering the room.

"What?" she asked.

"Something doesn't feel right." My head spun, my vision wavering. "Chaos? Are you picking up anything?"

Silence answered me.

"Now is not the time for you to go dormant, mister. Help me interpret these feelings." A wave of nausea washed over me, and I tightened my grip on Ember's arm. "I don't feel good."

My sister took both my hands in hers. "We're so close. Help me cast the magic-revealing spell, and you can sit out the rest of this adventure."

"This is bad, Em. I don't know what's happening." My vision tunneled, glowing red around the edges. "I can't…"

"C'mon, sis. I can't do it without the potion, so unless you've got one ready-made in that bag of yours…"

"Confess, expose…" I shook my head, and the room tilted.

"You've got this." Ember's power flowed into me, bringing everything back into focus.

"Confess, expose my magic sleuth. I call on you to reveal your truth." My knees buckled, and Ember helped me to the ground.

"I'm sorry. I held back as long as I could." My mouth formed the words. They filled the room with my voice. But I wasn't the one talking.

"Chaos?" I asked, but my mouth didn't work.

"We don't have much time." My body rose, a newfound strength running through my limbs, yet I had lost control.

"What's happening?" I asked.

"You are now the voice in *my* head," he said.

SIXTEEN

Well, wasn't that freaking fantabulous? I tried to take a step back, but the command from my brain didn't reach my legs. In fact, the idea didn't even seem to register in my brain or anywhere else in my body.

"What the hell, Chaos? You said we had more time than this."

"Obviously, I was wrong." He made my voice say the words, and it was the freakiest thing I'd ever heard. Kinda like when you hear yourself on a recording, only way worse.

"Wrong about what?" Ember asked, but she didn't wait for an answer. She stepped into the room and headed straight for the niche in the far right corner where sparkles clung to a shape like glitter on a drag queen.

"Tell her." I tried again to control something on my body, but it was pointless. I couldn't even make my pinkie finger twitch.

"There's no skull here." We walked into the room and stood

behind her while she stooped to examine a wooden box hidden by shadows.

"How do you know?" She waved her hand over the top of the box, thankfully not touching it. "It's sealed with magic. Maybe there's a cloaking spell on it too. Do your thing, and let's see."

Chaos inhaled deeply and exhaled slowly like he was fighting to hold in a growl. "We're wasting time here. We should move on to the next point of the star."

Ember looked over her shoulder at us. "What's gotten into you? Just do the spell so we can see. Skull or not, I want to know what's inside."

I started to recite the spell in my head, but Chaos cut me off and said it aloud himself. Nothing happened.

Ember narrowed her eyes. "Cast it for real."

"I can't use my magic unless I have control of my body. Give it back."

"I can't."

"Why not?" Ember asked.

"Why not?" I echoed her question. *"I was able to give you control for short times."*

"And that is what sped up the possession process. If I release control, we will bond even faster."

Ember blinked and tilted her head. "Is that what Chaos is saying?"

"Tell her."

He didn't.

Now it was my turn to growl. *"She needs to know."*

She stood, a look of worry creasing her brow. "Ash?"

Chaos tightened our right hand into a fist. "This body doesn't belong to Ash anymore."

"The hell it doesn't." She drew her sword, and flames erupted on the blade. "Bring her back now, or I'll…"

He crossed his…my…our arms. "Or you'll what? Stab your sister? Behead her?" He stepped toward her, and her hands trembled, the fire on the blade rolling back into her.

"Tell her I'm still here. You're scaring the bejeezus out of her."

He gripped the hilt of her sword and drew it from her grasp. She let him have it. Tears streamed down her cheeks, and she backed into the wall. "Ash," she whispered.

"Dammit, Chaos, if you don't tell her now, I'll…"

He chuckled. "You'll what?"

Friktity frak, he had a point. The demon was in complete control. Ember couldn't vanquish him without killing me. I couldn't control my body, so I was about as useful as mammaries on a man. Things just went from bad to the absolute worst they could be.

"Please tell her. I can't stand to see her cry."

He huffed, and the feeling in his bo…in *my* body—it was still mine, dammit, and I would regain control—went from *bwahahaha I'm finally free* to *wait, what am I doing?* "Ash is still alive for now."

Ember snapped her head toward him. "What do you mean, for now?"

"I have control of her body, but her consciousness is fully functional. Soon, though, my power will build, and her human form won't be able to hold me. She will die if we don't find my skull soon." He offered her the sword.

She yanked it from his grasp and held it at her side. "How soon?"

"A few hours. Maybe less, which is why we need to move on. My skull isn't here. I would sense it."

"It could be concealed." She gestured to the box. "Isabel was a strong witch. You said so yourself."

"You'll have to convince her if you're sure it's not here. She'll want to hack it open and release whatever's inside."

"Ash says you want to force it open." He kneeled by the box.

"She knows me well."

"Do you see this mark?" He pointed to a design carved into the wood. A series of crisscrossing lines and circles formed an intricate pattern about two inches wide.

"What about it?" She set her jaw, stubbornness obvious in her features.

"That is an adaptation of ancient Sanskrit combined with demonic sigils. It's a warning to her descendants that this one is a trap meant to kill any who attempt to free us."

Ember's eyes narrowed. "What would happen if I opened it?"

"Tell her that her face would melt off like the Nazis in Indiana Jones."

"Ash says your face would melt like something called a Jones Nazi." He rose and faced her.

Her eyes turned from narrowed in mild skepticism to slits of suspicion. "Is that what she says?" She crossed her arms. "Or are you just saying that? How do I know your skull isn't in there and you're saying it isn't so you'll get to take over Ash completely?"

"I want your sister to survive as much as you do." He raised a hand. "You have my word."

She blew out a hard breath. "The word of a demon doesn't mean much."

A spark of anger burned in our belly, the feeling both his and my own. *"She doesn't know you like I do."*

"You don't know me like you think you do."

Ember scoffed. "Then enlighten me, Mr. Prince of Hell. What's stopping you from trying to kill us both?"

He made my nostrils flare. "I was talking to Ash, but I will answer you. She and I share a bond. As long as it is intact, I will do whatever it takes to keep her safe...including taking out anyone who stands in my way."

"Jeez Louise. Don't threaten her, man. Ember loves to fight."

She tightened her grip on her sword, and flames licked down the blade. "And I suppose I'm in your way."

He closed our eyes, frustration, irritation, annoyance, and every other similar emotion flooding our system. "We are on the same side."

"No, we're not." She extinguished her sword and swung it at the box. Chaos caught her arm, keeping her from smashing it open, but the edge of the blade nicked the wood.

The magic surrounding the box pulsed orange before releasing a blast that knocked us on our butts. Chaos's demonic energy must've shielded us because he jumped to our feet and shook off the electrifying sensation crawling across our skin like it was nothing.

Ember didn't fare so well. She lay on her side, her eyes

closed, her sword sticking into the dirt wall like a toothpick in a meatball.

Chaos grunted, the sound extremely strange coming from my body. "My skull isn't here. We need to get to the next point." He pulled the sword from the wall and scooped up my sister, carrying her as if she weighed no more than a ragdoll.

"Whoa. I'm not this strong."

"I am." He marched back through the corridor, following our path out of the mall and to the van. He put her in the back seat, and she groaned.

"What happened?" She rubbed her temples.

"You foolishly disobeyed me and tried to open the box. It fought back." He climbed into the driver's seat and started the engine.

"Whoa. You've been locked up since before electric lights. You can't drive a car."

"Your sister in is no condition to be behind the wheel. Your body has muscle memory. We'll be fine." He slammed on the gas pedal and peeled out of the parking lot. "Enter the coordinates for the next location."

Ember sat up and handed him her phone. "My head feels like it's going to split in two."

"If I had allowed you to hit it with your full strength, it probably would have."

Everyone was quiet on the half-hour drive to the next location, which gave me time to ponder why we even went to that mall in the first place. The reason was obvious. I didn't inherit the power from my dad like we hoped.

"Tell her I'm sorry."

"What are you sorry for?"

"Nothing." Ember scoffed. "I don't trust you."

Chaos flicked his gaze to the rearview mirror. "My question wasn't directed at you."

She leaned forward, resting her hands on the console. "Is Ash talking? What's she saying?"

"It didn't work. I took us to the wrong location. I don't have Dad's power."

He relayed the message and added, "But you did know exactly where to look once we got there."

Ember's head bobbed in the mirror. "He's right, Ash. Dad couldn't locate things miles away, either. If it was in the vicinity, he could find anything, and that's exactly what happened with you. Twice. I shouldn't have pushed you to do something he couldn't do."

"Listen to your sister," Chaos said. "She is correct."

"And anyway…" Ember leaned back in the seat. "These locations are protected with wards. We tried scrying for them and came up with nothing. Even if the power did work at a distance, you probably wouldn't have picked up on it."

"I suppose."

"She's reluctant to accept the reasoning." He made a sharp right, and the tires squealed.

"Careful."

Ember buckled her seatbelt. "She's always had self-esteem issues."

"They're unwarranted. Your sister is more powerful than she thinks."

"Everyone knows that but her." Ember's face pinched. "We have to save her."

"That's the plan." He hung a left, taking the corner more slowly this time.

"Fair warning," my sister said. "If we don't save her, and you take over, I'll vanquish your ass right back to that dark prison. Then I'll find your skull and pulverize it."

Chaos chuckled. "I would expect nothing less."

SEVENTEEN

"Now *this* looks like a place for a witch to hide a demon skull." Ember began strapping on her weapons before Chaos stopped the van.

The next point on the map had directed us to a massive field. A few gnarled trees jutted up from the knee-high grass here and there, their knobs and bumps and crooked branches giving the area a spooky feel, driving Ember's point home. This *did* look like a good place to hide a skull.

It felt like it too. A low vibration, almost imperceptible, hummed in the air, and as Chaos killed the engine and slid out of the van, the hairs on my arms stood on end.

Not that there was much I could do about it. With a demon in control of my body and my vim, I couldn't cast a spell to save my life. Kind of ironic because that was exactly what I needed to do. How the hell was I supposed to exorcise him if I was nothing more than a fading voice?

Worry about one thing at a time, Ash. First, we had to get the skull, and I was certain it was here. What I wasn't sure about was whether *I* knew it or Chaos did. I could feel his emotions, sense his power building as if we were the same person. He was essentially absorbing me into his consciousness, and the scary thing was...I felt at peace with it.

"Why do I feel like ceasing to exist wouldn't be such a bad thing?" I asked.

"That would be a *very* bad thing." He stomped through the grass toward an overgrown mass of vines and weeds. "You have to fight this. Don't give up."

Ember jogged to catch up, my potion satchel bouncing on her hip with each step. "Do you have anything in here for headaches?"

"Tell her there's some pain powder in the blue pouch."

"Blue pouch," he said and continued his march toward the mess of brush.

Rage simmered in Chaos's chest, a barely contained inferno waiting to explode and take down everything in its path. Riding along with him in charge, I felt powerful...almost euphoric, which was weird because he wanted to tear Isabel and anyone else who knew about the skulls into a million tiny pieces and feed them to her descendants.

And if she wasn't turning to dust in a grave somewhere, he could do it. I had no doubt about that. Honestly, he'd be justified. I knew I was supposed to be about love and light...being a light witch and all...but the poor guy had been imprisoned for hundreds of years, all because a witch didn't want to pay when it came time to collect.

"It's here." He stopped a few yards away from the over-growth, and holy Hecate, there was a building beneath all those vines. He started forward.

"Wait! Stop!" Ember ran towards us, fumbling with a potion bottle. "We need to see what spells are protecting it before you barge in."

Well, look at that. Leap-first-look-later Ember actually thought before she acted. *"She's right."*

"I can withstand any spell she could concoct." He kept marching.

"Whoa. First of all, my body can't. It's not just you running into the fray. And second, you obviously can't withstand anything, or we wouldn't be in this situation."

Something hard hit the front of our shin, sweeping our legs backward out from under us. We faceplanted in the grass, and I got a good look at what had hit us. Ember's boot.

"You're not running in there and putting my sister in any more danger than you already have." She dropped the bag on the ground, cocking her head as if challenging him. "Let me do this first. Tell him, Ash."

Chaos growled and stood. It sounded way less menacing than when he used his real voice, but Ember bristled.

She fisted her hands. "Do not make me knock my sister out."

"Get out of my way," Chaos roared and shoved Ember aside.

Uh-oh. My body would not appreciate what was about to happen next. Ember screamed like a Viking warrior and ran towards us. She bent at the last second, shoving her shoulder into our abdomen and dragging us to the ground. The air left our lungs in a whoosh, and if I were the one in charge, we'd have stayed down.

Chaos did not. He called on his demonic strength and literally threw Ember off us. She landed five feet away with a grunt, but she shot to her feet and came back for more. This had to stop.

"Chaos, cut it out."

"I'm sorry, Ash." My sister swung, clipping us in the chin. Pain exploded across one side of our face, but Chaos laughed in spite of it. Or maybe because of it. I wasn't sure.

The rage he'd kept at a gentle simmer began to boil. Our fists tightened, the muscles in our arms coiling. *"Don't hurt my sister."*

His punch landed dead center in her stomach. She doubled over with a groan.

"Stop it, Chaos. I mean it."

Her head snapped up, and she lunged. He swung our arm, flinging her away. *"Enough!"* I shouted in our head, but his demonic nature was in full swing. I had to take back control before he killed her.

"You're wasting time." I focused on the fire in the core of my being. It was still there. *I* was still there. I let it burn as hot as I dared and imagined it filling my body, flowing down my arms and legs, and I used that fire, my inborn gift, to seize control.

My muscles burned with the strength of my ancestors as I ripped my body away from Chaos and threw up my hands. "Stop fighting. Both of you."

My breath came out in a rush, and a maniacal giggle followed. I'd done it. I'd taken my body back.

"Ash?" Ember took a tentative step toward me. "Is it you?"

I parked my hands on my hips. "Yes, it's me, and I'm pissed at you both. You've wasted ten minutes fighting when I only have hours left. What were you thinking?"

Neither of them answered me, but I didn't have time to listen to their excuses, anyway. I turned toward the building in the brush. "Confess, expose my magic sleuth. I call on you to reveal your truth."

My head spun, but I shook it off and waited for the golden dust to reveal what we were up against. It billowed like a cloud before swirling upward and descending over the structure like a dome.

"A cloaking spell? That's all?" Ember drew her sword and took a few cautious steps toward it.

I held out a hand to stop her and focused on the energy. One deep breath. Two. Then three. The low vibration I'd felt before hadn't grown any stronger. "Do you sense anything, Chaos?"

He was silent for a beat. Then he wheezed. *"You should not have taken back control. I can't hold back."*

"Oh, yes you can. Do you sense any demons close by?"

"The veil is thicker here. I don't sense anything but my skull."

"We're good." I nodded at Ember, and she slashed her sword through the spell, unraveling the camouflage. The decrepit building dissolved away, taking the overgrowth with it.

"Great. More grass." She sheathed her sword. "What now, Prince Harming?"

"He's in a timeout." My stomach rolled, and my peripheral vision grew hazy. His power was growing. I could tell he was holding back, but I had half an hour at most. "There has to be something here."

I swept my gaze across the grass and crept toward the space where the illusion of the house used to be. "That was a powerful cloaking spell if it could change with time and the environment."

"We've already established Isabel was a beast." Ember searched the ground with me. "What are we thinking? Did she cast a circle or hide it underground?"

"Where's the bag? I'll check."

"Oh, crap. It's over there." She pointed behind us.

"I'll get it." I jogged to the bag, and by the time I got back to my sister, my muscles trembled. My hands shook as I uncapped the bottle of perimeter dust, and as I blew it toward the space, a hacking cough racked my lungs. Oh, lordy. I should not have done that. Every ounce of energy, every iota of magic dried up like a gully in a drought.

Ceasing to exist didn't feel peaceful anymore. It felt like getting hit by a train.

"What's wrong?" Ember clutched my shoulders and then pulled me to her chest. "Tell me what to do."

"Magic. Drained. My vim," I said between coughs. "Chaos."

"Is he coming back?" Alarm filled her eyes, and I nodded. "Okay. Okay, let's get the skull. Let's...shit. It's a circle."

"Holding in or keeping out?" My knees buckled for half a

second before a surge of strength returned to my body. We stood, taking a step back, out of Ember's grasp, and straightening.

"I told you not to attempt regaining control," Chaos said with my mouth.

Fan-fluffing-tastic. The demon was back in charge.

"You were about to kill my sister."

"I wouldn't have killed her. Harmed her a little, perhaps. I was trying to subdue her."

"Yeah, well. You almost walked into a trap. You're welcome."

He sucked in an irritated breath like he was about to argue. "Thank you."

"Looks like we've got two choices." Ember drew her sword and eyed the perimeter. "Break the circle and risk turning loose whatever she has trapped in there, or step inside and take the chance of being stuck."

"Let's look at the pros and cons of each before we decide." I started to list them, but Chaos had another idea.

"Stay there," he said to Ember, and he stepped inside.

"What the eff, man? We're supposed to be working together." Ember fumed, but he ignored her, instead, locking his gaze on an area of disturbed ground.

"This is it. I can feel it." He kneeled.

I could feel it too. The pull in our belly like before, but also more. The vibration intensified, scattering my thoughts and sending my...our...emotions on a tilt-a-whirl. I needed to stop him. To insist he let Ember check the space for magic, but the desire, the need, was too strong. He...we...could finally be whole.

He felt the ground, swiping the dead weeds away to find a hatch. Anticipation built. I needed to say something, anything to caution him, but my scattered thoughts ping ponged off each other, making it impossible to think about anything but getting that skull.

"I'm coming in." Ember stepped toward the circle.

"Stay out!" Chaos boomed, stopping her short. "You will need to break this circle from the outside. The magic has trapped me in."

I wanted to argue that *we* were trapped, not just him, but he reached for the latch, gave it a twist, and opened the hatch. There, in the bottom of a rotting wood container, lay his skull.

This was too easy. I might not have been able to think straight, but the sinking sense of dread in my gut was unmistakable.

He reached inside. Something popped. A swarm of zombie fae shot out, slamming into our face and knocking us back.

"Son of a bitch!" Look at that. I'd found my words.

Chaos jumped to our feet and lunged for the skull, but the fae hadn't eaten in centuries. Did I ever mention how much they loved witch blood? And much like all the other creatures from across the veil, they didn't die unless they were beheaded, stabbed in the heart, or set on fire, so these suckers were ravenous.

They dive-bombed us, their tiny razor teeth slicing into our skin, taking little chunks of flesh before they retreated.

A few tried to escape, but the circle held them inside. They bounced off the wall and came back for us, more pissed off than ever. Chaos waved our arms, knocking them to the ground, but the starving little creatures would not be deterred. They wanted witch for dinner, and that was what they would have, goddess damn it.

"Ash! I'm coming in." Ember ran toward the circle. She slammed into the invisible wall, and dark magic pulsed, sending her careening into the ground three feet away. She landed with a thud, probably getting the wind knocked out of her.

Chaos kept swinging our arms, knocking the fae around, but they continued their assault. Our skin stung, and blood flowed in ribbons down our bare arms.

Ember tried again to cross the threshold, and again it knocked her back. Springing the trap kept anyone from getting in or out. Lovely.

Chaos roared, the sound way more guttural than I should have been capable of making. Our abdomen heated, burning hotter than my fire magic could go. He fisted our hands, crossing our arms in front of our chest. The heat felt like it would burn me alive.

Was this him taking over? Was he about to burn through my form and become a whole demon again? Goddess, I hoped not. Spontaneous combustion sounded like a painful way to go.

He roared again, throwing his arms out to the sides.

They erupted in flames.

He swung, moving faster than any witch was capable, turning into a tornado of fire inside the circle. Fae screeched, each one he hit tumbling to the ground, consumed by flames.

Exhilaration flowed through our veins, and I was pretty sure it was mine. My arms were *on fire*. Ember couldn't even do that. She could make fireballs and set objects ablaze like her sword, but this... Sure, it was the demon doing it, but holy Hecate, it was fun.

When the last fae hit the ground, its body shriveling and turning to dust, Chaos extinguished our arms and heaved in a breath. "Your body can't take much more."

"No kidding." Fatigue replaced all the excitement. He heaved another ragged breath.

"I'm trying, Ash. I'm trying, but I'm failing." He scooped his skull from the hatch and tucked it under his arm.

"You're doing great. Look, you've got your skull. Let's put you back together."

He huffed. "Ember, you can break the circle now."

"Can I? It seemed pretty adamant to keep me out." She rummaged through my satchel for a dissolving spell.

"While she does that, let's exorcise you."

"We can't do it here. You must cast me out in the same place I possessed you if you want to survive the exorcism."

"Well, shit."

"Well said."

The drive home would be forty-five minutes at best. *"How much time do we have?"*

He hesitated to answer. "Not enough."

CHAPTER

EIGHTEEN

"What's not enough?" Ember cast the dissolving spell and tore through the circle.

Chaos stumbled, and she clutched our arm, sending sharp pain shooting all the way past our shoulder, up the side of our neck, and into our head. He groaned. "Not enough. Time," he said through clenched teeth. "Get back...to house." Our knees buckled.

Ember clutched our shoulders, holding us upright. "Whoa, whoa, whoa. You are not burning through my sister right here in the field. You've got your skull. Do your thing."

"Can't do it here." He curled our hand, our nails digging into our palm.

My sister's lips parted, and her head wobbled like a bobble-head doll as she put the pieces together. "Right. Okay, you have to return to the place where you two were bound in order for you to separate completely. We need the spell book too, though it wouldn't surprise me if Ash had it memorized. Let's go."

"I can't." We dropped to our knees. Pain ripped through us. Not hot. Not cold. Searing.

"Oh, yes you can." She tried to drag us up, but the pain overwhelmed us.

I could not go out this way. We'd come too far. We had the friggin' skull for Hecate's sake. If only Ember had teleportation powers, we could...wait.

"Can't demons portal through space?" My voice sounded strained even though my failing body didn't utter the words.

"Not in this condition." We dug our fingers into the dirt as another wave of pain crashed through us.

Ember paced in front of us. "C'mon, Ash. You're a problem solver. How do we fix this?" She dropped to her knees in front of us, pleading with her gaze. "How, Ash? Please?"

"Okay. Umm..." My thoughts swirled, scattering like billiard balls every time I tried to grab hold of one. If only I could freeze them in place for half a second so I could pluck a useful one from the fray. Yes! That was it!

"Tell her to freeze us."

"Will that work?" he asked, his voice thin.

"It's the only idea I've got, so let her have it."

"She says freeze us." We collapsed onto our side and curled like a fetus. I could feel his effort. The strain. He really was trying not to split me open and crawl out of my belly like an alien.

"Right. Of course." Ember turned my satchel upside down and shook it. Bottles clattered to the ground, and she spread them out. "I'll never make fun of your label maker again." She uncorked the bottle, said the incantation, and tossed the dust onto us.

Normally, the binding spell stilled the mind along with the body. I assumed since I was three-quarters of the way to becoming a full-blown demon, Chaos's magic fought against the enchantment. I wasn't completely coherent, but the feel of dirt and grass across my backside as Ember dragged us to the van set my nerves on edge. Too many friggin' fae bites to count sent screams of agony to my brain. I'd need to bathe in antibiotic ointment when this was done.

If I survived.

Ember leaned us against the front tire and opened the van door. Hooking her arms beneath our pits, she hauled us into the backseat. Bottles clanked against bone as she dropped my satchel, filled with potions and Chaos's skull, on the floorboard, and if I could have winced, I would have. No doubt she'd dumped everything into the center pouch, not bothering to organize anything, but I would deal with that mess later. Hopefully.

"Please let this spell last." She peeled out of the field, flinging gravel in her wake, and floored it.

"*How's it going?*" I asked Chaos, but he didn't respond. Ember's spell had rendered him mute like it should have, which was a good thing. The fact I was coherent enough to see the streetlights pulsing through the windows as we whizzed past, not so much.

It should have been a forty-five-minute drive back to Salem. Ember made it in thirty and thank the goddess she did.

Right when she stopped in the alley behind our building, my pinkie twitched.

"Just hold on a little longer, Chaos." I had no idea if my words could soothe the savage beast he—we—were about to become, but I had to hold on to myself too. Talking in my head was the only thing I could do, so I turned into a chatterbox. *"Once this is done, I'll take you out for a steak dinner. Your resurrected body will be starving, right? Do you like beef? We could do seafood if you prefer, but I figure there aren't any oceans across the veil. Or are there?"*

"Here we go." Ember slid open the door and scooped me into her arms like a baby. If I'd had the use of my words, I'd have asked her why the hell she dragged me across the field if she was strong enough to carry me like this.

She finagled her arm just right so she could punch in the unlock code on the back door. She shoved it open and stepped through, but she didn't take my lolling head into account. My temple slammed against the jamb, and man, I wished I could groan.

"Sorry." She turned sideways and slipped inside, slamming the door shut with her foot before carrying me through the library and into my sigil studio.

Ember laid me and the skull on the floor and disappeared into the library before returning with her arms loaded down with supplies. "I'm going to put you in a circle before I unfreeze you."

Smart move. Who knew what condition Chaos would be in when he was finally free?

"I have to grab the exorcism grimoire. Give me two seconds." She darted out of the room again.

"One Witchissippi. Two Witchissippi. Huh. She's late." Three fingers on my left hand twitched. Sadly, I was not the one controlling them.

My hand curled into a fist. *"Chaos..."* Molten lava churned in my chest. *"Please hold on."* Hellfire rolled through my veins.

"Got it!" Ember raced in and opened the book on the table before flipping through the pages. "Here we go." She tapped the book and grabbed a canister of salt.

Speaking in Latin, she poured a ring around me, and I prayed to Hecate she was pronouncing the words right. Heaviness built inside the circle as she lit a bundle of sage and wafted it into the four corners of the room. Her voice grew in intensity. The energy inside the circle was suffocating.

"Okay." She set down the book and her supplies. "That should keep the demon in, but allow a witch to pass through. Is this the exorcism spell?" She held the book toward me, but I couldn't respond. "I'm unfreezing you in three, two...one."

She drew her magic inward, and we gasped. *"Yes, that's the spell."*

Dammit. Chaos was still in control. *"Let me take over."*

He groaned, tensing every muscle in our body. "I can't. I can't stop it."

"Then I will." I focused on whatever energy I had left. My own magic mixed with his, making it nearly impossible to tell my fire from the demon's. Maybe I could use that to my advantage. Did it really matter where the power came from as long as I could claw my way to the top?

No. No, it didn't.

I latched onto the heat, letting it fuel my consciousness. The hellfire raged, trying to consume me, but I rode it like a wave, letting it raise me higher.

"What. Are you. Doing, Ash?" Chaos ground out.

Ember lips curved into a half-smile. "She's digging her way to the top."

"Don't fight it. Let go."

"If I let go…" he said through teeth clenched like a vise. "You'll die."

"You're forgetting I'm a Holland witch. Let go."

He stopped straining. Our breath came out in a rush, and our body sagged. He sucked in a deep breath. The inferno roared.

I took the next breath. And the one after that. I scrambled to my knees, and Ember shoved the book toward me. I recited the words to rip him from my body, my mouth moving so fast I could have been speaking in tongues.

My muscles seized. I couldn't breathe for one second, two, three, four. Finally I exhaled and drew in another breath. I said the spell again. Then a third time, putting more vim than I had ever dared into the incantation.

A boom so loud it shook the house sounded from some-where…inside me, outside, I couldn't tell. The sigil on my arm burned down to my bones, and if I didn't know any better, I'd have said my entire body turned inside out before righting itself again.

I gasped, my lungs tightening like I'd inhaled fiberglass,

and when I exhaled, billowing black smoke rolled out of my mouth and nostrils to swirl around the skull lying on the floor.

Ember grabbed my arm and yanked me out of the circle while a storm brewed inside. Flashes of electricity pulsed and crackled. The dark cloud thickened, spinning like a tornado and gathering above the skull.

My sister's nails dug into my arm as we both stood there staring, unable to move.

The skull levitated, the tornado drawing it upward into the storm. The cloud took the shape of a man as the skull ascended. It billowed around the bone, and lightning cracked, blinding me for half a second. My vision wavered. The cloud dissipated.

My mouth dropped open at the sight of the demon.

CHAPTER

NINETEEN

"Release me!" Chaos boomed.

I needed to close my mouth, but my muscles wouldn't obey the command from my brain. Not because the demon had control, but because holy Hecate he was huge.

He stood seven and a half feet tall, with broad shoulders and a barrel of a chest. His skin, the color of red brick, stretched taut over the most defined muscles I'd ever seen. And his horns!

Thick, textured horns extended upward before curling around the sides of his head like a ram. My gaze drifted down his body to his... *Oh, my.* I swallowed hard, finally regaining my motor skills.

"Holy shit," Ember said. "That's what has been inside you all this time?"

I smiled. Hecate knew why, but I smiled. "Isn't he magnificent?"

"More like the stuff of nightmares." She clutched her sword and took two steps backward.

I moved toward the circle. "Chaos?"

"Don't get too close. That perimeter won't hold him forever."

"He won't hurt me. Will you, Chaos?" I didn't know why, but the temptation to step inside the circle and run my hand over his chest had me toeing the salt line.

"We had a deal, Ash. Let me go." His eyes glowed green, and his lips peeled back over pointy teeth.

"We need to vanquish him." Ember paced the perimeter of the circle. "It's too dangerous. I can feel his power from here."

He roared and lunged at my sister. She jumped like a frightened cat, but thankfully the circle held him in. "We had a deal."

"Okay, both of you, take a breath." I held up my hands. "Nobody's vanquishing anyone. We did have a deal, and I will uphold my end of the bargain once I'm sure you'll hold up yours."

His nostrils flared. "Of course I will."

"Don't trust him, Ash." Ember continued pacing. "Demons are liars."

"I'm not lying."

"How do we know?" I crossed my arms.

He closed his eyes like he was trying to calm himself down before he spoke. "We've been through this. You released me from prison. I am in your debt."

"Uh-huh." Ember stopped in front of him. "How do we know you won't be like Isabel and kill us so we can't collect?"

If looks could kill, Ember would've been nothing more than

a heap of flesh. Chaos grunted at her and then looked at me. "Your arm."

The sigil pulsed deep red. "Why is that still there?"

"We are still bonded."

I rubbed the design as if it were drawn on with marker and I could smear it. Needless to say, my effort was fruitless. "Take it off."

He waited a beat, two, three before he said, "As long as it's there, I belong to you. If you're so concerned about me going back on my word, I suggest you keep it intact until this is over."

I laughed. "You belong to me? As in..."

"I serve you." He said it matter-of-factly like it didn't bother him the slightest that he was mine.

For some reason, it didn't bother me either. I had my very own demon. Woo hoo! "I believe him."

Ember looked at me like I was the one with horns. "He's manipulating you. He's been in your head too long."

"I'm not," he growled.

"He's not." I tilted my head at Ember. "Trust me."

"But how do you know?"

"I just do."

She waved one hand flippantly. "Whatever. But he better find Cinder, or I'm sending him back across the veil where he belongs."

"Great. Now there's just one more issue." I put my hands on my hips. "You're not going anywhere looking like that. You said you're a prince, right? Is there a human form lurking anywhere in there?"

He glanced down at his body, curled his meaty hands into

fists, and smoke billowed around him again. When it dissipated, he'd shrunk to only six-foot-five. Thick, black hair replaced his horns, and sun-kissed skin covered his muscled frame.

My gaze wandered down his naked form, taking in the perfection that was Chaos. Heat pooled in my lady bits, and my stomach fluttered. When my eyes met his, I forgot to breathe. Emerald green with the same primal intensity as my dreams... Holy mother of magic, he was hot.

And, at least for the time being, he was *mine*.

A smirk lifted one corner of his mouth, and he arched a brow. "Is this better?"

I licked my lips. "Much."

COMMANDING CHAOS

FIRE WITCHES OF SALEM
BOOK TWO

CARRIE PULKINEN

CHAPTER 1
ASH

The buck-naked demon glowering in my studio should have scared the bejeezus out of me. A normal witch would have called on her magic, said a prayer to the goddess, and kicked demon ass. Or attempted to, at least. He was a Prince of Hell, so I doubted his ass would be the one getting kicked, but a normal witch would have tried. A smart witch would have run.

And me? I just stood there staring, trying not to drool.

In my defense, never had I ever seen so much raw masculinity in one person. One *naked* person. Smooth skin, defined muscles, jewel-green eyes so mesmerizing he wouldn't have to drag anyone to the depths of Hell. I'd follow him willingly.

I mean *they*. Whatever person he was trying to drag. Not me specifically.

"Ash." My sister's harsh voice registered at the edge of my mind like a ghostly echo. Nothing I needed to concern myself with.

Chaos's sigil pulsed on my arm, the heat of the molten red design spreading through my body, an unnatural calmness turning my muscles to mush while bringing clarity to my thoughts. I had just exorcized a demon from my body and lived to tell the tale. Holy Hecate.

"Snap out of it, Ash!" Ember's voice sliced through the serenity in my brain, and she latched onto the skin above my elbow, pinching and twisting at the same time.

Pain exploded down my arm, yanking me out of my quietude. "Mother plucker!" I jerked away, whirling to face her and rubbing the tender spot my dear, sweet sister had created. "What was that for?"

"You were in a trance. He's trying to control you."

"I'm not." Chaos's deep, rumbly voice drew my gaze back to the center of my studio. He stood in the middle of a circle meant to contain him, but I had a feeling if he wanted out, he could have smashed through our magic like the Kool-Aid man went through walls in the old commercials.

Instead, he crossed his arms. "You promised to release me."

I glanced at his eyes and turned my back to him. It was the only way I could keep my gaze from locking on his nether region again. "It's not him. It's this stupid sigil." I rubbed it as if I could wipe the magical ink away.

The contented growl rumbling from Chaos's chest reminded me just how strong our connection was. Temptation to turn around and ask him what part of his body he felt me touching when I did that had my shoulders threatening to swivel, but I maintained control.

"He needs clothes."

Ember scoffed. "He needs to be vanquished."

"Just..." I looked at Chaos and bit my lower lip. "Can you go get him some of Dad's pants? Anything to cover up..." I motioned to his junk, which earned me another smirk from the Prince of Hell.

"Dad was a beanpole compared to him." She crossed her arms, shifting her weight to one leg. "His clothes won't fit."

"Find something stretchy. Sweatpants, or hell, even a towel to wrap around his waist. *Something*." I tilted my head. "Please?"

She narrowed her eyes. "Do not release him while I'm gone."

I drew an X over my heart. "I won't. I promise."

After giving Chaos the stink eye and me a warning look, she turned on her heel and headed upstairs.

"If your father's clothes don't fit, I could stay naked...and you could join me." Heat flashed in his eyes, and for half a nanosecond, I considered his offer.

"Bad demon." I shook my finger at him. "You're not supposed to flirt with me, remember?"

He spread his hands to his sides. "I'm the naked one this time."

"We're even now. You've seen me; I've seen you. No more solicitations. I'm not interested."

"Then why do you keep staring at my dick?"

I flicked my gaze to his eyes, trying to keep a neutral expression. It was hard not to stare at it, especially since it had gone from flaccid to halfway hard in a matter of seconds.

He chuckled. "Admit it. You like what you see."

Who wouldn't? "That's irrelevant. I—"

Boots thudded on the stairs, saving me from making whatever rambling excuse I might've thrown at him, and he grumbled under his breath, his soldier returning to "at ease" as quickly as it had saluted. Ember rolled up a pair of sweatpants and swung her arm back, ready to throw them like a football, but I plucked them out of her hand.

"Gray? Really?" I started toward the circle, and she grabbed my elbow.

"Be careful. If he pulls you inside, you'll lose the perimeter's protection."

"Thanks. I know how circles work." Stopping a foot shy of the boundary and making damn certain my hand didn't cross the line, I offered him the roll of pants. My pulse kicked into a sprint as he reached for them, the shock finally—hopefully—subsiding and letting me focus on the problem and not the penis.

He took them gently and put them on before gesturing to his hips. "Better?"

"Yes." Not really. I mean gray sweatpants didn't do much to mask the package on a human man, much less when they were stretched too tight on a super-muscular demon prince. But they were Dad's sweatpants. My father's junk had been inside them.

Gross. I curled my lip. Yeah, that was enough to make me get my act together. Thanks, sis. "Okay. I'm going to break this circle, but remember... If you try anything stupid, Ember will send you across the veil faster than you can say hellhound. Got it?"

He fought a grin and glanced at my sister. Honestly, I wasn't sure who would win that battle if it happened. Ember was the toughest witch I knew, but she'd never fought a Prince of Hell before. Hopefully I wouldn't have to find out.

"You have my word and my mark." He stepped toward the salt line and held my gaze as if challenging me to keep my promise.

I pursed my lips and crossed my arms. "A deal is a deal."

Ember stood two feet behind me to my right. I could feel the tension rolling from her body, her fire magic simmering just beneath the surface.

I stared into Chaos's eyes, and he stared back at me. His smirk did things to me. Honestly, I couldn't say if his expression was one of anticipation or amusement, but it made my hormones flare way more than it should have. I scooted my foot closer to the circle. This was it. He'd either keep his word or tear us to shreds.

"Oh, for Hecate's sake, just do it." Ember stomped forward and swiped her boot through the salt, breaking the perimeter and freeing the demon.

Chaos blinked once, glanced at Ember and then me, and stormed forward. His shoulders slammed into ours as he pushed between us. They were rock-solid and sure to leave a mark.

I stumbled, catching myself on the table before planting my feet and clutching his forearm. "Where do you think you're going?"

He huffed and set his skin ablaze right where I'd grabbed him. Flames licked up my arm, singing my sleeve, and I tightened my grip. The nerve of this guy!

"You're lucky I'm immune to fire, mister, or you'd have burned me."

He extinguished the flames. "I wouldn't have done it otherwise. Release me."

"I did."

"My arm." He glanced at my hand before returning his gaze to mine.

Ember slid in front of the door in a wide stance, hands planted on her hips, her vim on the verge of going from simmer to boil.

The sigil pulsed, spreading that relaxing warmth through my body again, but this time, I fought against it, tightening my grip even more. "Whatever you're trying to accomplish when you do that, it won't work. This is our realm. We are in charge."

He narrowed his eyes, but he reeled in his magic, allowing my pulse to return to its sprint. "I must find Mayhem."

"We will, okay? But we have to have a plan. We can't go tearing through Massachusetts like a bunch of rogues, and you especially can't go out into near-freezing temperatures barefoot and shirtless." I let go of his arm, and Ember dropped her hands to her sides, curling them into fists.

Chaos relaxed a smidge, the tendons in his neck, which had

been as tight as guitar strings, loosening. "The cold doesn't affect me."

"Maybe not, but it does affect everyone else in town." Ember leaned one shoulder against the door jamb, crossing her legs at the ankles. I knew that stance. She might have appeared to let down her guard, but she could shift her weight to the crossed leg, spin, and kick in half a second flat.

"Just." I blew a hard breath, lifting my hands in a show of...I didn't know what. Not surrender. Innocence, maybe? Frustration? Whatever it was, all the adrenaline that was keeping me upright drained out with my heavy exhale. My shoulders slumped, my entire body seeming to fill with lead. "Can we sit down and talk?"

"The sooner we release my brother, the sooner we can collect our price." He looked from Ember to me, and I tilted my head. "And find your sister and end the curse. We will all benefit from retrieving Mayhem's skull."

My head spun, fatigue crashing into me like a cat-five hurricane. "You're forgetting this body is mortal. Not to mention I've been carrying around a Prince of Hell for the past week." I gripped the edge of the desk.

Chaos's expression softened, and the sigil on my arm heated. "You require rest."

"Whatever gave you that idea?" My lids grew heavy, and I swayed on my feet.

"Come on. Let's get you upstairs." Ember moved to my side and wrapped her arm around my waist. We started for the steps, but Chaos came up behind me, sweeping his arm beneath my knees and scooping me into a cradle carry.

"Don't hurt her." Ember stomped up the stairs behind us.

"I have no desire to harm you or your sister, but even if I did…" He carried me past the kitchen and settled me onto the couch before straightening and facing Ember. "As long as Ash bears my mark, hurting her hurts me. Our lives are bound."

She studied him, her eyes calculating. "If she died…?"

"I would immediately be drawn back to Hell. Our bond makes it so I can't exist in this realm without her."

"And if I vanquished you?"

I could barely keep up with their conversation, but when Chaos leaned down, running his fingers across my forehead to sweep the hair out of my face, my skin turned to gooseflesh.

"If you vanquish me, she will die." He said it matter-of-factly, as he tended to do, but his sorrowful expression said he didn't like the idea in the slightest. Thank the goddess he cared, because I could not keep my eyes open another minute.

"Plan of attack." I laid my head on a throw pillow and curled onto my side. "I'm going to take a nap. Ember, go buy Chaos some real clothes so he'll blend in with the humans. We'll figure the rest out when I wake up."

She gave me an *are you crazy?* look. "I'm not leaving you alone with a demon in the house."

"You heard him. Hurting me hurts him. Vanquishing him kills me. We're at an impasse, sis. Please do this for us."

"Us? So you're a unit now?"

"Please." Sleep begged to drag me under. "I'm safe."

"No harm will come to your sister." He slipped off my shoes and covered me with a blanket.

Going… Going…

Ember huffed "Fine. But if you try anything..."

"You'll vanquish me to the deepest depths of Hell."

"Exactly." She turned on her heel and headed toward the door.

Chaos settled into the accent chair. "She will learn to trust me like you do."

"I don't trust you..." And I was gone.

CHAPTER 2
CHAOS

If I wasn't immortal, I'd say this witch would be the death of me. She lay on the sofa, eyes closed, lips slightly parted, and all I could think about was how they might taste. How her body felt wrapped in my arms as I carried her up the stairs. How she commanded me as if she could actually control a Prince of Hell.

I chuckled at the thought. *Bad Demon*, she had called me. If she only knew...

Her sister, on the other hand, was a splinter in my side I'd gladly remove if not for her relation to Ash. Stubborn and strong-willed, she reminded me of Mayhem, always the reckless one. But I gave my word that no harm would come to her family or her coven, and as long as Ash bore my mark, I was incapable of breaking a promise to her.

I should *not* have been incapable of causing her turmoil. If she were any other witch, I could use my sigil to scatter her thoughts, blank her memory, and drive her to madness. But her power countered mine, turning chaos into order. As she had stood outside the circle, debating with her sister on when to release me, I had tried. I'd sent a small amount of magic through the sigil, hoping it would be enough to spark her into action.

Instead, it had done the opposite, calming her, helping her collect her thoughts rather than scattering them. I had never experienced such power from a witch. Not even Isabel.

At the thought of the insolent woman who'd banished us, a growl rumbled in my chest, and Ash stirred, a small whimper escaping her lips. Her face pinched, and she tensed, something in her dream distressing her.

I sent a pulse of magic through my mark. She inhaled deeply and let out a breath, her body relaxing, her sleep no longer disturbed.

What would my brothers say of this phenomenon? Of the way she turned my magic on its head?

That I should force her to remove my mark and kill her. She was dangerous to our kind. More dangerous than Isabel could have ever hoped to be.

Kill her...

Perhaps I would when this was through.

Lucifer knew I wouldn't make the same mistake twice. None of us would, which was why I needed to free my brothers, collect the debt owed to us, and return to Hell where we belonged.

Consorting with witches always ended badly.

Ember stomped up the stairs and returned to the living area

with her arms full of crystals. She placed them on the floor, encircling the sofa where Ash lay. Closing her eyes, she tilted her head upward and whispered.

I watched her for a moment before asking, "What are you doing?"

She finished her whispered spell and touched Ash on the shoulder. "Setting up wards so no evil can get to her while she sleeps. Nothing that's ever set foot across the veil can penetrate this." One brow arched over her eye.

"I won't allow any harm to befall her."

She scoffed. "I'm protecting her from you."

That much I knew, but I found no sense in assuring her more. Ember didn't trust me, nor I her. We would work together toward our common goal. Then I would decide what to do with these sisters.

"Try to touch her." She gestured at Ash.

I remained still. "Why?"

"So I can make sure it works. Try."

I crossed my arms. "You doubt your power?"

She mirrored my posture. "No, I'm proving it to you. Do it."

I hated to comply and give her the impression I obeyed orders, but the sooner I was clothed, the sooner I could slip away. Leaning forward, I reached toward Ash's head. My fingers met an invisible, solid surface. I pressed harder, sliding to the edge of my chair and pushing both palms against it. Ember smiled smugly.

I sat back. "Impressive. Why don't you cast these around your entire town?"

"It takes too much vim. I'm going to get your clothes now. If you try to break the ward, I'll know, and I'll be here faster than you can blink."

"I would expect nothing less."

She finally left, and I settled back into my chair and took in my surroundings. The structure in which they resided stood two stories high. We currently occupied the living area on the top floor, with a brown sofa where Ash lay, a smaller couch, and two dark green chairs. We had passed through a kitchen on the way to this room, and the scent of a plethora of herbs with magical qualities, along with some only used for cooking, filled the entire area.

Across the room stood a large, flat device the witches called a T.V. Blackness coated the front now, but when they pushed buttons on a palm-sized device, moving images appeared like magic. The technology of this time astounded me. Motorized vehicles, electric lights, indoor plumbing... I'd spent my time inside Ash taking it all in, learning as much as I could about their ways, their use of language, how their coven worked.

Aside from the ruptures in the veil and the monsters bleeding through, this seemed like a comfortable time to be alive.

Ash's eyes moved back and forth beneath her lids as I watched her sleep, and I longed to caress her soft skin, to run my fingers through her silken hair. Ember had done me a favor by casting this ward. I had to keep my distance from the blue-haired vixen, lest I succumb to the same fate as before.

Soft footsteps whispered on the stairs, pausing at the entrance. Ember peeked around the door jamb as if trying to catch me misbehaving. She stepped through the threshold, her boots in one hand, two white paper bags with brown handles in the other.

She dropped her shoes against the wall and strode into the living area, stopping in front of the couch and examining her sister. Seemingly satisfied Ash had not been disturbed, she turned to me and shoved the bags against my chest. "I got you boots and two sets of clothes. That's all you'll need."

"Is it?" I peered inside. A box occupied one of the bags, a mass of black fabric the other.

She rested a hand on her hip. "We know what we're doing now. As long as you don't get in our way, we'll get your brother's skull and find the other guy in two days, tops. Then, you're all leaving and never returning to Salem. If you do, I'll put a bounty on your heads."

I chuckled. "I assumed you wanted us to break your family curse first."

"That's a given."

I gazed at Ash, watching the gentle rise and fall of her chest. So much danger wrapped in so much beauty.

"She'll be out for hours, so I'm going to grab as much sleep as I can." Ember disappeared into the hallway and returned with a blanket and pillow. "You'll have to curl up on the loveseat tonight."

"I don't require sleep yet." I set the bags on the floor and remained in my chair.

"But demons do sleep?" She dropped the bedding onto the small couch.

"In this realm, our bodies require sleep, though not as much as yours. In our natural forms, in our realm, we do not."

"Good to know." She shrugged as if she didn't care, but I could see in her expression she had more questions. She chose not to ask them. "Come get me when she wakes up. I'm the first room on the left."

"No wards to protect yourself?"

"Of course. I'm not an idiot. Just yell from the hall." She flipped her hair over her shoulder as she turned and walked away.

I waited, watching Ash sleep, until no more noise sounded from Ember's room. With both witches settled into slumber, I dressed in the clothes she had given me and put on the boots, which surprisingly fit. I would retrieve my brother's skull while they slept and be back before either of them woke.

I rose, preparing to leave, but Ash stirred, drawing my attention to her delicate face.

"Chaos..." The sleepy sound of my name on her lips made me shiver. "Chaos, don't leave me."

"I'm here." I returned to my chair. Was she dreaming? Was she coherent enough to recognize I was about to walk out the door?

"Bad demon," she mumbled. "Stay."

How could I leave now?

CHAPTER 3
ASH

Sunlight streamed in through the window, coaxing me out of sleep. I squeezed my eyes shut tighter, hoping to catch a few more minutes of peace before I had to face the world...and the demon I could feel watching me intently. His low vibration reached down to my bones, making his presence impossible to ignore.

"Your breathing has changed. We know you're awake," Ember said.

Funny. I could feel Chaos in the room, but I somehow missed my sister's energy. I was still recovering from the exorcism. I needed more sleep, but I doubted these two would allow it. We had things to do, beasties to fight, demons to summon—yikes—so I reluctantly opened my eyes.

Chaos sat in one chair while Ember perched on the arm of the other. My demon was fully dressed now, thankfully, in boots, dark jeans, and a black shirt, and Ember wore her fireproof leather. She was ready to get this shit show on the road, but I could barely see straight.

I pushed to sitting, and the room spun. My mouth tasted like burnt dirt, and a crick had formed in my neck from sleeping on a throw pillow. Rolling my head from side to side helped ease the sharp pain, but I'd need to stand under a hot shower set to pulse if I wanted to work this knot out before we left.

"What time is it?" My vertebrae cracked, easing the tension a little more.

"It's ten." Ember rose to her feet as if she were ready to head out immediately. Yeah, that wasn't happening.

I rubbed my neck. "A.M. or P.M.?"

Chaos tilted his head. "Can you not see the daylight in the window? Have your eyes been affected?"

I'd asked a stupid question. Yes, I could see the daylight, but... "Affected by what?"

"Blindness is a common side effect of exorcisms." He spoke in a matter-of-fact tone that said he expected me to know this already.

"I'm not blind." I tried to run my fingers through my hair, but they got stuck in a massive tangle. "You could have warned me there'd be side effects before we performed it."

"Would it have changed your mind?"

I attempted to work the tangle out, but I made it worse. "No."

"I assumed a witch of your power and intelligence would know the possible consequences." He remained seated, calm as could be, while Ember paced in front of the television.

"We don't deal with demons much in Salem. At least, we didn't until Cinder..."

He corrected me. "I believe your parents were the first to summon one of my kind."

"It doesn't matter. I'm going to shower." I stood, bracing myself for the world to tip on its side, but it remained steady. Nice. I turned toward the hall, and the doorbell rang.

Ember tugged her phone from her pocket and frowned at the screen. "No messages. Did someone text you?"

"My phone is downstairs."

"Hey, Ash. You up there?" Shade's voice sounded from below, and I closed my eyes. I could not deal with his bullshit right now.

"Ember?" His boots fell heavily on the steps before he pounded on the door. Typical of Shade to assume he'd be let in if he showed up unannounced.

I caught a glimpse of Chaos glowering at the entrance, so I rested my hand on his shoulder. He relaxed, but his posture said he was on high alert, no doubt ready to wreak havoc on my mortal enemy if he so much as looked at me wrong.

I couldn't lie. Having my own personal bodyguard was pretty cool.

Shade pounded on the door again, and Ember rolled her eyes. "Take Chaos to the back of the house so I can see what he wants."

"Come on." I jerked my head toward the hall.

Chaos hesitated, cutting his gaze between the door and me. "I can solve your Shade problem."

"I know you can, but you won't." I grabbed his arm, solid, rock-hard muscle, and guided him to the hall.

We stopped at Ember's room, and I motioned for him to go inside while I stood in the hall so I could hear the exchange. Several pairs of shoes shuffled in. Fabulous. My nemesis had brought reinforcements.

"Where's Ash? We need sigils." I could practically hear Shade's lip curling. He hated depending on me as much as I hated tolerating him.

"She's lying down," Ember said. "Some advance notice would have been nice."

"I texted her." Miles was with him, of course.

"I tried calling." Ginger too. Fantastic.

"I'm not sure she's up to it," Ember said. "What's going on?"

"It feels weird in here," Ginger said. "The energy in your house is...off."

"It's probably Ash," Ember said. "She's got a stomach bug, and it's messing with her vim."

"No, it's something else," Miles said, and footsteps moved closer to the hall. "It's low."

"I feel it too." Shade this time, though I wouldn't be surprised if he was just going along, trying to start trouble.

Ember strode into the living room, and I peeked out to find her positioned between the other witches and the hallway door. "What do you need the sigils for? I assume, since you didn't bother to call me, it's something small."

"Two more gnomes spotted across the street from the first," Miles said.

"We didn't bother you since you're supposed to be researching where all these rifts are coming from," Shade said. "You are planning to call a meeting soon, aren't you?"

Ember scoffed. "Of course. I've been taking care of Ash, but I'm working on it."

"What is that odd vibration?" Miles moved toward the hall, Ember widened her stance, and I slipped out of view.

"I told you it's Ash. Her vim is messed up right now."

"They sense me," Chaos whispered behind me.

"Whatever gave you that idea?" I joined him in Ember's bedroom.

"Their reactions make it obvious." He reached above my head, resting his hand against the doorjamb and leaning forward to listen.

His close proximity made my stomach flutter, so I ducked and moved away. "We need to work on your grasp of sarcasm, but first we need to get them out of our house."

"With pleasure." A pulse of energy permeated from Chaos's body. A second later, all three visitors began talking at once. They used their normal voices at first, but it didn't take long before they were shouting over each other, sounding more and more like total...

"Chaos!" I backhanded him on the shoulder. "That is not what I meant. Stop it."

He reeled in his magic and shrugged. "Be more specific."

"I will get them out of here. You. Stay. Put." I poked my finger into his chest with the last three words, which earned me another mischievous grin.

Hecate on a hambone. What was I going to do with this demon?

First things first, I brushed a lock of blue tangles out of my face and strode into the living room. Shade, Miles, and Ginger stood there staring at Ember, a look of confusion clouding their eyes. Thankfully, it seemed people didn't remember exactly what happened when Chaos messed with their minds.

Ember gave me the side eye, knowing full well what had gone down, and I patted her shoulder. "I'm much better now. Gnomes, you said? So defense against venom and tougher skin? Those are easy."

I motioned for them to follow me and headed down the stairs. They shuffled across the floor, still confused as all get out, but I played it cool. Not cool, though, were the remnants of the exorcism still visible in my studio. The salt ring, still intact except for the spot Ember swiped her foot through, took up most of the floor. Was it too much to ask for her to clean this up while I slept it off?

Apparently so. I was the neat freak, not her.

The witches caught up with me, but I stopped them in the library. "Wait here a second. I got sick in my studio, and Ember didn't clean it up."

Shade curled his lip. "Make it fast."

"Do you want some help?" Ginger asked.

I shook my head. "It's kinda embarrassing. I'll only be a minute."

I closed the door between the rooms, grabbed a handheld vacuum, and sucked up the salt. The candles, which had burned out when Chaos reformed, sat at the five points of the former pentagram, so I swept them into my arms and stuffed them into a storage case. I spun around, checking for any more signs of light witches behaving badly, and grabbed the exorcism book before adding it to the case with the candles.

After a quick spray of air freshener to mask the fact I had not just cleaned up vomit, I opened the door and gestured for them to come inside. "All done. Who's first? Ginger?"

Her brows drew together in sympathy. "Are you up to doing three? I'm sure the guys can handle it. Want me to sit this one out?"

I waved a hand dismissively. "Nah. They need all the help they can get."

Both guys bristled, but they didn't say anything. I wasn't surprised. Chaos's playtime in their minds still had them off their game. They really did need all the help they could get.

I expected Ember to make her way down to reassure them they had not in fact sensed demon energy, but she never showed. I guess she trusted Chaos even less than I thought. His little display earlier didn't help.

Ginger sat like a champ, barely flinching when I reached the tender part inside her elbow. Shade ground his teeth, a whimper escaping his mouth at the sensitive spot. I suppose I could admit I pressed a tiny bit harder on his tattoo, but I couldn't resist him looking like a wuss in front of his man crush.

Miles went utterly still as I applied his sigil, almost as if he'd checked out of his body so he wouldn't feel the pain. I went even heavier on the tender spot to see if I could get a reaction out of him. He sucked a breath through his teeth and opened his eyes.

"You'll have to give a lecture on how to do that." I wiped the excess ink off his arm. "Some witches can't handle the pain."

No, I did not make a face at Shade, thank you very much. My statement wasn't a jab at him for once. We really did have a few in the coven who'd rather go in unaided than sit for a sigil.

"I don't feel the low vibration anymore, do you?" Miles rested his hand on Ginger's back.

She closed her eyes and breathed deeply before shaking her head. "It must've been residual from when Ash was sick. She's not putting off that vibe now."

"Yeah, it was one hell of a bug. I'm glad I got it all out." I picked up my Zippo and flicked it open. "Ready to light these babies up?"

They held their arms toward me, and I touched the flame to each, making them glow bright red before they faded to cool blue.

"Have fun gnome hunting." I forced a smile.

"I'll see you tomorrow morning." Ginger waved and followed the guys out the back.

I let out a huge exhale and slumped. The shop was closed on Mondays, but she'd be here bright and early tomorrow to open it. We had to get Chaos out before she returned. Who knew a kitchen witch would be so good at sensing demons?

I put my sigil gear away and headed back upstairs. Ember and Chaos sat in the places they were in when I woke this morning, and the tension in the room was so thick I felt like I was walking through mud.

"I told you we should have vanquished him." Ember stood and returned to pacing in front of the T.V. "It's too dangerous having him here. We almost got caught."

"You're right about that." I plopped onto the couch, exhausted from doing those simple sigils, and Chaos cut a steely gaze toward me.

I closed my eyes and pinched the bridge of my nose. "Not the vanquishing part. I don't have a death wish." I opened one eye to find his posture returning to normal, so I closed it again, relaxing.

"The female witch sensed me. I'm unsure about the males."

"Oh, Miles definitely did, but not until Ginger pointed it out." I opened my eyes. "They'll know what you are the second they see you."

"Which is why we should have—"

"You'd be dead if you tried." Chaos pinned his gaze on her, and she was lucky looks couldn't actually kill.

I let out a dramatic sigh. "C'mon, guys. We've been over this. We all need each other, so you two need to give up your grudges and learn to work together. I don't have the energy to play referee on top of everything else we have to do."

Her nostrils flared, but she gave me a tiny nod. Chaos spread his hands, conceding. Praise the goddess.

"You shouldn't have done those sigils." Ember returned to her chair. "Your body and vim have been taxed enough."

"If I hadn't, they'd be even more suspicious. Anyway, I had to do something after..." I glowered at the demon.

He waved a hand flippantly. "You said you wanted them gone. I obeyed."

"But they didn't leave, did they?"

He huffed. "They would have eventually."

"After they tore our house apart like Shade did my library?" I cocked my head.

Ember's mouth dropped open. "He's messed with Shade before?"

"And he *won't* do it again." I arched a brow at him.

He grunted. "Not unless it's necessary."

"And I get to determine when that is. Got it?" I held up my arm, reminding him of the sigil.

He glowered again, and damn it if he didn't look sexy doing it. "As you wish."

"Finally, we're getting somewhere," Ember said. "We have to find a way to hide Chaos. Get him out of town without the others noticing what he is. Then we can meet up with him later to look for the skull."

If he set foot outside anywhere near Ginger, she'd sense him. Who knew what other witches in the coven had that ability? It was too risky.

"You're in your own body now," I said. "Can't you portal to places?"

"Demons' abilities are limited in this realm. I could only portal back to Hell, which would kill you. I don't recommend it."

"He knows how to drive," Ember said. "We'll give him the keys to mom's car."

"And you trust him to wait for us and not run off to do his own thing?"

Her expression grew sullen. "No. What are we going to do with him then?"

I grinned. "I have an idea."

CHAPTER 4

ASH

"I remember seeing the spell in a book with a blue cover." I grabbed my phone off the desk and shoved it into my pocket, not bothering to check the messages. If anyone else needed a sigil, they'd have to wait. Operation Cloaking Chaos was in full swing.

Thankfully, both Ember and my demon had found enough patience to let me shower and change clothes. The hot water had worked wonders on my sore neck, and I was feeling fully refreshed after a bowl of yogurt and granola.

"There must be a hundred blue books in here." Ember pulled one from the shelf and flipped through the pages. "Do you remember what the spell was called?"

"I don't, but that doesn't matter." I took a deep breath and straightened my shoulders. "What was lost will be found. Near or far, show me where you are. Cloaking spell."

The energy in the room stilled, leaving only the tingle of the book with the spell. No, the books, plural. I felt a pull from three different volumes, which meant more than one spell of this kind existed. Perfect. If Chaos's power was too strong for one, I could cast all three. Surely that would hide his aura.

He stood next to Ember as I made my way down the first aisle of books. Irritation pricked at my soul. This mess would be the death of me if our escapades didn't kill me first. I stepped over a set of tomes strewn across the floor and tiptoed around a massive stack threatening to topple with the slightest disturbance.

Turning the corner at the end of the row, I found volume number one, a burgundy book with gold lettering. Not the specific one I was looking for, but I grabbed it just in case.

I made my way up the next aisle and found number two, a plain beige cover with a simple brown font. Tucking it under my arm, I focused on the spell's pull and found the blue one two rows over. "Got it!"

I couldn't help but grin as I bounded up the cleanest aisle and returned to the front. A quick search of the index found the cloaking spell in each book, and I spread open the volumes on my desk.

"Here we go." I tapped my finger against the page in the red book, then the beige, then the blue. "Three different cloaking spells. We can use these to mask Chaos's aura, so no one will know he's a demon."

Ember peered over my shoulder at the red book. "That might work if he was an artifact we needed to hide." She ran her finger down the page. "This is an invisibility spell for inanimate objects."

My heart sank as I skimmed the page. "Dang it. That's okay; we've got two more."

Chaos picked up the beige book. "I assume this one is for odor control. The title is Scent Cloaking."

I slammed the red book shut and took the beige one, setting them both aside. "No worries. This is the one I was looking for anyway." I read the spell, my heart sinking even more. Another object invisibility spell. "Well, crappity crap. I'll try the location spell again. "What's another word for cloaking?"

"Why don't you use your gift?" Ember rested a hand on my shoulder. "I'm sure if you focused, you could find exactly what you're looking for."

I shook my head. "This is how I always find books."

"That was before you learned how to use your power." Chaos put his hand on my other shoulder. "You found the skulls' hiding places by using your inborn magic."

I shrugged them both off and rose to my feet. "That was different."

"How so?" Ember crossed her arms.

"I had a demon in my head telling me what to do." I threw up my arms. "Now is not the time for me to try learning new magic."

"It's precisely the time." Chaos sent a pulse of energy through the sigil, instantly calming me. "You know the spell but not the name. Focus on your memory of it, and your power will guide you."

"It would be faster if I—"

"Do it, Ash," Ember said. "I know you can."

If Chaos hadn't been sending waves of calmness through me, I would have argued more. Instead, I decided to prove them wrong. I closed my eyes and thought about the spell. I'd been young, maybe seventeen, when I'd found it. I'd wanted to try it, but Dad wouldn't let me. He'd said I wasn't ready for a spell that powerful, and his words had nearly killed me. I'd felt like he didn't trust me, my magic.

Nobody trusted my fire and for good reason. I'd wanted so badly to prove I could handle the spell, but he'd refused, taking the book and hiding it amongst the stacks. He'd cloaked it, making it invisible.

Of course! I wasn't looking for a cloaking spell. "It's aura shrouding." Excitement tingled in my muscles the moment I felt the pull, and I practically ran through the stacks. A shelf at the back of the room stood empty, a layer of dust coating the wood.

"What else have you hidden here, Dad?" I reached for the invisible books, but my hand felt air. I traced my finger over the shelf, removing a stripe of dust. Nothing was there. My enthusiasm deflated like a three-day-old balloon.

I turned to Chaos and Ember, who had followed me through the library. "I told you I couldn't do it." I sounded like a sullen child, but I couldn't help it. For a few minutes, I'd had as much faith in my supposed inborn power as they had. I should've known better.

Chaos stepped toward the shelf, eyeing it skeptically. "Does your gut tell you the book is here?"

I shrugged. "I thought it did."

"Then it must be. Hold that thought." Ember turned and darted up the aisle.

Chaos examined the shelves above and below the empty one. "Your father didn't want you trying spells from this book."

"I already told you that." I leaned against the shelves behind me, waiting for Ember and whatever plan she'd concocted.

"Were there any other off-limits volumes?" Chaos asked.

"Anything he thought I couldn't handle, I guess." I shook my hands, preparing to cast the location spell again when Ember returned with a potion bottle.

"Don't waste your vim." She uncorked the bottle and splashed a yellow liquid on the shelf. "Spells cast are broken free. As I will it, so mote it be."

The shelf shimmered like heat coming off the asphalt during a hot summer. A spark glowed in the center, growing bigger until it popped like a gunshot. I flinched back, shielding my eyes against the light.

"I knew you could do it." Ember motioned with her head to the shelf, and my mouth dropped open.

The blue spell book, along with four others, occupied the once-empty space. I reached out tentatively, tapping the volume and jerking my hand away in case the magic fought back. With my heart hammering in my chest, I grabbed the book and opened it.

"Holy crap. It's been here all along." I flipped through the pages, and sure enough, there was the aura-shrouding spell.

"And you knew exactly where it was without casting a

spell. Come on." Ember turned and strode toward the front of the library.

"You're more powerful than you believe." Chaos gestured me forward and followed me to my desk.

"I didn't know a spell like that existed. Making things invisible to the eyes, sure, but to the touch?" I sank into my chair. "How did you know?"

"It's how they used to hide our Yule presents." Ember leaned on the corner of the desk. "I found the hiding spot every year so we could snoop. Once they caught on, they used magic. I watched Mom from the hallway when she hid them right beneath the tree one year."

I laughed. "And you figured out the spell to reveal them?"

She shook her head. "It was all magic above my level at the time. I remembered Mom making the potion, telling me it was for something boring. But it was bright yellow, and when she tossed it on the tree, suddenly all our presents appeared. It's an easy one to make."

Chaos frowned. "Your parents were kind enough to give you gifts to open on a specific day, yet you insolently found them in advance, ruining the surprise?"

She shrugged. "We were kids. Don't look at me like I'm a monster. Ash snooped too."

"Only because you were doing it. I was always so scared of getting caught, I had anxiety out the wazoo."

"And you turned out just fine." Ember squeezed my shoulders. "Anyway, the point is that you *did* know where the book was hidden, and I'm certain you would have figured out a way to reveal it if you'd had the time."

"You most definitely would have," Chaos said.

My cheeks heated. "Maybe." I read the spell, trying to ignore their praise. "I think we have all these ingredients in the kitchen. Let's go."

We returned upstairs, and Chaos sat at the counter while Ember and I gathered the ingredients. Bay leaf, lady's mantle, marjoram. Wolfsbane...boy, this was a powerful spell. Plants in the aconite family were only used in the most advanced light magic potions. They had all kinds of nasty uses for dark magic, uses which could sometimes turn out to be unintended side effects for us if we weren't careful.

"No wonder Dad hid this book away." I crushed the herbs and added them to the liquid Ember had mixed.

"It's going to take a lot of vim to pull off." She stirred the concoction and motioned to the final ingredient.

"Cast it together?" I picked up the bottle and pulled off the cap.

"Naturally." She smiled and held the bowl toward me.

I added one drop of cinnamon oil, causing the potion to pop and sizzle before turning to a fine pink powder. Ember poured half the contents into my palm and half into her own before holding my free hand.

"Are you ready for this?" I asked my demon.

He looked from me to Ember and back at me. "I trust you."

My chest gave a squeeze at his words, but I didn't have time to consider what that meant for us. Ember blew her dust at him, so I had to do the same, lest we waste it and have to start all over again.

We recited the incantation in unison, sharing our power.

"Aura strong, magic deep, we hide your essence from all who seek."

Ember's power flowed from her hand into mine, resonating in the core of my being while my magic poured into her. My body heated, magical fire flowing through my veins as we cast our power onto Chaos.

He stiffened, the charm taking hold. Sucking in a breath, his hands curled into fists, the tendons in his neck tightening, protruding as if he clenched his jaw.

"As we will it, so mote it be." Ember's and my breath came out in a rush, along with all the adrenaline that had built up in the excitement. That spell was no joke.

Chaos stilled, the rise and fall of his chest as he breathed the only movement he made. Closing my eyes, I focused on the energy in the room, expecting the low, bone-penetrating vibration to cease.

It didn't.

"Well, crap. It didn't work." I closed the spell book and slid onto a stool. "What now?"

"How do you know it didn't work?" Ember asked.

"I don't feel any different." Chaos's posture relaxed, his neck tendons returning to their normal position.

"I can still feel his aura," I said.

"I can't." Ember tapped her finger against her lips. "I'm not a pro at sensing demons like you are, but the energy in the room definitely feels lighter. Higher. I think I was sensing him before but didn't realize it."

Chaos ran his finger over the sigil on my arm, making it

tingle. "I believe you will always be able to sense me as long as you bear my mark."

"It worked, Ash. I know it did." She put the potion dishes in the sink.

I got up to wash them. "How can we be sure?" I turned on the water and rinsed the bowl.

Ember leaned on the counter next to me and flashed a conspiratorial grin. "There's only one way to find out."

CHAPTER 5
CHAOS

The hairs on my arms stood on end the moment we stepped onto the street. I'd grown accustomed to the sights and sounds of this modern world after sensing them through Ash, but her body did not respond to the thinning of the veil as mine now did.

It was October in this realm's time, which meant the curtain between worlds would only grow thinner in the coming weeks. Rifts would become more frequent and greater in size until the boundary ceased to exist.

I could not let that happen.

"It's a few streets over." Ember stopped near their black vehicle and turned to her sister. "Should we walk it?"

"I thought the point was to keep him out of sight and see if Ginger sensed him nearby." Ash pulled on the door handle, but it didn't open. "If we go parading him down the street, we'll risk someone else with the spidy-sense seeing him."

"Spidy-sense?" I asked.

Ash let out a small laugh. "It's an expression. I mean if someone else who can easily sense demons notices you."

"I see." The corners of my mouth turned upward against my will. Ash wore a corset, like women did in the previous centuries, which drew attention to the curves of her body. A sheer undershirt, tight black pants, and bulky boots completed her clothing ensemble, and her hair... The unnatural shade of blue somehow complemented her fair complexion, making it difficult to tear my gaze away.

This witch was an enigma. Pure of heart, yet tough and powerful, with a hint of...not evil per se. I believe the modern slang would be that she had a take-no-shit attitude, which I adored about her.

"We'll take the van." Ember pressed a button on her hand-held device, and the lock disengaged with a click.

Ash opened the side door for me before climbing into the front seat by her sister. I sat in the middle seat and closed the door, and we headed out of the alley onto the main thoroughfare. It took less than five earthly minutes to reach our destination.

Ember stopped on the side of the road before turning to Ash. "Tell your demon to stay put. He won't listen to me."

She was correct in that assumption.

"Don't leave the van until we know the spell worked," Ash said. "The windows are dark, so no one will see you in here."

I observed her for a moment. I could have easily let myself out and made the trek to find Mayhem's skull on my own, but their vehicle would get me there much faster. They needed to keep order in their coven, and though the idea went against my very nature, I conceded.

"I will await your word."

Ash's mouth twitched as if she wanted to smile. "We won't be long."

The sisters exited the van and jogged across the street where the trio of witches had sent the last gnome through the veil. Ash and Ember looked around as if they couldn't see the witches standing before their eyes.

Shade must have used shadow magic. Magic which I could see through. I would keep that information to myself for now.

Ginger's gaze locked on the van, and she picked up a sickle from the ground before crossing the street toward me. It appeared the shrouding spell didn't work. The sisters didn't see her leave the scene.

Now I had a dilemma. If this witch approached with the intention to vanquish me, I would have no choice but to kill her. Yet, I'd sworn to Ash no harm would come to her coven by my hand. I believed self-defense was a common reason for acquittal in this time. Ash needed me here in this realm to break the curse, so killing this witch would be in everyone's best interest.

The question was, fire or madness?

Ginger reached the van and slid the side door open. Without looking, she opened the hatch in the floor. Her head snapped up, her eyes widening.

Madness would cause the least amount of trouble with the human police. I primed my magic, gathering it in my chest.

Ginger straightened, her grip tight on the sickle. "Who are you?"

"I'm a friend of Ash." My power rose to just below the surface, ready to wreak havoc on her mind.

She dropped the sickle into the floor compartment. "I'm Ginger. What's your name?"

Had the spell worked after all? If she felt my demon aura, she would have swung the weapon rather than disposed of it. "I am—"

"Ginger!" Ash shouted as she darted across the street.

Ember stood talking to the men, the shadow magic having been lifted, but when her gaze snapped toward the van, she followed Ash.

"Hey!" Ash smiled harder than natural. "I see you've met my friend...umm..." She glanced at her arm where my sigil hid beneath her sleeve. "Mark. This is Mark, a new fire witch in town."

Ember stopped behind Ash, a look of alarm filling her eyes. "Mark. Yeah, he's with us."

"Hi, Mark." Ginger studied me. "You don't look like a witch."

"Well, he is," Ash's voice raised an octave. "He's staying with us while he's training for a new job in Salem. Right, Mark?"

"Indeed." I nodded a hello.

Ash's mind worked quickly. Her intelligence impressed me.

Ginger cut her skeptical gaze between the two of us. She was far too observant for my liking, so I held up my hand, igniting a controlled flame on my palm, proving my fire magic ability.

"Huh. Okay, well it's nice to meet you." She shrugged and closed the hatch. "Glad to see you're feeling better," she said to Ash.

"Much better. See you tomorrow, bright and early?" She forced another smile.

"I'll be there." With a wave, she retreated to join her friends.

Ash let out a massive breath before returning to her seat in the front of the van. "What did she say? Did she sense anything?"

"I don't believe she did. Not my demonic nature anyway." I gazed across the street where the witch in question had returned to the company of the men. She spoke, pointing to the van, and they snapped their heads toward us.

"Though she did find my presence abnormal. If I'm reading their body language correctly, the others do as well."

"Oh, she definitely finds you abnormal." Ember turned the key, starting the engine. "I'll call a meeting. We've got to give them something before they start making up their own stories about what's going on with the veil."

"The truth is far worse than anything they could imagine." I turned away from the window to peer out the front.

"No doubt." Ember put the vehicle in gear and pulled onto the road.

"Would you look at that?" Ash showed a genuine smile. "You two finally agree on something."

Her sister scoffed. "Don't get used to it."

"Indeed."

"Ha!" Ash pointed her finger from me to Ember. "You just agreed again."

CHAPTER 6
ASH

"I seriously can't believe we're doing this." I gripped the shopping cart in both hands, squeezing until my knuckles turned white.

"Grocery shopping together?" Chaos plucked a box of cereal from the shelf, curling his lip at the exaggerated cartoon bird on the front. "Neither can I. We could end this ordeal more quickly if we went straight for Mayhem's skull."

I snatched the box from his hands and returned it to the shelf. "Not shopping, doofus. Calling this emergency meeting to tell the coven 'someone' summoned a demon."

He snapped his head to the right and left, peering down the aisle. "Do you feel that?"

"Nervous? Like we're about to do something insane?"

He paced to the end of the row, looked from side to side, and paced back. "Dark magic. It's faint, barely tainting the air."

I groaned. "Please tell me a rift isn't about to open inside the supermarket."

"No, it's..." His brows slammed down over his eyes. "I don't feel it anymore."

"Thank the goddess. We're on strict orders from the High Priestess *not* to stir up any trouble."

While Ember stayed at the house to prepare for the gathering, she put me, and by default, Chaos, on snack duty. What did you serve a group of monster-hunting witches when you were about to deliver the news that a powerful demon walked among them? Calming foods.

"We need herbal tea. Come on." I steered us toward the end of the breakfast aisle, and Chaos dropped a different box into the cart. "Since when do demons eat cereal? I thought you'd feast on the blood of your enemies."

"You're confusing us with vampires." He wandered down the next aisle, so I followed him. "In this realm, we require food the same as you." He tapped the box. "And this one says it's 'magically delicious.'"

I laughed. "That's a figure of speech. You know there's no actual magic in that box, aside from the sugar high you'll get if you eat too much." Yeah, I might've known that from experience.

"I'll decide for myself. You mentioned herbal tea?"

"Chamomile, lavender. We need to get some calming herbs into the coven members before we drop a bomb like this. And foods with lots of tryptophan. Nuts, seeds, oh! I think they sell deviled egg trays in the deli."

He picked up a can of chili and read the label. "Most of these ingredients aren't food."

"Which is probably why cancer is on the rise." I took the can and returned it to the shelf. "Tea is on the next aisle over. C'mon."

"If you need the members to remain calm, why don't you simply cast a spell?"

I found the lavender and chamomile and dropped a few boxes into the cart. "They'd know. Just like I know when you're calming me. It works, but it feels unnatural. That would raise even more suspicion."

"Perhaps you should lie about the cause then. Mutiny in the fae realm. A necromancer raising too many dead. Fabricate a plausible reason for the rifts and leave it at that."

"Oh no. We can't do that. We're walking a razor-thin line as it is. If they catch on to what's really happening, and it's not the slightest bit close to what we told them it was, our coven will implode. Ember and I will be banished…or worse…and you'll never find your brothers."

"I suppose." He pursed his lips, looking thoughtful and kind of cute if I were being honest. If I had to be bound to a demon, at least it was to an attractive one.

"We have to give them a little nugget of truth." I held my thumb and forefinger close together. "We'll leave out the part about how we're the ones who summoned the demons and caused the rifts."

He arched a brow. "Lying by omission is still lying."

I stopped at the end of the aisle. "You're a demon. I didn't think that would bother you."

"It doesn't. But it will bother you."

"My self-preservation instinct is far too strong to worry over an omitted fact. Let's get the eggs and head home."

"Home..." He held my gaze with those unnaturally green, gem-like eyes, and, for a moment, I felt this ridiculous urge to take his face in my hands and plant one on him. Ludicrous, I knew. We were in the middle of the grocery store, for Hecate's sake, but the desire was there just the same.

In my defense, his full, luscious lips would have tempted any hot-blooded woman. Even fully dressed, he exuded this raw, rustic, panty-dropping masculinity that would entrance anyone.

Anyone except me, of course. Light witches and demons did not mix, so the sooner we could send him on his way, the better. Still, I could admit he was easy on the eyes. No harm in that.

His sharp inhale broke our mini trance, and he cleared his throat. "Why must you serve food at this meeting anyway? Shouldn't you get straight to the point?"

I picked up a tray of deviled eggs from the refrigerated case and set them in the basket. "Ember thinks it'll soften the blow. We always have food at our monthly meetings, so she doesn't want this one to be any different."

"But this is an emergency meeting, not your regular gathering."

"I know. Just go with it, okay? We're doing our best."

"Ash?" Chrys's voice sounded from behind me, and my breath caught.

I spun to face her, and Chaos moved in closer to me, resting his hand on my back protectively. Faking a smile, I said a quick, silent prayer to the goddess for his shroud to hold. "Hey, Chrys. You're coming to the meeting, right?"

"Yep. I popped in to get some spinach dip and crackers before I pick up Ginger and head that way. Should I bring anything else?" Her gaze cut between Chaos and me, the questions visible in her eyes.

"Just your lovely self." If I smiled any harder, my face might split.

"Perfect. And who is this tall, dark, and brooding stranger? I've never seen you before. I'm Chrys." She held out her hand to shake.

Chaos looked at her extended arm. "My name is—"

"Mark. His name is Mark, and he's an old friend of the family. Distant cousin maybe, I can't remember. His parents were friends with my parents..." Crappity crap. I didn't think to test if the shroud spell would stand up to touch.

"Well, don't leave me hanging." Chrys shoved her hand toward him, and he gripped it while I held my breath. "It's nice to meet you, Mark, friend of the family, maybe distant cousin."

"Likewise." He released her hand and returned his to my back. He stiffened, and if my corset didn't fit so snugly to my body, he'd have clutched it in his fist.

"See you in a bit." Chrys turned down an aisle, and I stepped away from my demon.

"What's with the possessive back grab? You're supposed to belong to me, not the other way around."

His eyes narrowed, and he stilled. "Protective, not possessive."

"Chrys is one of us, and she's super nice. I don't need—"

He held up his hand to silence me, and I laughed incredulously. I was about to tell him never to do that again, but he gestured to my right and said, "There. The dark magic I sensed."

I followed his gaze to find two women at the end of the deli case, staring. As soon as I looked at them, they jerked their heads down to examine a block of cheese. One wore a crossbody satchel nearly identical to my spell kit, and the other had a fanny pack slung over her shoulder.

I would never understand that trend. If you weren't planning to wear it around your waist, where it was made to be worn, why carry one? Bags and purses were much more fashionable, but what did I know? I was the blue-haired goth girl who got stared at everywhere I went, even in Salem.

Fanny Pack whispered something to Spell Satchel, who glanced quickly at me and dropped the cheese into the case before they both disappeared down the closest aisle.

"Hopefully they're just passing through. We don't have time to deal with dark witch shenanigans today. C'mon. Let's go pay." I led the way to the front of the store, and Chaos helped me put our groceries onto the belt.

"Do dark witches reside in Salem?" he whispered as we waited for the cashier to scan our items.

Beep...beep...beep. I swore the guy was moving like a sloth on purpose. That, or he was incredibly high. Ever since they legalized marijuana in Massachusetts, you never knew.

"Sometimes they try, but as soon as they perform unsavory magic, we give them a choice. Leave or be imprisoned and reported to the Higher Power. You can guess which option they choose."

"Indeed." He scanned the room, on high alert.

I fought a grin. Having Chaos around was a bit like having a guard dog. One that still needed a lot of training. If the dark duo tried anything here, I could imagine his way of handling it. "Best to let me deal with the confrontation if there is one."

"Hmm," was his only reply.

I paid for the groceries, and we grabbed the bags and headed for the exit. The glass doors slid open, the crisp fall air greeting us as we stepped outside, and Chaos returned his hand to my back. I looked to my right to find the witches standing on the sidewalk, talking.

Spell Satchel glanced at me and adjusted the strap on her shoulder, turning the bag and revealing a familiar emblem embroidered on the flap. I grabbed Chaos's arm and dragged him toward the van.

"Those are Boston Magic Society witches." I opened the door and threw the groceries into the back. "What on earth are they doing here?" I climbed into the driver's seat and started the engine.

Chaos sat next to me and buckled his seatbelt. "You did raid their library, tearing it apart in the process."

I pulled onto the street and headed home. "Yeah, but we didn't leave any evidence behind. Unless their golem can talk, they have no way of knowing it was us."

"Hmm," he said again.

"What?" I glanced at him before focusing on the road.

He pressed his lips into a thin line. "You tore a page out of a book relating directly to your coven."

"So?" I waved off his concern, hoping to send mine packing as well. "They had thousands of books. The chance of them opening that particular one is slim at best. They're probably just drawn to the thinning veil. It'll be fine."

"Ignoring a problem doesn't make it cease to exist." He watched the mirrors, making sure they didn't follow.

"One thing at a time." Because right now, we had too much on our plates to worry ourselves over a couple of witches visiting Witch City. "Maybe they just wanted to see where it all started." I parked in the back of the building, and Chaos helped me carry the groceries upstairs.

Ember sat at the counter, drumming her fingers on the surface as we entered the kitchen. "We can't lie, but we can imply, right? The kids in the woods summoned a demon. If the coven believes that was the start of it..."

I unpacked the bags and arranged everything on the counter before setting a pot of water to boil. "It started before that, but it has definitely picked up since then."

"It'll be fine." Chaos echoed my words from earlier. Always the helpful little demon.

Ember eyed the spread I'd set up. "Tea? Alcohol would have been a better choice for this. Everyone would chill the eff out."

"Right, because no one has ever gotten drunk and become belligerent and angry." I set a second pot to boil as backup and lined teacups and water glasses on the counter between the sink and stove. "Everything we bought has calming ingredients."

"Everything?" Ember raised her brows at Chaos, who leaned against the wall, shoving cereal into his mouth.

"That was his good boy prize. He didn't cause a panic at the grocery, so he got a reward."

"They're magically delicious," he said around a mouthful of Lucky Charms. "Speaking of the store…"

Boots thudded on the stairs before a knock sounded at the entrance. We'd have to tell Ember about the Boston witches later. That was a conversation that did not need to happen in front of the coven.

"Come in," Ember called, and Shade and Miles crossed the threshold.

Shade headed straight for the fridge and grabbed a beer, tossing it to Miles before taking the last one for himself.

Ember chuckled. "Told you."

"Whatever." The tea kettle whistled, so I turned off the heat and poured myself a mug of lavender dreams.

After taking a long pull from his beer, Shade lifted his chin at Chaos. "You must be Mark. I'm Shade, shadow witch." He tipped his beer toward my demon, not bothering to shake his hand.

"Indeed I am."

"Miles." He stuck out his hand, and Chaos shook it, and yes, I did hold my breath again. Miles had claimed to sense demonic energy when Ginger did. If anyone could feel through the shroud, it would be those two. "Nice to meet you."

I eyed Miles, looking for any sign he thought something was off. If he suspected anything, he was a master at hiding it.

"Likewise." Chaos set the cereal box on the counter, and it

tipped over, sending a few pieces to the floor. He turned as if he planned to walk away and leave the mess, and I almost blew our cover.

The words *bad demon* made it from my brain to the tip of my tongue before I realized my near faux pas. Instead, I cleared my throat, drawing his attention and looking from the mess on the floor to the one on the counter.

He pursed his lips, keeping his gaze trained on me as he crouched to pick up the clover-shaped marshmallows. After sweeping the mess off the counter and into his hand, he dumped it into the trash and closed the box. "Where do you keep this?"

"In the pantry." I pointed to the door.

He picked up a deviled egg and popped it into his mouth on his way, giving Shade a once-over as he passed. Shade bristled. If he had hackles, he would've raised them.

"Where is he sleeping while he stays with you?" Shade sneered at me. "In your bed I assume?"

"Ash is a Holland witch and Ink Master." Chaos returned to my side and glared at Shade. "You should remember your place when you speak to her."

Shade laughed incredulously before looming forward. "Oh, I know my place. It's her who needs—"

"Stop it! Both of you." I held up my hands and stood between them. "We're all on the same side, and as soon as Chrys and Ginger arrive, we can get down to business. In the meantime, have some herbal tea and calm the eff down."

Ember snickered, getting a kick out of me being the pivot

point in a hate triangle...because there was certainly no love among us.

"Let's grab a seat." Miles slapped Shade on the arm, steering him toward the living room.

A barely audible growl rumbled in Chaos's chest, and I cut him a steely gaze. "Behave yourself," I whispered.

"He started it." He crossed his arms and leaned against the counter.

I clenched my teeth. "Do I have to send you to your room?"

"Only if you plan to come with me." If eyes could actually twinkle, his would have.

My stomach had the audacity to flutter, so I grabbed my tea and joined the others in the living room. I leaned against the wall near the television, drawing the mug to my lips when Chrys plowed through the door, breathless.

"It's Ginger," she panted, her chest heaving with her breath. "I went to pick her up, but when I got there..." She inhaled deeply, and her entire body trembled. "She's dead."

CHAPTER 7
ASH

Ginger lived in the downstairs portion of a small duplex. With its pitched roof, pale blue paint, and white shutters, it looked like a quaint little cottage on the safest street in America. A massive juniper towered over the front sidewalk, and a white picket fence surrounded the structure, making it feel surreal. Murders weren't allowed to happen within the confines of white picket fences. Everyone knew that.

We'd all piled into the van and remained silent on the ride over. I let Shade ride shotgun, and I sat in the back, closer to Chaos than I needed to be, but having physical contact with him helped keep me calm.

Crazy, I knew, but the moment his thigh touched mine, I felt safe and confident. It was completely bonkers, and I blamed the damn sigil on my arm. Once I removed it, I'd come back to my senses. For now, I'd let this demon make me feel safe, even though I'd gotten along fine without him for twenty-four years.

Miles sat next to Chrys in the way back seat, his spine ramrod straight, his expression blank. No doubt the poor guy was in shock.

Ember parked on the curb, and we filed out of the van to stand on the sidewalk. "Thank you for not calling the police yet." She patted Chrys's shoulder.

"Magic was obviously involved." Her voice trembled as she spoke. "I figured it was better if we did our thing before the humans tromped all over the scene."

"Good call," I said before poking my head into the van. "Miles? Are you coming, or do you want to wait here?"

He sucked in a sharp breath. "Yeah. I'm coming." He climbed out and closed the door.

"It's gruesome. Prepare yourselves." Chrys opened the gate, and we followed her up the front steps. "I knocked for a good three minutes. When she didn't answer, I tried the door. It wasn't locked, so I let myself in." She grabbed the knob and gave it a twist.

"You shouldn't have touched that." Shade stepped into the foyer behind her. "Now your fingerprints are on it."

"I had already touched it. Come in before the neighbors get suspicious."

Inside the house, we all stopped in the foyer, going still, feeling, sensing. I searched for the low, bone-penetrating hum of demon magic, but I didn't pick up anything besides the one standing next to me. I looked at him, arching a brow in question. He shook his head, confirming no demon lurked inside.

"Someone used dark magic in here," Ember said. "And today wasn't the first time."

I opened my senses to witchcraft, feeling the icky, sticky energy running through the air. Someone used it very recently, and we were about to see the results. But residual dark magic also clung to the walls and ceiling. I could cast my revealing spell, but I wasn't sure I wanted to know exactly what had gone on.

"Ready?" Ember took point, and I swallowed the lump in my throat. My hands trembled as she led the way into the living room, and a collective gasp sounded from all of us...even Chaos.

"That is...brutal." I inched closer to the scene, and Chaos flanked me.

Ginger...or what was left of her...lay on the floor in the center of a pentagram. Red candles stood extinguished at each of the five points, and the wicked energy in the room was so thick, I gagged.

Her arms and legs, stretched outward to each point, reminded me of DaVinci's Vitruvian Man, but her face...burned beyond recognition...made my heart sink into my stomach, which then dropped into my shoes.

The rest of the space appeared neat and orderly. A white sofa sat beneath the window, the yellow throw pillows evenly spaced across the cushions. A bookshelf stood against the adjacent wall, with her titles arranged in alphabetical order by author, and a sunny landscape painting hung above it. Zero signs of a struggle. Poor Ginger didn't even get the chance to fight back.

Miles kneeled next to her, and a single tear slid down his cheek. "Who could do something like this?" His voice was barely a whisper.

I cast my gaze upward and then examined the wood around poor Ginger. "The only thing that burned was her. The floor and ceiling show no signs of flames."

"Magical fire." Ember paced around the circle, taking the gruesomeness in.

Shade snapped his head toward Chaos. "There were only two fire witches left in Salem until you showed up. Ginger said you were a fire witch too."

Chaos clasped his hands behind his back, widening his stance. "Indeed I am."

"Hold up. Are you accusing C...Mark of murder?" I stepped toward Shade, fuming, my hands curling into fists.

"The evidence is damning," he replied, shrugging one shoulder. "Unless you or Ember did it..."

The nerve of this guy! "Mark has been with me since the moment he arrived in Salem. Magical fire can be created with the right ingredients and a spell. Maybe you did it because she was getting in the way of your bromance with Miles."

"All right. Stop it. Both of you." Ember pulled out her phone and snapped pictures of the scene. "We're all on the same team. Act like it."

"Can you see what magic was used?" Miles asked, not taking his gaze off Ginger. He heaved in a breath, and his shoulders slumped.

"Sure can." I gave Shade the stink eye before stepping back into the room's entrance. I stretched my neck and wiggled my fingers, preparing myself for whatever goddess-awful magic I was about to uncover. "Confess, expose, my magic sleuth. I call on you to reveal your truth."

I sent my intention into the room, and it bounced back like a rubber band, slapping me in the face and shoving me against the wall. My head smacked the sheetrock, and my vision swam.

Chaos ran to my side, taking my cheeks in his hands, his concerned gaze traveling over my face. "Are you injured?" His palms were warm against my skin, and, once again, his touch gave me confidence and calmness.

"Whoever did this doesn't want us to know the method. I'll have to remove the cloak before I can reveal the magic." I grabbed a premade potion from my bag.

"Here." He slipped his hand into mine. "I'll help."

"No!" Alarm filled Ember's eyes, and she raced toward me. "I've got this. C'mon, Ash. We'll do it together."

She took the bottle and gripped my free hand, giving me a *don't do anything stupid* look. I suppose harnessing the power of a Prince of Hell in front of the coven warriors wasn't the best idea. Especially since, in their eyes, he was a prime suspect. I would've loved to feel his power running through me again, but I was a good girl, and I slid my hand from his grasp.

Ember threw the powdered potion into the air, and her energy built, flowing through me as mine flowed into her. My insides burned with magic, and I nodded at my sister before we said in unison, "Magic cloak, we now revoke."

Our spell shot outward, shoving against the cloaking hex the killer had put on the room. Pressure built. The hex fought back. Sweat beaded on my forehead as I pushed another wave of magic against the spell.

A loud *pop* reverberated in the space, vibrating against my skin before the hex dissolved. We cast the revealing spell together, and golden sparkles coated nearly everything. Ginger had practiced light magic a lot in this house, but the remnants of dark spells also hung in the atmosphere.

"The fire was definitely magical." Chrys stared at Ginger's charred face, where our incantation revealed the remnants of magical flames. "Can you tell if it was a fire witch or a spell?"

"Magical fire is magical fire, whether it comes from within or from a spell, so there's no way to know." I moved closer, kneeling by my friend's body, and Miles rose to his feet, backing away.

Ember kneeled next to me. "Why would someone do this?" she whispered.

My chest ached at the sight. If Chaos's theory about the Boston witches knowing what we did was true, I had an idea of who. A sob bubbled from my chest to my throat, but I swallowed it and rose to my feet. Could Ginger's death be related to the library incident? Good goddess, I hoped not.

"Do you see the red threads running from the points of the pentagram to her wrists, ankles, and neck?" I traced my finger around the scene to indicate the magic.

"She was bound." Chaos's deep voice sounded right behind my shoulder, and I jumped.

"Jeez. I didn't know you were standing there." I took a step away from him.

"Bound and tortured." Miles wiped a tear from his cheek. "There are cuts all over her."

"Someone was looking for information," Shade said.

My stomach turned. Information about who destroyed their library, perhaps?

"Or something nasty came through the veil." Ember looked at me. "Would a demon do something like this?"

I glanced at Chaos, who nodded. "If she wouldn't pay a debt she owed, maybe. If she summoned something—"

"She didn't summon a demon." Miles wrung his hands. "She wouldn't."

"How do you know that?" Shade crossed his arms. "There are dark magic remnants all over the place. She was obviously up to something."

She certainly was...

Holy Mother of Magic. Chaos's demonic nature must've been rubbing off on me because I had a diabolical thought. I felt absolutely mortified that it popped into my head, but we could use Ginger's death to our advantage.

We could blame the veil's weakening on Ginger summoning a demon.

No. No, that was terrible. Ginger was my friend, and she didn't deserve to die like this.

"Are you okay?" Ember's brows drew downward. "You look like you're either going to puke or you're severely constipated."

Chaos rested his hand on the small of my back, and I swallowed the bitterness from my mouth. Blaming her would solve one of our major problems. She didn't have any living family to disappoint...

Ugh! Moral dilemmas were not my strong suit.

"If she summoned a high-level demon," Chaos said as if reading my mind, "it would explain the weakening of the veil. In my research, I've found that major magic crossing it in either direction can upset the balance and cause rifts to form."

Nausea churned in my gut. He went there. He said it out loud, which shouldn't have surprised me. He was a demon for Hecate's sake, but I couldn't decide if a weight had been lifted or if I really did need to puke.

Ember raised her brows at me and shrugged. "It makes sense. I called the meeting today to tell you we thought someone had summoned a demon. Now we know who."

My sister went there too. *Dear goddess, please don't damn us to eternal suffering for this.*

Miles's expression blanked, his eyes not seeming to focus on anything.

"Ginger is the cause for all of this." Shade shook his head. "I never trusted her. She's always seemed off. Like she was scheming all the time, but summoning a demon?" He crossed his arms. "She got what she deserved."

"I knew..." Miles drew in a ragged breath. "I knew she was practicing dark magic." He blinked and looked at Ember, his lower lip trembling. "I should have turned her in. I should have said something, but they were minor spells. Money, luck, sex. I just..." His face crumpled. "I loved her."

Hexes and hand grenades. What had we done? Now, not only had we tarnished Ginger's name, but we'd have to deal with Miles's confession of knowing she was dabbling in the dark arts. I needed to buy a pair of thigh-high boots because the shit was getting deep in this coven. What would Cinder say about this tangled web we were weaving?

Not a damn thing because she was the one who started it all. I needed to remember that.

"What do we do now?" I asked Ember, who cut her gaze between Chaos and me. His hand still rested on my back, so I stepped away. I could see the gears turning in her mind. She hated the closeness between her little sis and a demon. I wasn't fond of it either, to be honest. Or maybe I was too fond of it.

"We hope the demon got what it wanted and went back to Hell," Shade said before ducking down the hall.

"I meant with Ginger." I paced to the kitchen and opened the cabinet doors, pretending to canvass the space for demonic clues. "If the media gets ahold of this story, rumors will spread about Satanic killings again."

"I'll call it in to the Chief." Ember pulled her phone from her pocket. "Search the house for anything that might explain why she summoned a demon."

Miles and Chrys went down the hall to join Shade, and Chaos stepped into the utility closet. Ember sank onto the couch and dialed the Chief, so I slipped into the closet with Chaos and closed the door.

"A demon didn't kill her," I whispered.

"No, none have been summoned in this space." He brushed a lock of hair away from my eye. "But one problem has been solved."

I crossed my arms over my stomach to hold myself together. "I can't believe poor Ginger is taking the fall for us."

"She's dead." He shrugged. "I doubt she'll mind."

"I know, but... The worst part of it is, I had the same idea. You had the guts to say it out loud, but I thought it."

He rested his hands on my shoulders. "Your friend was murdered. Nothing about that would change if she didn't take the blame. There is no shame in using a situation to your advantage."

I blew out a hard breath. "Says the demon."

"Perhaps this was a blessing from your goddess."

"No." I shrugged off his touch. "Light witches don't work that way. We—"

The door swung open before I could finish schooling the demon on how goodness worked, and Ember gaped at us. "What are you doing in here?"

"Talking privately." I brushed past her and returned to the foyer. I couldn't stomach the scene in the living room any longer.

"Higgins is on his way." Ember stood between Chaos and me, and the others joined us by the front door. "The humans will come up with a cover story that doesn't involve demons or devil worship. We have to clear out before they get here."

We filed out the front door and returned to our seats in the van. Ember started the engine, and we headed home, a heaviness hanging over us as we rolled down the road. I stared out the window, watching the trees go by. Their deep red and orange leaves contrasted with the gray tint of the cloudy sky. In a few more weeks, the branches would be bare.

My leg touched Chaos's again, and while I did enjoy the sensation it brought, I scooted away. I was getting too close to him, depending on him too much, and Ember could see it.

"Will the rifts stop opening now that the demon got Ginger?" Chrys asked.

Ember looked from me to Chaos in the rearview mirror, but I didn't know how to answer that question any more than she did. A demon didn't get Ginger, and the rifts wouldn't stop until we completed our quest. But we couldn't tell them that. Her death had bought us some time, but we weren't any closer to solving the problem than we were yesterday.

"I think that answers your question." Shade pointed out the window where the weirdest looking beastie I had ever seen crouched by a merry-go-round in the park, its gaze locked on a group of people across the street who were oblivious to its presence.

"I could use a good fight right about now." Ember rolled to a stop half a block away. "Get ready to cloak us, Shade."

CHAPTER 8
ASH

I opened the hatch beneath my feet and distributed the weapons: Ember's sword, Miles's and Shade's daggers, and Chrys's garden tools. I hung my spell kit over my shoulder while Shade closed his eyes, gathering his magic to hide us and the monster from the rest of the world's view.

"What the hell is that?" Chrys asked.

"That is a basilisk." Chaos set his jaw. "If a creature of that magnitude can pass through a rift, our situation is more dire than we thought."

"I'm ready." Shade slid out of the van, and the rest of us followed. A fog rolled over us and the beastie, casting everything outside our magic bubble in a grayish tinge.

Inside, we could see in full color, and dear goddess, this creature was weird. It stood as tall as a Clydesdale, with a green, scaley backside like a giant sea serpent. It had chicken legs and feathered wings with claws on the ends like a bat, and the screech coming from its rooster head nearly split my skull in two.

If Godzilla and Foghorn Leghorn had a baby, this would be it.

"What's the plan?" Miles clutched his daggers like he was ready to fight, but the distant look in his eyes gave away his sadness. The poor guy needed a hug and a good cry, but there wasn't time for either.

Ember swung her sword, and fire erupted down the blade. "Ash, you freeze it. I'll chop off its head."

"Will that vanquish it?" I asked.

"Indeed," Chaos said.

The basilisk let out a screechy roar and charged us before I got the chance to open my satchel. Ember swiped at its chicken leg, barely nicking its leathery skin, and it plowed past her, grabbing Shade in its beak and shaking him like a dog with a chew toy.

Chaos chuckled, and I elbowed him before grabbing the binding potion. "That's not nice."

"I wasn't trying to be."

Chrys kneeled, digging her claw rake into the ground. "This earth is too packed."

Shade hung limp in the creature's mouth as Ember and Miles rushed it, screaming like Scandinavian warriors. Their thrusts and stabs did nothing more than annoy the basilisk, and it tossed Shade aside to screech at them.

"I can't cast this spell with you that close to the monster. You'll all be frozen." I paced toward it with Chaos on my heels.

Foghornzilla screeched again and snapped its beak at Miles.

Ember threw a fireball, smacking it in the face, knocking its head aside in time for him to duck and cover.

"Incoming!" Chrys shouted, and the ground rumbled before exploding beneath the creature.

The basilisk careened backward, landing on the merry-go-round with a *thwack* and spinning in circles on its back. Boy, did that ever piss it off. It rolled to its feet and lunged at Ember, but I hit it with the freezing spell before it reached her. The beastie tipped over, thudding to the ground.

"Nighty night chicken snake." My sister lifted her sword above her head, ready to send the basilisk back across the veil where it belonged.

It jerked, and as her weapon came down, its massive serpent tail swung around, knocking into Ember and sending her flying across the park. She grunted as her back smacked earth, and she sat up, clutching her head, before crawling toward Shade, who lay motionless on the ground.

The beast rose, locking its gaze on Miles, who backed away like his life depended on it—which it did—and stumbled into Chrys. They both fell to the ground. The basilisk lowered its head in a predatory stance, tensing its muscles, preparing for attack.

I threw another spell at it, and it froze for a whopping three seconds.

Chaos sighed like he was bored. "Enough." He marched toward the basilisk and hurled a massive fireball at the beast. Hellfire exploded across its chest, lighting its feathers ablaze. The basilisk screeched. It flapped its wings, fanning the flames until they consumed every feathered part of its body. It looked like Kentucky fried Foghornzilla would be on the menu tonight...if witches were into eating creatures from Hell.

The basilisk spun, running first one way and then the other, the flames growing hotter and higher until they reached the trees. Fire spread across a spruce and jumped onto a maple.

Oh no. Not again.

"Cha...Mark!" I shouted and pointed at the inferno. At least it wasn't my fault this time.

He looked up, lifting a hand and calling the fire back into himself like it was the easiest thing in the world to do. For a Prince of Hell, I suppose it was. He extinguished the basilisk, but it still didn't die. Instead, it ran in circles like a chicken with its head cut off, which it was about to be. How fitting.

Ember gripped her sword in both hands and swung so hard she did a full three-sixty, lobbing off the beastie's head. Its charred body collapsed, and its head rolled to Chaos's feet. My demon shook his head at the creature, and with his hand at his side to hide it from the others, he made some sort of symbols with his fingers. In a flash of light and a pop that nearly burst my eardrums, the basilisk disappeared across the veil.

Cheers erupted from the crowd that had gathered around us.

The crowd...

Crappity crap, when the basilisk knocked Shade unconscious, his shadow magic went dark along with him. Thirty-plus people stood on the sidewalk clapping and whistling as if they'd just seen the best show of their lives.

"Well, that's a problem." Ember sheathed her sword.

"Was that a hologram?" a man shouted.

"Where's the projector?" a woman asked.

"Can I join your LARP group?" a teenager called.

They thought it was an act. That we were performing a Live Action Role Play. We could make this work. Just give them what they wanted and then be on our way.

"Go with it." I plastered on the biggest fake smile I could manage and took a bow.

Shade groaned and shuffled toward us, and Chrys looked at Ember, mouthing the words *"what do we do?"* Ember nodded, spread her arms wide, and did a half-bow half-curtsy. The others followed suit, and the crowd erupted in cheers again.

"Now what?" I asked Ember. "We need to find the rift, but we can't do it with all these people watching."

"There is no rift here," Chaos whispered so only my sister and I could hear. "This basilisk was summoned."

"Probably by the Boston Magic Society," I said under my breath.

"Summoned?" Ember frowned. "Boston?"

I nodded. "We need to talk privately."

"I think I've got enough vim to cloak us again." Shade rolled his neck. "But we'll disappear right before their eyes. Any idea on how to get them out of here so we can locate the rift?"

Ember pursed her lips, silently telling me to play along. "We may have to come back and look for it later."

"And leave this park susceptible to monsters that strong?" Chrys planted her hands on her hips. "No way."

"We could act like it's part of the show," Miles said. "Exaggerate it so when we disappear, they think it's special effects."

Chaos was being awfully quiet, so I elbowed him in the stomach and whispered, "Don't."

"Too late." He chuckled, and the crowd went nuts. They pushed and shoved, shouted and screamed. Some ran away while others threw punches.

Chrys gasped. "What in the goddess' name?"

Ember's nostrils flared, her jaw tensing as she flashed me a look that said *get that demon under control, or else.* "Quick, Shade. Do it now while they're distracted."

His gray fog rolled around us, concealing us from view, and my demon reeled in his magic. The crowd stilled, some in mid-punch, and looked at each other like the past thirty seconds were a blur. A few looked toward us, scratched their heads, and walked away, while others hung around, trying to figure out what the hell just happened to them.

A man in an oversized Army jacket touched his nose and looked at his fingers covered in blood. He shouted at a man in a peacoat before clocking him in the jaw. Peacoat fought back, and the rest of the crowd backed away, some filming the scuffle.

I grabbed Chaos's arm, digging my nails into his skin.

"It's not me." He pried my grip and squeezed my hand. "I swear."

Peacoat landed a punch that made Army Jacket double over, clutching his middle. When he straightened, he pulled a pistol from the back of his pants and fired three times, hitting Peacoat in the chest.

"Holy shit." Chrys moved next to me and gaped at the scene.

The crowd scattered, and Army Jacket picked up the shell casings, returned the gun to his waistband, and walked away as if he were on a Sunday stroll.

"Hurry up," Shade said through clenched teeth. "I can't hold it much longer."

My hands...no, my entire body...trembling, I pulled the perimeter location powder from my satchel, recited the incantation, and blew it into the air. Of course it all fell to the ground. Chaos already informed Ember and me that no rift existed here, but the others were expecting one.

"It probably closed when the basilisk passed through." I returned the empty bottle to my bag and adjusted the strap on my shoulder. "I've read that can happen when major magic crosses the threshold."

"I've heard that too." Miles gathered his daggers.

"I've read the same." Chaos grinned at me, and I glared at him. We would have words when we got home.

"I'm losing it," Shade said, his voice strained.

"Let's move." Ember jerked her head toward the van. "I do not want to deal with the police again today."

Shade's magic rolled away as we made it to our escape vehicle. He collapsed on the back seat, so Chaos sat in front and I joined Chrys and Miles in the way back, which was probably best. I was so pissed at Chaos, I wasn't sure I could hold it in if I had to sit next to him.

"What the hell happened to those people?" Chrys stared out the window, watching the scene get farther away.

I felt Ember's gaze flick to me in the rearview mirror before I saw her eyes. She was just as pissed as I was. Maybe more so.

Chaos turned in his seat. "I believe—"

Ember snapped her head toward him, giving him a look that could have melted skin from bone.

"They don't like each other much, do they?" Miles asked.

"Not at all." And at the moment, I didn't like him much either. "My guess is that the basilisk's magic affected them. It brought anger and chaos with it from the Underworld, and it bled into the crowd."

Miles raised a skeptical brow. "Then why didn't it affect us?"

"We're magical beings." I shrugged one shoulder dismissively. "Maybe we're immune to its madness."

Good goddess, the shit kept getting deeper. Forget the thigh-high boots. I needed waders.

I leaned my head against the headrest, closing my eyes and hoping to recharge my vim on the short drive home. I'd cast too many spells, one of them superfluous just so we could keep up this charade. Shade would be out for the rest of the night and half of tomorrow. If I'd worked sigil magic before this fiasco, I would be too.

The sun sank behind the horizon as we made it back to HQ, and Miles and Chrys carried Shade to his car to take him home while Ember, Chaos, and I headed upstairs.

"It's nearly full dark. Now would be the perfect time to retrieve Mayhem's skull." Chaos grabbed his cereal from the pantry and shoved a handful into his mouth.

"Not tonight," Ember said. "Not until we recharge, and definitely not before you tell me what you know about Boston."

"I need sleep. Now." I dragged myself through the kitchen

and into the living room before pointing at Chaos. "I will have words with you once I can form a coherent thought."

"I don't require rest yet. If you'll give me the keys, I can—"

"No, you can't." I shuffled toward the hall and turned around, resting my hand on the wall to keep myself upright. "You won't leave this apartment, understood?"

He grunted. "What will you have me do while the two of you sleep?"

Ember tossed him the remote. "Enjoy some pop culture. Maybe you'll learn a thing or two about empathy."

I walked like a zombie to my bedroom while my sister activated the wards she'd set up in the hall doorway last night. I should've helped her, but I didn't have an ounce of vim left in me, so I crashed onto my mattress and slept like the dead.

CHAPTER 9

CHAOS

"Your cold box is nearly empty. We need fuel." I closed the door and went to the food pantry. It didn't offer much in the way of sustenance either. "We cannot battle another creature on deviled eggs and Lucky Charms alone."

"It's called a refrigerator." Ash sat on a stool at the counter, her tone indicating a foul mood. "And we haven't had time to restock, thanks to you."

Ember paced behind her sister, her posture stiff, her expression sour, but she didn't speak.

I ignored the blame Ash tried to cast at me. She was still tired and extremely hungry, and if I had learned anything from watching their television all night, it was that people lost themselves when faced with both extremes at the same time. Also, those who went to bed angry always woke up that way.

They had both slept half the day, but their fragile mortal

bodies had been taxed beyond anything a mundane could withstand. Their magic was the only thing that kept them going thus far. They could not exist on their power alone.

"We should go to a restaurant." I closed the pantry door. "We will all think more clearly on full stomachs."

"Are you crazy?" Ash slapped her palm on the countertop. "We can't take you anywhere. Someone *died* yesterday."

"You know as well as I do who is responsible for your friend's demise."

Ember stopped and frowned at me before continuing her pacing.

Ash rolled her eyes. "I'm not talking about Ginger. We witnessed a human murder that never would have happened if you hadn't played with their minds."

A growl rumbled in my chest. Bound by my mark or not, I would not allow her to attribute a human's free will to my magic. "I told you I was not using my power at the time. You can't blame me for that."

"The hell I can't."

"Stop it." Ember grabbed a jacket from the wall rack. "While I despise agreeing with a demon, Chaos is right. We need food."

Ash moved her mouth as if she were chewing the inside of her cheek before she sighed. "Fine." She wagged a finger at me. "I'd make you promise not to cause trouble, but I doubt you'd keep your word."

How many times did I have to explain to this witch that as long as she bore my mark, I could not betray her? The panic I caused at the park was to help her, not cause her pain. "I will promise anyway."

"Like that means something." She rose and brushed past me before descending the stairs.

Ember arched a brow. "She's finally come to her senses."

Anger rarely came from sense, but before I could tell her that, she followed her sister outside. We exited the building, and the witches crossed their arms, tucking their hands beneath them as we walked two blocks to an establishment called Gloria's. Chilling air whipped down the street, the buildings on either side of us creating a wind tunnel.

Ash's hair blew into my face, wafting her intoxicating scent to my senses, reminding me why I'd had carnal thoughts about her from the moment I saw her through her own eyes. I was drawn to her on a primal level. Everything about her, including her infernal attitude, called to something deep inside me, making me want to raze this entire town and carry her to the depths of Hell to be by my side forever.

My brothers would call on Lucifer to lock me in the deepest cell of his most abhorrent prison for all of eternity if they discovered the way I felt for this witch.

I fisted my hands. The sooner we could end this and I could get away from her, the better.

We found a secluded table in the back of the restaurant. The server handed us menus, and as she walked away, Ember pointed at me and then Ash. "Not a word until you've eaten at least half of your lunch. Hangry talk is never productive."

"Hangry?" I inquired.

Ash opened her menu, not looking at me. "It's a combination of hungry and angry."

"I see."

"Uh-uh. Zip it." Ember cut her gaze between us.

Hungry and angry. That was exactly how Ash felt. How we all felt. Sometimes Ember made good points. I'd give her that.

The server returned with large glasses of water, and we ordered our meals. Ember asked for a hamburger, while Ash ordered grilled chicken.

"I would like the twenty-ounce prime rib, as rare as you can make it, two baked potatoes, and a dozen fried shrimp." I handed my menu to the server, and she hurried away.

"Good goddess," Ash said, still not looking at me. "We aren't made of money."

"You once promised me a steak and seafood dinner. This is my chance to collect."

She ignored me.

"What did I say about talking?" Ember snapped.

"I can make it so our meal is free." Scrambling the mind of an individual was easier than summoning hellfire. We could walk out the door, and no one would remember we were here.

"Absolutely not!" She finally made eye contact. Even narrowed into angry slits, they were mesmerizing.

I rested my forearms on the table. "Would you like me to change my order?"

"It's fine." Ember placed her hand on top of Ash's. "My last shift was a corporate ax-throwing party. They tipped well."

"People pay money to throw weapons?" I asked.

"Good money," Ember replied. "Neither of you listens very well."

We sat in silence until our food arrived. As she had requested, I ate half of my steak, one potato, and six shrimp before I spoke. "We should move under the cover of darkness tonight to the next point on the map. Now that I have a corporeal form, neutralizing whatever is guarding Mayhem's skull will not be an issue."

"Wait." Ember took a drink of water. "You said Boston summoned the basilisk. Why do you think that?"

Ash set down her fork, the muscles in her jaw tensing. "Can we please talk about what happened out there yesterday? Your playtime cost a man his life."

It seemed the food didn't help calm her down, so I sent a pulse of magic through my mark. Otherwise, we would never get anywhere having three conversations at once. Their sleep requirements had already wasted twelve hours of valuable time.

"Oh, hell no." She lifted her sleeve, showing me the sigil. "This is not for you to use whenever you please. Stop it."

How else would we focus on the issue at hand instead of her emotions? "I was trying to help you calm down so we can discuss our next steps rationally."

"Oh, you've done it now." Ember shook her head. "That was the worst thing you could have said."

I turned my palms up. "It is the truth."

Ash shot to her feet. "I can't do this right now. I'm going home." She stomped out of the restaurant, leaving me alone with her sister. Ember took a large bite of her hamburger, her right cheek protruding as she chewed.

Watching my witch walk away affected me in a surprising way. An ache formed in my being, twisting and stretching down to my stomach while tightening my throat. Had I disappointed her? Enraged her somehow? Never in my life had I cared how another person felt, yet it pained me to see her this way.

I waited for Ember to swallow her food before asking, "What did I do?"

She laughed. "You've caught on to the way things work in modern times pretty fast, but your knowledge of how women work is still in the stone ages."

"Please, enlighten me." I'd do anything to end the agony churning in my being.

"First of all, never tell a woman she needs to calm down. It will have the exact opposite effect of what you're trying to accomplish."

"Noted." I put down my fork, giving her my complete attention.

"Second, never try to manipulate her. Goddess knows why, but Ash has some weirdly fond feelings for you. She trusts you, even though she shouldn't, and I hate to admit that it...you... have been helpful. Try to control her, and all that will go down the drain."

My chest warmed. I knew Ash felt a kinship with me, but hearing her sister admit it caused the tightness in my abdomen to loosen. "My intention wasn't to manipulate her."

She shook her head. "Doesn't matter what you intended.

You did manipulate her. You made her feel something she didn't want to feel. She's entitled to her own emotions, whether you like them or not."

"Point taken. I won't use my power on her unless she needs it."

"No. Point not taken. You're missing it entirely." She filled her mouth with French fries, so I took a large bite of potato and contemplated her words.

Why would I not calm Ash if she needed calming? I would do anything to help her.

Ember took another drink and set down her glass. "You don't get to decide when she needs to calm down. The days of men blaming women's emotions on hysteria are over. Don't use your little manipulative trick on her unless she asks for it, and I doubt she ever will."

While Ash was the more logical of the two, both sisters operated on instinct and gut feelings. Not allowing her emotions to present would hinder her abilities. She needed to feel, whether the sentiments were pleasant or not. "I see."

"Do you?"

"I believe I do." And while Ember was speaking to me civilly, I should continue learning more about the witch to whom I was bound. "Tell me, why does she insist I caused the man's death at the park. I had released the crowd from my hold as soon as Shade created his cloak."

"There had to be remnants of your magic in them. It doesn't instantly go away, does it?"

"Indeed it does. The moment I release my hold, the human returns to normal. They'll be confused and won't remember what happened during the time I held them, but the other effects cease immediately."

She wiped her mouth with a napkin. "Okay, but if you hadn't caused the mass hysteria, the killer wouldn't have gotten a bloody nose and blamed it on the guy next to him."

I paused, the pieces to Ash's thought trail coming together in my mind. "And the men never would have scuffled. Therefore, he would not have pulled his gun."

"Bingo. You started the chain of events." She called to the server and asked for the check.

"True, but had I not held the crowd, Shade wouldn't have been able to cloak us without raising suspicion. I wasn't playing, as Ash accused. I was assisting your coven."

"A coven of light witches. We don't hurt or manipulate humans. Ever."

"Not even to keep your town safe from supernatural invasion?"

"Then who would keep them safe from us?" She paid the bill and rose, indicating I should follow her. "Anything that causes a human pain and suffering is off limits. The sooner you learn that, the sooner we can solve our problems."

I stood and tucked my chair beneath the table. "What about when the humans deserve it?"

She laughed dryly. "Not even then."

Considering the consequences of my actions went against my very nature, yet now that I had thought about it, I could understand Ash's logic. She made me look at the world differently, made me see how my actions affected others. Perhaps being bound to this witch was good for me. "It seems I owe Ash an apology."

She nodded. "A big one."

At the very least, if I could squelch her anger, she'd speak to me again. For reasons I would never understand, her fury, her silence, cut me to the core, and I couldn't deny it anymore. Ash wasn't just good for me...she was meant for me.

We exited the restaurant and returned to the blustery street. Ember flipped up her collar and held it tightly against the wind. "My turn to ask the questions. Why do you think BMS summoned the basilisk?"

I walked beside her, the cold having no effect on me. "A pair of their witches followed us through the grocery store before the events took place."

"How do you know they're from Boston?" Her hair blew across her face, and she tucked it behind her ear.

"Ash recognized their crest. I assume they're here because of their library."

She crossed her arms, tucking her hands beneath them. "Well, shit."

ASH

I'd never been more furious with anyone in my life. How could Chaos be so dense to not even acknowledge his hand in that man's death? And then he had the nerve not only to tell me to calm down but to try and force me to. This sigil had to go. It didn't matter if he was bound to serve me while I had it if he was going to go rogue and kill people anyway.

I slammed my bedroom door and fell face first onto my mattress where I could scream into my pillow without causing the neighbors alarm.

To think I trusted him. To think I was attracted to him. That I was starting to *like* him. I was an idiot. I should have listened to my sister from the get-go. She wasn't blinded by his good looks and charm. She saw the demon for what he was, and from now on, so would I.

At least, I wanted to. But he'd wormed his way into my

psyche, making me feel things I shouldn't for a creature from the Underworld. Things no one should, yet I felt them anyway. Ember may have seen the demon, but I saw the man beneath... and no man was perfect. Of course Chaos would make mistakes. Everyone did.

Ugh! I had to stop making excuses for him.

I lay there stewing for half an hour before a knock sounded on my door, and I groaned. "Go away."

"Hey, Ash." Ember came in anyway. Typical.

I sat up and found her lurking in the threshold with the door half-opened, her hand resting on the knob. "What?" I snapped.

"Chaos has something he'd like to say, and then we all need to talk."

"No, I don't want..."

She pushed the door the rest of the way open, revealing the demon, before she turned and walked away. He stepped into my room and clasped his hands in front of himself.

I gave him the maddest look I could muster. "I don't have anything to say to you."

"You need to listen." He paced across the room and sank onto the bed next to me.

I scooted away. "You don't get to tell me what I need."

"I know. That's why you need..." He took a deep breath and let it out slowly. "I would like to apologize if you'll allow it."

"You..." I clamped my mouth shut. Did he say apologize? The demon who justified his every misdeed wanted to admit fault? Oh, I had to hear this, so I waved my hand for him to continue.

He sat up straight, angling his body to face me and resting his palms on his knees. "You've had a trying few days. Yesterday, your friend died, and you watched two from your coven nearly be beaten by a monster that should have never crossed the veil. Your anger at me is justified."

"Hold on." I lifted a hand to stop him. "Is there an apology in there somewhere? Because it sounds like you're the one forgiving me for having feelings."

His hands fisted, and he growled. "Apologies are new to me. I am trying."

"He really is trying," Ember called from the hallway.

"I see. So my sister put you up to this. You can save it." I clutched a pillow to my chest.

"No." Ember stepped into my room. "We had a long talk, and he came to this conclusion on his own, believe it or not. I need you to hear him out so we can get past this and get down to business."

I narrowed my eyes.

She rolled hers. "If not for yourself, do it for the coven. They need us."

Damn her for throwing logic my way. I slammed the pillow onto the mattress. "Fine. Continue."

"Privacy would be nice," Chaos said.

"I'll be in the living room." She closed the door, and he waited for her footsteps to fade away before he spoke.

"I apologize," was all he said.

I crossed my arms. "For what?" Not that I actually expected him to know what he needed to be sorry for.

He took another deep breath and exhaled slowly. "I apologize for not listening to you. For suggesting you should feel any way other than the way you felt. For manipulating you with my magic. For not trying to understand your thought process, and for not considering the harm I could cause the humans while trying to assist your coven."

I opened my mouth to snap back at him, but I closed it, opened it again, and closed it. That covered everything I was pissed at him about, taking the wind right out of my angry sails. My boiling blood cooled to a simmer, but I tried to hang on to the clarity it had brought me. He might have been damn good at apologies, but he was still a demon.

He relaxed his fists, resting his palms on his knees again. "You are the light to my darkness. You make me consider things I would have never thought twice about, and I believe we are bound for a reason. You summoning me was no mistake, Ash. I am here to right the wrong I caused your family line. You have freed me from my prison, and I am meant to free you from your curse."

Well, crap. Whatever pissiness and clarity I had left flew right out the window. *Was* all this meant to be? Had the universe set this up...our parents summoning the wrong demon, Cinder making a deal with Discord and leading me to find the sigils and free Chaos, who could, in turn, free me?

"If that's true, why this elaborate scheme? Why didn't the universe just have me find your sigil on my own? Why did my parents and Cinder have to be lost? Why...?"

"Because it couldn't have happened any other way."

My mouth had gone as dry as the Mohave, so I swallowed hard. I knew I shouldn't trust him, but somewhere, deep inside my being, his words felt true. His theory felt...right. "Be straight with me. Do you really believe that, or are you saying it so I'll forgive you?"

"The seeds of this began sprouting while I was trapped inside you." He huffed like he wasn't pleased with his answer, but he held my gaze. "I fought it. I wanted it to be a coincidence, but seeing you angry, knowing it was I who wronged you, however unintentionally... I can't deny it anymore. These emotions...the way I feel about you runs deeper than our magical connection. You intrigue me in a way no one ever has."

"You've been imprisoned for centuries, and I'm the first woman you saw. Of course I intrigue you. You want to bang me."

"It's so much more than that." The sincerity in his eyes said he meant every word.

I pressed my lips together. This relationship was giving me a serious case of whiplash. The fact his words could turn my insides to mush when his actions had just ticked me off to no end was a huge red flag, yet there I was getting the warm fuzzies for a demon. Again. "It's kinda funny that the person who freed you is the one who's about to fall victim to your curse."

"It isn't funny at all. You were meant to free me, so you won't fall victim." He took my hand in his. "I truly am sorry. For everything."

"I know." My chest tightened, a new kind of heat spreading through my body. Yes, he was hotter than hellfire, and I had grown fond of him. I could admit that much, but this fate business...the universe wanting us to meet like this... "We can never be together, you know? When this is over, you have to go back to Hell, and I have to stay here."

"I know." His eyes smoldered, the jewel green undulating around his pupils, making my pulse kick into a sprint as his gaze dipped to my lips and returned to my eyes.

Warmth pooled below my navel, and I drifted closer to him. "As long as we're clear on that."

He cupped the back of my neck, tugging me toward him and crushing his mouth to mine. His internal temperature must've run twenty degrees hotter than mine because when he wrapped his arms around me, it was like being engulfed in an electric blanket. This was wrong. I knew it was, but I couldn't help myself. His skin was soft, his muscles firm, and he tasted just as I imagined...warm and spicy, like cloves and cinnamon.

A moan resonated from his throat, and he coaxed my lips apart with his tongue before sweeping it into my mouth to brush against mine. He slid one hand up my back to tangle in my hair while the other pulled me closer to his muscular frame, and I gave in, letting myself get lost in his embrace, reveling in the feel of his mouth exploring mine.

Knock, knock, knock. "Did you fall asleep in there?" Ember shouted.

I gasped and jerked away, touching my fingers to my lips. Good goddess, she would kill me if she knew what we'd just done. "Coming!" I shouted at the door.

Chaos chuckled. "You aren't, but I can help you with that."

My cheeks heated, and I smiled against my will. "Bad demon."

"You just wait and see."

Goddess dammit, I giggled. This was bad. Very bad. "Not a word of this fate stuff to my sister, okay?"

He drew an X over his chest.

"And this…" I touched my lips and pointed at his. "Can never happen again."

He arched a brow. "We'll see."

I shook my head and marched out of the room, leaving him grinning on my bed. What the hell had I just done?

Ember sat in a living room chair and motioned to the sofa, my usual spot. "Sit. Tell me about Boston."

Chaos walked in behind me, so I plopped into the chair. No way would I chance him sitting next to me on the couch. Distance. I needed distance and an ice-cold shower. He took the center seat on the sofa, spreading his arms across the back and resting his ankle on his knee like the cocky son of the devil he was.

"Two BMS witches followed us through the supermarket and watched us leave." I crossed my legs, trying to appear as casual as him. "I don't think it's a coincidence that we saw them in Salem right before Ginger was murdered and a basilisk was summoned."

Ember rested her elbows on the arms of the chair. "I thought you said a demon killed Ginger."

"I lied." He lifted his hands in an *oh well* gesture. "Demons don't rely on ritual or spells to wreak their havoc. If she summoned one of my kind, it likely would kill her, but not in that manner. Witchcraft killed your friend, not a demon."

"I don't know who else it could be but Boston." I clasped

my hands in my lap. "Chaos thinks they're here because of what we did to their library, but—"

"You brought home a page from one of their books," he said. "They could have easily tracked it."

"Their library was torn apart. There were hundreds of volumes all over the place, so I highly doubt they would have looked in that particular book and noticed a missing page." Maybe if I kept denying the possibility out loud, it would cease to exist. Otherwise, the guilt would crush me.

Ember drew her shoulders upward. "I wouldn't put it past them. No telling what kinds of spells they cast to figure out who did it."

My heart sank, taking my stomach down with it. "Come on. What are the odds they know?"

She tapped a finger to her lips. "Did you take anything else? We left the makeshift amulets behind, but could there be anything else linking us to their HQ?"

"The cards," Chaos said. "You put the cards from the drawer in your bag."

"Crap. You're right." I grabbed my satchel, opened it, and sure enough...all three cards from the catalog sat in the side pocket where I'd shoved them. "I don't think I closed the drawer either. They know which ones are missing."

"And they know who took them." Ember rubbed her temples. "Who else would be interested in Isabel's journals except the coven she cursed?"

I swallowed the sour taste from my mouth. "So they either killed Ginger in retaliation or to get information. Her death is our fault."

Chaos leaned forward. "They acted of their own free will. You are in no way to blame."

I held up a finger. "I know you're trying to help, but remember what I said about the guy who got shot yesterday?"

His lips formed a thin line. "I do. Actions can have unintended consequences."

"Poor Ginger." I pressed a hand to my chest, hoping to ease the ache. It didn't work.

"Let's not jump to conclusions." Ember chewed her lower lip, gathering her thoughts. "We found black magic in her house, remember? Miles said she'd been practicing, so maybe she had already been in contact with BMS. Maybe her death is unrelated to us."

"So...what? You think she was working with them? Trying to join them?" I liked this theory much better, but why on earth would she want to join a dark coven? She was happy here. Her boyfriend was here. Ginger was quiet and sweet and friendly... not dark witch material at all, even if she was dabbling.

"How long had she been a member of your coven?" Chaos asked.

"About a year longer than Miles, right?" I looked at Ember for confirmation.

"Yeah, so three years?" She stood and paced the length of the living room.

"Sounds right." I shifted forward in my seat. "She came from Michigan."

Chaos leaned back and clasped his hands on his knee. "Did she?"

"She had a Michigan ID. Wait." I straightened my spine, my

thought train joining his on the same track. "Are you saying she was a plant? A spy for the Boston Magic Society?"

Ember shook her head. "We would have known. There's no way a dark witch had lived in Salem…been a part of our coven… for three years without anyone knowing."

"Someone could have shrouded her aura like you shrouded mine," he said.

She squeezed her eyes shut and pinched the bridge of her nose. "Miles knew."

I drummed my fingers on the arm of the chair. Surely he wouldn't have kept *that* a secret. "He knew she'd been practicing. That doesn't mean he knew she was a spy."

"If she even was." Chaos returned his arms to their outstretched position on the back of the couch. "It's only one possibility."

"The other being they killed her because of us." And there went my heart again, back into my stomach.

"Let's focus on the spy scenario. Why would they send one?" Ember jabbed her fingers into her hair, fisting and pulling before letting go and dropping her arms. "And why kill her?"

Chaos leaned forward. "The question shouldn't be *why*, but rather *what* you're going to do about the events that occurred."

"I don't know." I covered my face with my hands.

Ember sank onto the arm of my chair. "Goddess, I wish Cinder were here. She'd know what to do."

"But she isn't here. You two are, and you're more capable than you give yourselves credit for. Both of you." Chaos gave me a pointed look, reminding me all this was happening according to the universe's plan. That was his theory, anyway.

"Maybe they were checking in on me, on the curse." I wrung my hands. "Someone could have stumbled across Isabel's journals and sent Ginger to see what was up. Ginger reported back that I was showing no signs of murdering everyone, but she was too ingrained in our coven for them to extract her. So they offed her instead."

"That sounds feasible." Ember stood and resumed pacing.

"But why the extravagant torture method? Why not kill her quickly?" I crossed and uncrossed my legs. My mind was going a mile a minute, making it impossible to keep my body still.

Chaos moved down the couch, closer to my chair. "You have two scenarios to choose from, and both involve BMS as the killer. Either they did it because of what happened to their library...which you cannot let your coven know...or they killed her because of her involvement in the dark arts. Labeling her as a spy is the least damning for us, regardless of the real reason."

Ember nodded. "He's got a point."

"What about the basilisk?" I asked. "Did Ginger summon it, or did BMS?"

"Boston did it as a distraction." She fisted and splayed her hands. "That'll be our story, anyway. They summoned it to keep us busy while they made their escape."

"So we're blaming everything that's happened on the dead woman, claiming she was a spy to keep the suspicion off us." My throat thickened, a lump forming in my stomach and stretching up to my chest.

"She's the only one of you with nothing to lose." Chaos

reached toward me as if to comfort me, but he dropped his hand on his knee.

Ember stopped pacing and put her hands on her hips. "We need to break the news to the others. If they do their research, they'll figure out a demon didn't kill her, no matter how big of one she summoned, so we've got to let them know we figured it out first. She summoned a demon, but it's not what killed her."

"She *didn't* summon one." I slid down in my seat.

"We already told them she did. That part of the story can't change." My sister crossed her arms. "Do you have a better idea?"

Aside from crawling into a dark hole and hiding until the world imploded? "No." I scooted upright. "It's going to crush Miles."

"He should have reported her dark magic practice to us as soon as he found out. This wouldn't have happened if he had."

I was certain Miles would come to the same conclusion and be even more devastated. He didn't need Ember's crassness to twist the knife harder. "Maybe I should talk to him, and you can tell Shade and Chrys."

She typed on her phone. A moment later, it pinged. "Chrys is at Shade's. Meet you back here in thirty?"

"Better make it an hour," I said. "He might need a shoulder to cry on."

ASH

Miles lived four blocks away, so Chaos and I went on foot. Thick clouds blanketed the afternoon sky, looking way too much like snow clouds for my liking. Frigid air stung my cheeks, my fall jacket not keeping me nearly warm enough.

"It's not supposed to be this cold in October." I tucked my hands beneath my armpits.

Chaos wrapped his arm around me, tugging me to his side, his demonic heat taming the prewinter chill. Warmth spread through me, both due to his external temperature and another, more inappropriate, reason.

"Uh-uh." I stepped out of his embrace. "That's too close. No hanky panky."

"I was merely trying to keep you warm." He dropped his arm to his side. "If you interpreted my actions another way, perhaps we should finish what we started in your bedroom."

"Fat chance."

"As long as there is one."

"There's not." There couldn't be, no matter how hot and bothered I got from simply being in his presence, and I would keep telling myself that until I believed it.

Miles lived on the second floor of a brown brick building from the early nineteen-hundreds not far from Salem Common. A white pitched portico covered the entrance leading to the foyer, and matching white frames trimmed the six small windows occupying the front façade.

Inside, the unoccupied ground-floor apartment door stood bolted to the right and a staircase stretched up in front of us. We climbed the steps and stopped outside his door. "Let me do the talking. He's going to need gentleness."

"I can be gentle."

I lifted my hand to knock and paused. "Can you?"

Chaos pursed his lips. "I don't know. I've never tried."

"Then keep your mouth shut." I knocked three times. He didn't answer, so I tried again. "Miles? It's Ash. Can I come in?"

Something thudded on the floor and scraped across wood. "Coming," he called, and footsteps sounded before the door swung open. "What's up. Another monster to fight?" He faked a smile.

"No, nothing like that." My brow creased in sympathy. At least, I hoped he viewed it as sympathy. He could have interpreted it as pity, so I tried for a neutral expression. "Can we come in?"

He looked Chaos up and down before nodding. "Sure. Can I

get you a drink? I think I've got some whiskey in here somewhere."

"No, thanks." I walked into the living room and sank onto the couch. I know, I know. I'd been avoiding being near Chaos, but Miles only had one other chair available, and his laptop sat in the seat.

"I'll take a whiskey." Chaos sat next to me. Our thighs touched, so I scooted away. That earned me a smirk.

Miles disappeared into the kitchen, and I took in his space. Brown furniture stood on hardwood floors that looked original to the building. Two black and white photos of a spooky forest hung above the couch. Otherwise, the walls were beige and bare.

A tan rug covered the floor. The corner closest to me had rolled under, causing a major tripping hazard, so I slipped my foot beneath it, untucking it before smoothing it down. An armoire stood against the far wall, one door slightly ajar, and I fought the urge to get up and close it. Instead, I straightened the coffee table.

Chaos chuckled, and I narrowed my eyes. "It didn't line up with the couch. It annoyed me."

"Sorry. I wasn't expecting guests." Whoops. I didn't hear Miles come in. He handed a glass to Chaos, set his on an end table, and moved the laptop to the floor before taking a seat. "How can I help?"

"We have news about Ginger's death." Chaos sipped his drink, and I gave him a warning look, which he completely ignored. "We believe the Boston coven is responsible."

Miles's eyes widened then narrowed. "What makes you think that?"

"Ahem," I said sharply before Chaos could continue. "When we were at the store, getting food for the meeting, two witches from the Boston Magic Society were following us. Their presence in Salem at the exact time of Ginger's murder makes us believe they're responsible."

He swallowed hard, his head bobbing slightly as he processed my words. "Why? What would they...?"

"You know about the curse on my bloodline, right?" Or rather, the story we were all told about me breaking the hex. Nobody needed to know the truth. Not yet. Not ever.

He nodded, so I explained our theory about Ginger being sent to check and see if the curse was really broken. "So we figure either she became too ingrained in our coven for them to extract her without us catching on, or she wanted to defect and stay with us full time. Either way, they decided their best option was to kill her. I'm so sorry."

He took a deep breath and scratched the back of his head, his mouth moving like he was trying to form words that wouldn't come. He blinked rapidly, and finally, he spoke, "I should have reported her. I could have saved her."

"Did you know she was a spy?" Chaos asked.

"No." He shook his head adamantly. "I knew she was experimenting with some spells she found online, but that's all. I guess..." He drew in a shaky breath. "I guess she lied to me about where she learned them. I didn't... I didn't know her at all, did I?"

His eyes glistened, tugging at my heartstrings.

"I'm sure you knew a good part of her." I patted his knee.

"We all have secrets we hide from those closest to us," Chaos unhelpfully added. I wanted to elbow him, but I thought better of it.

"What about you?" Miles inclined his head at my demon. "Where are you from? Ash told Ginger you were a family friend, but she told Chrys you were a distant relative. Which is it?"

My gaze locked with Chaos's, and I froze. Had I given them two different stories? Did I mention where he was from? Friggity frack. I was a horrible liar.

"She didn't mean a literal relative." Chaos saved the day. "Our families go back far enough in history that it feels we could be related, doesn't it?"

"Yep. That's exactly what I meant." Thank the goddess demons were good liars.

He continued, not missing a beat. "I reside in Maine, but I'm not part of a coven. I prefer to practice my magic alone...or with my brothers."

"A solitary witch..." Miles eyed him skeptically. "Where are your brothers now?"

"One is missing. The other is in prison."

Miles stilled, closing his eyes for a long blink before sizing up Chaos. Crap. Did he sense something? Honestly, I didn't know much about Miles at all. Maybe sensing demons came second nature to him. Maybe the shrouding spell we'd put on Chaos was wearing off.

He sipped his whiskey. "What's your brother in prison for?"

"We have some more investigating to do," I said before Chaos could spin an even thicker web of lies. "Once we can prove the BMS is responsible, we can report them and get justice."

"Or we can make them pay," Chaos said casually, as if that were a viable option.

"Anyway..." I rose to my feet. "We have to go, but if you need anything at all, let us know."

"I will. Thanks." He stood and followed Chaos and me to the foyer, closing the armoire on his way. Whew. Now I could sleep at night.

"Take care." I stepped onto the porch and waved. Thankfully, Chaos joined me and didn't put any more violent ideas into Miles's mind.

"He still suspects me," Chaos said as soon as we turned the corner.

"Whatever gave you that idea?" We crossed the street and headed home.

"The way he looked at me, questioned me. At one point, he opened his senses to detect my magic."

"It was a rhetorical question." I stopped outside an antique shop and drummed my fingers against my thigh. I hated that I'd fallen so far behind in my duties and that people had died because of it. Ember probably wasn't home yet; I could be in and out in ten minutes. "I need to check for artifacts really quick. Come inside."

A bell chimed, and the musty scent of old things greeted my senses the moment I stepped through the door. Rows and rows of books, knick-knacks, and dishes filled the room, the more valuable items locked in glass cases.

"We don't have time for shopping." Chaos examined a silver hairbrush.

"I'm not shopping; I'm doing my job."

"Ash! I haven't seen you in a while." Betty, the shopkeeper, glided toward us. She'd dyed her silver hair a soft pink, and the wrinkles around her eyes and mouth deepened with her smile.

"I know. Life keeps getting in the way of my shopping."

She grinned at Chaos. "Who's the hunk? Your boyfriend?"

"Goddess, no." I forced a smile. "This is Mark, an old friend of the family. He's visiting from Maine."

"It's very nice to meet you, Mark from Maine. I'm Betty." She held out her hand to shake, but Chaos brought it to his lips, kissing the backs of her fingers.

"The pleasure is mine, Betty." He winked, and she giggled.

"I have some items that you're going to love." She motioned for us to follow her. "I put them all together for you."

We stopped at a bookcase, and she gestured to the second shelf. "What do you think?"

A marble mortar and pestle, a book on modern witchcraft that you could buy in any bookshop, and a pewter candelabra with red wax clinging to the metal occupied the space.

"These are interesting." I picked up the candelabra, though none of the items had any magical qualities. I always bought something from Betty, whether I found enchanted artifacts or not. "I definitely want this one."

"I'll go wrap it up for you." She took the item and scurried to the cash register.

"Do you have to go up and down every row?" Chaos asked.

"I normally do, yeah." I strolled down the closest aisle.

He followed. "We don't have time for that. There are far more pressing matters, like finding Mayhem's skull and ending your curse. Or have you forgotten the true cause of your coven's turmoil?"

Nothing magical occupied these shelves, so I started down the next aisle. "It won't take long."

He clutched my hand. "Use your power. Tap into your magic and sense. If something is here, you will be guided to it."

"I...I'm not very good at it." I slipped from his grasp. Imposter syndrome was a real thing.

"Which is why you should practice."

Oof. He had a point. This would be the perfect place to practice. I nodded and closed my eyes, focusing on the fire in my being. Opening my senses, I reached out into the room, my intention set on finding anything magical. My chest tingled. It spread upward to my head, tugging me toward the far aisle.

I opened my eyes. "This way."

Chaos followed as I paced to the location I felt pulled toward. The closer I got, the greater the tingle, until I stopped in front of a cameo brooch. A magical aura shimmered around it, though I couldn't be sure what power it contained until I did some spell-casting at home.

I grabbed it from the shelf and handed it to Chaos.

"I told you that you could do it." He lifted the cameo, examining it. "Anything else?"

Closing my eyes, I sensed again, but nothing called to me. "I think that's it."

"Very good." He carried it to the cash register, and I paid for both items.

"See you soon," Betty called as we exited the shop.

"What did you detect on the brooch?" He took the bag from me, holding it by the little brown handles.

"I don't know. It's enchanted, but I'll have to do some spell work to see what it does."

My phone buzzed in my back pocket, so I tugged it out and found a text from Ember that read *Got another rift. Bring the van and the demon.* It buzzed again, and a pinned map came through.

"Eff me." I picked up the pace. Two more blocks to go.

"I would be happy to." Chaos shifted the bag to his other hand. "But from your tone, I sense you didn't mean that literally."

"You sensed correctly. There's another rift. We have to meet Ember." I unlocked the back door, and Chaos carried the bag inside.

"What are we battling this time?" he asked.

I paced to the library to grab the extra set of keys, and Chaos set the bag on my desk. "She didn't say. Just to bring you and the van." My sigil studio lay ten feet away, and I looked longingly at the door. I missed the days when the threats weren't immediate, and I could work my ink magic instead of battling beasties and sealing rifts.

I grabbed my travel kit, and we headed out back and climbed into the van. With the directions on my phone, I pulled onto the street, and we made our way toward the location

Ember pinned. "I hope they've got their weapons stocked in here. I didn't think to ask."

"If they weren't, she would have said so."

"No, she wouldn't." I pulled to the side of the road and put it in park. "She'd expect me to check, because that's what I do. I make sure the big kids have everything they need to fight the monsters." I crawled into the back seat and opened the hatch. Whew. It was stocked.

"Your power is far too great to be an errand girl."

I shrugged. "I don't mind."

"You deserve respect."

"The only person who disrespects me is Shade, and we've discussed why he does. It's fine. I promise." I returned to the driver's seat and pulled onto the road.

He pursed his lips, his face saying he didn't believe a word of it.

I tapped my thumbs on the steering wheel. "Question... When we summon Mayhem, isn't that going to make the veil even weaker? So we'll be dealing with more rifts?"

He didn't speak for five full seconds, which meant I was right. "Finding my brothers is the only way to break your curse."

I hung a right and stopped at a light. "Okay, but then what? You get your family reunion, convince your brothers to break the curse, and get your revenge on Isabel's descendants. The veil is still weak. The rifts are still happening. How can we fix the problem we started? Can we even fix it?"

He was silent for ten seconds, fifteen, twenty.

The light turned green, and I pressed the gas. "How bad is it? You always get quiet when I'm not going to like the answer."

"I'm thinking." He tapped his index finger on his thigh. "I believe it can be done."

"Care to enlighten me?" I turned left around a curve.

"Cinder is as powerful as you and Ember?"

"Put together, yes."

He nodded. "Combining your power, you should be able to revert the veil back to its original state on your side. It would require a time spell, but I believe it can be done."

"Whoa." I nearly missed a stop sign and slammed on the brakes. "Time spells are dark magic. Fully dark. They're not even a little gray. We can't do that."

"Not even to save your city? Possibly the world?"

I chewed the inside of my cheek and continued on my way. When he put it that way... "I mean, I guess if it came down to it, we could probably get away with one dark spell."

"My brothers and I will return to the other side and perform our own magic to restore the divide. The six of us together can end this."

"If you can convince your brothers to cooperate. They didn't spend a week trapped inside a witch's head, so they might not be as sympathetic."

"I'm aware of that hurdle."

"I guess we'll jump it when we get to it."

"Precisely."

"You have arrived at your destination," my map announced, so I rolled to a stop in front of a hardware store. One panel of glass in the front window was shattered, and the automatic sliding door went back and forth, back and forth, never opening or closing fully. The inside appeared completely normal. No commotion at all.

Chief Higgins marched to the van as soon as I put it in park. "It's about damn time."

"What's happening?" I slid out of my seat and opened the side door.

"Monkeys. That's the story."

"Monkeys?" I opened the back hatch and slung my spell bag over my shoulder before gathering as many daggers and gardening tools as I could.

Chaos picked up Ember's sword and tested its weight. "Very nice."

"You better take care of this fast." Higgins crossed his arms. "When the media catches wind, they'll swarm the place."

"That's what we do." I brushed past him, and Chaos and I walked into the store.

Gray fog rolled toward us, Shade engulfing us in his magic and bringing us into reality. Shelves had toppled. Nails lay strewn across the floor. A massive cut marred Shade's brow, and Ember's hair had been lobbed off on one side.

"What's happening?" I handed the weapons to Shade and Chrys.

Ember took her sword from Chaos. "A bunch of little shits. Twelve of them acting like gremlins. They killed the shopkeeper." She pointed at the dead man lying on the floor in a pool of blood. The hook end of a bungee cord pierced his cheek like a fish that had been caught, and chunks of flesh were missing from his arms and legs. His torn shirt revealed a gash in his stomach, and his intestines...

My stomach lurched.

An ear-piercing screech sounded from the left, and a beastie scrambled up the aisle before leaping onto a gas grill. I slammed the lid shut and groaned. "Not this guy again."

CHAPTER 12
ASH

"What are these things?" Chrys tucked her spade into her belt and took one of Shade's daggers.

"Imps." I put all my weight on the grill's lid, holding it tightly against the little guy's thrashing. "One got through a small rift in the library a while back."

"And now we've got a dozen." Ember ducked, dodging a flying hammer. It slammed into the wall behind her, embedding into the sheetrock.

Another screech, which sounded eerily like a *wahoo*, echoed through the store. Two imps rounded the corner, carrying a nail gun. One bore the weight of the tool while the other operated the trigger, sending nails shooting out like bullets. One hit the front of the grill, half an inch from my right hand. Another whizzed by my head.

"Shit!" I opened the lid, using it as a shield, and the little bugger inside jumped, yelped, and fell to the ground, a nail piercing its heart. It turned into a puff of smoke, and the rift sucked it through. "That's one way to do it."

The other two rushed toward us, but Ember swung her sword, taking off both their heads in one swipe. "That's for ruining my hair."

Their heads rolled, maniacal laughs emanating from their mouths, and their bodies kept going, firing nails all over the place.

Screech! Somehow, one of the heads found the momentum to roll toward Shade and launch itself up. It latched its pointy teeth onto his calf and growled like a rabid chihuahua.

"Son of a bitch!" He jabbed a dagger into its ear, but it kept growling and chewing as if Shade were a dog toy and it was determined to tear the squeaker out. "Why won't you die?"

"You have to pierce their hearts." Another array of nails flew toward us. One got me in the shin, and sharp pain exploded down my leg. "Mother may I!"

"You could have told us that from the beginning." Shade marched toward the headless gunmen, mini Cujo gnawing on him the whole way. He bent down and grabbed the gun, lifting it and the imps toward Chrys. *Bap, bap, bap.* Nails fired over her head.

"Bad dogs." She jabbed a dagger into one of the bastards, her gardening claw into the other. Their bodies plopped to the floor, and the head detached from Shade's leg before going up in a puff of smoke.

"Three down," he said.

"Nine to go." Ember gripped her sword in both hands, her muscles tensing as she prepared to go after the rest.

I yanked the nail from my leg, and blood squirted out in spurts. "Fabulous. It hit an artery." My head spun, and I leaned a hand on the grill to steady myself. I wasn't a faint-at-the-sight-of-blood gal, but seeing my shin turn into a fountain made my vision tunnel.

Chaos kneeled, gently taking my leg in his hands. He covered the wound with two fingers, applying pressure while I rummaged through my kit for an enchanted bandage. He pulled his hand away, looking at my blood on his skin.

"Don't even think about tasting it." I handed him a roll of gauze I'd infused with a spell to slow bleeding.

"Again, you're confusing me with a vampire." He wiped his hand on his jeans and wrapped my leg in the bandage. "They will obey me. I can order them back through the veil," he whispered.

"And then everyone will know what you are. We can't chance that." I grabbed three bottles of freezing spells, handing him one. "You'll have to fight like a witch."

"Understood." He gave the bottle back to me. "But I can't cast spells."

A racket of metal clanking sounded from above, and an imp swung from a light fixture, chittering at Ember and waving a toilet plunger like a sword.

"Are you making fun of me, you little shit?" She tested the sturdiness of a shelving unit and climbed up, jabbing her weapon at the imp. It screeched and jumped to the next fixture. Then it blew a raspberry at her.

No wonder Higgins called them monkeys.

"I've got three freezing spells ready to go." I left the safety of my grill shield and joined my friends. "We need to round them up so I can cast it on them all at once."

"I can help with that." Chaos disappeared down an aisle.

"Try not to burn the place down," Shade said before following my demon.

"Try not to burn the place down," I mocked and flicked Ember's hair. "What happened to you?"

"Garden shears. I think they were trying for my neck."

"We've got four cornered," Shade shouted, and we followed his voice to find him at one end of an aisle, Chaos at the other.

The slimy little gremlins faced their master, rocking back and forth and baring their teeth. I hit them with a binding spell so Chaos could release whatever hold he had on them before Shade got suspicious.

Screech! An imp dropped from the ceiling onto Chrys's head. It chomped on her scalp, snapping a tooth on her skull. Chaos plucked the creature off Chrys and held it toward her so she could jab a dagger into its heart. *Poof.* Another one turned to smoke.

"What are you? A demon tamer?" Shade knocked one of the frozen imps over and shoved a nail through its chest.

"Something like that." Chaos picked up another loose nail and vanquished a second one. Ember took out the other two.

Above us, thumping and scurrying sounded from the ceiling tiles. The last four had taken to the crawlspace.

I followed the sound toward the front of the store. "We can't let them escape."

Shade scoffed. "Obviously, genius."

"Watch your tone." Chaos puffed out his chest and loomed over Shade. "Ash is a powerful witch who deserves respect."

He clicked his tongue. "Says the guy who just happened to show up when everything went to shit. What are you hiding?"

Chaos's hand clenched into a fist, and he took another step toward Shade.

"Boys!" I shouted. "Same team, remember? We don't have time for you to compare dicks." Though I had no doubt Chaos would win the contest.

His fist relaxed, and as he brushed past Shade, he said, "Disrespect her again, and you will regret the day you met me."

"I can hear them up here." I pointed to the ceiling. "Can you give me a boost? I'll freeze them and toss them down to you."

Chaos laced his fingers together, and I stepped into his hands. He lifted me with ease. Too much ease, in fact, but I couldn't worry about that now. If Shade noticed, it would be one more weapon in his arsenal of mistrust. We'd burn that bridge when we got to it.

My spell at the ready, I pushed aside a ceiling tile and peered into the crawlspace. Two imps sat on their haunches, gnawing on electrical cables. One bit through the casing, and an electric jolt zapped them both. They laughed and did it again.

Goddess, help me. I was trapped in the movie *Gremlins*.

I said the incantation and threw the powder at them, and they dropped the cord. "A little higher?" I asked Chaos, and he lifted me far enough that I could crawl inside. Balancing on a beam, I inched toward the frozen imps and grabbed one by the slimy arm. I tossed it down and reached for the other one.

Thud, thud, thud. Screeeech! Imp number three barreled toward me, latching onto my shoulder. Its razor teeth pierced skin and hit bone. "Argh!" I took it in both hands and yanked, prying its teeth out of my flesh and losing a big chunk of skin in the process.

"Got a live one." I hurled it through the open ceiling tile. They could deal with that bugger. I shoved the last frozen imp through the hole next. That left one, the feistiest of the bunch.

It jumped from rafter to rafter, chittering and squealing, running around like it had chugged six energy drinks and a pot of coffee. I uncorked the last freezing spell and threw the powder at the imp. It dodged the granules, heading higher into the ceiling.

"Crap. Come here, you slimy bastard." I rose to my knees, then my feet, balancing on the beam. The imp hung from a rafter, just out of reach. On my tippy toes, I swiped my arm, knocking my hand against its butt and covering my fingers in slime.

At least, I hoped it was just slime. Gross.

"Here, impy, impy. It's time for you to go home." I reached again but missed.

The beastie peeled its lips back over its pointy teeth and hissed. Then it let go and landed on my face. I lost my balance and careened backward, falling through the ceiling. I tensed, bracing myself to smack the hard floor, but a pair of strong arms broke my fall.

Someone ripped the imp from my face, and I looked up, into Chaos's jewel-green eyes. I would go with the impact of his hard body taking my breath away, and not the cheesy emotional reason of being saved by the bad boy.

Ember stabbed the last imp, neutralizing the threat, but Chaos didn't move to put me down. He stared at me like he either wanted to kiss me or eat me, and neither option was appropriate at that moment.

"Thanks." I wiggled, trying to break free, but he didn't release his hold. "You can put me down now."

He inhaled sharply and blinked before letting me go.

"Holy Hecate." Ember slumped against a shelf. "It was easier to slay the basilisk."

"There was only one of him." Chrys sat in a patio chair. "And he didn't have weapons."

Shade eyed Chaos. "How did you control them? What are you?"

"Look at him," Ember said. "A dozen imps could feed on him for days. They were planning their attack."

My shoulder stung, and my leg throbbed. "I hope they're not venomous."

"They aren't." Chaos examined my wound. "Just annoying."

Ember cleared her throat at me, probably trying to tell me the demon was too close, but I was too tired to care. "Let's seal the rift and get out of here," she said. "Chrys, text Patrice and let her know we'll need healing."

"On it." She typed on her phone.

I had to cast a perimeter location spell and seal the rift. My body and vim told me to ask for help, but I'd be damned if I let

Shade one up me. Instead, I uncorked the bottle and blew the powder into the air before reciting the spell. The granules clung to the tear, and thankfully, there was only one.

"Who has the energy to seal it?" Ember asked.

"I do," I answered quickly before anyone else had a chance.

"I can assist." Chaos held out his hand.

"That's okay." Ember straightened. "I'll help you."

I looked into Chaos's eyes, and the sigil heated on my arm. Tapping into his magic would be an adrenaline rush, and it would be for a good cause. There was no harm in that, right? Besides, if Shade thought Chaos was casting a spell, maybe he'd lay off the *what are you?* routine.

I placed my hand in his. "We've got it."

The moment we connected, his power surged through me, reviving my vim. Heat rolled through my veins, his low vibration penetrating to my bones and making me shiver in a good way. He remained silent, closing his eyes as I cast the spell and sealed the rift. I stood there, basking in the vivacity of demon magic until my sister cleared her throat again.

"You can let go now. It's sealed." She crossed her arms, shifting her weight.

I hated to, but I pulled from his grip. Fatigue slammed into me the moment our connection severed, and I swayed on my feet.

"Go get the van and pull it around back." Ember gripped my shoulder, steadying me. "Higgins told the owner who survived they were monkeys, so we need to make it look like we took them with us."

I nodded and shuffled toward the exit.

"Mark, you stay here," Ember said.

"That's not happening." Chaos wrapped his arm around me and helped me out the door, and this time, I let him.

CHAPTER 13
CHAOS

Their insolent police chief, Higgins, stopped us the moment we exited the building. Ash lifted her head and showed him a weak thumbs up. "We'll get the van and take it around back to remove the monkeys."

"Took you long enough," he said with a toothpick in the corner of his mouth. His words dripped with enough disdain to take down the Minotaur.

I couldn't stop the growl from rumbling in my chest. "If you prefer to handle the supernatural yourself next time, that can be arranged. I'll give you an adversary to battle right now, and we'll see how you fair."

Ash patted my chest, ending my tirade. "Let's get the van."

Never in my existence had I encountered such a useless piece of flesh. His disrespect of the very people who kept his town safe made my blood boil, and if a crowd, including several people with recording devices, hadn't gathered outside the scene, I would have taught him never to disrespect a Holland witch again.

Ash stumbled, so I tightened my hold of her. I wanted to scoop her into my arms and carry her, taking away the burden of walking, but I didn't dare. She was finally coming into her power, her self-deprecation becoming less frequent. If she could walk after that ordeal, I would let her.

We approached the van, and she reached for the driver's side door. That, I would not allow. "You need rest. I will drive."

I attempted to steer her toward the other side, but she protested. "Ember will kill me if I let you drive."

"I have done it before."

"I know, but that was out of necessity." She stepped out of my grasp and fished the keys from her pocket. She swayed, clutching her head. "Whoa. Okay, maybe this time is a necessity too."

I helped her around to the passenger seat and buckled her in before getting behind the wheel and starting the engine.

"How do you learn so fast? You haven't existed in this time more than a few weeks, yet you understand all our technology."

I chuckled. "I am a Prince of Hell."

"Commander of armies, destroyer of all who vex you, yada, yada, yada." She rested her head against the window and offered a teasing smile. "It doesn't mean you have to be so smart."

"Powerful, smart, good-looking..." I returned her grin and drove toward the back of the store. "Hard to resist, I'm sure."

"You have no idea." She laughed and winced, gingerly touching her injured shoulder.

My face fell, my mood darkening. "I could have ended that battle with a snap of my fingers. You didn't need to get hurt."

She closed her eyes. "We've been over this."

"Indeed. It doesn't mean I have to like it." I stopped the vehicle in the lot behind the store, and the other witches climbed in.

Ember's jaw tightened when she saw me behind the wheel, but she remained silent as she returned her weapons to the hatch and buckled her seatbelt. "Here." She shoved her phone toward me with the directions open on the screen.

Ash snored softly, an endearing sound, on the way to their healer's home. Her lips parted slightly, and as I stopped the van, she snorted, waking herself. I held in my laugh. I had never experienced this much silence from these witches, which meant they were all in need of rest and healing. It also meant finding my brother's skull would be delayed even longer.

The urge to leave them all here and retrieve it myself had me gripping the steering wheel in a vise. But as Ash lifted her head and smiled at me sleepily, I knew I could not leave her side.

A fist of pain curled in my chest. I would have to leave her eventually. Returning to Hell was the only way to restore the veil to its natural state.

I couldn't think about that, or I might raze the city and take her to the Underworld with me. As my attachment to her grew, the option sounded more and more appealing.

"We have arrived," I said to the sleeping witches in the back.

Shade groaned, and Ember let out a growl to rival a demon.

Chrys opened the side door, and they filed out, not bothering to close it behind them on their way inside.

Ash opened her door and paused, turning to me. "Thank you for helping us today."

"I would burn down the world to protect you."

She swallowed, her gaze flowing over my face. "Let's hope it doesn't come to that."

"Indeed." Though I wouldn't hesitate if it did.

She slid out of her seat. "Are you coming in?"

"I will wait with the van. I'm afraid your healer may discover more than she needs to know about me if I come inside."

"Good idea." She closed the door and shuffled to the house.

Half an earthly hour later, they returned. Ash's complexion once again had a pink hue, and the others walked upright, rather than stumbling. Their healer was undeniably talented.

"Feeling better?" I asked Ash as she buckled her seat belt.

"Still exhausted, but Patrice put a healing salve on our wounds, and it's already working." She indicated her freshly bandaged leg.

"You need rest."

"We all do." Ember offered her phone again. "Take Shade and Chrys home first. Just follow the map."

"Aye, aye, Captain," I said, and Ash laughed.

I glanced in the rearview mirror, and Shade ground his teeth, his pinched expression sour, as it tended to be. He inhaled deeply and let out his breath in a huff. "Why are you the only one who didn't get hurt?"

"Cool it, Shade," Ember said over her shoulder.

"No, someone's got to say it, and since you all are blind to this guy, I will. I don't trust him. He hardly lifts a finger to help in a fight, but when he does… There's something going on, and I don't like it."

"There's nothing going on with him." Ash turned in her seat to glare at her adversary. "You're just jealous he's stealing some of your thunder, that you're not the big strong man on the team anymore."

"Enough!" Ember straightened, showing each of them a palm. "I am too tired to deal with this shit. I want everyone to go home and get some sleep. That's an order."

"Sounds good to me," Chrys said.

We rode in silence as I followed Ember's map first to Shade's home and then Chrys's. When we returned to the coven headquarters, Ash turned in her seat and opened her mouth to speak.

Ember held up a hand, stopping her. "Shade is suspicious, and that's a problem. We'll deal with it tomorrow."

Ash nodded. "Miles is too. Chrys hasn't mentioned anything, but…"

"Tomorrow." Ember exited the van and slammed the door. She was already in her room by the time Ash and I made it upstairs.

"Her injuries must have been extensive." I took a cup from the cupboard and filled it with water before offering it to Ash.

She drank the entire contents. "Thanks. Yeah, I think it's stress too. She's responsible for the coven right now, and everything is going to shit. She feels alone."

"She has you." I opened the pantry and gestured inside, but she shook her head.

"Ember always feels alone. I need my bed before I pass out in the kitchen." She turned and walked down the hall.

I followed closely in case she stumbled. She made it to the bed and fell face-first onto her mattress. I waited for her to sit up and remove her boots, but she didn't move. Kneeling at the end of the bed, where her feet hung over the edge, I untied her laces and slid her shoes off, revealing pink stockings with purple kittens and yellow hearts. I couldn't help but laugh.

"What?" The mattress muffled her words. "Do my feet stink?"

"Your stockings surprised me."

"We call them socks." She drew her knees toward her chest as she rolled to her side and moved higher on the bed. "Good night."

"My body also requires rest. Where would you like me?"

She sighed heavily and lifted her head, her gaze flowing down my form. "I'd say the couch, but you wouldn't fit." She closed her mouth, her jaw moving as if she were chewing the inside of her cheek. "You can sleep next to me *if* you promise to keep your hands to yourself."

My mouth watered at the thought of all I could do if she hadn't added the stipulation. "Your sister will have a conniption."

"She'd have a fit if I put you in Cinder's or our parent's bed too. At least here I can make sure you don't sneak out and wreak havoc on Salem."

"Havoc is my cousin." I toed off my shoes and lay next to her before she could change her mind.

"Is he a prince too?" She returned her head to the pillow.

"A duke."

A beautiful smile played on her lips. "When I said, 'hands to yourself,' I meant all parts of your body. Tentacles and tail included if you have them."

I chuckled. "I have neither."

She held me with her gaze, her bright blue eyes filled with secrets I would love to unravel. "Goodnight, Chaos."

Perhaps, in time, I would get the chance. "Goodnight, Ash."

CHAPTER 14
ASH

I slept like the dead, waking on my side, in the same position as when I'd closed my eyes last night. Chaos lay beside me, utterly still, aside from the even rise and fall of his chest. I ran my hand down my side, checking my clothes. Everything was in place. Unless he'd used his magic to keep me asleep, undressed and redressed me, he'd kept his hands to himself.

I kind of wished he hadn't.

No. No, I didn't. I was beat, and he was respectful, and that was the way it should be. Still, the thought of a Prince of Hell ravishing me, having his way with me, made my lady parts tingle and my mouth water.

Only *this* Prince of Hell, though. Geez Louise, I had the hots for the very thing I was supposed to keep Salem safe from. For the thing that cursed me. *Get yourself together, Ash.*

But Chaos wasn't a thing. He wasn't some mindless demon, hell-bent on destroying our world and everyone in it. He was a person. He had feelings, opinions, a sense of humor that matched my own.

Not to mention his smoking hot body.

He'd be returning to Hell when all this was through. How bad would it be if I enjoyed him while he was here?

He lay on his side, facing me, and I hovered my hand above his shoulder, moving down to his hip. Not touching…just feeling his warmth. The tiny hairs on his skin stood on end as I passed my hand over his arm, his body reacting to mine, even in his sleep.

His face was a work of art. He had a chiseled jaw, strong cheekbones, and deep-set eyes. My fingers hovered above his cheek, and I couldn't help myself. I brushed the tips to his soft skin, tracing them down his jaw, toward his lips.

I could still feel his mouth pressed to mine, taste the warm spice of his tongue. I moved my fingers up his face to brush a lock of dark brown hair off his forehead.

"You're allowed to touch me, but I can't touch you? That hardly seems fair."

"Oh crap." I jerked my hand away, and he opened his eyes. "I'm so sorry."

A flirtatious smile played on his lips. "I don't mind."

"No, no. Consent works both ways. I shouldn't have done that." I sat up and smoothed my shirt down my stomach.

He propped his head on his hand. "You have my consent to touch me whenever…and wherever…you please."

Heat spread across my cheeks, no doubt turning me beet red. "I should take a shower."

"Would you like company?"

Yes. "Not a chance."

He returned his head to the pillow. "I'll be here if you change your mind."

"Don't hold your breath." I got up, grabbed some clean clothes, and locked myself in the bathroom.

Good goddess, I looked a mess. The pillow not only smushed my hair into a rat's nest on one side, but it created a lovely crisscrossing pattern down my cheek. A bit of dried drool clung to my lip—good thing I didn't try to kiss him—and my makeup looked like a five-year-old had tried to give me smokey eyes.

I brushed my teeth, detangled my hair, and stared at my raccoon mask in the mirror. With a wet washcloth, I wiped away yesterday's makeup, which would have easily come off in the shower. *What are you doing, Ash?*

Tugging up my sleeve, I looked at the sigil on my arm. The mark of Chaos. The thing that made him mine. If I removed it, would I still want him this badly? Would he still want me?

I looked at the lock on the door. If I opened it, invited him in, how far would we go? All the way, if I were being honest. An image flashed in my mind of him turning from his demonic to human form. Good goddess, he was a sight to see.

Could he hold onto his human form if we did the deed, or would he transform right in the middle of it? Would I mind?

I squeezed my eyes shut, shaking my head. I couldn't think like this. Not while our town had gone to shit and my sister and parents were missing. *Focus, woman.* I tossed my dirty clothes into the hamper and hopped into the shower, turning it as cold as I could stand it.

I took my time applying makeup and drying my hair, not ready to face the demon in my bed or my sister's wrath for letting him sleep next to me. When I couldn't put it off any longer, I opened the bathroom door. Chaos sat on the edge of the bed, his hands on his knees, his eyes closed.

"Are you meditating?" I got a pair of orange striped socks from the drawer and sat next to him to put them on.

"In a way." He opened his eyes and inhaled deeply. "I was fighting the urge to send my magic through my mark in hopes that you'd open the door and let me join you."

"I appreciate you putting up a fight." Because if he'd done that, I most definitely would have opened the door. "Your turn."

He rose. "My other set of clothing is in a bag somewhere in your home. I left it by the living room chair."

"I'll get it, and...take your time. I'll have to defuse the Ember bomb before we leave the house."

"I wish you luck with that feat."

"I'll need it." I left Chaos in my room and headed toward the living room. Ember's door stood open, and my stomach clenched. This would not be fun.

She sat at the breakfast table, clutching a mug of coffee and glaring daggers at me. She didn't say a word as I picked up Chaos's bag and returned to my room. When Ember didn't have anything to say, that meant one thing.

She was livid.

I left the bag near the bathroom door, which Chaos had left partially open. "Nice try, but no."

"You can't blame me," he called from beneath the shower.

No, I could not. I swallowed the thickness from my throat and returned to the front of the house. Ember still didn't speak as I poured a cup of coffee and a bowl of cereal. I sat at the table and shoved a spoonful into my mouth. My sister stared at me, one brow lifted, her bitch face on point, though she wasn't resting it. This was her active bitch face. Her *if you weren't my sister, I'd chop off your head* face.

"I didn't sleep with him." I took a sip of coffee, watching her over the rim of the mug.

She licked her lips, narrowing her eyes. "That's funny because I found him in bed with you when I opened your door this morning."

I really needed to start using the lock. "And we were both fully clothed, weren't we?"

"What's going on with you, Ash? I thought you were smart. Smarter than *this*." She gestured to the hallway.

"I let him sleep next to me because there was nowhere else for him to rest. He's too big for the couch."

She leaned back in her chair and crossed her arms. "This isn't one of your 'there's only one bed' romance novel tropes. You could have put him in Cinder's room."

I flattened my hands on the table. "I was exhausted and wasn't thinking straight. It didn't feel right to put him in there when we're trying so hard to bring her back." And maybe I wanted him to sleep next to me. We did share a bond, however manufactured it might be. I didn't dare tell her that, though.

"You're getting too close to him."

"So what? It's not like we can live happily ever after. When this is through, he and his brothers will go back across the veil, and I'll never see him again." I shoved another spoonful into my mouth, my shoulders slumping at the thought.

"What if he decides to stay? What if he falls in love with you?"

I fought my mouth. I really did, but the corners turned upward against my will.

"See?" Ember gestured at my face with her palm up. "You like the idea. That's bad, sis. Really bad."

"Even if he did...and he won't...it wouldn't matter. He and his brothers have to cross the veil to mend it. They'll fix it from their side, and we'll fix it from ours. The six of us together can set it back to its original state."

I leaned forward, resting my chin on my fists. "There will be an end to this. To all of it. I swear."

She nodded, her expression softening, and she matched my posture. "What if you fall in love with him?"

I took a deep breath. "I'm sure I won't. Once I remove this sigil, I bet I won't even find him attractive."

"Yes, you will." She sipped her coffee.

I folded my arms on the table. "How can you be so sure?"

"Because *everyone* finds him attractive."

I laughed. "He is easy on the eyes, isn't he?"

"Thank you. I try." I snapped my gaze up and found my demon standing three feet away.

"How much of that did you hear?" I got up and poured him a cup of coffee.

"Not nearly enough." He glanced at my bowl on the table and retrieved his Lucky Charms from the pantry. "You eat this with milk?"

"Usually, yeah." I took his mug to the table and returned to my seat while he prepared his breakfast. He sat next to me, and Ember's eyes flicked between us.

"Has the bomb been defused, or should I explain?" He took a bite of cereal and nodded his appreciation. "This is good."

"I might have just lengthened the fuse, but we're okay for now." I turned to Ember. "Do we have work to do before nightfall?"

"Shade brought more shadow spells by this morning, so we can head out to the next point as soon as you're done."

I nearly choked on my cereal. "Does he know we used the other ones?"

"No. He said he bottled them for us because the rifts are happening more frequently. He thought we might have to split up to fight the beasties coming through...the three of us as a team, he, Chrys, and Miles as the other."

Lovely. Now he was going to lure Chrys to the asshole side. "Is Miles okay to fight after...?"

She shrugged. "We'll see."

We finished our coffee and breakfast, and Chaos helped me carry the dishes to the sink. I turned on the water and squirted dish soap on a sponge. "Grab that towel. I'll wash, you dry."

His playful smile made my stomach flutter. "No one in my entire existence has attempted telling me what to do."

I laughed. "Welcome to the twenty-first century."

Ember stomped behind us. "Leave it. Let's get this over with."

"It won't take us five minutes. I'm not leaving a mess." I handed a bowl to Chaos, and he dried it before setting it in the cabinet.

Ember huffed, but she knew how I felt about order. Instead of pressing the issue, she grabbed my satchel and rummaged through, adding Shade's shadow spells before lifting my bottle of rosemary oil. "This one needs a refill. I'll do it."

"Thanks." I offered the last mug to Chaos for drying, and his fingers brushed mine as he took it. That tiny bit of contact made my insides buzz, so I stepped away, drying my hands on my pants.

What if I did fall in love with him?

You simply can't let that happen, woman. Get your hormones under control and fight these urges. That was what I would do.

"Ready?" I slung the refilled satchel over my shoulder and grabbed the keys from the peg. "Who's driving?"

Ember took them from my hand. "I am. You're shotgun."

We filed down the stairs, and I stopped at my desk to grab a piece of paper and a marker. "Hold on. I need to make a sign for the shop door."

"The one that says 'Closed' is good enough." Ember crossed her arms and tapped her foot.

"We've been closed for three days. We need to let people know it might be a while before we open again." I wrote *Due to a family emergency, The Holland Witchery will be closed for the foreseeable future. We apologize for the inconvenience* in large block letters, centered on the page. "That should do it."

I paced to the front of the building and taped it to the door before returning to the library. A quick glance at the stacks had my lip curling. One mess at a time. That should be my new motto.

"The brooch." Chaos opened the antique store bag and pulled it out. "Perhaps it could be useful."

Ember took it from his hand. "When did you have time to shop?"

"She used her power to find it in fewer than three minutes." He snatched it back and handed it to me. "I believe shopping is one of her duties in the coven, is it not?"

She screwed her mouth to one side, but she didn't reply.

A quick magic-revealing spell wouldn't hurt. I recited the incantation to reveal a simple beauty enhancement charm. "Unless I want to make myself more attractive, I don't think it'll help."

Ember grabbed it and strode to the back of the library. She returned a moment later, wiping her hand on her pants. "No one needs magic like that right now."

Chaos raked his gaze down my body. "You especially, Ash."

My sister blew out a hard breath, closing her eyes and shaking her head. "Let's go."

We headed out the back door, and as soon as I locked it, Shade and Miles came around the corner, wearing their black spandex beastie-battling attire.

"Did you find another rift?" Miles asked.

"No, did you?" I gestured to his outfit. "You look like you're ready to fight." Or attend goth yoga. It would work for both.

"With the frequency it's happening, I didn't want to ruin

my good clothes." Poor guy. He was trying so hard, but he couldn't hide the sadness in his eyes.

"Smart move." I descended the back steps. Ember stopped halfway to the van.

"Where are you going?" Shade glanced at my travel spell kit before looking at my eyes. "We'll tag along."

"Umm..." I adjusted the strap. "That's okay. We've got it. Hey, thanks for the extra shadow spells. Ember said we're splitting up?"

"Only if we have to." He turned to Ember. "Where are we headed?"

She made a noncommittal gesture with her shoulders. "Nowhere important."

He crossed his arms. "It must be important if the three of you have to go together."

I clenched my jaw. "It's private."

He scoffed. "I thought there were no secrets in this coven. Look what happened when Miles kept one. No offense, man."

"Yeah." His posture deflated. Poor, poor Miles. I would never understand why he subjected himself to Shade.

My brain scrambled, trying to come up with anything to get him off our backs. Of course, I had nothing. My mind inconveniently blanked right when I needed it most.

"If you must know..." Chaos moved beside me. "My mother passed away recently. We're going to spread her ashes at sea."

"Where's the urn?" Shade would not let up. I clenched my teeth.

"We will pick it up from the undertaker on our way." Chaos

inclined his chin. "It's a private affair, which you are not invited to attend."

Shade sniffed. "I'm sorry for your loss."

"I'm sorry too," Miles said. "We'll handle anything that breaks through today. Take your time."

I grabbed Chaos's arm and tugged him to the van while Miles and Shade walked away, once again thanking the goddess demons were good liars.

CHAPTER 15
ASH

The drive to the next point on the pentagram took twenty minutes with traffic. From Boston, it would take nearly an hour, which meant it would have taken Isabel at least half a day to get there by foot. More if she were traveling from one of the other points on the star. I couldn't imagine her state of mind as she hid the skulls of the demons she had tricked.

I also couldn't believe Ember and I were helping them exact revenge on her innocent relatives. "How will you find Isabel's descendants once your brothers are freed? What will you do to them?"

I turned in my seat to see Chaos's expression as he answered. He held my gaze for a moment before looking down. "The three of us together will sense them."

Ember tightened her grip on the steering wheel.

"Remember this is for the greater good. Every war requires sacrifices."

"I know." It didn't mean I had to like it. "Will you kill them all?"

Chaos took a deep breath, flicking his gaze to mine. "It's within our right to take them all."

I swallowed the lump in my throat and nodded before turning back to the front.

"However..." Chaos rested his hand on my shoulder, stopping me. "I feel that one will suffice. My brothers may feel otherwise."

"What if they don't know about the curse? What if they're completely innocent? Light witches like me and Em?"

His eyes darkened, and he moved his hand to his lap. "A debt is a debt. It must be paid."

"Okay." I turned around and stared out the front window. One life in exchange for thousands of others. It made sense, I guessed.

"This is it." Ember put the van in park. "Get out and see what you can feel."

I did as I was told and exited the van to stand on the sidewalk on a historic street in Marblehead. Two- and three-story buildings dating back to the seventeen hundreds lined the road on both sides, and trees with golden leaves that would soon fall to the ground dotted the spaces between buildings.

Straightening my spine, I inhaled deeply and set my intention on finding Mayhem's skull. I held still, searching the vibration in the air. I felt nothing. No tickle, no pull. Nada. I expanded my intention to include a possible trap laid to vex anyone who tried to revive the demons. Still nothing.

I got back in the van. "Let me look at the map. I'm not getting anything here." Isabel's pentagram ended at a point roughly near this area, but with everything that had been built, torn down, and rebuilt since her time, it was impossible to tell how close we were.

"It's farther north," Chaos said.

I returned the maps to my bag. "How do you know?"

"I can sense it. The pull is unmistakable. Mayhem is near to the north."

It wasn't so unmistakable for me. I felt zip. "Guess I've got work to do if I want to develop this newfound power." If I even could. I never developed my fire magic, and I'd been working on that all my life.

Ember put the van in drive and continued north. "You'll get it."

"Will I?" Maybe the antique store was a fluke. Maybe I could only find insignificant things.

"Don't you dare start that again." She gave me the side eye as she drove.

"You will master your magic," Chaos said. "Mayhem is my brother. It's not surprising I would sense him first. I'm familiar with his vibration. You are not."

"Yeah, okay." He had a point. It took me years to master sigil work. I shouldn't expect this to come easily either.

"Here." He tapped the back of Ember's seat. "I believe she hid his skull in there."

We stopped in a parking lot in front of Fort Sewall, a coastal fortification circa the sixteen thirties, now a public park. It was used in just about every war fought on American soil, but the current structure, which wasn't much, didn't exist when Isabel would have been here.

Ember climbed out and opened the side door to gather her daggers. "How do you think she infiltrated a military base to hide a skull?"

"Isabel was a powerful witch, who practiced dark magic." Chaos exited the van, and we stood outside as Ember strapped on her weapons, hiding them strategically inside her jacket and in her boots. "She could have used a number of spells to render the soldiers catatonic."

I slung my bag over my shoulder. "Or she used her feminine wiles to get inside. Witches don't need magic for everything."

Chaos made a *hmph* sound, solidifying my suspicion that he and Isabel were lovers. She probably used her feminine wiles to trick all three of them. I had to give her props for that, despite the fact she cursed my bloodline. She commanded three Princes of Hell. I could barely manage one.

"It's this way." Chaos started toward the entrance, but I grabbed his arm.

"Hold up. This is a public place. We have to do this with finesse."

"He's here. I must find him." He jerked from my grasp and continued walking. "I can handle the bystanders."

"Stop!" I parked my hands on my hips, and he turned to face me. "Bad demon. You swore you wouldn't hurt anyone else."

His lips twitched, and he blew out a hard breath.

"Well, shit." Ember closed the door and locked the van. "Chrys texted. More Boston witches were spotted hanging around our HQ."

"They're planning something else." I took a shadow and a binding spell from my bag. "Let's do this so we can protect our territory."

"Hold on. She said Miles talked to them, and they left." She used both thumbs to type a message before returning her phone to her pocket. "I told her to set up a ward around the building. We'll strengthen it when we get home."

"Go gently," I said to Chaos. "Don't draw attention."

He stormed away, a demon on a mission, and I had to scurry to keep up. A squat, white structure built into the surrounding hills stood in front of us, but Chaos passed it and continued into the base. He stopped in the middle of the fort and spun in a circle, his expression both menacing and determined.

I suppose if I'd been wronged like he had, and my sister lay yards away beneath the ground, I'd look the same way. Since he'd stopped, I opened my senses, searching for the skull or the trap. My gut tingled slightly, a tiny pull calling me toward a flat-topped triangle built into a mound of grass-covered earth. A rusted metal door covered the entrance to the underground, and when I pointed at the location, Chaos nodded and paced toward it.

"I told you that you'd get it." Ember walked beside me. "You just needed to be closer."

"I don't know. It feels different than the other places. Something is off." We stopped outside the door.

"So this one is a trap?" Ember looked from right to left. A couple with a five-year-old walked by and headed up the steps toward the ocean.

"This isn't a trap. Mayhem is here. I can feel him." Chaos gestured at the door. "Are you going to do this with finesse, or shall I rip it off its hinges?"

"Down, boy. We'll take care of it." I looked at the bottled shadow spell. "I hate to waste this. Ember, take lookout while I unlock the door. Maybe we can slip inside without being noticed."

I moved in front of the door, and Chaos stood behind me, facing out, shielding me from prying eyes. "Confess, expose, my magic sleuth. I call on you to reveal your truth." No magic blocked the entrance.

I could have used an unlocking spell, but I took my lock-picking kit from my satchel and slid the tools into the keyhole instead. The padlock disengaged easily without magic, but the lever keeping the door shut had rusted in place.

"We're clear," Ember said.

I tried the lever, putting all my weight into it, but it wouldn't budge. I could put together a lubrication spell, but I had a feeling the beastie guarding this hidey hole would be a doozie. I needed all my strength. Chaos had plenty to spare.

"Without breaking the door, can you release this rusted lever?"

He grabbed the metal, lifted, and pulled, swinging the door open without any effort at all. Then he disappeared inside.

"Wait for us." I followed him, and Ember joined us, closing the door behind her and casting us in total darkness.

I turned on my phone's flashlight and shined it around the corridor. Packed earth created the walls, and brick arches provided support so the whole thing didn't cave in. Apparently, demons could see just fine in the dark because Chaos paced ahead, going farther and farther down.

"He's going to get us killed." Ember turned on her flashlight and strode behind him.

"Wait up!" Again, I had to scurry. Powerful, badass witches didn't scurry. I needed to work on lengthening my strides.

We reached the end of the corridor and found a doorway that had been bricked over. Ember ran her finger over the mortar, and I cringed. "That could have been boobytrapped."

"This is new." She rubbed her thumb and finger together. "It's been sealed off recently."

"Mayhem is in there." Chaos fisted his hand, drawing back like he planned to punch a hole through the wall.

"Wait." I put my hand on his bicep, and he relaxed slightly. "Let me check it for magic first. Ember and I aren't immortal like you."

He looked at my arm where my shirtsleeve covered his mark. "Proceed."

I cast my spell again, and the golden sparkles fell to the ground, collecting on a pile of bricks to the left of the doorway. "There used to be a ward. Look." I pointed.

Ember kneeled by the bricks. "These are much older. Someone broke in recently and recovered the entrance."

"I don't like this." That uneasy feeling I'd had before, telling me something was very off, expanded from my stomach to my chest. "I think this is a trap."

"It's not. I feel him." Chaos reared back and smashed his fist into the bricks. They fell inward, the wall crumbling with his single punch, and he grabbed the remaining few, pulling them away from the opening.

"Whoa." I knew he was strong, but damn.

"The mortar wasn't set yet." Ember shined her flashlight into the hole. "Whoever put up this wall did it less than two days ago."

Chaos stepped inside, and Ember followed before I could check for hexes. It was just as well. Let the demon go first; he could survive anything. Then again, if he got vanquished to Hell, I'd have to go with him.

"Be careful!" I hung outside the entry for a beat or two, listening for sounds of a scuffle. All I heard was their footsteps receding, so, against my better judgment, I stepped over the discarded bricks and trod down the hall.

The smell of dank earth made the room feel stuffy, suffocating. I hurried to catch up with the leap-first-look-later crew and opened my senses, searching this time only for a trap.

And a trap we had found. I was sure of it.

Then again, Chaos was so sure it was Mayhem, maybe I was wrong. It wouldn't be the first time my magic didn't work properly.

"Hold on," I said, and they kept walking. "Chaos, stop."

He froze, and Ember slammed into his back. "Good goddess, man. A little warning next time?"

"I obey Ash's orders." He turned, giving me an irritated glare.

"Can we talk about the fact that this place was sealed up

recently? You aren't the slightest bit concerned that someone has been in here?"

"Not when I can sense my brother ten feet away." He turned.

"Wait."

"You are testing your luck with these commands." He glowered. "You won't always bear my mark."

"Oh?" I crossed my arms. "And what are you going to do to me once it's removed?"

He mirrored my posture. "Once we're no longer bound, I could kill you."

"You made us a promise," my sister said, alarm filling her voice.

Chaos shrugged. "I'm a demon. We lie."

Ember bristled, but I laughed. "Really? You think you could kill me?"

His lips puckered. "Hmpf. No." Was that a pout I detected in his voice? "You know I couldn't. I wouldn't."

"That's what I thought. We need to think before we bust in this time. Someone was here. They left and sealed it back up, but they didn't bother putting up another ward. Why?"

Ember tapped her finger to her lips. "Because they already found the skull, so there's nothing to protect?"

"Not likely." Chaos dropped his arms, fisting his hands. "Mayhem *is* here."

"So maybe they came for the skull, but they couldn't defeat whatever Isabel has guarding it," Ember said.

I rolled the idea around in my mind. "That's a possibility, but why brick it back up?"

"To keep the mundane away," Chaos said.

Ember shook her head. "If the Boston witches really know what we're after, and they're the ones who were here, they wouldn't care if a few innocents got hurt."

"Maybe, maybe not," I said. "Could've been someone with a conscience."

"Indeed," Chaos said. "I'm going to get my brother now."

"Okay. Just be careful. I still don't like this setup." I motioned for him to continue, and I walked behind Ember until the corridor spilled out into a small chamber.

Chaos stopped outside the entrance, stilling as he sensed the energy in the space. I did the same, searching for signs of a demon other than mine, but I came up short. Before he could step inside, I cast my magic-revealing spell one more time, sending golden sparkles into the room. They gathered in two places: on an ornate wooden box in the center of the space, just big enough to hold a skull, and around a niche carved into the dirt wall at the other end of the room.

I clutched the freezing spell in my right hand, my left holding the cork, ready to pop this baby open at any moment. Chaos stepped inside, and Ember and I fanned out around him. Her daggers in each hand, she rocked on her feet, her muscles tense and ready for a fight.

"Come out, come out, wherever you are," she sang.

Something in the niche grunted, and I opened my senses again, trying to ascertain what we were up against. It wasn't demonic, whatever it was, so Chaos wouldn't be able to control it like he did the imps.

One witchissippi. Two witchissippi. No one made a move.

I shifted on my feet, and Chaos held out his arm, warning me to stay back. Now did he believe me this was a trap?

"Oh, for goddess's sake." Ember hurled a dagger into the niche.

First a yelp. Then a guttural roar. Boy, she'd done it now. Out from the alcove stepped a five-foot-tall, green-skinned monster with a pig-like nose and tusks protruding from both its upper and lower jaws. Blood trailed down its arm where the dagger had gotten it, and it yanked the knife from its flesh before tossing it to the ground.

"Sweet Shrek, is that an ogre?" I uncapped the potion, but it was too far away for the spell to reach.

"A troll." Chaos cracked his neck. "They're usually docile creatures, but your sister has agitated this one."

"As she likes to do." I inched toward it, but Chaos put out his arm again, warning me back.

"At least the action has started." Ember took another dagger from her jacket.

"This is odd," Chaos said. "Trolls aren't used as guards."

Ember pointed a blade at the beastie. "This one is."

The troll roared and barreled toward her. I hit it with the freezing spell, and its eyes widened before it face-planted in the dirt. This was too easy. Way too easy.

"If I had my sword, I'd lop off its head. Will a knife to the heart do?" She rolled it onto its back and looked at Chaos for confirmation.

"Indeed," he said, his voice growing wary.

I looked away while Ember did her thing. Thankfully, she was quick, and the monster only let out a single yelp before it expired. But the foreboding feeling in my gut had grown almost unbearable.

"Chaos." I spun to face him, but I was too late.

He ripped the lock off the box and threw open the lid. Reaching inside, he cradled something, drawing it out and holding it even with his face. A skull.

Looked like I was wrong after all.

A high-pitched ringing pierced my ears. Ember clutched her head and dropped to her knees a half-second before the skull exploded in Chaos's hands. White light flashed, blinding me. A pulse of dark energy slammed into my chest, knocking me back. I hit the wall, my breath whooshing from my lungs, before I pitched forward and hit my head on something hard. Splitting pain exploded in my skull. The world slipped away.

CHAPTER 16

CHAOS

"Ash!" Ember shot to her feet and rushed to her sister's side. "What the hell was that?" She held Ash's face in her hands, wiping away the blood that marred her forehead.

I stared at my empty hands where Mayhem's skull once sat, attempting to comprehend what happened. It would not have exploded, disappearing without a trace. It could not.

"Chaos!" Ember's shout drew me from my trance, and I dropped to my knees beside my witch. Her eyes were closed, her breathing shallow.

"That was a trap, as Ash knew." The blood had come from a small cut, one that would easily heal on its own, but her internal injuries could be far more severe.

I gripped her hand in mine, a crushing weight pressing on my chest, threatening to crumble me. "This is my fault."

"You're damn right, it is." I expected nothing less from

Ember. "Why didn't you listen to her? You keep saying what a powerful witch she is, yet when she warned you this was a trap, you ignored her."

I traced my fingers down the side of her face, and her lids fluttered. "I'm sorry, Ash."

A soft moan emanated from her throat, and she swallowed.

"I should have heeded your warning. My rage and desire to free my brother blinded me, and I fell into the trap. I was wrong, and you were right." Pressure built in the back of my eyes, threatening to turn liquid.

Her lids fluttered open, and a small smile curved her pink lips. "You're getting really good at this apology thing. I don't even feel like saying 'I told you so.'"

"Oh, thank the goddess." Ember slumped. "Are you okay? Is anything broken?"

"I think I'm good." She struggled to sit up, so I took her arm, helping her. "I've got a salve in here somewhere. Here it is." She retrieved a small jar from her bag.

"Allow me." I took it and opened the lid.

Ember offered an eye roll, but she didn't argue, instead rising to her feet and retrieving her daggers.

I dipped my finger into the salve and gently applied it to Ash's wound. "If you had not recovered, I would not have forgiven myself."

"Really?" She arched a brow and took the jar, returning it to her bag. "Because you threatened to kill me ten minutes ago."

"And you knew that threat was idle." I cupped her face in my palm.

She rested her hand on mine. "Yeah, but Ember doesn't

know that, so watch what you say around her, 'kay?" She clutched my hand, removing it from her face. "Help me up."

I did as she asked, aiding her to her feet. "I am sincerely sorry."

"I know, but we need to talk about why you were so sure Mayhem was here." She dusted off her backside. "What happened?"

"I sensed him. He was…" I exhaled hard, tracing my gaze across the room. The troll lay in a pool of blood next to the empty box. Isabel knew the docile nature of trolls; she kept one as a pet, and this wasn't it. "Perhaps a spell gave off the same vibration as Mayhem?"

"That would be one hell of a spell to trick a Prince of Hell." She adjusted the strap of her bag.

"Wouldn't be the first time Isabel pulled one over on him," Ember said.

"Want to help figure it out?" Ash held out her hand, and her sister took it as they recited a spell in unison. Their joined magic clung to the box, and they both crouched to examine it.

"This can't be Isabel's spell." Ash pointed at the wood. "For one, these nails are from this century. And the magic is fresh."

"Cast two days ago fresh?" Ember rose, brushing off her pants.

"Exactly." Ash stood. "They must know what we're doing. That we're after the skulls, and this blast was meant to stop us…to kill us."

"Someone has a copy of the map you stole." I closed the troll's eyes. The poor creature's death was unnecessary.

"Come on." Ember moved toward the doorway. "We're

burning daylight; we can discuss this in the van on the way to the final point."

"Hold on." Ash pointed at the troll. "We can't leave the beastie here for the humans to find, and I am not bricking up the entrance. Someone want to cremate him?"

Ember sighed heavily, and Ash said, "I'd do it myself, but we'd probably choke on the smoke."

"I will do it." I summoned hellfire and directed it at the troll. It incinerated in seconds, turning into a pile of dust.

"I would love to be able to do that," Ash said.

"I can teach you." Because I was certain she could if she only had the confidence to learn.

Ash walked beside me as we made our way to the surface, and she rested her hand on my arm. "They beat us here, so I'll bet they've already made it to the last point."

I placed my hand over hers. "I must see for myself."

We reached the door, and bright sunlight slashed across my eyes as Ember pushed it open. Ash moved ahead of me, but both sisters froze in the exit.

"Hey!" a man shouted. "You're not supposed to be in there."

I peered over Ash's shoulder, where a security guard paced toward us, his hand on his holstered weapon.

"Hey, John," he called to another man in the same uniform.

"Crap." Ash reached into her bag and uncorked a shadow spell. "Hide from sight our magical plight. With the power of Shade, my intent is conveyed."

I rolled my eyes at the ego he put into the incantation. He wrote it that way to vex Ash, of that I was certain. Despite his arrogance, the spell worked perfectly, making us invisible to the human eye.

"What the hell?" The guard stopped short, and the one called John joined him. "I swear two women were coming out of that door."

"I told you this place was haunted." He shook his head and returned to his post.

We made our way to the van and climbed inside, undetected, leaving the security guard scratching his head. I couldn't help but smile. Ash had thought quickly, using passive magic to allow our escape, where her sister would have used force. They were so different, yet they worked so well together. And Ash...

I would be more careful. I couldn't stand it if I lost her. My brothers would not be pleased with this emotional development, but they would have to tolerate it if they wanted out of prison and home in the Underworld where we belonged.

My chest ached at the thought of never seeing my blue-haired witch again, but there was no other way to restore balance to our realms. My brothers and I had to return home.

"Shit." Ember typed on her phone before placing it in a holder and displaying a map. "Boston witches showed up at Miles's place. Shade was there, and they fought them off."

A look of alarm widened Ash's eyes. "Were they planning to kill him too?"

"I don't know. We need to check out the last point on Isabel's map and get back." She shifted into gear and pulled out of the parking lot. "It sounds like they're declaring war."

CHAPTER 17
ASH

"They must know we've got Chaos." I pulled the cards from the Boston coven's library from my bag and fanned them out. "It's the only thing that makes sense."

"Maybe. Maybe not," Ember said. "We can't rule anything out yet."

I scoffed. "The magic in that hidey-hole was recent. Someone was in there, and they set a trap. Chaos was the only one who sensed Mayhem. If they thought it was only you and me following the map, they would've cast a different spell. Or none at all. They don't know I'm developing this sensing power."

Ember's jaw ticked. "I see your point."

"Or..." Chaos shifted in his seat, missing a few beats before he continued. "Perhaps Mayhem's skull was there, and that is what I sensed. You said the magic and mortar were no more than two days old, correct?"

I twisted around to face him. "So someone found the skull, battled the beastie, and set the trap. And they grabbed a troll to plant inside so we wouldn't question it being unguarded."

"That has to be it." Ember ended the directions on her phone. "The troll looked healthy. Well-fed. It would have been starving if it had been down there since the sixteen hundreds." She did a U-turn. "We don't need to go to the last point."

"Yes, we do." Chaos leaned forward.

"They've already got his skull." She continued driving toward Salem.

"We aren't certain of that," he said.

"I am." Ember shrugged one shoulder, and Chaos flashed a *help me out here* look, which was funny coming from a demon. I didn't imagine he needed help with very much when he was allowed to be his fiendish self.

Good thing I was keeping him on a tight leash. "He's right, Em. Nothing about this is certain. We need to check."

She let out a long, irritated sigh, but she relented, pulling over and handing me her phone. "Punch in the coordinates again. I'm sure I'll be saying 'I told you so,' but my little sister is nothing if not thorough. I admire that about you."

"As do I," Chaos chimed in, and Ember glared at him in the rearview mirror.

"Stop it." I rolled my eyes and brought up the directions. "You're making me blush."

An hour and a half later, we found ourselves in a crowded

parking lot in the middle of downtown Worcester. It looked like we'd be invading someone's basement to find the next hidey-hole. We did our usual routine, Ember strapping on weapons, Chaos and I opening our senses, trying to detect the location.

A tug formed in my stomach, pulling me toward the street. "It's this way. Do you feel it?"

"I do not," Chaos said grimly. If he didn't sense Mayhem, his brother most likely wasn't here either. Still, I felt something, so we couldn't leave without checking it out.

We hung a right, following the magical pull until it drew me into the middle of the road. A car horn blared, and Chaos grabbed my arm, yanking me back onto the sidewalk.

"Don't lose your other senses while focusing on the one."

"Good advice." I crossed my arms and stared at the pavement.

"Where to now?" Ember asked.

"It's below ground."

"Obviously, but where? Can you tell which building it's beneath?" She pulled her hair back in a band, but the part the imps cut off swung forward into her face. "Damn gremlins."

I drummed my fingers against my arm. "It's not beneath a building. It's under the road."

Her lip curled. "Under the road is the sewer. Surely Isabel wouldn't have..."

"The sewer didn't exist then," Chaos said. "She either dug or found a cave."

Ember yanked the band from her hair and wrapped it around her wrist. "Well, shit."

"Literally." I paced up the sidewalk until I spotted a manhole cover in the road. "We can get down through there."

"Or we can not. Chaos doesn't sense him. Why expose ourselves to the rats and feces if we don't have to?" She shuddered. "I hate rats."

I dug a shadow spell out of my bag. "You know we have to do this."

"*You* know there's nothing down there, and when I'm proven right, I'll expect you to do all the cooking for the next month."

"I do all the cooking anyway." I uncorked the spell and recited the words, and gray fog engulfed us. "Chaos, you remove the cover. We'll go down first, and you put it back in place when you join us. We can't be wrecking any cars in the process."

We waited for a garbage truck to roll by, and when the coast was clear, we darted into the street. Chaos lifted the cover as if it were made of Styrofoam, and Ember climbed down first. I followed, and we all met at the bottom.

The sewer looked exactly like all the sewers in every movie or television show I'd ever seen. The arched tunnel had raised walks on both sides, and a stream of liquid and sludge flowed down the middle.

Rats squeaked and chittered somewhere in the darkness, and a splash sounded a few yards away. Was it a giant alligator? A Ninja Turtle? I didn't plan on staying down there long enough to find out.

"Good goddess, it stinks." Ember pulled her shirt over her nose to mask the sulfurous stench.

Chaos inhaled deeply. "It reminds me of home."

"Any thought I ever had about visiting you in the Underworld just flew out the window. Gross." I turned on my phone's flashlight and followed the tug.

"You've thought about visiting me?" Surprise lifted Chaos's voice, but I didn't turn around to see his face.

"No, she has not." Ember stomped behind him. "My sister would never be so stupid."

I grinned, giving her a hard time. "Cinder did it. I don't see why I couldn't."

"She went to find Mom and Dad, not to visit a demon." I could practically feel the pain in her jaw as she spoke through clenched teeth. "Ahh!"

I spun around in time to see her rip a rat out of her hair and fling it into the water. She shined her light at the ceiling, revealing a swarm of rodents on the ledge above her, and she squealed. Rushing forward while looking up, she slammed into Chaos. Her foot slipped off the walk, and she fell knee-deep into the sludge.

Chaos caught her before she went in completely, and he laughed as he tugged her back to safety. "I've seen you battle a hoard of imps, a shedim, and a basilisk without flinching, yet you're afraid of a harmless rodent."

She huffed and jerked from his grasp. "Rats are not harmless. They carry the plague and who knows what else."

"A kid at school found a dead one on the playground and dropped it down the back of her shirt when they were in third grade. She never got over it." I shined my light to the right where I felt the tug and found a narrow tunnel dug into the wall. Crumbled bricks lay scattered around the opening, and a pile of dirt stood to the right.

"This looks fresh." I kicked the earth. "We aren't the first people to find this place."

"No kidding, Captain Obvious." Ember kicked her leg, throwing sludge off her boot. "This is where I say, 'I told you so.'"

Scraping that sounded an awful lot like the manhole cover being removed echoed behind us, and a beam of light flashed into the tunnel. Boots thudded on the walk, and we killed our lights, pressing our bodies to the wall.

"How many shadow spells do we have left?" Ember asked.

"Two. Come on." My heart racing, I slipped into the tunnel, and Chaos followed. "Hopefully they're workers, and we can hide out until they're done."

"It just had to be in the sewer, didn't it?" a woman asked. "No telling what we might catch down here with all these rats."

"See?" Ember whispered and joined us in the tunnel. "It's not just me."

"How are we going to make this thing do our bidding?" a man asked.

"We're setting it free. It'll be in our debt," the woman replied.

"Crap. Not workers then." I inched deeper into the tunnel. This was so not me, going first without checking for hexes or wards. I stopped and turned around, hoping to make my way past Chaos to let him lead, but the passage was narrow. I couldn't get around him.

"Do you sense anything?" I whispered. "Demons? Trolls?"

He shook his head. "Do you?"

"No."

"Keep going," Ember said. "They're almost here."

"Wait." I recited a quick revealing spell. Sparkles clung to the walls and drifted into the darkness. "There was a ward, but someone broke it. I can't see the rest without light."

"Just go," Ember said. "I'd rather face whatever is in here than dark witches. They don't fight fair."

An image of poor Ginger flashed through my mind. Ember made a good point. With my hands stretched out in front of me, I carefully trod down the path until a ray of light slashed through the darkness from above.

"We're right below a storm drain." A ceramic container lay shattered on the ground, my spell clinging to it, revealing a shroud. "Damn it."

Roots protruded from the wall on the left, and a dead beastie hung tangled, a machete penetrating its heart. It stood at least six feet tall, with green skin stretched tightly over bulging muscles that gave Chaos a run for his money in the beef department.

My demon stood in front of it, clasping his hands behind his back. "That is a proper guard."

"What is it?" I asked.

"A goblin." He turned away from the carnage. "A troll's meaner, more aggressive cousin."

"I thought light witches didn't mess with demons." I spun around to find a woman with curly blonde hair sneering, twirling a knife in her hand. "Step aside. This one's ours."

Ember drew her daggers, assuming a fighting stance. "The hell it is."

Chaos stood in front of me, his arms to his sides like he was about to summon hellfire. I rested my hand on his bicep, hoping to calm him. His muscles tensed even more.

"Don't," I whispered. "You'll blow your cover."

He growled, but the fire inside him simmered. "How did you know to look here?"

"How did you?" the man asked.

"It doesn't matter." I moved beside Chaos and pointed at the shattered jar. "We're all too late."

"You're the cursed one, aren't you? We know your secret." The woman looked from me to Ember to Chaos. "Do they?"

Of course they knew. Why else would we be there?

"How do you know who I am?" I slowly slid my hand into my satchel, hoping to grab a freezing spell, though, honestly, I'd have taken anything. The confrontational energy building between the four of them was about to hit critical mass, and I had no doubt Chaos could wipe them out...and us in the process...with a flick of his fiery fingers.

The man scoffed. "You're part of the wrongfully ruling family. Everyone knows who you are, no matter how much you try to hide."

"We don't have time for this." Ember flipped a dagger in the air, catching it by the handle before flipping it again...like she did when she was about to throw it. "Turn around, walk away, and we'll pretend we never saw you. Otherwise, you can join the goblin pinned to the wall."

My fingers curled around a potion bottle. The woman

snapped her head toward me, and before I could get the spell out of my bag, she grabbed a bottle from the strap across her chest, opened it, and hurled the contents at me.

Green slime splashed across my arm, burning through my sleeve and clinging to my skin. It sizzled, the intense heat and scent of burning flesh making my stomach turn.

Ember threw her first dagger, embedding it in the woman's shoulder. She yelped and thrust her knife, but my sister darted right, roundhouse kicking the woman's arm and knocking the knife to the ground.

Chaos's sigil heated on my arm, fighting against the poison trying to eat my flesh. He grunted, the energy in the chamber shifting as he called on his fire.

"Please don't." I bit the inside of my cheek, making it bleed.

He looked at me, his nostrils flaring, and returned his menacing stare to the dark witches. Without moving a muscle or doing anything at all to indicate he'd called on his other power, he sent out a pulse of magic.

The woman's eyes widened, and she turned away from Ember to shove the man. "This is your fault. We'd have been here sooner if you didn't have to take a shit before we left."

He pushed her back. "We wouldn't be here at all if I hadn't told you about it. Typical Cami, riding on my coattails and blaming me the second something goes wrong."

"How dare you?" Her expression was wild, a dozen different emotions crossing her features, mixing and melding, her mind no doubt a garbled mess of chaos.

"How dare *you*?" The man threw the first punch, hitting her in the stomach. Cami recovered and went for his throat, slamming him against the wall.

Ember sucked in a breath, looking at Chaos like she wanted to scold him. Instead, she pointed to the storm drain. "Think we'll fit through that?"

The guy made choking noises. Cami's hands tightened on his neck. He grabbed the dagger still protruding from her shoulder, yanked it out, and slammed it into her chest. She sputtered. Blood ran from her lips.

My arm screamed with agony. If I didn't apply an antidote soon, the poison would eat through my flesh and dissolve bone, but I couldn't let these two kill each other. I used my teeth to uncork the freezing potion and threw it at them. "Standing tall or on your knees, in the name of the goddess, I force you to freeze."

The man went still as a statue like he should have, but the woman dropped to the ground, limp. Lifeless.

Fabulous. Yet another death was on my hands. Maybe the curse was already happening. Maybe I wasn't meant to go on a murderous rampage, but I'd be indirectly responsible for the destruction of my coven, witch by witch.

Crap.

Chaos scaled the wall and slammed his fist into the storm drain cover. It cracked, sending powdered concrete raining onto us.

"Wait!" No telling who might be walking by above us. With my good arm—the other was paralyzed—I dug through my bag in search of a shadow spell.

"Here." Ember sheathed her dagger and peered into the

satchel, snatching the potion and activating it, turning the world grayscale. "Get us out of here, Chaos."

"Stand back." He punched the concrete again. More powder rained down.

I backed away, my foot knocking into Cami's head. She didn't move. Her empty eyes stayed open, staring at nothing. Who would die next because of me?

Chaos hit the drain cover again, and it shattered. Chunks of concrete fell to the ground, and when the dust settled, he hoisted himself out of the tunnel and offered his hand to Ember. She took it without hesitation, and he hauled her up so she could climb out.

He dropped to the ground next to me and eyed my arm, his expression livid. The tendons in his neck tightened as he turned his attention to the frozen man.

"Please don't." I took his hand and tugged him to the opening. "Help me up?"

He thought about it. I could practically see the gears turning in his mind. "They hurt you."

"She did, and now she's dead. Leave him be."

He huffed. "As you wish." Wrapping his hands around my hips, he lifted me. Ember reached down, taking my good arm, and they got me to the surface. Chaos jumped, grabbing the sides of the hole and hauling himself up.

"Quick, before the shadow spell wears off." Ember paced away from the mess we'd made.

When we reached the van, I dumped the contents of my satchel onto the back seat. An old ceramic jar with a pentagram and fire symbol on the lid tumbled out, and my breath came out in a rush.

"I hope this hasn't expired." I opened the jar and spread the neutralizing salve over my arm.

"Your magic can expire?" Chaos watched me intently, his expression grim. No doubt he battled his nature, wanting to return to the crime scene and take out the other witch.

"I mixed this two years ago. This is the first occasion I've had to try it out." The moment the salve touched my wound, a cooling sensation spread through my arm. The poison dissolved, leaving behind raw, charred flesh. I wiggled my fingers.

Chaos's brow slammed down over his eyes. "That looks painful."

"No worse than the burns when we got electrocuted." I scooped the rest of the potions into the bag and climbed into the front seat.

Chaos got in the back. "I remember the agony. It was unbearable."

"I'll be fine." At least the chemical burn only covered my arm, rather than my entire body.

Ember started the van and drove toward home. "I'd say it's time for Plan B, but we don't have one."

I wrapped a bandage over my burns. "Can we call Patrice over when we get home?"

"Of course. We need you in peak shape so you can figure out a solution to our problem."

I laughed dryly. Good old Ember. Always the compassionate one.

CHAPTER 18
ASH

Since we were down one fighter, we recruited Patrice to join us. She didn't have the physical skills to replace Ginger, but she was a badass with spellwork. Not to mention she could heal us on the spot when we got injured.

When *I* got injured. Because we all knew I'd be the first to go down.

After we all showered off the sewer sludge, she'd met us at our place, used a spell to draw out the rest of the poison, and bandaged me up.

"I haven't seen this sigil before," she said as she wrapped the gauze around my forearm and taped it in place. "What does it do?"

Ember locked eyes with me, flashing a warning look, as if I didn't know telling Patrice I'd summoned a demon was a bad idea.

"I was trying a new form of protection, but it didn't work, obviously." I gestured to the bandage.

"Shouldn't it have faded by now? You've had it for more than a week." She returned her supplies to her kit and set it on the coffee table.

"It wouldn't activate. Since it's dormant, I'm stuck with it until I have time to remove it."

Chaos nodded his approval from the kitchen where he shoveled Lucky Charms into his mouth. I guess I was getting better at lying. Fabulous.

Patrice sat back on the sofa next to me. "I can't believe they attacked you on our home turf. Do they want a war?"

Yeah, that was another lie courtesy of yours truly. After the Boston witches had followed Chaos and me in the store, it only seemed natural to blame my latest injury on the bad guys hanging around Salem.

"Knock, knock," Chrys called before she stepped through the door. Miles and Shade followed her in, and they took seats in the living room for yet another session of lies. Yay.

Ember cracked her neck and paced in front of the television. "Start from the beginning, Miles. You saw the Boston witches outside and confronted them. What did they say?"

His face was solemn, his mouth tight. "Someone broke into their library and tore it apart. They're blaming me."

"What? That's ridiculous." My voice raised an octave or two, and Ember shot another warning glare. I cleared my throat. "What would make them think it was you?"

"I didn't..." He fisted his hands in his lap before splaying them on his knees. "I didn't want to tell you this, but I've been there before."

Ember stopped pacing, a look of alarm flashing on her face before she composed herself. "Why did you find yourself inside a dark witch coven's headquarters?"

He drew his shoulders toward his ears. "When Ginger started doing dark spells she found online, I was worried. You never know what kind of crap people post. Maybe a spell she thought would bring her wealth was some teenage witch's idea of a joke and it would blow up in her face."

"I can see where this is going, and I do not approve." Ember crossed her arms.

He lifted his hands and dropped them in his lap. "I knew you wouldn't. That's why I did it in secret, but I swear I did not destroy their library."

Shade clapped him on the shoulder. "We believe you, man. He was with me when they claim it happened. The night of the Hunter's Moon."

"I thought if I could get her some legit spells, it might curb her appetite. Let her see the kind of toll dark magic takes on a witch." He covered his face with his hands. "I'm sorry."

Chaos straightened his spine. "And now they're starting a war on this coven because of your insolence."

"He didn't do it." Shade shot to his feet. "I told you he was with me that night. Where were you? The way I see it, all this shit started happening right before you showed up. How do we know you're not to blame?"

"Sit down, Shade." Ember was getting good at this commander-in-chief thing. "So Boston figured out you stole spells and gave them to Ginger. They killed her, and now they're after you because they think you are responsible for the vandalism of their library."

Miles swallowed hard. "In a nutshell, yeah."

"How did you get into their library?" Patrice asked. "Did you break in? Because that would be grounds for them to declare war whether you trashed the place or not."

I pressed my lips into a line. *Thanks for the reminder, Patrice. Why did we recruit her again?*

"I made friends with one of their low-level witches. I told her I'd take her out on a date if she let me in." He lifted his hands in defense. "But that was weeks ago. I haven't been back since. I... What can I do to make this right?"

"You tried talking to them." Ember resumed her pacing.

"Yeah. They didn't believe me."

"So they showed up at your door." I drummed my fingers on the arm of the couch. "They know where you live."

"When I answered," Shade said, "I attacked them before they set foot inside, and I scared them away. If I hadn't been there, he'd be dead too."

I rolled my eyes. "Right, because Miles is completely incapable of self-defense."

"Apparently Ginger was." Shade arched a brow.

"Too soon." I stood and joined Ember in front of the television. I hated to admit it, but Miles's transgressions did make him the perfect scapegoat for our situation. Of course, we knew he wasn't to blame for the library mishap, and it sucked that he and Ginger were taking the fall, but they did kind of bring it on themselves by dabbling in the dark arts.

Good goddess, would you listen to me? I'd had a demon in my head for way too long.

"You need to call a meeting with their High Priestess," Patrice said. "No one from our coven destroyed their library, but they are attacking our witches. Convince her this has to stop."

"That's an excellent idea," Chaos said.

No. No, it was a horrible idea, and the face I made at him said as much. Lying to our own coven members was one thing. Their High Priestess would put us under a truth spell, and we'd admit to everything. Or worse. She might force us to falsely confess to a whole slew of magical crimes.

Ember rubbed her forehead. "Yeah. Yeah, okay. I'll work on that. In the meantime, we need to protect Miles. He can't go home."

"He'd be safest here," Chrys said. "With all the wards I put up today, nothing with malicious intent is getting inside."

Again... No. Absolutely not. "Don't underestimate that coven. They've already attacked me, and they know where our headquarters is."

"Can I stay with you?" Miles asked Shade.

"Of course. You'll be safer with me anyway."

"I can come too," Chrys said. "Safety in numbers."

"We're good." Shade rose to his feet and looked at Ember. "Let us know when you get a meeting."

"I will."

Shade and Miles headed downstairs, and Chrys shook her head. "The ego on that one keeps getting bigger, doesn't it?"

"Indeed," Chaos said.

Patrice rose and grabbed her bag. "You can stay with me, Chrys. I could use a little safety."

"Gladly." She stood, and they left the house too.

"Holy Hecate." Ember dropped onto a chair and leaned her head back, closing her eyes. "So we're on the same page…" She lifted one lid. "A meeting with the Boston High Priestess is *not* happening."

Thank the goddess. I sank onto the arm of Chaos's chair. "Why did you say it was a good idea?"

"To buy us time and remove suspicion when we return to Boston," he said.

"Why would we go back there?" Ember sat straight. "We know everything about the curse."

"But we don't know who has Mayhem's skull." I tapped my foot. "They've obviously put the pieces together. The missing cards from the catalog, the torn page from Isabel's journal. They have a copy of the stolen map since they found the hiding spot. They know what we're up to."

"And they have his skull." She dropped her head back on the chair.

"Maybe not," I said. "Those were Boston witches in the tunnel. I saw their emblem tattooed on the man's wrist. They didn't know the skull was already gone."

"Yeah, but they didn't sound official. That was definitely a covert operation. Those two wanted the skull for their own reasons." She stood and started pacing again. "The only thing we know for certain is that *someone* got to it before we did, and it happened recently. We have to find it."

"Wait." I tapped a finger on Chaos's shoulder. "Do we really?"

"Our entire plan hinges on it, so yeah," she said.

Chaos tilted his head, flashing a conspiratorial expression. "Once they summon my brother, I will sense him. The hunt for his skull is unnecessary. We'll find him once he is whole."

Ember opened her mouth like she wanted to argue, but she paused. "It'll be that easy for you to find him?"

"Indeed." He steepled his fingers.

She sank into her chair. "So we wait?"

"Seems like the best course of action at the moment," I said. "Rest, recharge, let someone else summon the demon for once."

She pressed her fingers to her temples. "But if we aren't the ones who free him, he won't owe us a debt. What if he won't help?"

"Chaos can convince him." I rested a hand on his shoulder. "Then we find Cinder and Discord, lift the curse, and mend the veil. No one has to know we're responsible for any of it. This actually worked out in our favor."

Ember's gaze locked on my hand touching his shoulder. Her features pinched, but then they softened. "I don't like it. People are dying, but...you're right. Why risk our lives trying to find the skull when we can let someone else do the dirty work?" She laughed dryly. "What would Cinder think of us now?"

"That you're doing the best you can to end Ash's curse and keep the city safe." He placed his hand over mine.

"It feels like we're missing something, though." Ember closed her eyes for a long blink before lifting her hands and letting them fall to her lap. "I need to think. With Chrys's wards up, you should be safe without me for a while." She stood and grabbed her house keys.

"You're not worried about leaving me alone with a demon anymore?" I lifted my brows.

"If he had malicious intent, he wouldn't have made it past the wards. The rest…" She shrugged. "You're a grown woman. Do what you want."

"Where are you going?" I asked.

"For a walk. I think better when I'm moving."

"Obviously." Chaos chuckled. "I'm surprised you haven't worn a hole in the floor with your pacing."

She twirled the keys around her finger. "The library incident was weeks ago. Why are they here now? What are we missing?"

I squeezed my eyes shut. Enough talking in circles. "I don't know, and I'm too tired to think about it."

She nodded. "Sleep, and don't open the door to anyone who's not in our coven."

"Don't worry about me. I've got a big scary demon to keep me safe."

"Yeah. Because he's done a fabulous job so far." She closed the door, locking it behind her, and Chaos stiffened.

I massaged his shoulder. "She's tired. She didn't mean it."

"Yes, she did, and she's right. I vowed no harm would come to you, yet you continue getting injured."

I laughed. "Believe me, that's nobody's fault but my own. I'm still the same witch who burned down the cemetery and possessed myself with a demon."

"And I am very glad you did." He grabbed my waist and pulled me into his lap before wrapping his arms around me.

I could have struggled. I probably should have gotten up, but I sighed contentedly instead, relaxing into his embrace. "I'd have preferred to meet you under different circumstances. You know...so you didn't almost take over my body and make me cease to exist."

He searched my eyes, though I couldn't tell you what he was looking for. "It couldn't have happened any other way. You are my salvation."

"Can demons be saved?"

He lowered his gaze to my lips, and my insides tightened. "I would like to find out."

"It doesn't hurt to try."

He took my face in his hands and kissed me tenderly, as if I were the most fragile treasure he'd ever held. I suppose I was, if I were to believe everything he'd said. Closing his eyes, he moaned softly into my mouth, the vibration turning my skin to gooseflesh. One hand slid down my arm, but when he reached my bandage, he gasped, breaking the kiss.

"It's okay." I brushed my lips to his. "It doesn't hurt anymore. Look."

I untaped the gauze, and he unrolled the bandage slowly, inch by inch, revealing my scarred skin in such a seductive way, heat pooled below my navel. He ran his finger over the scar and turned my arm over, caressing his mark and making me shiver.

"You drew it perfectly." He traced his fingertip along the dips and turns, and it heated, glowing a soft red.

"I am an Ink Master."

"That you are." He inhaled deeply and looked into my eyes, his gaze penetrating to my soul. "It looks good on you."

My breath shuddered. "I never should have…"

"But you did." He slid his hands up to my shoulders, gripping them gently.

"I'm a light witch," I whispered. "It's wrong."

"Then why does it feel so right?" His gaze flowed over my face, returning to my eyes with an intensity that nearly melted me.

"It does, doesn't it?" My voice was barely audible over the pulse rushing in my ears. "I want you, and I'm tired of fighting it."

"As am I." His grip on my shoulders tightened, and he pulled me to his chest, planting his mouth on mine.

I wrapped my arms behind his neck and rose to my knees, straddling his lap. He groaned and kissed me harder. I was no longer his fragile flower. Now I was his last breath of air. He slid his hands to my back knotting, them in my shirt. I moved to tug it over my head, but he pulled, ripping it apart and tossing it aside.

I gasped. Normally I'd be pissed if a man did that to my clothes, but the feral look in his eyes made my heart sprint and my clit throb. "Take me to the bedroom."

Without a word, he rose effortlessly. I wrapped my legs around his waist, and he bent to pick up my discarded shirt. "So we don't alarm your sister."

I was glad he could think clearly because the feel of his rock-hard length pressed between my legs scattered my thoughts like a dandelion in the wind. He carried me to the bedroom, kicking the door shut behind us and slamming my back against it. The impact only made me want him more.

I lowered my feet to the floor, and he leaned against me, clutching my hair and angling my mouth upward to meet his. His cock pressed into my stomach, and I grabbed the hem of his shirt, my nails scraping his skin as I drew it up his back.

His body shuddered. Leaning back, he yanked it over his head, revealing the chiseled abs and defined pecs I hadn't been able to get out of my head since he'd stood naked in my studio. He licked his lips, his gaze blazing a trail of heat down to my chest. Cupping my breasts, he teased my nipples through my bra, hardening them into pearls.

I reached behind my back and opened the clasp, letting it fall to the floor. His pupils dilated. His nostrils flared on a deep inhale, and he bent, taking one nipple into his mouth, bathing it in heat while pinching the other between his fingers. Electricity exploded in my chest, cascading downward and filling me with an urgency I'd never felt before.

"I need you," I rasped.

"You'll have me." He sucked my other nipple into his mouth, and I moaned.

"Right now."

"Is that an order, or can I take my time?" He trailed his tongue up my neck and took my earlobe between his teeth.

The sensation made my knees buckle, but he didn't let me fall. He scooped me into his arms and tossed me onto the bed, a wicked grin lifting one corner of his mouth. After taking off my shoes, he undid my pants and yanked them down, leaving me in nothing but a pair of yellow panties.

He devoured me with his eyes, the hunger in them palpable as he took me in. "Even better than I remember." With one hand, he unbuttoned his jeans and shoved them to the floor, taking his underwear with them.

My gaze locked on his dick, long and thick, and I licked my lips.

"I can take you now, as you command…" He grabbed his cock and stroked it twice. "Or I can ravish every inch of your body, showering you with the attention and ecstasy you deserve."

Well, when he put it that way… "Ravish away."

The green of his eyes glowed softly, his smile that of a predator who'd cornered his prey, and Hecate have mercy, I had never been so turned on in my life.

He pulled my underwear off, grabbed my hips, and flipped me to my stomach before climbing onto the bed and covering my body with his. The demonic heat of his skin enveloped me, and as he nuzzled against my neck, goosebumps rose on my arms.

I turned my head to see him, and he descended, pressing his lips between my shoulders. He moved achingly slow, his coarse hands memorizing my body, his mouth gliding along my skin. He nipped my shoulder between his teeth, and I gasped. He chuckled and did it again.

"You're killing me," I said into the sheets.

"No." He trailed his tongue down my spine, stopping just above my butt. "I'm showing you how to live."

He bit the top of my left cheek, and another pleasure explosion rocketed through my body. I cried out and bit a pillow. He laughed and kissed his way down the back of one leg, circling his tongue around the sensitive flesh behind my knee, nipping it before continuing down and working his way up the other.

Sitting up, he straddled my legs, and I imagined him stroking his cock as he ravished me with his gaze. I started to turn over to see, but he held my shoulder down, keeping me on my stomach. My entire body ached with so much need I thought I would explode.

"It isn't often you relinquish control." His hands slid up and down my back. "Why do you now?"

"I..."

He spread my legs with his knees.

I parted them willingly. "I don't know."

He lowered his body, hovering just above me and rubbing the tip of his cock between my folds. "Are you afraid?"

"No." My core tightened, anticipation building, becoming nearly unbearable.

"I will stop at your command."

"I don't want you to."

"Good." He rose and turned me onto my back. The tip of his cock glistened with my wetness, and though my mouth watered to lick it, I stayed still, giving him complete control.

"What do you want me to do?" His voice was rough, thick with need.

"Anything you want." Mine was breathless.

He arched a brow and raked his gaze down my body. "Where to start?"

A bead of moisture gathered on his tip, and he swiped it with two fingers and pressed them to my clit. He rubbed circles before slipping them inside me, pumping twice, and returning to my sensitive spot.

I moaned and gripped the sheets, but he made a *tsk* sound. "Not yet, my little witch. I'm not ready for you to come."

Good goddess, hearing those words from his lips was hot. And knowing that, at any moment, I could flip the switch and take control made it that much hotter.

I reached for him, and he gripped my wrists, pinning them above my head as he straddled my hips. Leaning down, he hovered his lips a scant centimeter from mine, teasing me, his breath warming my skin. I opened, and he slipped his tongue into my mouth to tangle with mine.

A pleased growl rumbled from his chest, and he released my wrists, sliding his hands down my arms to cup my breasts. He broke the kiss, pressing his forehead to mine and breathing deeply as if trying to control himself.

A masculine grunt emanated from his throat, and he moved down, giving my front the same attention he'd given my back. He kissed and licked, nipped and sucked, working his way across my chest and down my stomach.

My muscles tightened, and he spread my legs, settling between them and wrapping them behind his shoulders. His wicked grin said he wanted to tease me more, but the moment his tongue met my folds, he groaned.

"Gods, you taste good." He licked again from bottom to top before sucking my clit between his lips.

Electricity zipped through my body like pinballs bouncing off nerves I never knew I had. I gasped and clutched the sheets again, but this time, he kept going, licking and sucking, working my sensitive nub in circles as he pumped his fingers inside me.

I tangled my fingers in his hair as the orgasm coiled in my core. He twisted his hand, making a *come here* motion with his fingers, and I lost control. Ecstasy exploded in my body, flames of passion consuming me from my head to the tips of my fingers and toes.

My hips bucked, but he held on, relentlessly pleasuring me until I couldn't take it anymore. "Please," I rasped, and he rose to his hands and knees, his eyes smoldering, the green undulating like hellfire simmering just below the surface.

He slid off the bed, pulling my hips to the edge and turning me onto my stomach again. My feet stood on the floor; my body bent over the mattress. I watched him over my shoulder as he took his dick in his hand and rubbed the tip against me. He slipped it inside halfway, and a pleasurable ache spread through my core.

Two short pumps, and he pulled it out again. I moaned in protest, and he chuckled. "Do you want all of me, little witch?"

"Goddess, yes."

Gripping my hips, he slammed his cock inside me. "You feel so good wrapped around me."

I tried to respond, but all I managed were a few garbled syllables. He pumped his hips, filling me completely with each thrust. The sounds of skin slapping skin and his grunts of pleasure filled my senses, rendering me incapable of coherent thought.

He pulled out suddenly, and before I could protest, he

flipped me over, tossing me onto the center of the mattress. "I want to see your face when you come."

I managed a small whimper before he covered my body with his and thrust inside me. He kissed me passionately as he took me, holding my face in his hands and drinking me in like I was the last drop of wine on Earth.

I gripped his shoulders, digging my nails into his skin as another climax built inside me. "Chaos…"

He looked at me with passion-drunk eyes. "Come for me, Ash."

I cried out, tossing my head back onto the pillow as wave after wave of sheer carnal pleasure ricocheted through my body.

His rhythm increased as he rose onto his hands, his gaze never straying from my face. I moaned again and wrapped my legs around his waist. He slowed, pulling out halfway and pumping three times.

He thrust into me hard, the sexiest growl-groan I had ever heard escaping his lips as he collapsed on top of me, finding his release. He stilled, pushing deep inside me, his breath coming out in huffs.

Wrapping my arms around him, I kissed the side of his head and held on like he'd disappear if I let go.

"You're a goddess," he whispered against my ear.

"Just a fire witch."

He rolled onto his back, tugging me to his side. "There is nothing *just* about you."

I draped my leg across his hips and rested my head on his shoulder. We lay there silently, basking in the afterglow of the hottest sex I'd ever experienced, and he traced his fingertips along my arm.

Night had fallen, and the waning moon cast a silvery glow in my bedroom. The kitchen door opened and closed. Boots thudded on the hardwood, going silent before the footsteps reached the hall. A door clicked shut. Finally, Ember gave me privacy.

Chaos kissed the top of my head. "Your sister won't approve of this development."

"She doesn't get a say in my sex life." I snuggled closer to my demon and fell asleep in his arms.

A thud, followed by a man whisper-shouting, "Shit," drew me from my slumber.

I sat up, and Chaos shot out of bed to put on his underwear. "You're alarmed. That's not a normal sound in your home." He put on his pants.

"Maybe Ember brought a guy home, and he's trying to sneak out."

My doorknob twisted, and I clutched the sheets to my chest. If this was my sister checking up on me, I swore to Hecate...

The door swung open.

It wasn't Ember.

CHAPTER 19
CHAOS

"Shade." I glared at the insolent man standing in Ash's doorway.

Surprise lifted his brows, indicating I had just given away my secret.

"What the hell, Shade?" Ash asked before he could question my ability to see through his shadow screen. She clutched the sheets to her chest, and I stepped in front of him, blocking his view of my witch.

"How dare you sneak in here?" She rose, keeping the sheet firmly wrapped around her, and disappeared into the bathroom. A few seconds later, she returned wearing a blue robe cinched tightly around her waist. "And hiding yourself with shadow magic? What are you doing?"

"I knew it. I knew he wasn't some long-lost cousin." Shade moved deeper into the room, dropping his cloak. Ash sucked in a breath, finally able to see him, and I stopped him with a hand to his chest. He attempted to knock my arm away. When he couldn't move it, he scoffed and stepped back, straightening his shirt.

"How did you get in here?" Ash stood next to me, resting her hand on my arm, reminding me to behave.

"I have a key. Duh."

I bit back a growl.

"Not to the upstairs, you don't." She tightened her grip on my arm.

"You're not the only one who can pick a lock. I knew something was going on between you." He paced toward the bed.

"So what if it is?" Ash crossed her arms. "Why are you here?"

"I was suspicious. Something is off about him, and I'm going to find out what it is." He matched Ash's posture. "No witch can see through my magic. What are you?"

"What in Hecate's name?" Ember stood in the doorway and glanced at each of us. "Do I even want to know?"

"Shade broke into your home and cloaked himself in shadow." Anger ignited in my chest. "How dare you violate these women in their private space?"

He laughed dryly. "I'm not the one who did the violating. Did she beg for it? Did she show you the notches on her headboard?"

My hands clenched into fists. He walked a razor-thin line with his disrespect, and I would not tolerate more.

"That's enough." Ember paced into the room. "What's going on?"

He gestured to the disturbed bedding. "They were obviously banging."

"For goddess's sake, Shade." Ash opened a drawer and put on underwear and sweatpants beneath her robe. "Get over yourself and get out of my room. It's none of your business."

"It is when his presence is affecting our coven. I can see why you're blind to his involvement in the chaos, but you, Ember? Unless you're banging him too." He watched Ember, waiting for a response. When she gave none, he continued, "No? Ash is still the only slut in the family?"

My tolerance for his audacity ran out. Ash had commanded me not to harm him. She didn't say a word about scaring the hell out of him.

I grabbed the front of his shirt in my fist and yanked him toward me. "You will respect your superiors."

A hint of fear flashed in his eyes, but he quickly recovered. "They aren't my superiors. This coven has gone to shit since Cinder disappeared."

"Get out." Ash pointed at the doorway, so I released my hold, shoving him away.

Shade did not obey. "You're in on it, aren't you?" He stalked toward my witch. "You're working together to take down this coven. First your parents and Cinder. Then Ginger. Now you're trying for Miles, but he's under my protection. You won't lay a finger or a hex on him."

Ash straightened her spine. "What the hell are you talking about? Too many hits with the basilisk's tail has made you delusional."

"You didn't break the family curse, did you? All of this...the rifts, the deaths...you're picking off our coven one by one, and you're using him to do it." He shoved her. She stumbled back.

All logical thought drained from my mind, blind rage replacing it.

I clutched his shoulder, spinning him around before wrapping my hand around his puny neck. I could have easily snapped it. Instead, I lifted him from the ground and threw him across the room. The mirror hanging on the wall shattered with his impact, and he grunted and slid to the floor.

"Enough, boys." Ember paced toward Shade and helped him to his feet. He rewarded her with a fist to her jaw.

She clutched her face. "Get the hell out of our house."

Ash grabbed my arm, her way of reminding me of my promise, but I could not uphold my end of that deal when the sisters' lives were in danger.

"What's your end game?" He shoved Ember and stalked toward me. "You must be the mastermind because these two don't have the brain power to pull off something like this."

I growled. My eyes heated, my demon form rising to the surface, threatening to expose me. I fought to keep it subdued.

Shade pulled a potion bottle from his pocket and recited a spell.

"Shade..." Alarm filled Ash's voice. "What are you doing? We don't want to hurt you." She tried to take the bottle, but he jerked his hand back.

Ember grabbed his wrist. He spun and punched her in the stomach with his free hand. She released her hold, and he turned toward me, malice filling his smoky gray eyes. "You're not going to destroy this coven."

"Neither are you." I hit him with my mind magic, and he froze, dropping the potion bottle to the floor. The contents spilled and sizzled, purple smoke rising from the liquid, billowing out across the floor.

"Shit. It's a nerve hex. Come on." Ember motioned for us to follow her out of the room.

"Crap! It's on my feet." Ash lifted one leg and then the other. "Ow, ow, ow."

I felt nothing from the spell, so I lifted my witch from the smoke and carried her into the hall. Shade stood in the middle of it, the chaos in his mind not allowing the pain to register. He grunted and swiped his arm across the top of Ash's dresser, knocking her possessions to the floor.

"You're such a control freak. Everything has to be in its place." He went for the bedsheets, stripping them from the mattress.

"Chaos, stop," Ash commanded, so I released my hold on him. Ember stomped into the room, grabbed Shade by the arm, and dragged him to the safety of the hall, closing the door behind them.

"Chaos?" Shade squinted at me. "What did you do to me? This..." He clutched his head. "This has happened before."

"Ash, go make an antidote." Ember doubled over, resting her hands on her knees. Both women's bare feet swelled, patterns of purple and black extending across the skin and rising to their ankles. Ash padded toward the kitchen, wincing and sucking air through her teeth with each step.

"What's *your* endgame, asshole?" Ember sweated, her jaw tensing, tendons protruding on her neck. "What are you trying to accomplish?"

He had harmed my witch and her sister. Hellfire sparked on my fingertips. I landed a punch in his gut. He grunted, careening backward into the wall.

"Holy shit." He wrapped his arms around his middle. Sweat beaded on his forehead, the pain from his nerve hex finally registering.

I wanted to kill him. To save the world from his miserable existence, but my connection to Ash wouldn't allow it. My demon form, however, insisted I morph. I fought it with all my might, but talons protruded from my fingers. I fisted my hands.

Shade's eyes widened. He swallowed hard. "You're not a witch." He shook his head, inching away from me and locking his gaze on my hands. "Chaos. She called you Chaos."

I loomed toward him, extending my fingers. My talons grew.

"You...you started all this. The rifts." He backed to the other side of the wall, flattening himself against it and jerking his head toward Ember. "You summoned a demon."

"A Prince of Hell to be exact." My eyes heated, the green undulating in my irises.

"We didn't start it," Ember said through clenched teeth. "We're trying to stop it."

He shoved her toward me, attempting to flee. I grabbed the back of his neck, my talons encircling it as I lifted him from the ground. He flailed, his legs and arms thrashing, knocking against the wall.

Ember sank to her knees, the poison climbing her legs like a vine on a lattice. "Let him go."

"He knows our secret." I tightened my grip.

He clawed at my talons, attempting to pry them from his neck.

"I can't..." Ember's eyes rolled, and she crumbled to the floor, unconscious.

I carried Shade into the living room. Ash stood in the kitchen, leaning on the counter next to a large copper bowl. "Let him go."

"Are you certain you want me to do that?"

"Yes, do it." Her lids fluttered shut. She swayed on her feet. "Antidote is done." She fell to the floor.

"You will pay for this." I dropped Shade, and he rushed out the door without looking back. He would pay, indeed.

My hands returning to their human form, I paced into the kitchen and took the container, dropping to my knees beside Ash. Reaching into the bowl, I scooped a handful of the thick liquid and applied it to her feet, smearing it up her legs. Sparkles gathered around her, and the purple and black faded, the swelling disappearing nearly instantly.

She sucked in a breath, opening her eyes. "Ember?"

"I will assist her. Will you be okay?"

She nodded and sat up, so I carried the bowl to the hallway and applied the antidote to Ember. She awoke with a start, scrambling to her feet before running into the living room. "Where is he?"

"I let him go, as you requested." I set the bowl on an end table.

"Shit." She paced. "What are we going to do?"

"I hate to say it…" Ash joined us in the living room. "But there's only one thing we can do."

I nodded. Finally, we agreed. "Shall I kill him quickly, or slowly?"

CHAPTER 20
ASH

"We're not killing Shade." Ash sat on the arm of a chair. "We have to bring him in. Tell him everything."

Ember stopped pacing, her expression incredulous. "The hell we do. Are you crazy?"

Chaos looked at me like I'd grown horns. "He could be in cahoots with your rival coven. If you tell him everything, he will use it against you."

Ember cocked her head, her brow crumpling. "I never considered that. It would explain his pissy behavior lately."

"And why he broke into your home, cloaking himself in shadow," Chaos said. "I doubt he 'scared away' the Boston witches. He's working with them."

"Shade is always pissy, but I do see your point." I padded to the kitchen and put on a pot of coffee. "But he knows we have Chaos. So if he's *not* working with Boston, he's going to spread the word that we're harboring a demon. Hell, he'll probably report us to the Higher Power. We need to explain it all to him to keep him from tearing our coven apart."

Ember took three cups from the cabinet and set them next to the coffee pot. We watched the machine drip for a while before she said, "What if he is working with Boston?"

"What's that saying? 'Keep your friends close and your enemies closer.' If we bring him into the fray, we can keep a better eye on him." The machine beeped, so I poured the coffee and carried a mug to Chaos.

"I don't like it. We can't trust him." Ember sipped her brew, tapping her finger against the mug. "He broke into our house for Hecate's sake."

"But if he was working with Boston, he wouldn't have made it past the wards." I sat on the couch. "Nothing with ill intent could get through."

She scoffed. "His intent seemed pretty ill to me."

"I bet it wasn't when he snuck in." I gulped my coffee, thankful I couldn't burn because it was way too hot to drink. "Everything changed when he found Chaos in my bed."

"We should capture him. Torture him for information," he said.

I shook my head and laughed. That Chaos. He was full of ideas.

"All right. Let's do it." Ember grabbed her phone.

"I'm glad you agree." Chaos chugged his drink and went to the kitchen for a refill.

"I was agreeing with Ash," Ember shouted behind him and

dialed Shade's number. "Straight to voicemail. I'll text him that we need to talk."

I leaned my head back and closed my eyes. Seriously, could this situation get any worse? Never mind. I already knew the answer to that, and it was a resounding *yes*.

"Are you okay?" Chaos put his mug on an end table and sat next to me, lifting one of my legs, and then the other, running his hands over my skin. "You recovered quickly after the antidote, but your adrenaline may be waning, revealing more injuries."

"I'm okay." As good as his hot palms felt rubbing on my legs, I doubted my sister appreciated the show. I tugged his hands from my calf and held them both in his lap. "Ember, we—"

She held up a hand. "Your love life is the least of our worries right now." She focused on Chaos. "How were you able to punch Shade when you said you couldn't break a promise to Ash? You promised her you wouldn't hurt him."

"My vow to protect her surpasses any other promise. You both were in danger. I defended you."

I squeezed his hand. "He saved our lives."

She arched a brow. "I'm aware. Shade isn't replying."

"Would you? He tried to kill us." I grabbed my mug and finished my coffee. "We'll have to go to him."

Ember worried her lip between her teeth. "I can't wrap my mind around that. Shade is a grade-one, narcissistic asshole, but he's not a killer." Her gaze flicked to mine. "Is he?"

I took a deep breath, my cheeks puffing as I blew it out. "I didn't think he was."

"Perhaps the nerve spell was meant for me," Chaos said. "My presence in your coven threatened him."

Ember shook her head. "I still don't think he'd resort to murder."

"Maybe he thought he was protecting us." I collected our empty mugs and stood. "Sitting here speculating won't solve our problems. Let's get dressed and go find him."

She looked at her phone and frowned. "You're right. I'll hit the shower and meet you in the kitchen to restock the travel kit."

I set the mugs in the sink. "Sounds like a plan."

Ember disappeared down the hall, and Chaos joined me in the kitchen. "I will wash these. You go shower."

"What's this? No offers to wash my back?" I playfully poked his stomach. I might as well have poked granite.

He brushed my hair away from my forehead, tucking it behind my ear. "Nothing would please me more, but if I joined you in the shower, we would be there all day."

"That sounds like paradise."

"Indeed." He stroked his thumb down my cheek before turning to the dishes. "Go. I will be here."

I wiped the dreamy look from my eyes and strode to my bedroom. Now was not the time to go cuckoo for Chaos, but damn it felt nice to be appreciated. I twisted the knob and pushed the door open, hanging back in the hall. My magic-revealing spell showed Shade's hex had dissipated. Only a few sparkles clung to the floor where he'd dropped the bottle, so I went in, careful to avoid that spot.

I gathered Chaos's clothes and set them on the quick wash

cycle before hopping in the shower. It was done by the time I got out, so I wrapped a towel around myself and padded down the hall to the laundry room to transfer them to the dryer.

"Mmm…" Chaos stood by my bedroom, enough heat in his eyes to melt my panties right off if I were wearing any. "I suggest you get dressed before my instincts take over and I ravish you."

My, oh my, wouldn't that be fun?

"Oh, for Hecate's sake." Ember stepped into the hall, drying her hair with a towel. "We've got shit to do."

I couldn't help but grin as I tiptoed past him into my room. "Give me three minutes." I closed the door and threw on a pair of black leggings, a long-sleeved shirt, and my favorite corset. Reaching behind my back, I clutched the ribbons and pulled, tightening it around my waist before tying them.

When I opened the door, I found Chaos waiting patiently, my sister glaring at him. "Come on." I motioned for him to enter before smirking at Ember. "We've got shit to do."

My demon strode inside, dropping his clothes to the floor on his way to the bathroom. Yes, I stood there watching him strip. Hey, if he didn't want me to, he'd have closed the door. Good thing I had enough self-control for us both because the temptation to follow his tight, round butt into the shower had me licking my lips.

I scooped up this set of clothes and threw them into the washer. "Why didn't you buy him more clothes?"

Ember crossed her arms. "I didn't expect things to be this complicated."

"Neither did I." After putting on my boots, I joined her in

the kitchen to restock the spell kit. I mixed a binding potion and bottled it, pursing my lips. "I expect he'll be belligerent and need to be held down to reason with him. I don't think this is the spell for that. He won't remember anything."

"Pack it anyway, just in case." Ember refilled the bottle of peppermint oil. "Maybe your new molasses spell?"

"I haven't tested it on anyone's memory, but it's worth a shot." I mixed the ingredients and bottled them.

"I assume, since we have shit to do, you don't plan on me remaining naked?"

I snapped my head up to find Chaos standing across the counter, wearing nothing but a towel around his waist. I tried not to react. I really did, but a whimper emanated from my throat against my will.

Ember sighed hard, and I cleared my throat. "Check the dryer. Actually, here. I need to move the wet ones over."

I tried not to look at his abs as I passed him and headed to the laundry room. The dryer had a minute left on the timer, but that was just cool-down time, so it would be fine. I couldn't handle a minute more of his bare pecs. I grabbed the clothes and shoved them at his chest.

He chuckled. "Thank you."

"My pleasure." Why the hell was my throat so dry? "Shoo. Get dressed in my room." I motioned for him to go away because if he dropped his towel right there, I might drop to my knees. *Woof.*

Thankfully, he obeyed. I moved the rest of his clothes to the dryer and returned to the kitchen and Ember's judging gaze.

"What?" I snapped.

"Nothing." She handed me the restocked bag, and I slung it over my shoulder. "Still no response from Shade."

"Still didn't expect one." I grabbed three energy bars from the pantry and handed one to her. "One of these days, we'll have time for real meals again."

"I sure hope so." She broke it in half and shoved a piece into her mouth.

I tossed one to Chaos when he joined us in the kitchen.

He curled his lip. "What is this?"

"Breakfast, and probably lunch. Eat up." I tossed my wrapper into the trash and took a bite.

"Your means of sustenance are lacking." He shoved the entire bar into his mouth.

"Let's go." Ember grabbed the keys from the hook, and we headed downstairs and out the back door.

Chaos took the back seat, and I climbed in front next to my sister. "Where do you think he is?" I asked.

"I figure we'll try his house first. If he's not there or at Miles's place, we'll have to scry for him. I'd rather not waste our vim on that, but if we have to, we will."

I nodded, and she backed out of the alley before heading to our first destination. We stopped on the curb across the street and eyed Shade's house, a squat one-story painted white with green shutters. His black Mustang sat in the driveway, and his porch light was still on from the night before.

Ember turned in her seat and made a stop motion with her hand to Chaos. "Wait here."

"Not happening." He reached for the door handle.

"She's right." I touched his shoulder. "He likely won't

answer if you're standing on the porch. Let us try to smooth things over before we bring you in."

He grunted. "Either your memory is short, or you have no regard for your own lives. He nearly killed you both."

I winced. He had a point as well. "Okay but hang back on the sidewalk until we calm him down."

"That request, I can accommodate."

Ember and I hurried up the front walk while Chaos stayed back like a good demon. She rang the doorbell and knocked, but, of course, Shade didn't answer.

"Open up," she shouted. "Your car is in the driveway; we know you're home."

"Perhaps he walked somewhere," Chaos said, which earned him a "shhhh" from my sister.

She knocked again and peered through the window. "I don't see him. Maybe he's in the back." She started around the side of the house.

"Wait." I took a deep breath, centering myself. "I know we're saving our vim, but if I have this inborn power of location, it won't tax me."

Ember nodded. "Do it."

Closing my eyes, I opened my senses and searched the vibrations in the air for Shade. I felt Chaos easily. Ember as well, but when I sent my magic outward, I felt nothing. "He's not here."

"Are you sure?" She climbed on a wooden box to peer through a side window.

I laughed dryly. "You've spent the past weeks convincing me I have this power, and now you're questioning it?"

"If Ash doesn't sense him, he isn't here." Chaos joined me on the porch and took my hand. "If you want to scry for him, I can share my magic with you. Use my power so you don't deplete yours."

"That's a big, fat nope. Let's go." Ember paced across the street and stopped outside the van. "Now."

"We're wasting time," he said under his breath.

"Humor her." I descended the steps, and we climbed into our respective seats.

Ember glared at me as I buckled my seatbelt, giving me my eight-hundredth warning look since Chaos came into our lives. I ignored her, and she drove to Miles's house in silence.

"Same plan." She slid out of the driver's seat and gently shut the door.

I turned to get out, but Chaos touched my shoulder. "Is he here?"

"I don't know. I think I need to be closer." I joined Ember on the porch as she knocked.

Once again, I centered myself and focused my energy on finding Shade. Again, I sensed nothing. Not even Miles. "He's not here either. It's time to scry."

She sighed heavily. "If he tries to pull anything, we might be too weak to…"

"Chaos can help." I moved down the walk toward him.

"I'm not using demon magic, and I'm sure as hell not letting my baby sister do it." She brushed past us, the stubborn set of her jaw telling me she'd die on this hill. "You had him in your head long enough. Now you've had him in your coochie too, and I won't risk you being any more corrupted. We'll do it ourselves."

"I've never met a more stubborn witch," Chaos grumbled.

"Neither have I." I pulled a bottle of water and a copper bowl from my bag. "Let's do it here. No need to go all the way home when Miles's backyard is free."

We walked up the driveway and through the chain link fence. A wrought iron table with two chairs stood beneath a maple tree. That was as good a place as any. Dry leaves crunched beneath my boots as I paced toward it, and I set the bowl in the middle of the table before filling it with water.

"Chaos, will you be our lookout?" I shoved the empty bottle into my bag. "We'll be in a trance while we search."

"Which is why we always do this inside." Ember sat in the chair across from me. "This is dangerous."

"Compared to everything we've been through the past few weeks?" I held out my hands, and she placed hers in mine. "Chaos has our backs."

"Indeed, I do. No harm will come to either of you."

She arched a brow. "I've heard that one before."

Chaos clamped his mouth shut, his nostrils flaring.

"Ready?" she asked, and I nodded. "Hecate, goddess of magic, we call on you to protect and guide us."

I stared at the bowl of water, letting my gaze relax and blur. "We search for Shade, in dire need. Take us to him, hear our plea."

"As we will it, so mote it be," we said in unison.

The feel of Ember's warm hands in mine and the coolness of the metal seeping through my sleeves ceased. I floated in nothingness, the water turning black beneath my gaze. The wind no longer rustled in the trees, my magic attuning to nothing but Shade's energy.

Blackness surrounded him like a void. I searched with all my senses, feeling the vibrations, listening for clues to his location. He gave none.

"What the hell?" Ember's voice registered in my mind. *"Can you see where he is?"*

"It's like a vacuum around him. I can't sense anything." I tried again, sending out my magic, draining my vim even more.

"This isn't working. We need to pull out before we exhaust ourselves."

A hand gripped my shoulder, and a low vibration flowed through me, filling me with Chaos's essence. A surge of energy heightened my senses, and an image came into crisp focus in my mind.

Ember broke our connection. I gasped, my physical senses returning in a rush as the scrying session ended. Chaos's hand still rested on my shoulder.

Ember shot to her feet. "What. The. Actual. Eff?"

I stood and stumbled. Chaos caught me by the arm.

"That's why we couldn't see anything." Ember marched toward him. "You messed with our magic. You stopped us from seeing Shade."

I stepped between them. "He's at home."

Ember flinched like I'd slapped her. "What?"

"When Chaos touched me, I saw him. He's been at home the whole time." I dumped the water from the bowl and returned it to my bag. "He's shrouded in dark magic, hiding.

That's why I couldn't find him. Why *we* couldn't find him without Chaos. He helped us cut through the spell."

Ember shook her head. "Shade doesn't practice dark magic."

"We didn't know Ginger did either."

Chaos moved next to me, a sinister grin on his lips. "Now can I kill him?"

CHAPTER 21
ASH

The pit of my stomach churned like an acid pool in the deepest recesses of the Underworld. My hands trembled, the blast of demon magic Chaos had sent me fighting with fatigue for control. My nerves felt raw, exposed, and I closed my eyes in meditation, hoping to revive my vim enough for whatever was about to take place.

Ember sat in the back seat, also meditating, while Chaos drove to Shade's home. The van stopped, and I blinked open my eyes, squinting against the bright morning light.

"That wasn't nearly enough time to recover," Ember said, her eyes still closed.

"Should we go home first so I can work sigil magic? I can give you energy and stamina."

She looked at me. "And then you'll sleep the rest of the day. No way. You used just as much vim as I did scrying. I'll call Chrys for backup."

"No." I twisted in my seat to face her. "We need to squash this problem like the cockroach it is and move forward with our plan. Chrys still trusts us. Don't give her a reason not to."

"Miles is probably in there." She laughed, unbelieving. "Why was he willing to take the fall for Shade's involvement in the dark arts?"

"Shade brainwashed him. They were spending more and more time together. I wouldn't be surprised if he'd brainwashed Ginger too."

"If he can cast a shroud strong enough to keep two Holland witches from finding him, I'm not sure we'll have the strength to contain him." She opened the hatch beneath her feet.

"You're forgetting our secret weapon doesn't have to stay secret anymore. Chaos won't have to hold back."

She gave him a pointed look. "Nobody dies."

He eyed her through the rearview mirror. "If your lives are threatened—"

I rested my hand on his thigh. "Then you'll do your best to stop the threat without killing anyone."

He grunted. "I will do my best."

Ember pursed her lips, unconvinced.

"That's the best we're going to get from him," I said. "And we can't do this without him."

"We don't even know exactly what we're doing." She drew out her sword. "We don't know if he's involved with Boston, if he has Mayhem's skull, if he killed Ginger..."

"It's most likely all of the above." I hung my satchel across my body.

"But why?" She took four daggers from the hidey-hole and

strapped them to her legs. "He was born into our coven. He's an elite fighter. He holds the highest rank someone not of our bloodline can hold."

"Ego," Chaos said. "He wants more power, and dark magic can give it to him."

Her jaw clamped shut with an audible click. She inhaled and blew out a hard breath. "All right. We go in and contain him. I want him alive."

"If he knows where my brother is, so do I." Chaos exited the van, and Ember and I followed.

We didn't say a word as we crossed the street. Shade's car still sat in the driveway; his porch light still burned. No signs of dark magic pricked at my skin as we approached the house. The morning felt peaceful, serene.

"His power is strong to mask this well," Chaos said.

"No kidding." Ember reached for the knob, but I caught her arm.

"Always check for magic first," I said. When she stepped back, I cast my spell, "Confess, expose, my magic sleuth. I call on you to reveal your truth."

Golden sparkles gathered in the air, turning the world around us grayscale, revealing the real condition of the scene. He'd used shadow magic to cloak his home, making it appear normal, but that wouldn't have kept us from finding him when we scried.

"The door is open." Ember pushed it with her boot, jerking her foot back as soon as it creaked. No hexes or boobytraps blocked the entrance. "Whatever he's doing in there, he didn't expect to be found."

"Or he set a trap." Chaos's brows slammed down over his eyes. "This doesn't feel right."

"Sure doesn't." Ember started inside, but Chaos brushed past her, leading the way.

"Whatever happened to ladies first?" she grumbled and went in after him.

"I guess we're throwing caution to the wind yet again." I took up the rear, leaving the door open for a quick escape if things went any further south than they already were.

Eerie silence engulfed us as we made our way through the foyer. A small study stood empty to the right, and framed sigils lined the wall to our left. The entry hall spilled out into an unoccupied living room. A bookshelf filled with crystals, powdered charcoal, and other granules he used for shadow magic stood against one wall, and a black faux leather sofa sat beneath the window. Morning sunlight seeping in through the closed blinds provided the only illumination in the room.

"Shade, are you here?" Ember called out as if she had never seen a horror movie in her entire life.

"Of course he is," I whisper-shouted and grabbed her arm. My pulse thrummed, and enough adrenaline rushed through my veins to make me forget all about my depleted vim. I flipped on the light switch because I had seen just about every horror movie ever made.

"Where?" Chaos stopped. Ember ran into his back, and I smacked into hers.

"Don't do that." She rubbed her shoulder, and they both turned toward me.

I opened my senses and searched the space, but once

again, I felt nothing. "He's still cloaked." I tried to sense the powdered charcoal to see if my newfound power even worked in this house. It didn't. "He's blocking everything."

Footsteps sounded from the bedroom, and Shade appeared in the doorway, wearing the same black spandex and boots he'd worn we he infiltrated our house. His pupils had bled outward until the gray of his irises was merely a thin ring around them, and his brows smushed together in concentration.

He spread his arms dramatically. "Welcome, infidels."

Seriously? Infidels?

Ember scoffed. "You're the one who's turned his back on his faith. How long have you been practicing dark magic?"

He lifted a finger to point at Chaos, really laying on the theatrics. "That demon belongs to me."

"The hell he does." I reached into my bag, wrapping my fingers around the freezing spell.

Chaos stiffened. I could almost feel the hellfire simmering beneath his skin, so I moved next to him, touching my arm to his.

"He has Mayhem," he tried to whisper, but everyone heard. "I can feel it."

"I have him." Shade lifted his chin and sneered. "I'm going to free him, and he's going to destroy the rest of the Holland bloodline."

Ember tightened her grip on her sword. "The rest of the bloodline is standing in front of you. Why don't you end us yourself?"

Chaos puffed out his chest. "You'll have to get through me before you lay a finger on these witches."

What was it with these two? They literally asked him to fight when we needed information first.

"Did you kill Ginger? Are you working with Boston?" I should have mixed up a truth serum to blast him with. That would have moved things along much more quickly.

"Ginger got what she deserved. She knew too much." He took two steps into the living room.

I, the rational one, took two steps back. Ember and Chaos moved toward him.

Shade chanted something in Latin and held his hands together, a black ball of smoke gathering between them. I'd never seen him work that kind of magic before, but I didn't have time to contemplate it. Before we could react, he hurled the smoke bomb toward us.

It hit my shoulder, knocking me back before it exploded, filling the room with darkness. Blinded, I focused on my sense of hearing. Hurried footsteps rushed toward us. My heart shot upward into my throat. The air around me shifted.

A smack like a fist hitting a jaw sounded. A grunt. Someone hit the ground.

The blackness rolled back into Shade. He sat on the floor, clutching his jaw. "Don't make this harder than it has to be." He shot to his feet and did a spinning jump kick, Jean-Claude Van Damme style, his boot colliding with Chaos's head.

Whoa. I'd never seen him do that before either.

He landed and threw a punch, hitting me in the stomach. The steel bones in my corset absorbed the brunt of it, but the pain was enough to make me double over. Where the hell was he getting this strength?

My demon growled. Goosebumps pricked his skin, and his fingers lengthened, turning to talons.

"Standing tall or on your knees, in the name of the goddess, I force you to freeze," I whispered and threw the powder at Shade.

He held out his hand, said something else in Latin, and the granules blew backward, into me.

"What the...?" My muscles tensed. I couldn't move. If I didn't get out of this soon, I'd have no memory of what happened next.

Shade whirled toward Ember, an energy ball forming between his hands. She spun and struck out, smacking him in the head with the flat side of her sword. He went down. Chaos's hands turned full demon, and horns protruded through his hair.

My vision blurred. "Ember..." I ground out.

"I got you, sis." She grabbed my shoulder and recited the undoing spell, releasing me.

Shade scrambled to his feet and lunged at Chaos, wrapping his arms around him as if trying to tackle him. Chaos stumbled, but he didn't go down.

"His strength is unnatural." My demon's voice grew deeper, more gravelly. He grabbed Shade by the scruff of his neck and jerked him back. Seams ripped. Fabric tore. Chaos morphed into his demon form.

Shade kicked, clawing at Chaos's talons, but he'd encircled

his entire neck. He started to speak in Latin. Chaos tightened his grip, choking off the hex.

Shade's arms flailed, and my gaze locked on the inside of his forearm. A sigil unlike any I had ever drawn glowed deep purple on his skin. His lips turned blue. His arms and legs stilled.

"Stop." I clutched my demon's shoulder. "Put him down. He's being controlled."

Chaos's fiery gaze snapped toward me, malice filling his eyes. His expression softened, and he released his hold. Shade fell to the floor with a *thump*.

Ember dropped to her knees beside him and rested her ear on his chest. "He's not breathing."

"Good," Chaos said.

"Not good. Look." I kneeled and lifted his arm, showing him the sigil. "I recognize this part of the mark. It's used in exorcisms to gain control of the demon."

Ember bent over and blew a breath into Shade's mouth. His chest rose and fell. She tried again. And a third time. He coughed, rolling to his side and gasping before sitting up abruptly. His pupils shrank to their normal size for less than a second, long enough for me to see the alarm in his eyes before they bled outward again.

He screamed and launched at me, clutching my shoulders and knocking me onto my back. My breath came out in a woosh. His hands wrapped around my neck.

Chaos yanked him off me and hurled him into the wall. The sheetrock cracked, and he slid to the floor before jumping up again and speaking Latin.

"Stay down, Shade." Ember smacked him in the back with her sword and brought the pommel down onto his head, knocking him unconscious. She caught him as he fell and dragged him to the couch.

"He will pay for the pain he caused you." Chaos threw his arms out to his sides, and fire erupted on his skin.

"No! Bad demon." I stepped in front of him, pressing my palms against his chest. If I wasn't a fire witch, my hands would have melted. His skin was hot as magma. "We need him alive."

Ember turned over Shade's arm. "Can you neutralize this?"

"No. It'll have to wear off on its own." I gave Chaos a look, telling him to calm the eff down. He took a deep breath and blew it out hard, but he relaxed. A little.

"I thought Shade was a better fighter." We spun around to find Miles emerging from the bedroom.

He wore a black cloak with the hood pulled down low, casting his face in shadow. Strolling into the room like he owned the space, he made a *tsk* sound and stopped in front of Chaos. "If you want to see your brother again, you'll kill these witches and come with me."

My mouth hung open, so I snapped it shut. Miles was the villain in this horror movie? Sweet, quiet, helpful Miles?

"Where is Mayhem?" Chaos growled and clutched his robe, twisting it in his hand.

Miles let out a sinister laugh and flung his arm toward me. A blast of energy knocked me backward into the bookcase, collapsing the shelves. Powdered charcoal rained onto my head, billowing around me in a black cloud.

Shade's eyes fluttered open, and he wheezed out an incantation in English. His magic struck me a half-second before another blast from Miles would have rendered me unconscious. The charcoal activated, absorbing the magic and shielding me from the hit.

His eyes rolled back, and he passed out again.

Chaos roared and set Miles's robe ablaze. Hellfire rolled over him. He screamed and flailed, his robe disintegrating in the flames, revealing fireproof clothing beneath. His bare arms blistered, but I caught a glimpse of purple glow before the skin deformed.

"Stop!" I commanded.

Chaos obeyed instantly, extinguishing the flames but keeping a tight grip on his fireproof shirt. "Where. Is. Mayhem?"

"You'll never know if you kill me," he ground out.

I rummaged in my bag for the magical burn salve I always carried. Yes, I had accidentally burned more than cemeteries in my twenty-four years. It was why I rarely used my fire. I slathered the salve onto his forearm while his feet still dangled in the air, and sure enough, the same sigil as the one on Shade marred his skin.

"What the hell?" Ember gripped her sword in both hands and peered into the bedroom. "Who else is in there?"

Miles spoke in Latin, a black ball forming between his hands. Chaos gripped his throat, but he flung out the energy, knocking all three of us from our feet. We careened back in different directions, smacking the walls in unison. My head hit the shelf, making my vision swim.

"The mark is their connection." Chaos hurled a fireball at Miles, but his clothes absorbed the flames. "He is the one controlling Shade."

Ember screamed like a Valkyrie and plowed toward him. He dropped to the ground and kicked out, knocking her off her feet and landing a punch to her back. She groaned.

I played dead while Chaos went still, using his silent power to scramble Miles's mind.

Miles tilted his head, another sinister laugh emanating from his throat. "You don't think I prepared for your magic, demon?"

I whispered the molasses spell and hurled a handful of dust at him. His eyes widened, his enlarged pupils shrinking to their normal size as his movement slowed to a sloth's pace.

"I guess you didn't plan for mine." I stood and brushed the charcoal from my hair. My entire body ached. Stabbing pains pulsed in my back, arms, and neck, and whatever vim I had left retreated deep inside my being. I wasn't just spent. I was in magical debt.

Ember moaned and rolled to her side before pushing up to sit, clutching her head.

A growl rumbled in Chaos's chest. "The moment we find Mayhem, this witch is dead."

"We need to tie him up." I unplugged an extension cord that lined a wall and handed it to Ember. "That spell won't last long. I barely had the vim to cast it."

She stood and shoved him into a chair before wrapping the cord around his wrists and securing him to the seat. I rummaged through the kitchen drawers and found a roll of duct tape. I wrapped it around his chest and the back of the chair and then secured his ankles together.

He tried to say another spell, but when the first word of Latin crossed his lips, I slapped a piece of tape over his mouth.

Chaos stomped into the bedroom, ducking in the doorway so his horns wouldn't hit the jamb. A moment later, he stormed back out. "Where is Mayhem?"

Miles shook his head as quickly as my spell would allow, panic filling his eyes as he cut his gaze to the open front door. The sun shone into the dark hall, blinding us to the outside.

The house rumbled. The floor shook beneath our feet, the wood cracking and splitting with the violent tremors. Pictures fell from the walls, their glass frames shattering.

I looked at Ember. "Earthquake?"

Massive roots shot up from beneath the foundation, spiraling up Chaos's legs, wrapping around his body like a boa constrictor.

Boots thudded in the entry, and a silhouetted figure came into view. "I should've known not to send men to do a woman's job."

CHAPTER 22
ASH

"Chrys?" Ember's voice sounded incredulous, as I'm sure mine would have if I could make words. No way was Chrys the mastermind behind all this. She was our friend, Cinder's *best* friend, the nicest witch in the coven. She came to our family dinners when my family was still whole, for goddess' sake. She was...

The one who "found" Ginger dead. The one who *said* she'd set up the wards on our house, yet Shade got in with ill intent. Calliope on a cracker. How could we be so blind?

She strolled into the living room, twirling a garden tool in her right hand. "You didn't think these guys were strong enough to pull this off, did you?" She shook her head in disappointment. "I should have kept Ginger alive and killed him instead." She nodded at Miles.

Chaos erupted into flames, and I half-expected Chrys to go up too. I should've known better. She simply laughed, tossing her head back like he was the funniest little beastie she'd ever seen.

He drew his fire inward, and the roots holding him weren't charred in the least. "Release me, witch." Disdain dripped from the last word like it had when I'd first summoned him.

"Now, why would I do that, when I finally have you where I want you?" She strolled toward Miles and clicked her tongue. "I'll be taking my power back now, boys."

Holding one hand toward Shade and one toward Miles, she bent her fingers into claws. The guys screamed as the purple sigils ripped from their skin, the magic turning to smoke before rolling into her hands.

Ember sent flames up the length of her sword, but she barely took one step toward Chrys before roots spiraled up her legs and around her body, pinning her arms to her sides. Her sword extinguished and clattered to the floor.

"Why are you doing this?" I asked, scrambling for time. Shade lay on the couch, his eyes closed, but they moved beneath his lids. He was either dreaming or scheming, and I sure as shit hoped it was the latter.

"Please." She rolled her eyes and opened the bag hanging from her shoulder. "Do you expect me to monologue like a movie villain?" She took a skull from inside and ran her hand over the top.

"Mayhem." With a guttural roar, Chaos flexed. He groaned and pushed, his tendons and veins protruding as he tore the vines to shreds and lunged at Chrys. She stepped back and to the left, but Chaos tracked her. His arms swung out, his talons ready to tear through her flesh.

She flicked her wrist and spoke four words in Latin...four words I knew. Chaos slammed into an invisible wall. She'd trapped him in a containment circle.

He roared again and slammed his shoulder into one side and another. "Release me!"

"Here's one for you, Ash. Confess, expose, my magic sleuth. I call on you to reveal your truth." She blew a power onto the ground around him, revealing not only a salt circle with a pentagram and everything else needed to trap a demon, but the cloaking enchantment my dad had used to hide the powerful spell book from me.

"Please, Chrys. We're friends." I inched toward Chaos, my hands raised in surrender. "Whatever you think you need him for, I'm sure we can figure it out."

"Yeah?" She returned the skull to her bag. "The Holland witches are allowed to summon a demon, but no one else is?"

"That was an accident." I swept my foot toward the salt line. Chrys was faster.

With a flick of her wrist, she called on more roots, trapping me like she'd done to my sister. "How did you do it without their sigils?"

"I didn't mean to." The roots tightened, squeezing the air from my lungs. I struggled against the pressure.

"Let us go," Miles said, his voice weak. If we hadn't tied him up so well, he might've been able to help.

Chrys grabbed my arm. Chaos's mark glowed deep red. "This is how. Where did you find his mark?"

I clamped my mouth shut. If she refused to explain herself, so did I.

She moved to Ember and pressed the tip of a spade to her chest. "Tell me where to find the others, or your High Priestess is dead."

"Don't tell her anything." Ember worked her arm downward toward the dagger strapped to her thigh. Half an inch farther and she'd reach it.

Think, Ash. Think. My thoughts were scattered. I couldn't grab onto anything that might help me figure a way out of this. I needed to calm down. To think rationally. To...

"Chaos," I said and cut my gaze to my arm.

Without a word, he sent a pulse of magic through his mark. I welcomed the unnatural calmness, letting it loosen my muscles and clear my thoughts. If only I had another freezing potion in my pocket.

Then again, I'd done that spell so many times in the past few weeks, I might not even need the powder anymore. It was worth a shot. "Standing tall or on your knees..."

"We'll have none of that." Chrys sent a root snaking around my neck and across my mouth. I kept my lips closed tight, but when she snapped her fingers, the root squeezed, forcing itself into my mouth like a gag.

Bitterness flooded my tongue, making me cough.

Chaos slammed his shoulder against the circle over and over, trying to break through. He punched and kicked the invisible wall, but it held strong...stronger than any circle I could have created.

I needed to cast this freezing spell. It was the only way to stop her. I bit down hard on the root, working my jaw from side to side, sawing through it with my teeth, cringing against the sharp, pungent taste.

Chrys moved the tip of her spade to the soft spot beneath Ember's chin. "I know you're the ones who raided Boston's library. You tore the pages from the journal. Where are they?"

Ember spit in her face.

She flicked it off her cheek and took a dagger from Ember's leg harness. "If you had told me, I might've let you live. Now I'll have to tear apart your house to find it."

Chrys cut the satchel from my shoulder and moved into the entry hall. She took two bottles from her own bag and hurled them into the living room. They shattered, and magical fire blazed around us, licking up the walls and setting the curtains alight.

I kept chewing. Almost through...

She tossed my bag into the flames, incinerating it and all the inactivated potions inside it before pointing at Chaos. "I'll come back for you once they're dead."

"We're fireproof, asshole," Ember said.

Chrys laughed. "I know, but the smoke will kill you before the flames ever could. Later, witches." She ran out the door and slammed it behind her.

I bit through the root and spit it out. "Crap! Shade, wake the eff up!"

I struggled against the roots, which was pointless. If Ember couldn't bust out of them, there was no way I could. Smoke billowed on the ceiling, creeping downward at a pace much too fast for my liking.

"Shade!" Ember shouted, but he didn't move.

My nostrils and eyes stung. "Chaos, can you wake him?"

"I can." He stilled, activating his chaos magic.

Shade gasped and shot up, his eyes wild as he spun right and left. "What the...?"

Chaos released him, and he blinked, confusion contorting his features until he took in his surroundings. "Shit!" He untied Miles, ripping through the tape and glaring at me. "What did you do?"

"It wasn't them." Miles picked up Ember's sword and hacked at the roots holding her. "Chrys did this." He freed one of her arms, and she grabbed a dagger to saw at the root holding the other.

"Chrys?" He looked from Miles to me to Chaos, and his eyes widened in disbelief.

"A little help please?" I said.

His brow crumpled, but he grabbed a knife that had fallen from the shelf when I crashed into it and sliced through the roots holding me. My feet hit the ground, and I swiped a boot through the circle, releasing my demon. We ran for the door.

Chaos stopped inside the foyer to morph into his human form, and we darted toward the van, his noodle flopping along the way. Yep, he was naked, and I didn't have the energy to care. Thank the goddess he didn't bust out of his boots too because those were his only pair.

We piled into the van and closed the doors. Shade's house, still cloaked in magic, looked as quiet and peaceful as it had when we arrived. Beneath the shroud, an inferno raged. I sure hoped he had insurance.

Ember floored it, heading home, and I clung to Chaos's

arm, trying to keep my eyes open. I couldn't recall a time when my vim had been depleted this much.

"What the hell is going on?" Shade sat in the front seat, his glaring gaze bouncing between all of us.

"Chrys was controlling you." I lifted my head from Chaos's shoulder. "She killed Ginger."

"Bullshit." He looked at Ember. "Why are you harboring a demon?"

"It's true," Miles said from the way back. "She admitted it. She tried to kill us all."

"I can't..." Shade shook his head.

"Neither could we," Ember said, "yet here we are."

She parked in the alley behind our house. The back door stood ajar. We crept inside, staying close to the walls in case she hurled another potion at us. My library had been torn apart. All the contents from my desk lay strewn about the floor. She'd emptied the drawers, turning them upside down.

Ember kicked things out of the way so she could pace. "Where was the sigil page?"

I kneeled and turned one of the drawers upright. "In my bag, which she threw into the fire."

"Okay. We can work with that." She hauled me to my feet.

My studio and the shop in front lay in the same disarray as the library. Upstairs, she'd emptied our herb cabinet and taken every spell-making supply we owned. She'd dumped our drawers, turned furniture on its sides.

Chaos went to the laundry room for his clothes, and the rest of us gathered in the living room.

Shade raked a hand through his hair. "I need to know what's going on. Why are you harboring a demon?"

Chaos stepped into the room and stood next to me. "Because I'm the only one who can break the curse."

I sighed and returned the cushions to the sofa. "Sit down, guys. We've got some explaining to do."

"Oh no." Ember grabbed my arm. "Where's Patrice?"

CLAIMING CHAOS

FIRE WITCHES OF SALEM
BOOK THREE

CARRIE PULKINEN

CHAPTER 1

ASH

"Poor Patrice." My heart hammered in my chest as we crept toward her house. Chrys didn't bother with shadow spells or cloaking for whatever she'd done inside, and the icky, sticky dark magic funk bled out into the yard, making my stomach lurch.

A knee-high leaf pile stood to the right of the walk, a discarded rake lying next to it. The wind had blown through the mound, scattering half the leaves she'd gathered across the yard. One crunched beneath my foot as I stopped at the bottom of the porch steps.

Yep, I had taken point on this endeavor, which was *so* not me. But I could reveal her spells without a potion, so there I was, leading the way into who knew what madness. I still couldn't wrap my mind around Chrys being involved in this ordeal...especially not her being a murderer. She was Cinder's best friend, for Hecate's sake.

Chaos stood behind me, so close I could feel the heat radiating from his skin. Ember positioned herself behind him, with Miles and Shade taking up the rear. I cast my spell, sending magic onto the house, and golden sparkles gathered around the door and windows.

"Of course there's a ward." Ember bounded up the steps ahead of me and examined the magic. "Have you seen anything like this before?"

I joined her on the porch. "See how the energy moves in waves, rather than shimmering? She cast it with a lower vibration than a light witch would dare. It reminds me of the electrification spell BMS has on their library."

"Hold on." Shade brushed past Miles, giving Chaos a wide berth before squeezing his way onto the small porch with us. "*You're* the ones who trashed their library? Ginger died because of you."

The back of my throat heated as I blew out an irritated breath. We should have left him at home. "Boston didn't kill Ginger. Chrys did."

"We'll explain everything after we find Patrice. She's our first priority." Ember picked up a pinecone and tossed it at the ward. The magic fried it like an electric bug zapper, and it exploded into tiny pieces. "I hope you have black tourmaline and horehound in your bag."

I clenched my teeth. Chrys had burned up my favorite satchel, so I'd had to stock one of my old ones that wasn't nearly as comfortable on my shoulder. "I don't, and I doubt it would work. This spell is different. I'm sure she wouldn't have cast one she knows we can get through. We need to unravel it."

I followed the trail of magic down the jamb and across the porch where it penetrated the ground.

"She's an earth witch," Chaos said, following my gaze. "Her magic originates in the land."

I hopped off the porch and brushed the leaves aside. "The ward gets its power from the earth here. It's not very old. Maybe we can dig it up. Neutralize the source."

Ember paced around the house, and the guys joined me on the ground. Wavering energy disappeared into the grass, but I had no idea how deep it went. Honestly, I'd had no idea how powerful Chrys was until today. She'd hid her magic well.

"I'm sure I can make it through." Chaos eyed the front door. "We survived the electrification ward."

"Did you not see what happened to that pinecone?" I shook my head. "No way."

"Let him," Shade said. "If he wants to blow himself to bits, I say go for it. Let him get vanquished."

I crossed my arms. "Except if he gets vanquished, I die. This plot is deeper than you can imagine, so please just play along for now."

"Got shovels." Ember returned to the front yard, her arms full of gardening tools. "Patrice has a shed in the back." She dropped them at our feet.

Chaos picked up the biggest shovel and started to dig right over the magic.

"Wait." I grabbed his arm. "Dig around it, not on it. If you hit the spell, it will fight back."

He moved the tip of the shovel and planted it into the dirt.

Five minutes later, we could see where the magic rooted, three feet deep. Gotta love demon strength.

"And?" Ember kneeled, cocking her head at the source. "Can we unplug it?"

"I think I can neutralize it." I set my satchel on the porch and rummaged through it for the ingredients. Angelica, basil, garlic, and a drop of myrrh oil would do the trick. I crushed and mixed the herbs before adding the myrrh. The potion popped and sizzled, turning to flakes like crushed red pepper.

I poured it into my hand. "We're all spent after what happened this morning, and who knows what we'll encounter inside."

"You may use my energy." Chaos held out his hand.

I looked from Shade to Miles. "This isn't the time to freak out over a demon. Believe me, he's the least of your worries right now." I slipped my hand into his.

Shade stiffened, his lids flying high, his brow shooting toward his hairline. "You can't."

Ember motioned for him and Miles to move back. "I don't like it any more than you, but she's right. We need to save our vim, so we're going to let her channel Chaos. She's done it before."

Shade's head moved back and forth so quickly, he probably didn't realize he was shaking it.

Miles nodded. "Do it. We can't let another witch die."

Chaos squeezed my hand, and a surge of demon power flowed into me, setting my nerves ablaze. I focused his chaos magic, channeling it into my being and casting my spell.

"Uproot and end this magic source. Allow us to tread our intended course."

I dropped the flakes into the hole, and a pulse of energy shot out, whipping my hair back and stinging my cheeks. A high-pitched ring filled my head as ice flushed my veins. I rubbed my watery eyes, trying desperately to bring my vision back into focus.

"What just happened?" Ember asked.

I blinked, looking toward the house. The ward was gone. "I think that was an alarm."

"Indeed." Chaos ascended the porch steps. "She knows we're here, so we must move quickly." He disappeared into the house.

"Let's find Patrice and get out of here before she comes back." Ember followed him inside.

I slung my satchel over my shoulder and swallowed the dryness from my mouth before whispering a prayer to the goddess that we'd find our healer alive. Opening my senses, I inched forward, searching, feeling, trying to predict what might lie ahead. A current of dark magic ran over the remnants of Patrice's light, creating a choking sensation in my throat.

"It's thick in here," Miles said as he and Shade crept in behind me. "Fresh."

The foyer opened into a dining and living area. A wooden table with six chairs occupied the space to our left, and a blue sofa with white accent chairs stood to the right. Beyond that lay a kitchen and a short hallway with three doors.

Chaos came out from one of the rooms. "She isn't on this floor."

Ember appeared from another. "She's got a basement, right? I saw an entrance outside."

"Is she here?" Chaos asked me.

"We won't know unless we look." Shade went into the third room and returned to the hall. "Doesn't look like she has basement access from the inside."

"Is she here?" Chaos asked again.

I inhaled deeply and centered myself before searching the atmosphere for Patrice's energy. A tingle in my abdomen shot up to my head, pulling me into the kitchen.

"She's in the basement." A door stood closed between the fridge and the sink, and I opened it to find the pantry. Chaos stepped in behind me, and Ember wiggled past him.

"Is there a hatch in the floor?" She pulled a cord, turning on an overhead light, and stomped on the wood. "It sounds solid."

"It's here." I tugged one of the shelves, and the whole unit swung toward me, revealing a set of stairs. I cast my revealing spell. No magic blocked our descent, so I motioned for Chaos and Ember to take the lead.

"If you knew where the basement door was, why didn't you say so?" Shade came down behind me, with Miles on his heels.

"I didn't know."

Patrice's basement looked exactly how I imagined a healer's would. To the right lay the mundane: a washer-dryer, water heater, and furnace taking up most of the space. To the left stood a massive shelving unit filled with every kind of herb and oil imaginable. Mixing bowls, jars, and instruments lay atop a nine-foot, wooden table in front of the shelf, and more bundles of herbs and flowers hung from the ceiling, drying.

I walked past her workspace to the back of the room. From the entry, the walls appeared to meet, ending the basement, but as I got closer, I found an opening around the corner that led into an unfinished space with a dirt floor. Whether it was a random optical illusion or built this way on purpose, I couldn't be sure, but it didn't matter. I'd found Patrice.

"Oh, my goddess." Ember rushed in and dropped to her knees before I could check for protection spells. Thankfully, nothing exploded when she touched our healer's forehead.

Patrice lay on her back in the dirt, a mess of roots criss-crossing over her body, pinning her down. Thick shoots covered her legs, stomach, and chest, while smaller sprouts crawled across the rest of her, creating a web around her that almost looked like a cocoon.

Ember grabbed a root in one hand, a dagger in the other. "Help me get her out."

"Wait." I paced toward my sister and clutched her shoulder. "Look." I gestured to webs pulsing softly against her skin. "If the roots are drawing out her energy, and we start hacking away at this setup, we could kill her."

Miles hung back in the doorway. "Is she…" He cleared his throat. "Is she alive?"

"I hope so." I kneeled next to Ember and studied our friend. She was a natural redhead and always pale, but her complexion had taken on a milky, ashy tone. Patrice lay utterly still, so I bent down, aligning my eyes with her chest. It rose and fell infinitesimally, nearly impossible to detect.

"I think she's breathing. You check." I moved so Ember could look.

"Yeah. It's shallow, but she's alive." She stood and dusted off her knees. "Anybody know another earth witch we could call for help unraveling this spell?"

"True elemental witches are rare," Chaos said. "Even more rare are those who don't run their own covens."

"Like Chrys." I walked around Patrice, following the patterns of the roots. There were too many of them for my uprooting spell to work, even with chaos magic giving me a boost. "She wants control of Salem."

"Elementals aren't the be-all, end-all." Shade squatted by Patrice and examined her condition. "This web isn't drawing nutrients from her. It's putting magic into her."

"How can you tell?" Ember bent down beside him.

He pointed. "Look at the direction of the pulses."

"They're moving toward her." She straightened and turned to me. "Chrys is using them to sedate her."

"She wants her alive," I said.

"And if the roots aren't drawing from her, ripping them apart won't kill her." She reached behind her back and unsheathed her sword.

I took a step backward. "Hack away."

With both hands, Ember raised the sword above her head and swung it down onto the biggest root, just above where it met the ground. The blade sliced halfway through, so she tried again, severing it with the second blow.

Miles grabbed the loose root and pulled, the webs dissolving as he yanked it away from Patrice's body. The ground shuddered, and the root Ember had cut shimmered, sprouting three tendrils where there used to be one. They snaked their way toward Patrice, and Miles sliced one with his dagger. Three more shoots grew from the cut.

"These roots behave like a hydra," Chaos said. "Cutting them will only make your healer's situation worse."

"Burn them," Shade said before cutting his gaze to me. "Ember, not you."

"Oh, that's right." I crossed my arms. "You slept through the whole ordeal. She makes them fireproof."

"We can try." Ember lit her sword ablaze and swung again. "Cauterize, bitch." The root sizzled, and three more grew in its place.

"Perhaps hellfire." Chaos gathered a flame in his hand and shot it at the base of the offending root. Heat blasted against my face, and if I wasn't fireproof, it would've singed my eyebrows. Lucky for Miles and Shade, they stood far enough away to avoid the brunt of it, but they both backpedaled into the wall behind them.

"What the hell?" Shade wiped the sweat from his brow and sneered at the undamaged root. "Are you trying to kill us all?"

"Just you," Chaos said so low only I could hear. "Your adversary is well-prepared against our power. Fire will not work."

"She couldn't have thought of everything." I rummaged through my spell kit, though I couldn't tell you what I was looking for. An idea. An inkling. Anything to get Patrice out of this mess. "My molasses spell got through her defenses. What else might she not expect?"

"Weed killer." Miles paced toward the exit. "The roots are charged with magic, but they're still roots."

"That's genius." Ember followed him out the door. A minute later, they returned with a gallon-sized jug of plant poison.

Miles poured it in a circle around Patrice, focusing on the biggest roots. With the jug empty, we gathered around, willing it to work its mundane magic. The smallest root by her left foot began to shrivel, the webs spinning out from it dissolving, and we held a collective breath. A few more webs retreated, but we'd need twenty gallons of the stuff to pry her loose.

"They're sucking the poison up into the plants above ground." Shade kicked the single shriveled one aside, freeing Patrice's foot. "Even if we had enough poison to kill whatever is making this trap, it would take days."

"Who's got another idea?" Miles asked.

Chaos huffed, and his mouth pinched. "It pains me to say this, but one of you can speed the killing along." He looked at Shade. "Plants require sunlight. Shadow extinguishes light."

"I don't think making it dark is going to kill this thing," Ember said. "Otherwise plants would die every time the sun sets."

Shade arched a brow at Chaos, his expression conspiratorial and not the least bit sour. "Shadow magic can do more than block light and conceal things."

My demon nodded. "It can draw light out, destroying the life it helped sustain."

Shade laughed once, like he couldn't believe what he was

about to say, and he looked at me. "If you can pinpoint which plant she used to create this trap, I can kill it."

"What?" Ember stood next to me and crossed her arms. "Since when?"

"Since Chrys had me try. Come on." He walked out of the room, leaving us standing there, gaping.

Wait. What? Chrys had been coaching Shade on using dangerous magic. Who else had she gotten to?

"Go ahead," Miles said. "I'll stay with Patrice."

"What the hell, Shade?" Ember stomped up the stairs, with Chaos and me on her heels.

We followed him out of the house and into the yard before he explained. "She told me I was helping test her magic. She wanted to find a way to fight off dark magic with her earth powers in case we were ever under attack."

"When really she wanted to learn how to counter you." I rubbed my forehead. Were there any of us she hadn't fooled? "You weren't the least bit suspicious?"

He shrugged. "She never gave me reason to be."

She'd never given any of us reason to believe she was anything but kind, sweet Chrys. "Was she ever successful in countering you?"

"No." He lifted his head in pride. "I'd never dared tap into that side of my magic. Too many shadow witches end up going dark. But she convinced me it was for the greater good, so…" He lifted and dropped his shoulders again as if shrugging off any blame we might want to throw at him.

"Wow." Ember peered up at a tree. "Okay. Let's do it then. Which one is she controlling?"

I focused, centering myself and searching for the offending tree. Only, it wasn't a tree at all. The tug in my mind carried me to a rose bush in the flowerbed. "It's this one."

"This isn't the time for jokes." Shade turned toward the maple. "There's no way that little bush is doing that much damage."

"It's not a joke, Shade." I parked my hands on my hips.

"You didn't even cast your little spell." He wiggled his fingers, mocking me.

Chaos stiffened, curling his hands into fists, and I patted his shoulder.

"She's developed our dad's power." Ember wrapped her arm around me. "She hasn't been wrong yet."

"If you want to kill a perfectly good tree, be my guest." I gestured to the maple. "I hope you'll have enough vim left for the real problem when you're through."

He narrowed his eyes, offense all over his face. Then he softened and walked toward me. "I won't have any vim left at all. It's the most taxing magic I've ever cast. This one, you said?"

I nodded.

"I'll be useless after this. Can I trust you to have my back?" He looked from me to Ember.

"We've got you," she said.

"You can trust us." I stepped back, giving him space to work his spell, lest he accidentally cast his shadow too far and suck the light out of me in the process. Chaos rested his hand on my back, and I leaned into his side, letting his warmth envelop me.

Shade took a few deep breaths, nodding as if either convincing himself he could trust us or that he could accomplish this feat. Maybe it was both.

He lifted his hands in front of his chest, and black smoke billowed between his palms. With his fingers outstretched, he widened his arms, the shadow magic growing between them. He whispered a spell, but I couldn't make out the words. The shadow stretched outward to the rose bush, cascading around it and enclosing it in darkness.

"How did you know he could do this?" Ember whispered.

"All shadow witches have this ability." Chaos slid his hand across my back to rest on my hip. "We're lucky he already knew how to use it."

The tendons in Shade's neck tightened. He groaned and then wheezed.

"Are you okay?" Ember called, and he gave his head a tiny nod.

Two full minutes passed before he let out a hard exhale and doubled over. We rushed to his side, and Ember and I helped him stand as the shadow rolled back into his chest. The rose bush shriveled and crumbled to dust.

We took Shade to the porch and lowered him onto the steps. Sweat dripped from his brow, and he heaved in a ragged breath. "Patrice?"

"I'll go check." I hurried inside and down the stairs into the unfinished part of the basement. The roots around Patrice had crumbled, and Miles wrapped his arms beneath her shoulders, hauling her toward the exit.

"Let me help." I grabbed her feet, and we carried her out of the room.

The energy shifted, and I turned around. The air shimmered as a rift opened, and a set of long, thick talons pushed through.

"Well, crap."

CHAPTER 2
ASH

"Chaos!" I shouted as we positioned Patrice in a chair. "Ember, Shade, we need you."

Miles grabbed two knives from his shoulder harness and stormed back into the room. Patrice's head lolled to the side, so I pushed it upright, balancing it on the back of the chair. "Hang tight. We'll come back for you." I started for the unfinished room as my sister and my demon clomped down the stairs.

"What happened?" Chaos raced to my side. "Are you hurt?"

"Surprisingly, no. I've made it this far into our current adventure without a scratch." I stopped outside the entrance. "But there's a rift. Something nasty wants to come through."

"It's already through," Miles yelled before he grunted and his knife thudded on the ground.

"Get binding and sealing spells ready." Ember marched past me and followed Chaos into the room.

"What's happening?" Shade stumbled down the stairs.

"A rift. Wait with Patrice." I grabbed both potion bottles and stepped inside.

Chaos stood face to face with the fiend. It had a wide, pug nose, spiraling horns, and charcoal-colored skin, making its species unmistakable.

"Not this guy again." Ember stood two feet behind Chaos, clutching her sword in both hands. Miles rocked from foot to foot, gripping his knives so hard his knuckles turned white.

"Tell me that's not the same shedim we already vanquished." I stood back, giving them room to fight, but I was ready to mend the rift the moment they sent the bastard back through.

"It's not the same." Chaos stepped toward it. The fiend moved back.

"Holy mother of magic." Shade stood in the doorway, slumping against the jamb. "What is that?"

"It's a shedim." Chaos took another step forward. It moved back again.

"Bind it." Ember moved next to him. "I'll vanquish it."

"That won't be necessary." Chaos grabbed the shedim by the neck and lifted it from the ground. It hung limp in his grasp, not even trying to fight back as he shoved it through the invisible rift. "You can seal it now."

"Wha..." My mouth hung open. Ember scratched her head, and Miles gaped at Chaos.

"That's it?" She sheathed her sword. "All this time, you've been able to just shove them back through?"

"When I don't have to hide my true identity, demons will

not be an issue." The shedim's talons protruded through the invisible rift. "No," Chaos said before winking at me. "Bad demon."

I laughed. "I'll have to cast a perimeter location spell first to make sure I get it all. I can't see the rift." I grabbed the premade potion from my satchel.

"Let me." Miles held out his hand. "I'll locate; you seal. We should share the tax on our vim."

"Let the demon do it." Shade slid down the wall to sit on the floor. "He doesn't need to recharge like we do."

"Can you seal it?" Ember asked.

Chaos shook his head. "Not from this side, no. But I can share my magic with Ash to help her."

I wasn't sure I could handle another burst of adrenaline like that, so I handed the location spell to Miles. He uncorked it, releasing the smoke into the air and reciting the incantation. It billowed and gathered around a four-foot tear in the veil. After popping the top on the mending potion, I poured it over the tear and said the spell. The fibers of reality wove back together, and the energy in the room lightened. We all exhaled as if the weight pressing down on our chests finally lifted.

"What's going...?" Patrice said from the other room before a thud sounded, like a body smacking concrete. "Oof."

Shade's legs stretched across the doorway, so I stepped over him and ran to her side. "Oh, honey. Here." I held her shoulders and helped her sit upright.

She clutched her head, her eyes pinching like she had one helluva headache. "Chrys."

"We know." Ember paced to us, and we helped Patrice into the chair. "Tell us what to mix to heal you."

"There's a headache powder in the brown jar on the second shelf. That and twelve hours of sleep should do the trick."

"I'm so glad you're alive." Miles had Shade's arm over his shoulder, and he led him to the table, leaning him against it before letting him go. "What did she say to you?"

Patrice shook her head, squeezing her eyes shut. Chaos rested his hand on my back.

"We'll have time to talk when we get home." Ember brought a mug of water with dissolved headache powder to her. "Chrys knows we're here. We need to get home quickly, and then we'll discuss what we know."

"Home, where Chrys set up who knows what kind of wards." I took the mug from Patrice after she drank it and handed it to Ember. "I never thought to check what she'd done."

"You didn't think you had reason to," Chaos said.

"Let me grab a few necessities, and we can go." Patrice stood, took a bag from a cabinet, and filled it with herbs, oils, and powders before heading upstairs. We followed her up, and she took more vials and herbs from the kitchen. "I think I'm good."

"Pack some clothes," Ember said. "You're sleeping at our place for a while."

We waited in the living room as she packed, all of us silent, including Shade. When she finished, Chaos carried her suitcase to the car, while Miles helped Shade into the front seat. Ember drove to Miles's house and parked in the driveway.

"Do you have enough vim for one more revealing spell?" She twisted in her seat to face me. "We need to make sure his house isn't booby-trapped before we go inside."

"Yeah, I think so." I opened the side door and climbed out.

"I can assist you." Chaos followed me onto the pavement.

"Thanks, but I'm good." I had to use my demon's magic sparingly. Too many rushes of power from him, and I might turn to the dark side too.

"What about me?" Shade asked. "My house and all my clothes are ashes now."

"We're the same size. I'll get enough of mine for both of us." Miles exited the van, leaving Patrice and Shade alone.

I rested a hand on Chaos's chest. "Will you wait here? They're defenseless right now."

He nodded and crossed his arms, widening his legs into a bodyguard stance.

I said the incantation. No magic protected Miles's home, so he opened the door. One last spell on the inside revealed nothing sinister. "Unless something is cloaking the nastiness, I think it's safe."

"Wait at the van." Ember clutched her sword just in case. "I'll go in with him."

"Gladly." Because my vim was nearly spent, and I still had to figure out what Chrys had done to our house. The twelve hours of sleep Patrice mentioned sounded like pure heaven. I climbed into the van, and Chaos stayed on guard duty until Ember and Miles returned with two giant duffel bags.

I rested my head on Chaos's shoulder on the short drive home, letting his warmth soothe me. He carried everyone's bags upstairs, leaving Patrice's in Cinder's room and Miles's in my parents'. Once we got everyone settled in the living room, I ordered three large pepperoni pizzas, gathered some supplies, and went with Ember to check the wards.

Outside on the sidewalk, Ember slipped her hand into mine, sharing her vim with me as I revealed what Chrys had done. Golden sparkles gathered around the perimeter of the building, coating the doors and windows.

My sister laughed, unbelieving. "She set up a ward to keep out the fae? That's it?"

"Apparently so." I rubbed oil on four railroad spikes and handed her two with a hammer. "You do the back, and I'll do the front."

"Sounds good." She headed to the back of the building, and I hammered a spike into the slim space where the cobblestone met the foundation. After placing the second one at the other corner, I joined her around back to cast our spell.

"Protect this space from malice and harm. If our ward is broken, we will be warned." We pushed our magic toward the building, hoping to wrap it in a cocoon of protection, but our spell hit a barrier and bounced back, stinging my cheeks and blowing through my hair.

"Oh, for Hecate's sake." I threw my hands into the air. "What the hell did you do, Chrys?"

A meaty hand landed on my shoulder, sending my heart into my throat. I squealed and whirled around, throwing a punch at the same time. My knuckles met Chaos's rock-hard chest, nearly crushing my bones.

"Ow! Son of a bison." I shook my hand. "You scared me to death."

"I require more clothing if I'm to blend in with your world." He gently gripped my fingers, brushing his over the tops before bringing them to his lips. "And we need to work on your self-defense skills."

Yes, my stomach fluttered. So what?

I tugged from his grasp and glanced at Ember. She gave me a reluctant nod and shrugged as if the simple movement of her shoulders wore her out. I understood exactly how she felt...

Spent.

"There's a store two blocks over." I laid my hand on his chest where I'd hit him. "I'll give you my card after you help us unravel whatever Chrys did to our building."

He peered at the roof before raking his gaze over the property. "I take it she did not cast a ward to keep out ill intent."

Plopping onto the back steps, I rummaged through my bag for supplies. "She put multiple layers on the building. The outermost is a ward to make sure we wouldn't suspect, but it's only to keep out the fae."

"The fae?" He arched a brow.

"Next is probably a cloak to hide whatever's beneath it." Ember sat next to me and crushed the herbs I'd dumped into the bowl.

"We need to remove the ward first, and then we'll figure out the next layer, unravel it, and hopefully get to the final layer." I poured in the oil, and the potion sizzled.

"And you need my assistance to ascertain her spells?"

Chaos placed his palm against the wall. "I feel dark magic, but I'm no witch. I can't tell you what hexes she cast."

"Not exactly." I stood and tugged Ember up. "We need to borrow your power to undo her darkness. We're running on fumes."

His brow furrowed. "Fumes?"

"We're tired and hangry," Ember said. "Whatever is underneath the ward fought back and wouldn't let us set up another one."

I tossed the potion onto the faery ward and held Chaos's and Ember's hands. My poor sister was as drained as I was, but as Chaos's demon magic flowed through me, I opened up and shared it with Ember.

She gasped. "Whoa."

"It's a rush, isn't it?" My entire body heated, especially my nether region, and I could only hope Ember didn't feel that part of Chaos's essence too. It didn't matter at this point. I just wanted to get our house protected so we could eat and crash.

Ember and I recited the undoing spell. Thankfully, the ward unraveled easily. We cast the magic-revealing spell, and it hit Chrys's cloak. Similar to the one Cinder had placed in her room, it fought back, sending out a pulse so strong it rattled in my chest.

I mixed up the next potion and blew the powder at the cloak before we joined hands again and spoke the incantation. I couldn't tell you if Chrys's spell was weaker than Cinder's, or if Chaos's power made us that much stronger, but the cloak dissolved, leaving only the final layer. Hopefully.

"Hold on. I need a break." Ember sat on the steps and

rubbed her palms on her pants. "My nerves feel like they've been dipped in alcohol and rubbed with salt. How are you still standing?"

"Ash's magic counters mine," Chaos said. "She is the epitome of order. I believe the human expression would be 'she is the yin to my yang.'"

She pursed her lips and nodded. "I can see that."

"We can do the next one." Clutching my demon's hand, I recited the revealing spell one more time. Golden sparkles clung to the windows and doors, revealing an icky, sticky, dark magic hex.

"Good goddess." Ember stood and moved next to me.

"What is it?" Chaos asked.

"It's a…" I tilted my head, squinting at the magic. "It looks like a vim-draining spell. Or maybe not draining but making it hard to replenish. She's been keeping us weak." And that explained so much.

My sister's hoarse laugh sounded forced, and she crossed her arms, irritation evident in her tight expression. "How long do you think it's been here?"

I traced my gaze along the tendrils of the hex. "It's stuck on pretty well. See how it slips between the building and the cobblestone? She rooted it in the earth."

Ember sighed heavily. "Of course she did. And we can't dig it up without breaking the cobble and having the city on our asses."

"Maybe we don't need to. Wait here." I darted inside to the library and walked straight to the book I needed. I'd have to ponder how easy that was later. I returned to the back of the building and opened the book right to the spell I wanted. So friggin' easy!

Tracing my finger over the page, I read the list of ingredients while Ember retrieved them from my satchel. Basil, garlic, Solomon's seal. I crushed and mixed, and the potion puffed, a light blue cloud floating upward and spreading across the hex.

I laid the book on the top step and took their hands again.

"Hold on," Ember said. "Her hex fought back against our protection ward. What if it happens again?"

"We've got Chaos this time. We can neutralize it."

She pursed her lips and inhaled. "Okay."

We read the incantation in unison. Nothing happened, so we tried again. Still nothing.

"One more time," I said. "The power of three."

We recited the words, channeling Chaos and sending out as much magic as we could. My insides burned, and my nerves felt electric with all the demon power I channeled. Was it bad that I enjoyed the rush? Maybe, but we couldn't do it without his help. And this *had* to be done.

The building rumbled. A dark film stretched over the brick, pulling tighter and tighter and tighter until it popped and dissolved.

Chaos drew his magic back in, and I sagged against his side.

"Let's set up this protection ward before the adrenaline wears off." Ember tugged my hand, and I straightened.

We recited the incantation in unison once more. "Protect this space from malice and harm. If our ward is broken, we will be warned."

This time, the ward held. Thank the goddess.

Ember jerked from my grasp and rubbed her palm on her pants. "I hope to never need to do that again."

The sentiment wasn't the same, but I didn't tell her that. Instead, I tugged my credit card and house keys from my bag and handed them to Chaos. "Can I trust you to not cause any trouble?"

He fought a grin. "I will do my best."

"Straight to the store and back. Do not go rogue. Do not hurt or kill anyone." I tapped my finger against his chest. "That includes messing with their minds."

"You have my word." He winked and walked away while Ember and I went inside.

"Thanks for doing that," I said as I dragged myself up the steps.

"We didn't have a choice." She followed me up. "But seriously, sis. You can't keep channeling him. His power could be addictive, and with your curse still active..."

I waved off her concern. "I've got it under control."

"Do you?"

Good question.

CHAPTER 3
CHAOS

I returned from the clothing store to find a man holding three flat boxes and knocking on the front entrance door. He huffed and rang the buzzer, shaking his head before looking at his phone. His mouth drew downward, and lines creased his forehead.

"Are you the delivery person?" I approached with caution, opening my senses to detect any magic he might exude. I found none.

"I've been knocking for five minutes. Here." He shoved the boxes at my chest before stepping back and holding his hand toward me, palm up.

I'd seen plenty of people on the television return the gesture by slapping the outstretched palm, so I hooked the bags onto my fingers beneath the pizza boxes and "gave him five."

He scoffed, his attitude growing more fowl by the second. "My tip, man. What the hell's wrong with you?"

My eyes heated, the green undulating around my pupils. If I hadn't given Ash my word that I would harm no one, this delivery boy would be nothing more than a pile of soot. Instead, I straightened my spine and leaned toward him. "I suggest you treat your elders with respect. You never know what we're capable of."

His eyes widened, and his throat bobbed with his hard swallow. "Never mind. We're good."

I tilted my head slightly, and he took two stumbling steps backward before turning and running to his vehicle.

"Chaos! What did you do?" Ash stood in the doorway, her arms crossed over her chest.

"He insisted on a tip, so I gave him one." I shrugged and stepped inside. "I didn't use my power on him if that's what you're asking."

She arched a brow. "Did he have blond hair and a scar on his lip?"

"Indeed. And an attitude worse than Shade's."

"That's John. He's an ass." She locked the front door and led the way to the stairs. "Come on up. We're so hungry, we're about to eat our shoes."

"Surely you have something else to eat in your kitchen. Leather is an animal product, but it's not for consumption."

She stopped and turned to me, laughing, her entire face lighting up with beauty. "It's an expression."

I couldn't help but smile. "Is it?"

"Well, if it isn't, I just made it one." She continued up the stairs.

In the kitchen, I set the boxes on the counter before taking my clothes to Ash's bedroom. When I returned, she handed me a piece of round, stiff paper and set three slices of pizza on it. With our plates full, everyone settled in the living room. Ash sank onto the sofa next to me, and our legs touched. Normally, she moved away when this happened, but not this time. She rested her shoulder against mine, and warmth filled my chest before a fist of dread squeezed it tightly.

This witch would never be mine. Not unless I took her to Hell with me, and I knew without a doubt that she would never leave her sisters. But perhaps, with a little convincing…

"It's time for answers," Shade said around a mouthful of food. "What's going on?"

"We should ask the same of you." Ash took two gulps of water and set her glass on the coffee table. "What the hell were you doing in our house, and why did you hit us with a nerve hex?"

He leaned forward in his chair. "I came here because you're harboring a demon. The spell was meant for him."

"What made you think I was a demon? You seemed surprised when you figured it out." I folded a slice in half and ate half in one bite.

"Chrys thought…" He clamped his mouth shut.

Chrys. He'd fallen victim to a dark witch's whims. Who was I to judge him for that?

Miles sat next to Patrice on the smaller sofa, his shoulders moving toward his ears. "Ginger told her we sensed something off in your house. Maybe she..." His eyes glistened, and he inhaled a shaky breath.

"Maybe we should start from the beginning," their healer said. "It sounds like we all have pieces to the puzzle that the others are missing."

Ember traded a glance with Ash. "Do you want to tell them, or should I?"

She set her empty plate next to her cup. "I will. It's all about me, anyway."

"You—" Shade began to quip, but he closed his mouth again.

Ash took a deep breath and straightened her spine. "I didn't break the curse on our coven. I *am* the curse."

She told them about Isabel's wrath, about how every High Priestess in the coven had lied about the curse and claimed a third-born daughter would die in infancy. Patrice watched her tell the story, sympathy creasing her forehead as she listened. Miles sat stoic, undoubtedly trying to hold back tears for his deceased girlfriend, and Shade's face pinched in his signature sour expression.

Ash shrugged, the sharp movement making her bounce on the cushion. "So our parents tried to find these guys and failed." She pointed her thumb at me. "Cinder figured out how to summon them and convinced Discord to take her across the veil to rescue Mom and Dad. I found the sigils and accidentally summoned Chaos into my mind. We retrieved his skull and got him out of my head, and now we need to get Mayhem's skull, which Chrys has."

Ember set her empty plate on the table. "Once we summon

Mayhem, we can bring everyone back to this side of the veil, end the curse, and put everything right again. That's all we know. Who's next?"

"Hold on." Shade pinched the bridge of his nose. "If Cinder summoning Discord started the weakening of the veil, and Ash summoning Chaos made it worse, won't Mayhem tear it to shreds?"

"Your situation will get worse before it improves." I glanced at Ash's hands folded on her lap and fought the urge to hold them in mine. "However, once my brothers and I return to our realm permanently, the Holland sisters have the power to mend the veil. Everything will be as it was before."

"Except it won't." Miles stared at the half-eaten pizza on his plate. "Ginger will still be dead."

And I would live the rest of my existence knowing my perfect match could never be mine. The ache in my chest reached up to my throat.

"Miles." Ash shifted forward, leaning toward him. "I know it's hard to talk about, but do you think Ginger was working with Chrys?"

"I don't." He shook his head. "I mean, Chrys could have been the one who got her into dark magic, but Ginger would never hurt anyone."

"Why is Chrys even doing this?" Shade asked. "What does she want with Mayhem's skull?"

"My guess," Ember said, "is that she's working with Boston. She's either a member of their coven, or she's using their knowledge to try and take control of Salem."

Once again, Ember and I agreed. "That's a plausible explanation. It is rare for an elemental witch to be content without ruling."

Patrice nodded. "When she got to me, she said she wanted me alive because she'd need a good healer when she took over the coven."

"There you go," Ash said. "She knows about the curse. Hell, she and Cinder were close friends so it wouldn't surprise me if Chrys knew about her plans to free the demons and save me."

"And she's using it to her advantage," I said. "Without Mayhem and Discord, I can't lift the curse on Ash."

"She's hoping Ash will do the dirty work and take out all the light witches for her." Ember stood and began pacing. "But you two." She pointed to Miles and Shade. "How did she get to you?"

Shade's brow slammed down over his eyes. "She manipulated us, convinced us to be suspicious. She's the reason I came here last night. I thought I was saving you, that you didn't know what he is, but when I saw Ash in bed with him, I lost it."

He flicked his gaze to Ash. "I'm sorry."

She flinched. "Umm. Thanks?"

"I don't know how she got the sigils onto us," Miles said. "I don't even remember her coming inside. I guess she used a binding spell?"

"A doozy of one," Ash said. "I could never have guessed how powerful she is. She fooled us all."

"What are our next steps?" Patrice rose and gathered the empty plates before taking them to the trash can.

Ember looked at me. "Do we let her summon Mayhem herself?"

"I don't think she can," Ash answered. "From what she said, it sounded like Isabel kept the sigils separate from the map. The book in our vault must've had the only copy."

"Can she summon him without the sigil?" Shade asked.

"Our marks are required for us to pass across the veil. She will either continue searching for the one you had, or she will look elsewhere. Isabel didn't create our marks. They've existed as long as we have."

Shade lifted his hands and dropped them in his lap. "She wants to take over Salem, and she's working with Boston. That much I follow, but why does she want to summon another demon? She knows it'll only make the veil weaker."

"Maybe that's part of her plan. Who knows how dark witches think?" Ash rolled her neck. "Besides, have you not seen how helpful Chaos is? Having a demon in her back pocket would level the playing field."

The only reason I'd been helpful to Ash was the bond I shared with her. I doubted my brother would feel for his witch the way I did about mine.

I was about to say as much when Patrice spoke, "Can I make a suggestion?"

"Please." Ember dropped onto the couch and pressed her fingers to her temples.

"We're all exhausted. No amount of healing I can provide will replace a full night of sleep." She clasped her hands in front of her chest. "I think we should rest and talk about our next steps in the morning."

"Yeah." Miles stood. "We'll be useless until morning. Let's get some sleep."

Shade drummed his fingers on the arm of the chair. "You can sleep with a demon in the house?"

Ash opened her mouth to speak, but Miles answered, "They set up the wards while he was outside. If he had ill intent, he couldn't have come back in." He turned and headed for the hall.

"Good night, everyone." Patrice followed.

I stood tugging Ash up with me. "No harm will come to any of you by my hand tonight."

"He means it," she said.

"You're safe here." Ember rose to her feet. "You can stay in our parents' room with Miles."

His face pulled into a frown. "I'm fine on the couch."

"Suit yourself." Ash led me to the hallway while Ember retrieved the same blanket and pillow she had offered me my first night here.

We stepped inside Ash's bedroom, and she closed the door, locking it before sliding her arms around my waist and resting her head against my chest. I held her tightly, pressing my lips to her hair and breathing in her intoxicating scent.

"I don't know why it is..." My shirt muffled her words, so she lifted her head and looked into my eyes. "But touching you always brings me a sense of calmness and safety."

I brushed a strand of hair from her forehead. "It's the bond we share."

"Your mark."

"No." I trailed my fingers down her cheek. Her skin felt as

soft as down. "It's so much more than the ink on your arm. It's…"

"Fate?" She brushed her lips to mine.

"I believe it is." I moved my hand up her back to slide my fingers into her silky hair. "Do you?"

"I don't know what to believe." She stepped out of my embrace, and I immediately missed her warmth. "What I do know is that I'm in desperate need of a shower." Her tongue slipped out to moisten her lips as her gaze trailed down my body and up to my face. "Want to come wash my back?"

I inhaled deeply, the mere thought of seeing hot water rolling down her delicate skin making my dick twitch. "Your body requires rest."

"And I'll sleep so much more deeply if you help me relieve some of this stress. Don't you think?" She ran her finger down my abdomen, stopping at the top of my pants.

My stomach clenched. Who was I to deny her a restful night of sleep?

I removed my shirt and dropped it on the floor. "Lead the way, little witch."

She grinned and held up a finger. "Only if you promise to be quiet. I don't have enough vim to cast a silencing spell."

I dropped my pants. "I will try my best."

Her gaze locked on my dick, and her pupils dilated as she stripped. Heat pooled in my groin, making my cock ache with need. She drew her bottom lip between her teeth and wrapped her fingers around my length, stroking it three times before turning and slinking into the bathroom.

I watched as she started the shower, testing the water with the inside of her wrist before stepping beneath the stream and beckoning me to join her. Water ran in rivulets over her shoulders, curving around her breasts and cascading down to her toes. She applied a floral-scented, liquid soap to a cloth and ran it over her face before turning her back to me and letting the water rinse her cheeks.

The view of her backside was as glorious as her front.

"Would you mind?" She handed me the cloth and moved her hair over her shoulder, giving me access to every dip and curve of her skin.

I did as she asked, cleansing her back before reaching around to her stomach. "I believe you missed a spot," I said into her ear, and her skin turned to gooseflesh.

"I believe you're right." She twisted in my arms and crushed her mouth to mine.

A growl rumbled in my chest, reaching upward to my throat as I coaxed her lips apart and tangled my tongue with hers. She fit in my embrace as if she were made for me, and the more time I spent with this witch, the more convinced I became that it was true.

Breaking the kiss, she trailed her tongue down my neck, nipping at my shoulder while her hands roamed over my chest. Her touch electrified me, sending flames of desire coursing through my veins. Pulling back to gaze at me, she grinned wickedly, one brow arching over a deep blue eye.

She ran one hand up to cup my cheek, while the other slid down to my stomach. I held in a groan as she inched her fingers closer to the prize, and when she wrapped her hand around my cock, stroking it like she owned it, I moaned.

"Bad demon." She stopped and squeezed me hard. "You promised not to make a sound."

I ground my teeth. "I promised to try my best."

"Try harder, or I'll have to send you to bed without your supper."

My eyes heated, the molten green of my irises undulating at her words. Not once in my entire existence had a lover told me what to do. I would never have obeyed if they tried, but this little witch...

I would do *anything* she told me to do.

I nodded, and she licked her lips before turning me around, so the water hit my back. Then, she lowered to her knees.

Gripping my dick with one hand, she flicked out her tongue, swiping it over my tip. The sensation felt like warm velvet against my skin, and I let out a slow exhale. She did it again, this time circling her tongue around the head before sucking the first inch into her mouth.

I held my breath to stop my moan.

She looked up at me as she took me into her mouth as far as I could go, and she closed her eyes, drawing her head back, her teeth grazing my length before she released me. My knees nearly buckled when she took me back in. She released me again, looking up and running her tongue from the base to my tip.

My nostrils flared, and I reached down, hooking my finger under her chin and guiding her to her feet. She smiled and ran her hands up my body, tracing the cuts of my muscles, her fingertips memorizing my form.

"Your body is exquisite." She rose onto her toes, brushing a kiss to my lips. "Take me to bed."

Her whisper made me shiver. I shut off the water and grabbed a towel, wrapping it around her back, my length pressing against her stomach as I drank her in. She cupped my face, returning the passion in our kiss before pulling away and grinning. "Now, please."

A primal grunt rumbled up from my core, but I squelched it before it passed my throat. Scooping her into my arms, I carried her to the bed and lay her on the mattress, but she rose to her hands and knees, slinking backward like a cat.

"I love it when you look at me like you want to devour me." She nodded toward the empty space on the bed. "Lie down."

I did as I was told, lying on my back and fighting the urge to throw her down and take her. She wanted to be in control this time, and I would relinquish it to her for as long as she wanted it tonight.

She crawled toward me, straddling my hips and rubbing her slit over the length of my dick as she kissed me. Every muscle in my body tensed. I wanted to groan. To tangle my fingers in her hair and make her scream my name.

"Mmm..." she said softly against my lips. "Good demon."

Rising onto her knees, she guided me to her folds and took me in slowly, inch by inch until nothing separated us. She was tight and wet, and as she rose up and down my length, I couldn't tear my gaze away from her beauty.

Her lips parted, her breath quickening as she rode me.

Grabbing my hands, she placed them against her breasts and closed her eyes, her expression one of sheer ecstasy as I caressed her.

"Oh, Chaos," she whispered and moved one of my hands down her body.

I pressed my thumb to her clit, and she gasped. Her rhythm increased, and she opened her eyes, biting her bottom lip and leaning forward to rest her hands on my chest. My entire body hummed with the need to feel her release.

I circled her sensitive nub, bringing her closer and closer to the edge until she pressed her lips together and moaned. She rode me hard and fast, tossing her head back as she found her release. I gripped her hips, holding her still and pounding into her, the orgasm twisting in my core, threatening to burn me alive if I didn't release it.

But I waited. I continued thrusting into her until she inhaled deeply, pinning me with her deep blue gaze and nodding her approval. I thrust two more times and let go. Ecstasy exploded inside me, rolling through my body like wildfire and setting my soul ablaze.

Panting, she collapsed on top of me, sliding her arms beneath my shoulders and holding me tightly. I traced my fingers up and down her back, reveling in the feel of her wrapped around me, of her body still one with mine.

"Never in my life has sex been this good," she whispered.

"We were made for each other, little witch."

"Mmm... It feels that way sometimes." She rolled to her side and snuggled against me.

For me, it felt that way all the time. Ash was the light to my darkness. The order to my madness. The one I wanted to spend eternity with.

My chest pinched with agony. There had to be an answer. Fate would not lead me to her and then tear her from my arms. I would do anything to spend my existence with her, no matter what the cost. It didn't matter what I had to do...

Ash would be mine.

CHAPTER 4
ASH

Voices and dishes clanking roused me from sleep, and I squeezed my eyes shut, willing myself back under. I lay on my side, the heat of Chaos's body against my back making me feel safe, cozy even.

A month ago, if you'd told me I'd be in bed with a demon, I would have laughed and called you cuckoo. Yet, there I was, wrapped in his strong embrace and enjoying every minute of it.

"The others are up." His deep voice, raspy from sleep, made me shiver in a good way.

I turned toward him, snuggling into his arms, my head fitting perfectly beneath his chin. "Tell me this is all a bad dream."

"If it were, I wouldn't be here."

"Tell me everything except you is a bad dream." I closed my eyes, breathing in his warm, spicy scent. "I just want it all to go away."

Five seconds passed before he responded. "I can make it go away."

I laughed. "Without killing everyone."

Another long pause, and he kissed the top of my head. "Come to Hell with me."

I laughed again.

"I'm not joking."

I pulled back to see his face. He looked as serious as could be.

"We're meant to be together, Ash." He held my gaze with emotion-filled eyes. "We don't need my brothers to end your curse when I can take you away. Your coven will be safe if you're in Hell with me, and we can be together forever."

"You can't be serious." I scooted away, my brow furrowing. Surely he didn't think that was a viable solution.

"It would solve all your problems." He reached for me, but I rolled away and got out of bed.

"It most certainly would not. Too much sugary cereal has affected your brain. I'm not going to Hell with you." I opened my drawers and put on a bra and underwear.

He sat up, the sheets falling away from his statue-perfect body, and I fought the urge to shut him up by sitting on his face. Why did he have to be so frigging hot? I turned back to my drawers and shoved my legs into a pair of black pants.

"Why not?" He stood, all his glorious nakedness taunting me.

"The fire and brimstone, for one thing." I threw on a fire-proof black shirt and wrapped a corset around my waist, hooking it in the front.

"It's not as bad as you think." He pulled on his jeans. "We could be happy there."

"I could not be happy in Hell." I fumbled with the ribbons in the back of my corset as he finished dressing. "I'm not leaving my sister or my coven no matter how hot a fire you light in my core. What is wrong with this damn thing?" It wouldn't tighten the way it was supposed to.

Chaos moved behind me and took the ribbons, pulling and tugging until it tightened perfectly. "You're meant to be mine."

"Whoa." I turned to face him. "I thought we agreed we'd have a little fun when we could, and then you'd go home and I'd stay here. That was the deal."

"I'm not sure I can exist without you." The sincerity in his eyes nearly buckled my knees, and Ember's words echoed in my mind.

What if he falls in love with you? What if you fall in love with him?

Hell, no. That wasn't happening. I couldn't let it. "Let me make this very clear. I am *not* going to Hell with you or anyone else, so get that idea out of your head right now."

He looked at me silently as I put on my socks and boots. Maybe sleeping with a demon wasn't such a good idea after all.

"I hear your words." He opened the door and walked out of my room.

He heard my words? Was he implying that I didn't mean what I said? If so, he didn't know me as well as he thought he did. I'd always been a *say what I mean and mean what I say* gal.

I joined the others in the kitchen. Shade cut his gaze from

Chaos to me, but thankfully he kept his mouth shut. It was too early in the morning to deal with his bullshit. Patrice stood at the stove, frying bacon, and Miles took two slices of bread from the toaster, adding them to the stack, while Ember poured two more cups of coffee, offering them to Chaos and me.

I accepted the mug and sank into a chair at the table. "Where'd all the food come from?"

"Miles and I stepped out this morning and went to the corner market." Patrice added four more slices to the pan. They sizzled and popped, filling the room with their delicious aroma and making my mouth water.

Patrice plated the food and presented us with a spread of scrambled eggs, bacon, and toast with jam before joining Chaos, Ember, and me at the table. Miles and Shade sat at the counter, and we ate in glorious silence. When we finished, I collected the empty plates and carried them to the kitchen. Chaos picked up a dish towel and joined me at the sink.

"I've got it." I snatched the towel from his hands.

He grabbed it back. "You wash; I'll dry."

I gritted my teeth. "I was planning to put them in the dishwasher."

He stepped away and opened it, gesturing to the racks already full. Dammit, I'd forgotten to empty it.

Shade clutched his coffee in both hands. "Are we not going to talk about the fact that Ash is sleeping with a demon?"

Ember refilled her mug and leaned a hip against the counter. "It's irrelevant to our problems, so no. We're not going to talk about my sister's sex life."

Hallelujah.

I finished washing the dishes and poured the last of the coffee into my mug. "We have two options. We can wait it out, let Chrys find the sigils and summon Mayhem, and then hope Chaos can get to him before she uses him to destroy us. Or, we can go on the offensive."

"Being offensive is our best bet." Chaos dried his hands on a towel and dropped it on the counter.

I hung it in its proper place. "You don't even know—"

"We find her, kill her, and take the skull." He said it matter-of-factly, as if it were the only viable course of action.

"She nearly killed all of us," Miles said. "That won't be an easy feat."

"And good luck finding her," Ember added. "Scrying for Shade took so much vim we didn't have enough left to fight."

I blew out a long, slow breath and pressed my lips into a line.

"That's not what you meant, is it? You prefer to wait it out?" Patrice carried the frying pan to the sink and washed it. At least *someone* wanted to hear my suggestion.

"No. If she gets control of Mayhem, who knows what she'll do. We can't let her summon him." I sipped my coffee, waiting for them all to look at me. "We have to do it first."

"How?" Ember asked. "We don't have the sigils either. They burned up in Shade's house. Do you remember what they look like?"

"Not exactly, and we can't risk doing it wrong. Who knows what might happen if we did." I drummed my fingers against my mug and flicked my gaze to Chaos. "Can you draw them?"

His brow furrowed. "I believe so."

"That didn't sound convincing." Ember opened a drawer and pulled out a pad of paper and a pencil.

"I've never tried." He took the paper and gripped the pencil in his left hand. "Mayhem's mark is similar to mine, so it would start with a curve at the top." He laid the pad on the counter and began to draw.

I sipped my coffee and watched the sigil take form. The treble clef shape looked like Chaos's mark, but Mayhem's had sharper edges and more straight lines. When he got to the bottom, he looped it around to the right and paused.

"I think it goes left." I set my mug on the counter and pointed to his mistake.

"It most certainly goes right. What comes after this loop is why I paused. Mayhem and Discord have the same angles here, but they are reversed. I can't remember which is which."

"Well, that's a problem." I crossed my arms. "And I still think it goes left."

"It goes right."

"It doesn't matter." Ember tore the page from the pad and tossed it in the trash. "If neither of you remembers exactly, we're screwed. We'll have to get another copy of them."

I leaned against the counter. "Prince of Hell sigils won't be easy to find. If they were, Chrys would have them by now."

"If anyone can locate them, it's you." She returned the pencil to the drawer.

"Say you do find them," Shade said. "Then what? We still don't have the skull."

Chaos leaned against the counter next to me, and I fought

the urge to scoot away. I was still miffed at him for the way he acted this morning, and miffed was good. It was better than the alternative, anyway.

What if you fall in love with him? No, no, no.

"One step at a time." I paced to the opposite end of the kitchen. "Chrys is looking for the sigils. We need to find them first, and then we can work on locating her and the skull."

"How will we find them first?" Miles asked. "She's probably been searching the witchy web since she figured out who Chaos is. That's a big head start."

"Chrys is just an earth witch." Ember wrapped her arm around me, giving me a side hug. "We've got a librarian on our team. Ash can find anything."

Finally a task I was confident I could handle. "Give me an hour. If there's a copy of those sigils somewhere on this continent, I'll find it." I headed for the stairs.

Chaos followed me down to my office, and I huffed, plopping into my squeaky chair. He needed to learn how to read the room. "I don't need any help."

He stood next to my desk, his gaze traveling from my eyes to my fists clenched on the surface. "I've upset you."

"Whatever gave you that idea?" I fired up my laptop, hoping to Hecate it still worked after Shade threw it on the floor. The familiar start-up ping sounded, and I let out a breath. *Thank you, goddess.*

"I assume your question was rhetorical." He picked up the drawers Chrys had pulled out and returned them to their rightful places in my desk.

Another sarcastic comment rolled through my mind, but it

didn't make it past my lips. We didn't have time for games. If I wanted to keep this demon on my team, I needed to be straight with him. "You freaked me out up there."

"I didn't mean to."

A hairband sat loose on the edge of my desk, so I grabbed it and tied my hair into a bun. "I know you didn't, but..." I blew out another breath. "I like you a lot, but my loyalty lies with my coven. Going to Hell with you is not an option, and the fact you even suggested it is a huge red flag."

He rested his fingertips on my desk. "The suggestion was harmless."

"No, actually, it wasn't. I told you 'no,' and you implied that my 'no' didn't mean 'no.' That's not cool."

"I see." He clasped his hands and said nothing more.

I guess expecting yet another apology from a demon was asking too much. When he didn't offer one, I pulled up the witchy web and began my search. Looking for the demons' names didn't help. Chaos, Mayhem, and Discord were normal words, and all I got were definitions and listings for the Discord social media site. I tried *prince of hell, demon prince sigil,* and a few similar search times, but those gave me paranormal romance novels written by witches. Believe it or not, only a handful of magical authors wrote stories about magic. Most paranormal romance writers were human. Go figure.

"Does your Higher Power not monitor searches like this?" Chaos leaned down, resting one hand on the back of my chair and the other on the desk. "Will you and your coven not be investigated for looking up demons?"

"I use an encrypted browser, and there isn't enough magic

in the world for them to constantly spy on every coven's activity. We're fine." I swiveled my chair, and he straightened, stepping back. Maybe a reverse image search would bring better luck. I grabbed my phone and snapped a photo of the mark on my arm before uploading it to my laptop.

Twenty minutes later, I'd found nothing. I slumped in my chair while Chaos returned the books Shade had knocked down to the shelves. "You don't have to do that," I said. "When this is all through, I'm going to reorganize the whole library."

He put another book on the shelf. "The disarray bothers you, and this part of it was my fault."

I pursed my lips. How could he be such a brute and then turn around and do something thoughtful? So annoying. "Thank you. I've exhausted the witchy web. Either we had the only copy of those sigils, or whatever book they might be in isn't listed."

He placed another volume on the shelf. "Was your dark grimoire listed?"

I dropped my head back on the chair. "No. Any coven who understands how powerful you are would hide it. Damn." I should have realized that before I even tried.

"If you can't find a copy, I doubt Chrys can either." He sat on the edge of my desk. "We should kill her."

And the brute was back. I pinched the bridge of my nose. "We don't kill people...on purpose."

"We should accidentally kill her."

I laughed, but I doubted he was joking. Then it hit me. "Hold on." I sat upright. "Magical beings would understand how dangerous summoning a Prince of Hell can be, but humans wouldn't. Your sigils could be sitting in a book in the Salem library, right under our noses. Let me check."

My fingers flew across the keys, my heart sprinting in my chest. Why hadn't I thought of this before? It took a few different search strings to get it right, but ten minutes later, there it was. "*The Complete Encyclopedia of Demonic Legions as recorded by Father Timothy Carson.*"

"Mortals keep an encyclopedia of my kind?" He leaned closer to the screen and read the description. "'Explore the hierarchy of Hell from Lucifer down to the smallest fiends. Includes sigil artwork for each demon and summoning precautions.' Hmm. Sounds promising."

"It better be. It's the only thing I can find that comes close to what we need, and there's only one copy on record in all of North America." I opened another tab and searched the title on the web. No hits returned for this continent, but one came back from France.

"Is it in Salem?"

"Sadly, no. It's in New Orleans." I returned to the library site and clicked the entry. "And it's classified as a reference book, so we can't get it through interlibrary loan."

"Is New Orleans far?"

"Fifteen hundred miles. I'll have to fly there." I closed the laptop and shoved it into its case.

"You..." Chaos straightened, confusion pinching his features. "You have the ability to fly?"

"In an airplane, yeah." I rose and paced to the stairs. "What? Did you think I meant on my broom?"

"Of course not." He followed me up the steps. "But you made it sound as if you had an ability I was unaware of."

"There's a lot you don't know about me." I opened the door to find Ember and the others packing up to leave. "What's going on?"

"Higgins called about another rift." She handed me my bag. "What did you find?"

"There's a demonic encyclopedia with sigil artwork in New Orleans." I set my satchel on the counter. "It's in the public library."

"Is it legit?" Miles asked.

"I'll have to go there to see. It's in the reference section."

"So they won't let you check it out." Ember tapped her foot. "You'll have to steal it."

My stomach clenched at the idea of stealing from a library, but she was right. If the book was legit, it needed to be held under lock and key, not sitting out available for anyone to play with.

"If Chrys hasn't already taken it," Shade said. "She's smarter than you think."

I rolled my eyes and swiped open my phone to bring up the New Orleans Public Library website. I clicked the number and pressed the speaker button.

It rang three times before someone answered. "New Orleans Public Library. How can I help you?"

"Hi. I'm calling about one of your reference books. It's called *The Complete Encyclopedia of Demonic Legions as recorded by Father Timothy Carson.* Do you still have that?"

The sounds of a keyboard clicking filled the silence. "Yes, ma'am. It's in our catalog."

"She could have stolen it already," Shade whispered. "They might not know it's gone."

I nodded. "Yeah, I saw it there online, but would you mind checking to see if you still have it in your possession? I'm going to travel a long way to look at it, and I'd hate to make the trip if it was transferred to another building."

"Hold please." Jazz music blasted through the speaker, so I turned down the volume. Five minutes later, she returned to the line. "Yes, ma'am. It's in the reference section on the second floor."

"Thank you." I pressed End and returned the phone to my pocket...without making a face at Shade, thank you very much.

"Good." Ember grabbed her keys from the peg. "Take Chaos with you. We'll hold down the fort until you get back."

"I can go alone. It's just a library." I needed to put as much distance as possible between us. His whole *I can't exist without you; you're meant to be mine* speech still had me reeling.

"I won't leave you unprotected," Chaos said.

I whirled to face him. "I've done just fine without you for twenty-four years. I don't need protection."

"Yes, you do," Ember said. "Sorry, sis, but the circumstances have changed. We're on the buddy system from now on, and you're the only person he listens to. Whatever lovers' quarrel you're having needs to end right now."

"Okay." I threw up my hands in surrender. "Take the premade spells from my kit. I'll put together some more before I...we...leave."

Patrice held up her phone. "There's a flight out of Boston in three hours. Do you think you can make it?"

Ember looked at the screen. "She can. Book it for her and Shade. Here's my card."

"Shade is not accompanying us." Chaos crossed his arms.

Honestly, I'd almost rather have gone with Shade at that point, but I knew what my sister meant. "You're going to use his ID, or they won't let you on the plane."

"Whoever *they* are, they can't stop me."

I opened my mouth to argue but thought better of it. Instead, I turned to Shade and held out my hand.

His expression pinched, growing even more sour, but he took his driver's license from his wallet and handed it to me. "Don't let him tarnish my name."

"No promises," I grumbled and gave it to Chaos. "I'll cast a glamour spell on the photo to make it look like you. When we're at the airport, your name is Shade."

He peered at the license before sliding it into his back pocket. "Understood."

"The flight is booked," Patrice said. "The return trip is tomorrow evening, but you can always change it if you need more time. I'm sending the boarding passes now."

Ember pulled me into a tight hug. "Don't forget to book a room and try to stay away from other witches."

I laughed and pulled away. "You do realize we're going to New Orleans, right?"

"Do your best to stay off their radar. Fire and water don't mix."

"I will."

Ember and the others left, leaving me alone with Chaos. I looked at him, and he looked at me, and for the first time since I'd met him, awkwardness expanded between us.

I didn't like it.

Not at all.

CHAPTER 5
ASH

I left two days' worth of bottled spells on the counter before we headed to the airport. At least, I hoped it would last two days. Between the rifts, Chrys, and Boston trying to get revenge for their library—if that was even why they were involved—I had my doubts. But they had Patrice now, and Miles was good at spell work. They'd be fine without me.

Hell, they might even be better off. Hecate knew their lives would be a helluva lot easier if I'd never been born. I lowered my gaze to my hands clasped in my lap. Chipped black polish partially coated my nails, which irritated me almost as much as the disarray in my library. I picked a piece off my thumb and flicked it to the ground.

A pair of black boots came into view in front of me, and I lifted my head. Chaos handed me a cup and sank into the chair next to me. Our flight boarded in twenty minutes, so I'd sent him on a coffee run to give me some space.

"I was hesitant to try this concoction you call a pumpkin spice latte, but I'm glad I did. It's decadent." He pressed the cup to his lips and tipped it, closing his eyes as he sipped. "It's only available during this time of year?"

"That's part of what makes it so good." I took a drink and lowered the cup to my lap, toying with the paper sleeve. "What's it like in your realm?"

"I'm not sure anymore. It's been centuries. Why do you ask?"

"What was it like before you were imprisoned? Where did you sleep?" I cut my gaze toward a man practically yelling into his phone. Would it be bad of me to cast a silencing spell on him? If I were only doing it for myself, yes, it would. But, surely, I wasn't the only person who wanted to throw his phone across the room. Maybe for the greater good...

"In my realm, I don't require sleep. Otherwise, it isn't all that different from here. The only humans there are those who sold their souls into torture, but we have food and drinks, games, and entertainment. I assume it hasn't changed."

I peeled apart the insulating sleeve and dropped it into my lap as a sickening sensation formed in my stomach. "Are my parents and Cinder being tortured?"

He inhaled deeply, going silent for a full three seconds. "I don't know."

I set my cup and the ruined sleeve on the table next to me. "They're in Hell because of me. If they're being tortured, it's my fault."

"No." He clutched my hand.

"Yes." I pulled from his grasp. From the moment I possessed myself, my life had been nothing but go, go, go. Adrenaline rushes, vim depletion, danger, sex, exhaustion, sleep. This was the first time I'd had downtime in weeks, and sitting there in the airport, waiting to get on a plane, my mind finally had a moment to contemplate how much of a mess I'd made of my family, my coven, my town.

He set his cup on the floor at his feet and rested his hands on his knees. "Your family is in Hell because of the choices they made."

"Choices they wouldn't have *had* to make if not for me." I stared at the man yelling across the way, willing him to end the effing call for goddess's sake. The woman next to him huffed, glaring at him as she gathered her carry-ons and moved to the next row.

"Ash..." Chaos angled toward me.

"Screw it." I whispered a silencing spell and directed my magic at the cacophonous culprit. He yelled a silent *hello* a few times into the phone before shouting *can you hear me* twice. Jabbing his thick finger onto the screen, he ended the call, looked at the teenager next to him, and spoke, but no sound emanated from his lips.

"Freak." The teen scoffed and moved two aisles away.

"Maybe you're right." I turned to Chaos. "Maybe I should go to Hell with you. I could trade places with them. I stay, and they go home. My mom can help my sisters mend the veil from their side. I'm not there to destroy them all." I shrugged. "It makes sense."

He shook his head. "It's not a viable solution, and I never should have suggested it."

They called our flight for boarding over the speaker, so I stood and slung my bag over my shoulder. "I cause nothing but trouble everywhere I go. C'mon. Let's see what kind of mess we can make of New Orleans."

Patrice had booked us on a budget airline with no assigned seats. The man I'd hexed sat in the second row, and I whispered an undoing spell as I passed, moving to the back of the plane, as far away from him as possible. I found an empty row and scooted in, claiming the window seat. Chaos took the middle, leaving the coveted aisle seat empty. A woman saw the free space and made her way toward us, but when her gaze locked on Chaos, she swallowed hard and turned around to find another seat. The same thing happened with a man in a suit and a teenage boy in a hoodie.

I elbowed Chaos. "Are you doing something?"

"Just giving us privacy so we can talk freely."

I wanted to argue it was rude, but I had to admit if I could warn people away without wasting my vim, I'd do it all the time. "If the flight's full someone will have to sit there."

Thankfully, it wasn't full. I shoved my bag beneath the seat in front of me and buckled my seatbelt. "Do not, under any circumstances, use your chaos magic on this plane. No fire either."

"What is the purpose of a seatbelt? If the plane falls from the sky, I doubt remaining in our seats will provide safety." He buckled up and angled his body toward me.

"Sometimes there's turbulence. The plane will hit pockets

with different air pressure and jerk down and up. Seatbelts keep us from falling all over the place."

The plane took off, and Chaos watched the world fall away through the window, his eyes full of wonder. His lips curved upward into an adorable smile, and he leaned closer, looking all around. "Humans have evolved so much since I was imprisoned."

"I'm not sure evolved is the right word. Our technology has grown by leaps and bounds, but we're not any better at being human beings. People still suck."

"You consider yourself human?" He leaned back in his seat and looked at me.

"Yeah. I mean, aside from having some magical abilities, witches aren't much different than humans. We're mortal, we exist in their world, hold their jobs, play their games, follow their laws. Most of us do, anyway."

He sighed. "You wouldn't be happy in Hell."

"Then why did you insist I come? Because that's starting to sound like the best thing I could do for my coven."

He leaned his head against the seat and closed his eyes. "Because I'm selfish. It's my nature to take what I want without regard to how it affects others."

"So you thought you could take me, whisk me away from my family, and keep me for yourself, never mind how I might feel about it." I shook my head. This right here was why I needed to keep my feelings for him in check.

He opened his eyes and pinned me with his gaze. "The thought crossed my mind, yes. Many times. I would raze the world to keep you safe."

Dammit if my stomach didn't flutter. "I don't want you to raze the world. As dysfunctional as it is, it's my home. I like my life in Salem."

"I know. That's why I never should have suggested you come to Hell. I will have to figure out another way to make you mine."

I laughed. "Good luck with that."

He lifted one shoulder. "Besides, even if we could find your parents and sister and release them, Mayhem would still be trapped. Chrys would find a way to summon him, and your coven would be destroyed."

"And I can't let that happen." I slid the window cover down, blocking the blinding light shining through.

"You won't. You're the only one who can defeat the earth witch."

I laughed a little harder. "You're still a funny little demon."

He arched a brow. "Nothing about me is little. I think you're aware of that."

"No kidding." Heat flushed my cheeks, and I shifted in my seat. Holy Hecate, how could a simple raised brow get me hot and bothered?

He leaned his left elbow on the armrest. "Chrys underestimates you. Everyone except Ember does."

"They just know what a magical klutz I am. They've seen me flub more times than they can count." I waved a hand flippantly. They knew what I was and wasn't capable of, and they were right to judge me for it.

He pursed his lips. "You underestimate yourself as well."

I shrugged. "I know my limitations."

"You limit yourself. If you had more confidence, you could be the most powerful witch in your coven."

"That's the thing though." I twisted toward him. "I don't care about power. I'm happy in my library and my studio. Ink is my jam."

He nodded. "I'm sorry for upsetting you this morning."

I searched my heart for a reason to stay mad at him, but I couldn't find one. Chaos was a demon. I couldn't expect him to behave like a human man. Hell, he actually behaved better than a lot of men. My brain couldn't find a logical reason to stay miffed either. For once, my heart and mind agreed on something.

"You're forgiven."

He took my hand, and this time, I let him hold it. I liked Chaos a lot. Too much, honestly, but knowing our relationship had an expiration date made it okay in my mind. He would leave me in the end, but first, he would save me.

My chest tightened, and an ache spread through my body. My heart didn't want him to leave. My brain told me he had to, but I would deal with that pain when the time came. For now, I would enjoy being wanted, because it sure as hell felt good.

We landed at Louis Armstrong Airport at six in the evening, right when the library closed. Since breaking and entering wasn't on my to-do list, we gathered our bags and took an Uber to our boutique hotel in the French Quarter. The two-story building sported yellowish-beige paint with white trim, and a wrought iron fence that looked like cornstalks surrounded the property.

After checking in, Chaos carried the bags and we headed upstairs to our room. A king-size bed in an antique frame sat next to the window, and a matching armoire stood against the wall across from it.

Chaos sat on the edge of the mattress and ran his hand over the duvet. "I do hope we can make use of this tonight."

My stomach fluttered again, and heat pooled below my navel. We could make use of it right then and there if I wasn't famished. "If you're a good demon, maybe we can."

The green in his eyes rippled like water disturbed by a pebble. "I'll be very good."

Sweet spirits, was it hot in here? I grabbed my satchel and slung it over my shoulder. "Food first. I'm starving."

We left the hotel and made our way down Royal Street in search of a restaurant. Tourists milled about, and music and laughter from a block over filled the air. It was warm out... almost muggy...which was odd to a girl from Massachusetts. I pulled up my sleeves and tied my hair into a ponytail.

"This city is thick with magic. Not all of it is good." Chaos rested his hand on the small of my back.

"I know. New Orleans is like a beacon for the supernatural. A lot of vampires and shapeshifters live here, along with three different classes of witches." I found a restaurant, and we went inside. The scents of Cajun spices filled the air, making my mouth water.

We sat at a table by the window, and Chaos looked at me over his menu. "Light and dark witches. What's the third?"

"Voodoo. It's a lot like witchcraft, but they have their own spirits called loa. They have different rituals and beliefs, but they tap into the same energy from the universe as witches."

"Fascinating."

The server arrived to take our order, and I asked for the sampler platter with red beans and rice, etouffee, and jambalaya. Chaos ordered the biggest steak they had and a bottle of wine.

When the server filled our glasses and walked away, I took a sip of cabernet. It was bold and dry, and it warmed me from the inside out. Kind of like the man sitting across from me.

I set the glass down and let out a long sigh. "It feels so good to take a break. I kinda feel bad for Ember though. She's out there fighting monsters and sealing rifts, and I'm sitting in a French Quarter restaurant, enjoying a glass of wine with the hottest man on the planet."

"Something tells me Ember enjoys fighting." He picked up his glass and took a sip.

I laughed. "Oh, she definitely does. Maybe not this often, but fighting is in her blood."

"And ink is in yours. You all have something useful to contribute to your coven, and we are here, enjoying a glass of wine, because your skills require us to be here. Guilt is a useless emotion. You should let it go."

"I would if I could." Our food arrived, and I dug in. I'd been to New Orleans once before, but like most people in their early twenties in this city for the first time, I'd let the good times roll and drank more than I ate.

I shoveled a spoonful of etouffee into my mouth, and it was a spicy, savory flavor explosion on my tongue. Every bite of every morsel tasted almost orgasmic. Chaos nodded his appreciation with each cut of meat he ate, and we devoured our meals more quickly than a newbie in a maximum-security prison.

"That was so good." I reluctantly pushed my plate away. "I can't eat another bite."

"May I?" He picked up his fork.

"Have at it." I downed the rest of my wine and took a sip of water.

After paying the tab, we walked down Royal, looking in the shop windows and acting like a normal couple in a normal world, which was weird as weird could be. The shroud we put on his aura hadn't faded, so no one had a clue a Prince of Hell walked among them.

"Where is the music coming from?" he asked.

"Bourbon Street, one block over. It's wild after dark. You'd love it." I stopped at an art gallery to admire a painting of a swamp scene.

"Then we should go." He stood behind me, resting his hands on my shoulders.

I gazed at his reflection in the glass. "I'm not sure you could control yourself. It's chaotic enough at night."

He slid his arms around me, hugging me from behind, and whispered, "I already promised to be a good demon."

His breath against my ear made me shiver. "Okay. But just for a few minutes, and then we go back to the hotel."

"Where I can be a bad demon?" He flicked out his tongue to lick my earlobe.

Hecate have mercy, my knees nearly buckled. I turned to face him. "Only for me."

He drew an X over his heart. "I swear on the throne of Hades."

"I thought Lucifer was king."

"He has many names." He took my hand and guided me toward a side street. Quaint little houses in pastel shades lined the sides of the empty road, and a streetlight cast a hazy glow over a giant pothole.

Chaos tightened his grip on my hand and yanked me behind him. "Don't move."

"What's wrong?" I started forward, but he put his arm out to block me.

"Shadow magic. A group of witches are battling an orc."

"What? Right here around all these houses?" I gripped his arm and followed his gaze to the supposed scene. I saw nothing but a quiet street. "Let's turn around so they can do their thing. We're not supposed to engage here."

"Indeed, I can," he said to the invisible witches. At least, I assumed it was them because I still saw and heard nothing.

"Allow me to be of assistance." Chaos strode toward them and lit a fireball in his hand.

Crappity crap. What part of *fire and water don't mix* did he not understand? The New Orleans covens despised Salem. They swore their city was the magical epicenter of North America, even though Salem had the first witches and the thinnest veil.

I had no idea what they said in response to his display, but he tossed the fireball onto what I assume was the dead orc. The flames blazed and dissipated in seconds. A moment later, the shadow magic rolled away, and I could finally see.

A woman stood with her arms crossed, eyeing Chaos suspiciously, and a wet spot lay on the concrete where Chaos had tossed his fire. Oh jeez. Of course he had to do that in front of a water witch. Way to stay off their radar.

"You." She pointed at me. "Come here."

I held in a groan and walked toward them. "Sorry for the intrusion." I clutched Chaos's arm. "My boyfriend is overly helpful sometimes. We'll be on our way."

She widened her stance, and the three men who were with her fanned out around us. "You saw through our shadow and can summon fire. You're not going anywhere but our coven headquarters. The High Priestess will decide what we do with you."

"That's really not necessary." I squeezed Chaos's arm, reminding him of his promise to be a good demon. "We're just here for a little vacay. If we're not welcome, we'll leave first thing in the morning."

"How did the orc get here if there's no rift?" Chaos asked.

The woman tilted her head, studying him. "We sealed it yesterday. This was the last monster who got through." She cast her gaze to me. "Fire witches who know about the rifts. You must be from Salem."

"No." I shook my head adamantly. "We're from Maine, actually. We're solitary."

She put her hands on her hips. "First an earth witch infiltrated our library, and now we have fire witches in our midst. If Salem wants war, that's what we'll give them."

Shit. Chrys was here. This was bad. So very bad. "Hey, honey?" I squeezed Chaos's arm again. "Remember that promise you made?"

His energy shifted, his magic rising to the surface. "Indeed."

"It's okay if you want to break it."

"Understood." He didn't move, didn't give any indication that he was doing anything at all, but the water witch's eyes widened, and her hands clenched into fists. She looked at us, confusion creasing her brow, and she whirled to face one of the men.

"What are you doing?" she screeched.

The man stiffened. "What are *you* doing."

One man shoved the other, and I tugged on Chaos's arm. "Time to go."

We turned and pounded pavement back to Royal Street before making a sharp right and heading for the hotel. Inside, I cast a ward to shroud our magic and hoped to Hecate they didn't see which way we ran.

"Chrys believed the book was with the coven." He sat on the edge of the bed. "Why?"

I shook my head and paced the small room. "She must have used magic to search. A location spell might show her the general area, but it wouldn't be precise." I stopped and dropped down next to him. "She has Mayhem's skull. I bet she used it as a conduit to scry for his mark. Good gravy, she's a strong witch."

"Not as strong as you." He grasped my hand. "Why did you not scry for it?"

"Because searching for it the mundane way was faster and

didn't use any vim. If she figures out it's in the public library, we're screwed."

"Then will have to get to it before she does."

I sighed hard. It looked like breaking and entering was on my to-do list after all.

CHAPTER 6
CHAOS

Donned in all black, Ash had tied her hair into a knot on top of her head and pulled a knit cap over it, concealing her blue locks. With her bag of spells slung over her shoulder, she crept down the road, her gaze bouncing this way and that, her muscles tensing more than I'd ever seen them before.

I walked beside her, resting my hand on her back and wishing I could send her a pulse of magic through my mark to calm her. But I'd made a promise never to use magic on her without permission, and I would uphold it. I would do anything for her.

"I understand that you're saving your vim, but the amount of stress you're feeling right now will deplete your energy as well."

"It's fine. We're almost there." A light indicated we could

cross the six-lane thoroughfare, and Ash jogged to the opposite side. I followed, and after another block and then a right turn, the library came into view.

The multistory building had darkened windows, save for one on the bottom floor near the front entrance. Ash looked at it, scrunched her nose in an adorable way, and paced past the doors and around the side.

Stopping at a service entrance, she took my hand and pulled me into the shadows. "There's probably a security guard in there. If he catches us, can you handle him without hurting him?"

"I will do my best."

She tugged her lock-picking kit from her bag. "I'm serious. Just scramble his mind long enough for us to grab the book and make sure he doesn't remember what we look like."

Interesting. She'd gone from *don't use your magic under any circumstance* to my power being her first line of defense. "I can't guarantee he won't destroy any books. I know you are particular about libraries."

Her shoulders dropped with her hard exhale. "You're right. Change of plans. We find the guard first. I'll cast a binding spell, and we'll haul ass upstairs, grab the book and get out before he knows what hit him."

"That is an excellent plan."

She slid two pieces of metal into the lock and moved them around until it clicked. The handle moved down when she pressed it, but the door didn't budge. "Dammit. It's deadbolted from the inside. I'll have to use magic to unlock it."

"Might there be an alarm system?"

"Might you have mentioned that concern before I tried to open the door?" She straightened and adjusted the knit cap on her head. "If there is one, the keypad to turn it off isn't going to be here. There must be another door the employees enter through. Come on."

We crept along the back of the library and turned up the left side. Another door with a light above it stood near the front corner. "Will you be able to disarm the alarm without the code?"

Her mouth screwed to one side as she took out her lock-picking tools. "I think so. If not, we'll have to run. We've already put ourselves on the coven's radar. We can't risk getting into trouble with the law too."

The law didn't worry me in the slightest. Ash might not approve of the ways I could handle them, but she didn't need to worry about the police. I was about to tell her as much when she opened the door, and an incessant beeping sounded in the entry.

She grabbed my arm, pulled me inside, and shined her phone's light onto the wall. A panel with illuminated numbers screeched, and Ash held her hands over it, whispering a spell. It beeped three more times in quick succession before glorious silence filled the room.

"Whew. I am so glad that worked." She paced across the room and pressed her back against the wall before peeking through the doorway. Waving her hand, she told me to move aside, so I joined her against the wall.

"What's your plan?" I asked in a hushed voice.

"The security guard is coming this way." She clutched a potion bottle in her hand and removed the cork. "Standing tall or on your knees, in the name of the goddess, I force you to freeze." She tossed the potion at the guard, and he immediately stilled, his eyelids the only part of him that could move.

"How long will your spell last?" I asked as I followed her down the hall and toward a staircase.

"My vim is stronger since we got rid of Chrys's hex on our house, so ten to fifteen minutes. Let's grab the book and jet."

I couldn't help but smile as we ascended the stairs and Ash made a sharp left toward a doorway. "You know where to find the book. Your newfound power has grown exponentially."

"It's so weird." She plucked a thick volume from the shelf and laid it on a table. "I hardly have to try anymore."

She opened the book to the index and ran her finger down the page before tapping it and flipping through. "Thank the goddess this book is legit. Do those look right to you?"

She turned the book toward me and pointed to the entries about my brothers and me. Multiple paragraphs described our physical appearance and our place in the hierarchy. How in Hell's name did humans know so much about us?

"The sigils do look correct."

She pointed to Mayhem's mark. "I told you it curved left."

"Hmm. I stand corrected."

She took her phone from her pocket and snapped a photo of the page.

"I thought we were removing the book from public access."

"We are, but I'm not taking any chances. I'm texting the picture to Ember now, so we'll be ready when we get his skull. I don't want to lug this giant book around everywhere we go." She closed it and put it in her bag.

"Very smart."

"I tend to be." She winked, making my chest heat, and nodded toward the stairs.

We made our way down and past the security guard who still stood frozen in the hall. He blinked but otherwise seemed incoherent of what happened around him.

"That is a handy spell," I said as we exited the building.

"Sure is."

Ash closed the door and stayed close to the wall, slinking toward the back of the building. "We'll take this to the room, and I'll see if I can get us an earlier flight tomorrow. The sooner we can get out of New Orleans, the better."

"Leaving so soon? But the party just started." Chrys stepped out from the shadows and rested her hands on her hips.

Ash gasped, stopping in her tracks and stepping backward into me. I clutched her shoulders and moved her aside so I could block whatever magic Chrys might throw at her.

"Hand it over, Ash. Don't make this difficult." She clutched a knife in one hand.

"You have no idea what you're dealing with." Ash stepped forward. "If you summon Mayhem, the veil will be torn to shreds and Salem will be overrun with beasts. Surely you don't want to destroy the entire town."

Chrys scoffed. "Says the woman who already summoned Chaos. I'd hoped he'd plow through my hex on Patrice's house.

Vanquishing him then would have saved me a lot of trouble, but this actually worked out in my favor."

"How so?" Ash slipped her hand into her bag.

"You led me right to the book I needed. Scrying only gets you so far, as I'm sure you know. Now, give it to me."

"You'll have to kill me first." Ash took a bottle from her satchel, but before she could activate it, Chrys threw her knife. The blade sliced into her hand, knocking the potion to the ground, where it shattered, rendering the spell useless.

Talons protruded from my fingertips as fury ignited an inferno in my soul. My horns extended from my skull, and as my muscles coiled, preparing me to lunge, a gunshot exploded from behind me and pain ripped through my shoulder.

I roared and whirled around to see the culprit: the security guard, who now trembled in his boots. With a grunt, I scrambled his mind. He turned and ran, his head slamming into the brick wall with such force, his skull cracked and caved inward. Blood poured from the gash on his forehead as he thudded on the pavement, dead.

Ash used the distraction to her advantage, running and tackling Chrys. She groaned as her back hit the ground, and Ash pinned her shoulders, holding them down with her knees. "Why are you doing this?"

Chrys struggled beneath her weight. "I need the demon."

"Chaos, can you hold her?" Ash shouted.

I rotated my shoulder and stormed toward them. Chrys groaned again, and a root from a nearby magnolia tree snaked around Ash's waist, jerking her to the ground. The earth witch yanked the bag from Ash's shoulder and scrambled to her feet, shouting in Latin and raising her hand toward me. A pulse of dark magic slammed into my chest, making me stumble back.

I pushed forward, and another pulse hit my head, then my injured shoulder. The next pulse stopped me in my tracks. Magic wavered in front of me, a wall that could have been made of steel.

"Stop right there, demon." Chrys curled her other hand into a fist, and the roots tightened around Ash. The ground rumbled, the pavement splitting open like a fissure, revealing the earth below. "Or I will bury her so deep no one will ever find her body."

Ash struggled against the roots, grunting as she strained, while Chrys poured a circle of salt, speaking in Latin again. I slammed my shoulder against the spell and broke through, rushing to my witch's side. Gripping the roots, I pulled, trying to free her, but the harder I pulled the tighter they became.

She wheezed, shaking her head. "Any tighter and I can't breathe."

I rose and faced Chrys. "Release her."

The spell complete, she dusted off her hands. "Or what?"

I called on my chaos magic, sending it toward her and trying to scramble her brain. It had no effect. She had figured out a way to block me. "I'll kill you," I growled.

"No, you won't. Earth magic doesn't die with the caster. Those roots are very much alive, and if I stop controlling them, they'll return to the ground...taking Ash with them."

"It's true," Ash said. "Just like my fire would continue to burn."

"If you want to save your girlfriend, step into the circle."

Chrys gestured to the containment ring she'd drawn on the ground.

"Don't do it," Ash ground out. "She'll vanquish you, and I'll die anyway."

Surprise flashed across Chrys's face. "The sigil connects you? I assume that works both ways then?"

Ash pressed her lips together, refusing to speak.

"We can always find out." She flicked her wrist, and a root snaked around Ash's neck. "If you die, and he gets vanquished, I can easily summon him back now that I have the sigils. What will it be, lover boy? I'm about to snap her neck, so make up your mind."

I looked from Ash to Chrys. "Will you release her if I comply?"

"Of course." She waved a hand flippantly. "You have my word."

"Chaos, no! She's lying."

My stomach soured as I watched the root tighten around her neck. Chrys wanted to command me, to force me to do her bidding, and Ash's life was her currency. Stepping into her circle gave Ash her only chance at survival. "Agreed."

"Please." Ash struggled, her adrenaline causing her fingertips to spark, and a tiny flame danced across a root, charring the surface. It seemed our adversary hadn't bothered to make her trap fireproof.

"Allow me to say goodbye." I took a tentative step toward my witch. When the roots didn't tighten, I continued, kicking dirt over the small amount of smoke rising from the burned area. Kneeling beside her, I pressed a kiss to her forehead.

"Everyone underestimates you, but your fire will continue to burn."

"Don't," she whispered.

Chrys laughed. "Ash's fire. That's funny."

Her dismissal confirmed my suspicion. I stepped into the circle. "Let your fire burn."

CHAPTER 7
ASH

Let my fire burn? Was he serious? Surely he didn't just offer himself up to a dark witch, thinking I could burn my way out of this mess, because I had already tried. All I'd managed was a miniature flame that barely singed the root, and then he'd kicked dirt over it.

Wait... My little spark had burned the root. She didn't bother with a fireproofing spell because, as Chaos said, she underestimated me. Everyone underestimated me, and that was his plan. For me to somehow tap into my dysfunctional fire magic, burn my way out of this trap, and defeat an earth witch whose power was stronger than anyone I'd ever seen...even Cinder.

Riiiight... I should have gone to Hell with Chaos when I had the chance.

Chrys popped the top off a potion bottle and recited

Shade's spell, "Hide from sight our magical plight. With the power of Shade, my intent is conveyed."

Shadows rolled around us, casting the rest of the world in grayscale. If she'd done that from the beginning, maybe the security guard would have survived. Not that she cared about the lives of others, but I did. And my body count was adding up.

She crossed her arms, screwing her mouth to one side. "This is a conundrum. I'd planned to force you into submission and kill Ash. Now, I'll have to keep her alive in order to use you."

Chaos growled. "Ash has claimed me. No spell you could cast will change that. I belong to her and her alone."

She cocked her head. "Careful, demon, or I'll send you back to prison with your brother."

"You don't have the power." He curled his hands into fists, his talons and horns retreating, returning him to his full human form, and I couldn't begin to fathom why.

Well, I guess I could. He was counting on me to save the day for some goddess-knew-why reason, but he was stronger in his demon form. Why on earth would he limit himself?

"You don't have a clue. None of you do." Chrys took a grimoire from her bag and opened it to a bookmarked page.

I wiggled beneath the roots, trying to free my arm. If I'd thought to strap a dagger to my thigh, I might be able to cut my way out of this, but no. I'd hyper-focused on getting that damn encyclopedia and didn't consider that Chrys might follow us. That we might lead her right to it.

"Why are you doing this?" I asked for the umpteenth time.

"Cinder was your best friend. Our coven, our family, has been nothing but good to you. We treated you like a sister."

"Quit your whining." She snapped the book shut and returned it to her bag. "Cinder betrayed me, Ember's ego is more than I can bare, and you screw up everything you touch. Salem will be a better place without the three of you."

She snapped her fingers, and the roots tightened around me, the dirt beneath me rumbling, turning to quicksand. "I'll be calling on you again soon," she said to Chaos before turning on her heel and darting into the night, no doubt heading back to Salem to enact her plan.

And here we were again. Chrys had decided to kill me after all, and why not? With the sigils and Mayhem's skull in her possession, she could summon him and Chaos in one circle. Hell, she could probably drag Discord away from Cinder if she wanted to. It would have been the perfect time to say *I told you so* if I wasn't in the process of being buried alive.

Chaos slammed his shoulder against the circle's magic, letting out a roar when it didn't shatter. Maybe if he set his inner demon free, he'd have a chance, but no. He stayed in his human form. "Burn through, Ash. You can do it."

Dirt piled up around me as I sank farther and farther into the earth. My pulse sprinted, my chest squeezing like a vice until I could barely breathe. Did I ever mention being buried alive was at the top of my phobias list?

Burn through. How could I do that when a tiny spark was all I could ever manage? "I can't."

"You can." He punched the invisible wall, and the magic

shimmered. "Search your soul. It's deep inside you, ready to come out. Use the adrenaline in your veins, and light those roots ablaze."

"Thanks for the pep talk." The roots pulled me deeper. Dirt covered my legs. If I waited much longer, whatever fire I could summon wouldn't have the oxygen it needed to burn.

I took a deep breath and focused on my inborn power. Either nothing would happen, or I'd turn New Orleans into an inferno. I'd have to chance it.

"Goddess, please help me." I drew magic from the core of my being, raising it to the surface. My veins heated, and sparks formed on my fingertips.

"You can do it, Ash." Chaos slammed against the circle again. "I know you can."

I had to, and I could. At least I thought I could. I had to think I could, or it wouldn't work. I was like the Little Engine. *I think I can. I think I can.*

Curling my fingers toward my palms, I gathered my fire, igniting a ball in each hand. I let the fire roll down onto the roots, but the dirt shifted, dousing the flame before it could do any damage.

A fist of dread clenched in my stomach. That was all the fire I'd ever been capable of summoning, and with my legs covered in dirt, it was useless. "There's no way."

I sank deeper, deeper. My grave covered my hips and hands.

"There is a way." He pressed his palms to the ring of magic containing him. "Remember when I was inside you. The fire ignited on your arms as we fought the fae."

"That was you." I wiggled some more, making my dire situation worse.

"No, Ash. That was your fire. I accessed it, but it belonged to you."

Yeah, right. "I can't do that. Believe me, it was all you."

"So you're going to let Chrys destroy your coven? She'll murder your sisters and turn your town dark, and you're going to lie there and take it like an impotent runt?" He lit his hands on fire and bashed them against the circle. The magic shimmered but didn't wane.

Anger sparked in my chest, battling my fear for control. "I'm *not* an impotent runt."

"No?" His talons extended, and he jabbed them against the magic, making it pulse. "Are you sure? Because that's exactly how you're acting. Like a useless, spoiled runt."

My teeth clenched tightly until a sharp pain shot through my jaw. Where did he get off calling me a runt when he was trapped in a containment circle? A circle he *voluntarily* walked into, even though I told him she'd kill me anyway.

Fury billowed in my chest, making my blood boil and my fire magic rise to the surface.

Chaos's hands returned to normal, and he held them up in surrender. "Go ahead then. Let Chrys win. Let her murder your coven for you. You'd have done it yourself eventually."

My rage surged, coursing through my veins. "I would *never* hurt my family."

"How many people have already died in your wake?" He crossed his arms. "How many more will?"

"I haven't killed anyone!" I strained. Every muscle in my body tensed. Fire churned in my gut and rolled down my arms, gathering in my hands and turning them hotter than a crematorium. Hotter than they'd ever been before.

Flames exploded from my palms, sending dirt flying through the air.

Magical fire rushed up my arms, circling my chest and turning Chrys's roots to soot. I screamed and slammed my flaming arms onto my legs, incinerating the rest of my organic chains before scrambling out of my grave. Thank the goddess I wore fireproof clothes.

My body still ablaze, I marched toward the circle, my nostrils flaring as I clenched my hands into fists. "Don't you ever call me a runt again. I'm an effing Holland witch."

Chaos smiled, nodding his head like a proud papa. "The shadow magic is retreating. I suggest you douse your flames before someone sees you."

"I..." My standard answer of *I can't* nearly crossed my lips, but I looked at the fire dancing on my arms and sucked in a trembling breath. I'd done it. I'd burned my way out of Chrys's death trap and lit half my body ablaze. Even Ember couldn't do that.

"Take a deep breath." Chaos demonstrated as if I didn't know how to breathe.

I did as he said, inhaling as deeply as I could and letting it out slowly. When nothing happened, I did it again.

"Focus on the core of your being, where your magic resides. Do you feel the source of the flames?"

I concentrated and searched, finding the cradle of my magic

directly below my breastbone. Resting my hand on the spot, I took another breath.

"Call it back inside. Don't try to force it. Just allow it to return home."

Relaxing my body, I closed my eyes and centered myself, imagining the source opening and allowing the fire to return.

"You're straining. Relax your jaw."

I parted my teeth and took another deep, cleansing breath. The fire rolled back inside me, gathering in my chest and calming to embers. Holy crap.

A laugh blurted from my throat. "That was insane."

"That was your magic."

I shook my finger at my demon. "I've got a good mind to leave you in the circle, mister. What you said was cruel."

He shrugged. "I said what I had to say to force you into acting."

"It wasn't nice."

"I wasn't trying to be."

I kicked my boot through the salt ring, freeing him, and tugged my phone from my back pocket. Whew. It was still intact. If I'd set my whole body on fire, it would have melted and we'd have been screwed.

"Let's get back to the hotel. We'll head for the airport first thing in the morning and try to get on an earlier flight." I texted Ember, telling her to be on the lookout for Chrys.

"You aren't worried Chrys will summon Mayhem tonight?"

"She won't do it here. Taking over Salem is her goal, so she'll want to have him there. She thinks I'm dead, which would mean you're vanquished. It would be a helluva lot easier to control you both if she didn't have to transport you fifteen hundred miles." I led the way out of the back alley, and we crossed Canal Street before heading into the French Quarter.

"She has a head start and the sigils. She could make it to Salem and summon my brother long before we return if we wait."

Crappity crap. He was right. After everything that just went down, my mind was reeling. I couldn't think straight. But I'd set my arms on fire! "We'll grab our stuff and head there now."

Chaos took my hand. "I hope you know I didn't mean a word of what I said back there."

I waited for a horse-drawn carriage to pass the intersection before darting across the street. "Didn't you though?"

He held his thumb close to his pointer finger. "Maybe about your behavior, but I have never believed you're useless."

"I know, and apparently, I needed to hear it. Though it freaks me out to think it took absolute fury for me to unleash it. That's not a good quality in a light witch."

His brow furrowed, but he didn't offer an answer. I didn't have one either, and we didn't have time to ponder it. Maybe after we saved the world, I could try to figure it out.

We made it to the hotel without incident—thank the goddess—and grabbed our bags. Well, I grabbed my bag of clothes. Chrys had, once again, taken my satchel full of spells. At least she didn't destroy it this time.

Then again, she now had an arsenal at her disposal. Not that she needed the help. She'd managed to arm herself against Chaos's brain-scrambling magic and nearly killed me. Twice.

I cast a longing look at the comfy, king-sized bed and

allowed myself a moment of regret for not letting Chaos be a bad demon when I'd had the chance.

He wrapped his arms around me and brushed his lips to mine. "We will have another opportunity to play."

"Will we?" I rested my head on his shoulder. "Seems like everything will be nonstop from here."

"Everyone has to sleep at some point, and I will make certain you're relaxed enough to slumber when that time arrives."

The feel of his strong arms wrapped around me and the warmth of his embrace made me ache all over. I wanted him more than I'd ever wanted anyone in my life, and not just in a playtime kind of way. He complemented me in a way I never dreamed anyone could.

Yeah, he'd royally pissed me off back at the library, but it was exactly what I'd needed to save us both. He always knew what I needed.

Chaos made me a better witch. A better woman.

I swallowed the lump in my throat and pulled from his embrace. "We should go. I don't have the ingredients to cloak us on the way to the airport, and I'm certain the local coven we ticked off is looking for us."

I swiped open the Uber app and called for a ride. "Should be here in five. Let's head down."

Outside the hotel, a cast-iron table with two chairs stood beneath a magnolia tree. How nice it would have been to enjoy a nightcap in the warm fall air before going inside and letting this Prince of Hell bang my brains out.

We passed the table and stepped outside the fence to wait

for our ride. A group of women wearing hot pink sashes walked by, two of them helping the one with a white veil remain on her feet. Across the street, a man with a scraggly beard sat against the building, balancing a cardboard sign against his legs as he dozed off.

Both New Orleans and Salem were tourist destinations teeming with magic, yet the atmosphere, the vibe, couldn't have been more different. A fist of regret tightened in my chest because I would never get to explore the magic and wonder of this city with the man by my side.

Oof. I had to stop thinking about the end. Regret was another one of those useless emotions Chaos mentioned. It did absolutely no good, so I needed to make like Elsa and let it go. We'd be home in Salem before I knew it, battling a dark witch for a demon skull and literally breaking Hell loose.

Goddess, help us all.

I checked my phone. The Uber sat in traffic a block away. I was about to suggest we go to it when a fog rolled over us, casting the world into grayscale.

"Shit." My heart hammered in my chest, and I clutched Chaos's arm, dragging him toward the car. "Is it Chrys?"

"You tell me." His gaze darted around the shadow spell's perimeter.

Right. I could locate people close by as easily as objects now. With a deep inhale, I focused on Chrys's energy, searching the area for her vibration. "I don't sense her."

The Uber stood four yards away. Just a few more steps...

My muscles seized mid-stride. A heaviness pressed down on me, squeezing, making me completely immobile. I cut my gaze to Chaos. He was frozen too. The Uber turned the corner, heading toward the hotel, and I tried to shout. My voice didn't work. My vision tunneled. The only sound I heard was my pulse whooshing in my ears.

Then silence.

CHAPTER 8
ASH

My brain throbbed in my skull, and I pressed the heels of my hands to my temples, countering the pressure. I opened my eyes to bright white light, and my stomach lurched. Sitting up, I dry heaved, thanking the goddess my dinner didn't splatter on the floor.

"Ash?" The familiar voice calmed me, and I looked up to find Chaos standing behind a set of iron bars.

I blinked and rubbed my eyes, trying to focus. "Where are we?"

"Are you okay?" He started to grab the bars but fisted his hands, dropping them to his sides instead.

"I think so. What happened?" My vision returned to normal, and the pounding in my head lessened to a dull ache.

He exhaled, some of the tension releasing from his shoulders. "We're imprisoned in a coven house. The cells neutralize magic, even mine, and the bars are enchanted with some sort of pain spell. I don't advise touching them."

"Sounds like you know that from experience." I stood and took in my surroundings. My cell had three wooden walls and an iron gate. A cot sat on the hardwood in the middle of the small space, and an unnecessarily bright light fixture hung from a beam above.

Chaos stood across the hall in an identical enclosure, his jaw tight, a vein protruding from his forehead. "Only an elemental witch would be powerful enough to contain me for this long."

"Yeah, the New Orleans covens are run by water witches." I turned to the back wall and lifted a hand to knock my fist against it.

"Don't."

The moment my knuckles met the wood, an electric jolt zipped up my arm and exploded through my body like a million needles jabbing me from the inside out. "Son of a bitch!"

I clutched my chest, making sure my heart still beat. The sensation felt a lot like the electrification spell in Boston.

"The walls are enchanted as well," Chaos said.

"No kidding." I opened and closed my fist, the pain slowly subsiding as I rolled my neck. "I don't remember anything after the shadow rolled over us. Do you?"

"I was mildly coherent through it all. Though my vision blurred too much for me to identify the culprits, their voices sounded like the ones we encountered yesterday."

"Yesterday?" I snapped my gaze to his eyes. "We've been here all night?"

"When I leaned against the bars, I saw the door at the end of the hall. I assume daylight illuminated the edges, though it could have been a yellow electric light."

"Crap. Crappity, crap, crap, crap. Chrys must be in Salem by now. Has she summoned Mayhem? Can you sense him?"

"I sense nothing outside these walls."

"We need to warn my sister." I slapped my back pocket. Of course they'd taken my phone. "Ugh! What are we going to do? Chrys could be using Mayhem to destroy everything as we speak. We have to get you home. You're the only one who can stop him."

His lips twitched. "They have not only electrified the bars and neutralized our magic, but they have also cast a containment circle around each cell. I'm afraid we're at their mercy until they arrive to retrieve us. They want to question us."

"Of course they do. We're fire witches who know about the rifts." I sank onto the cot and pinched the bridge of my nose. "Okay, let's get our story straight. I had no idea the rifts were spreading, and they'll surely blame us. Who knows what Chrys told them."

He crossed his arms. "My chaos magic normally works through any containment or suppression spell. Unless they know what I am and have guarded themselves against my power, I will be able to drive them mad. If you'll allow me, I can make it so they don't remember we were ever here."

"And then what?" I dropped my hands into my lap. "Unless you can control their minds and make them let us out, we'll still be stuck in here."

He frowned. "No, my magic is about disorder, not control. I cannot command anyone in a maddened state."

"They'd end up killing each other, and we'd be left to rot."

He arched a brow. "Unless one of the witches who dies is the one whose magic has trapped us."

I laughed dryly. That Chaos. He always looked on the bright side of destruction, didn't he? "As tempting as that sounds, I think our best bet is to tell them what's going on. We can blame it all on Chrys, tell them she's summoning the demons, and we have to go to Salem to stop her."

He pressed his lips together, nodding as he considered my plan. "And you believe they'll simply let us go?"

"If we're convincing enough, why wouldn't they?"

He clasped his hands behind his back. "You are forgetting that New Orleans contains both light and dark covens, and we don't know which one has imprisoned us."

"Then I guess we'll have to play it by ear."

"If they're dark witches, my plan will—"

"We'll play it by ear."

We would have to because the door at the end of the hall swung open and sunlight flooded the corridor. I cocked my head, giving Chaos a look that I hoped to Hecate said *let me handle this*. He opened his hands, palms toward me, conceding control...at least for the moment.

"Here they are," a woman's voice drifted down the hall, and three or four sets of footsteps followed. It was hard to make out just how people planned to interrogate us until they came into view.

The brunette water witch we saw yesterday evening, two of

the men who'd accompanied her, a big beefy guy I'd never seen, and a tall, lanky blonde, who had to be their High Priestess, made five. Damn. This was serious, and I couldn't tell if they were dark, light, or something in-between, thanks to the hex they'd placed on these cells.

And how the hell did they remember who we were? Chaos must've been holding back when he fried their brains.

"They claimed they were from Maine," our elemental friend said. "But their IDs show Salem addresses." She handed the little plastic cards to the High Priestess.

"Thank you, Sandra." She looked at our IDs, her brows lifting as she read mine. "And this one is a Holland witch." She strolled toward me. "A member of Salem's founding family, causing trouble and telling lies in our city. Explain yourself."

"We didn't come here to cause trouble." I started to reach for the bars, but I remembered what had happened when I touched the wall and thought better of it.

The Priestess handed our IDs to Sandra and crossed her arms. "Then tell me, Ash, why are you and Shade here?"

I flicked my gaze to Chaos. I'd forgotten about the glamour on Shade's license. Thank the goddess it hadn't worn off. "Just a little vaycay."

She tilted her head like a disapproving mother. "That's not what your earth witch told us when we caught her in our library."

I crossed my arms to mimic her posture. "Whatever she told you was a lie."

"Says the witch who's been lying since she got here." A man with curly black hair stepped forward. "How can you see through my magic? I'm a master shadow caster. No one can penetrate my spells."

The High Priestess put her hand against his chest, pushing him back. "Calm down, Umbra. They're elementals. They have power you can't imagine."

He narrowed his eyes. "Elementals aren't all that."

Oh, for Hecate's sake. Was it a requirement that all shadow witches had egos for days? "I can't see through your magic. Shade can because it's one of his inborn powers. I don't know how he does it."

Chaos shrugged, acting cool as an icicle. "I have always been able to see through shadow."

"Nobody has that much power," Umbra said.

"He obviously does." The Priestess gave him a pointed look, and he backpedaled to join the other four.

"Look." I raised my hands in surrender. "It's true we aren't here on vacation. We lied because we didn't want to stir up any trouble, but we obviously made it worse by not being upfront. We aren't the enemy."

"The earth witch you found in your library is the true adversary," Chaos said. "She is the reason the veil is weakening, and she plans to destroy it when she returns to Salem."

"Funny." She rested a hand on her hip, shifting her weight to her right leg. "That's the same story she told us about you."

My hands instinctively curled into fists. "She has an encyclopedia of demons. She's planning to summon a Prince of Hell, and if we don't get back to Salem soon, she'll do it. You think the rifts are bad now? Wait and see what happens if you don't let us go."

She looked me up and down. "Your friend told me about your curse." She held a hand toward my chest and inhaled deeply, calling on an inborn power, I assumed. "It's as I suspected. Someone...your mother, maybe...blocked your fire magic. She did everything she could to stop you from fulfilling your destiny, but destiny...fate...can't be avoided. You will be responsible for your coven's demise one way or another."

I tried to keep a neutral expression, but damn. My mom blocked my magic? All these years, I'd thought I was defective, when my power had been bound all along. What the actual eff, Mom?

"You didn't know." She pressed her lips together, looking at me with pity. "It doesn't matter. I won't let you summon more demons. We've already had to join forces with the other covens to fight off the monsters coming through. It ends now."

"It's Chrys you want," I said. "She has the book. She's going to summon the demon."

The High Priestess turned, flipping her hair over her shoulder and lifting a hand as she walked away. "Kill them."

That answered my question. We'd landed ourselves in a dark coven's prison.

"Fast or slow?" Umbra cracked his knuckles and stood in front of my cell.

A wicked smile curved Sandra's lips. "Slow deaths are always sweeter."

"Works for me." He shoved his hand into his pocket and pulled out a handful of one-inch-long capsules in red, purple, blue, and green. With a chuckle, he touched each one, no doubt trying to decide which spell he wanted to throw at me first.

He closed his fist around them and searched his pocket for another one, and I had to admit packaging spells like that would be convenient. They took up a helluva lot less space than the bottles I used, but the thing I was most envious of was his pocket size. He could hold fifty spells in each one, with how deep they went. If my pants even had pockets, I'd be lucky if they were three inches. Maybe I should start wearing guys' clothes if I made it out of this in one piece.

"Here we go." He held a black capsule between his thumb and forefinger.

"Don't use that one." Sandra held her hands in front of her chest, gathering the moisture from the air between her palms and creating a ball of water. "I want her to watch her boyfriend die."

Chaos crossed his arms, looking bored. Unless Sandra could sharpen that ball into a sword and stab him through the heart, she would be sorely disappointed.

Umbra's jaw tightened. "If she's blinded, she can only hear his screams. That'll be even better."

She whirled to face him. "She watches. Put your shadow away."

His nostrils flared as he blew out a breath, but he returned the black capsule to his pocket and decided on the purple one. Without even whispering a spell, he wound his arm back and threw it like a baseball. I half-expected it to bounce off the hex surrounding the cell, or at least to fizzle out upon impact. Instead, it sailed right between the bars and exploded against my stomach, and let me tell you, that little pill felt more like a cinder block slamming into my gut.

I careened backward, my shoulders slamming against the electrified wall, sending a jolt rocketing through my body. Fabulous. Their magic could get in, but I couldn't even summon mine, much less throw it at them.

I stretched my neck and shook off the pain. "I didn't know New Orleans witches were such cowards. Why don't you let us out so it can be a fair fight?"

Umbra glared at me and reached toward the lock.

"Don't," one of the henchmen finally got the courage to speak. "They'll burn us alive."

Sandra sent a blast of water with the force of a firehose at Chaos's chest. I was sure she meant to knock him back into the wall like Umbra had just done to me, but my demon held his ground. Her magic soaked his shirt but didn't hurt him in the least.

He laughed. "Is that the best you can do?"

"I'm just getting started." She hurled a stream of water at him, but he stepped out of the way. It splashed against the back wall, the electricity spell zapping the liquid and turning it into steam.

"Javon, freeze them both." Sandra stepped back, letting a henchman approach Chaos's cell. Umbra handed him two green capsules, and Javon cast a binding spell on my demon.

Honestly, I couldn't tell if the hex worked on him or not. He didn't move a muscle, so he was either pretending so he didn't reveal his true identity or it did work and we were screwed.

Javon pinched the capsule and threw it at me before reciting the binding spell. On me, it definitely worked. Starting at my feet, my muscles seized. I tried to wiggle my toes inside my boots, but I'd lost control. The magic crept upward, freezing my legs, my abdomen, my neck. I was a fish in a barrel, and Umbra was about to cock his gun.

Sandra shot another stream at Chaos. It hit his arm and sliced open the skin, but he didn't reward her with a reaction. She hit the other arm and then his shoulder, ripping his shirt. He still looked bored AF, even with blood dripping down his arms.

"Give me a nerve spell." She held her hand toward Umbra, and he placed a red capsule in her palm. "Let's see if you stay stoic with this one."

Oh, dear. Unless they knew of some secret ingredient for that one, he most definitely would stay stoic. Nerve spells didn't affect the Princes of Hell. Not this prince, anyway.

She cast it, and Chaos closed his eyes, his face pinching. Again, he could have been faking. "I expected dark witches to practice more unsavory magic. Especially an elemental. Has someone bound your power too?"

Holy crap, he could talk. "Way to blow your cover." I clamped my mouth shut. I could talk too. And my mind worked perfectly. If we got out of this mess, I'd have to swipe those capsules to see if I could reverse engineer their binding spell.

"Cover?" Sandra faced Chaos. "What is she talking about."

He inclined his chin, refusing to speak.

She turned toward me, her eyes calculating. "Change of plans. He's going to watch her die. Hit her with everything you've got."

"Gladly." Umber gathered shadows between his palms that

looked way too much like Shade's when he'd summoned his magic to kill the rose bush.

I willed my legs to move, to let me step back, away from the icky, sticky funk of dark magic, but they didn't budge. He sent the shadow toward me, and it rolled around my body, encasing me in agony as it dimmed my inner light, sucking the life out of me.

"Chaos," I wheezed, hoping that was enough to let him know he could use whatever magic he needed to get us out of this place.

Umbra's eyes widened, and he blinked three times. His magic released me, the shadows rolling back into him. I heaved two heavy breaths. If I hadn't been frozen, I might have collapsed to the floor. Ouch.

"Umbra!" Sandra shouted. "What are you doing?"

He spun around. "I'm done taking orders from you."

"The hell you are." She shoved him into the bars, zapping him like a mosquito in a bug trap.

He roared and barreled toward her, knocking her into Chaos's bars. She screamed and peeled herself away. Javon threw a punch at the other henchman, clipping him in the jaw. He fought back, and the four of them brawled like they were in a bar fight.

Chaos had bought us some time, but without the use of my magic, I couldn't unlock these doors. He couldn't bust through them, thanks to the containment circle, so we were still stuck. *Think, Ash. Think.*

I looked down, my head finally able to move. The binding spell was wearing off slowly, but these witches would kill each other before I could come up with a plan. Maybe, if the one who cast the spells to keep us in died in this fight, we'd be able to get out like Chaos said. But I had a feeling the High Priestess herself set up this prison. Only someone with immense power could deny an elemental access to her inborn gifts.

My shoulders moved, and I gazed at my arm. My sleeve covered Chaos's mark, but it heated in response to his magic. I wondered...

"Do you think our bond works both ways?"

He walked toward the bars. "What do you mean?"

Sandra sent a wave of water toward Umbra, knocking him off his feet. Javon kicked him while he was down, landing a boot in his stomach. The other guy kicked his head.

"I'm going to try sending my power to you. Hopefully my magic will counter yours, and you'll have control of their minds." It sounded logical, anyway. He was madness; I was order. It was worth a shot.

He raised his brows. "That might just work."

My fingers moved. Then my wrists. Finally my arms were free. Lifting my sleeve, I ran my hand over the mark. Chaos let out a slow exhale. One day I'd remember to ask him what that felt like.

I centered myself, taking three deep breaths and focusing on my connection to my demon. I couldn't summon magic from the core of my being inside this cell, so instead, I thought about Chaos. I imagined the way my body reacted when he sent his power into me. The way it calmed me and helped my mind focus.

"Do you feel anything?" I rubbed the sigil again.

His gaze locked with mine, his expression going from concentration to wonder. He turned his head toward the fray and said, "Order."

The witches stopped fighting, Javon in mid-swing, and turned toward Chaos. Umbra groaned in a pool of blood on the floor.

"Release us," Chaos said.

"I…" Sandra's brow furrowed in confusion.

"Open the gates and let us go," my demon commanded.

"Yeah." She held her hands over the lock and recited a spell. The door swung open, breaking the ring of salt, and Chaos stepped out of his cell.

"Now her." He gestured to me, and Sandra shuffled to my side before casting the same unlocking spell.

I hauled ass out of there and clutched Chaos's arm. "Ask her for our IDs."

He held out his hand, and Sandra dropped the licenses into his palm. "Our bags," he said.

"They're in the main house."

I took the IDs and shoved them into my back pocket. "Can you make it so they don't remember any of this?"

"Not while I'm channeling you."

"Okay. I'll let you go." I pulled down my sleeve, and drew my energy inward, breaking the connection. "Come on." I tugged him toward the exit while Sandra and her gang turned on each other once more.

We stepped into the daylight, and I squinted against the brightness. A massive stone fountain bubbled in the center of a cobblestone courtyard, and decorative troughs lined the perimeter, with water pouring from stone heads mounted to the walls. Muffled shouts echoed from the carriage house where we'd spent the night, but the rest of the air hung soundless, still. Someone had cast a silencing spell over the entire property, allowing nothing out or in.

"Forget about our bags, let's find a cab and get to the airport." I clutched his hand and made my way toward a gate. "Don't let them kill each other."

"The moment we step off the property, I will release them."

"You're not going anywhere." The High Priestess appeared from the main house and lifted a hand toward the fountain. A tidal wave blasted toward us.

CHAPTER 9
CHAOS

I shot a line of hellfire onto the ground and raised my hands. The flames surged, creating a barrier to counter the witch's magic. My fire consumed her wave, turning it to steam the moment it met the flames.

"Impressive." She crossed her arms. "I collect elementals, you know. Perhaps you'd like to stay." Her gaze flicked to our right, where another witch hid in the shadows.

A single root ruptured from the earth and snaked toward Ash before looping around her ankle.

"Hecate on a Hellhound, this is getting old." Ash shook her leg and then bent down yanking the root free. Another one shot upward to her wrist, but she easily removed that one as well. The Priestess might have collected elementals, but her earth witch was either very young or very weak.

Another root snaked toward Ash, and she stomped her boot on it, pinning it to the dirt. "Listen, you do not want to see me use my fire magic right now, because I will burn your entire coven house to the ground and it won't even be on purpose."

I held in a laugh, certain she meant that she would lose control of whatever fire she created. In reality, she could raze this entire city if she could summon the fury to counter the block her mother put on her power.

"So Salem does want war. We can accommodate that." The Priestess pointed at Ash and turned her hand over, curling her fingers one by one toward her palm.

Ash gasped, and sweat beaded on her forehead before gushing from her pores. Tears rained from her eyes, and each exhale released a puff of steam.

I called my wall of fire back to me and stepped between them, blocking her magic from reaching my witch.

"She was dehydrating me." Ash sucked in a giant breath. "I need water." She lunged for the fountain, scooping the water into her hands and sucking down as much as she could.

The Priestess pointed at me before making the same motion with her fingers. "I'm the most powerful elemental on this continent. No witch can defeat me."

This time, I didn't hold in my laugh. "No, you are not, and I am not a witch."

I unleashed my chaos magic in full force, sending it outward to cover the entire property. A panicked scream ripped from the Priestess's throat, and the earth witch stepped out from the shadows, clawing at her face and making it bleed.

Ash tried to stand, but she stumbled, falling backward onto the cobblestone. With our adversaries going insane, I scooped her from the ground, bent her over my shoulder, and carried her through the gate.

"Turn it off." She tapped my back. "It's affecting me too."

I took a deep breath and drew my magic inward. The force with which I had hit them would render them incapable of remembering the past four hours. Possibly the past twenty-four. When we reached the end of the block, I lowered Ash to her feet, holding her tightly until she regained her bearings.

"Will they survive?" She clutched my biceps and swayed.

I pulled her to my chest. "Their minds will recover, though they'll have no memories of the events. I have no way of knowing what they did to each other while I held them."

She nodded and wrapped her arms around my waist. "I need water. Maybe a hospital."

Her skin felt dry, and as I brushed my thumb across her face, it flaked. "You need a healer."

"Well, Patrice is a thousand miles away, so..." Her pallor turned ashen.

"You said there is a light coven here. We'll find it and ask—"

"No." She pulled back, squinting her eyes against the sunlight. "No more witches. I just need a bag of IV fluids, and I'll be fine."

"IV fluids? What are they? Where can I get them?"

"A hospital, but that would take too long. I bet there's an IV bar or three around here somewhere." She turned and took a single step before swaying on her feet and clutching her head. "I can't. I can't walk; I'm too woozy."

"I will carry you." I made to pick her up as I had carried her before, but she shook her head.

"That'll draw too much attention. I'll have to ride piggyback." She motioned for me to turn around, so I obeyed. With her hands on my shoulders, she lifted one leg toward my hip. "Pull me up."

I helped her onto my back, and we ventured deeper into the city.

"Hang a right here. Once we get closer to Bourbon Street, we can ask for directions."

Music grew louder as we approached, and the sidewalks filled with people. The sun hung high in the cloudless sky, illuminating the smiles of the humans walking by.

"Excuse me," Ash said to a woman in a black t-shirt with the name of a bar embroidered on the breast. "Can you point me toward an IV bar?"

Sympathy creased the woman's brow. "Rough night, huh?"

"You have no idea."

"Two blocks that way, on the right." She pointed down the street. "They swear they've got a forty-five-minute hangover cure. Thankfully, I've never had to try it."

"Sounds like exactly what I need. Thank you."

"Anytime." The woman continued on her way, and I walked in the direction she had pointed.

"Oh, crap." Ash tightened her grip on my shoulders. "I don't have a way to pay. My wallet was in the satchel Chrys took."

I continued my trek. "Yet the ID cards and phone were in your pocket. Why not carry everything of importance on your person?"

Her laugh turned into a cough. "Have you seen girl pockets?"

"Apparently not."

"I put the IDs in my back pocket because a lot of places here want to see them before they'll let you inside. My phone went in the other one, and nothing would fit in my front pockets, especially in these pants. They're two inches deep."

"What's the point of adding them to clothing if they'll be of no use?"

"Right? There it is." She pointed to the next building. A sign that read *The Original Forty-Five Minute Hangover Cure* hung above a blue door. She groaned. "I have to stop talking. My throat is so dry."

"Then stop talking."

"But we still don't have a way to pay."

"We won't need to pay."

"These are innocent humans. You can't scramble their brains. Maybe I can get some free water at a fast-food restaurant."

"You can't even walk, Ash. If this will make you better, you'll have it." I opened the door and stepped inside before she could argue. "My girlfriend requires hydration."

"It's fine. I really don't think—"

"Is payment required in advance?" I asked the man behind the counter.

He stood and motioned me toward a reclined chair. "You can pay on your way out. Have a seat."

I situated Ash in the chair, and he handed her a plastic card. "Have a look at the menu, and I'll get a tech for you."

He walked into a back room, and Ash glared at me. "You can't keep hurting people. That's not how this works."

"If you are hydrated, will your magic function properly?"

"Yeah. I haven't used any vim today, but—"

"When it's time to pay, connect with me the way you did in the prison. We will simply convince them that we don't need to pay."

She opened her mouth to argue but paused and closed her lips.

I took her hand. "It's for the greater good. You are the only one who can defeat Chrys, and I am the only one who can reason with Mayhem. We must make you well so we can return to Salem."

"Fine. Just this once but give me the cheapest one." She handed the menu to me, and I scanned the offerings.

A woman wearing a beige shirt and pants smiled as she approached. "Hi, I'm Ashley. What can I do for you?"

"She'll have the deluxe hydration and vitamin package." I gave the menu to her before Ash could see that I requested the most expensive option they offered.

"Perfect. Let's get you hooked up." She took Ash's left arm and pushed up her sleeve. "That's a beautiful tattoo."

Ash's eyes widened in alarm, but when the tech didn't say more, she relaxed. "Thanks."

The woman rubbed alcohol on Ash's skin at the bend of her elbow before sticking her with a thick needle. Ash winced, and the woman removed the needle, leaving a piece of plastic tubing in its place. "It takes about forty-five minutes to complete. Can I get you some water while you wait?"

"Yes, thank you."

"You got it." She opened a small refrigerator and offered some to us both. "Are you going next?"

"No, I feel fine." I accepted mine and twisted off the cap.

She nodded and returned to the back room as Ash drank her entire bottle.

I took a sip and brushed a strand of hair from her face. "Is your full name Ashley like hers?"

"Nope. Mom stayed true to the fire theme when she named us. I asked her why we didn't have normal names once. She said it was because we aren't normal women." She shrugged and leaned her head back, closing her eyes.

"She was right about that." I watched her rest, the color returning to her cheeks as the fluids replenished her system, the anger I felt toward the High Priestess for doing this to her growing with each passing second.

I couldn't begin to imagine the pain Ash must have felt. If I hadn't intervened, she would have died an agonizing death, and for that, the dark witch would pay. I could make good on Ash's threat to burn their entire coven house to the ground, including every witch inside.

The fluids would take another half hour to replenish her. I could kill them all and be back before it was done.

"Don't even think about it." Ash opened her eyes, pinning me with a familiar look. "You're staying right here."

I relaxed the tension from my shoulders. She knew me too well. "She deserves to suffer."

"No. Bad demon." She fought a smile.

"How could you tell what I was planning?" I took her hand in mine.

"Your energy changes when you get mad and start plotting. Plus, the tendons in your neck get so tight I could pluck them like guitar strings."

"I see."

"When this is done, we're getting on the plane, and we are never coming to New Orleans again."

"It's a shame. I rather like this city, aside from the infuriating witches hellbent on destroying you." I sat back in my chair, and we watched a program on the television while the fluids dripped into Ash's arm.

When the bag emptied, the tech removed the tubing and wrapped a pink bandage around her elbow. "How do you feel?"

"Much better, thank you." Ash stood and took two tentative steps forward.

"You can check out at the front desk. Have a great day." The tech smiled warmly and gestured us toward the man behind the counter.

We approached, and I looked at Ash, waiting for her to create the connection. She ran her finger down my mark, and I shivered as the sensation of her caressing every inch of my skin at once washed over me. A moment later, her magic flowed into me, and I activated mine, sending it to the man at the desk. He snapped his gaze to me and blinked twice, awaiting my command.

"The treatment was complimentary," I said. "We'll be leaving now."

He looked at Ash and then at me. "Yeah, of course. Don't forget to give us a good review on Yelp."

"I will. Thanks." Ash took a business card from the desk before walking out the door.

I met her on the sidewalk and took her hand. "We make a good team."

She shook her head. "We can never do that again. Mind control isn't the light witch way."

"How do you plan to travel to the airport then? I'm afraid it's too far to walk."

"Crap." She waved at a yellow car. "Okay. We'll do it one more time."

CHAPTER 10
ASH

"You're joking." Ember paced the length of the kitchen. "Tell me you're joking."

"I wish I was." I sat at the counter next to Chaos and took a sip of beer. Patrice had gone shopping again, and our fridge was now fully stocked. She'd also emptied the dishwasher and swept the floors while we were gone. Maybe we could keep her around...

"You had one job. Go to New Orleans, get the book, and come home." Ember stopped and rested her hands on the counter. "And I specifically told you not to interact with the witches there."

I rolled my eyes. "It's not like we went looking for trouble."

"You don't have to. Trouble follows him everywhere he goes." She grabbed a beer from the fridge and popped the top before taking a long pull. "Mind control, Ash? That's not just bad. That's goddess-smiting-you bad."

"It was for the greater good, so I think I'll be okay." I hoped I would anyway. Besides, even the goddess had a few shades of gray in her.

She sighed, her shoulders drooping with her exhale. "Don't do it again."

"I don't plan to."

Chaos downed his beer and set the empty bottle on the counter. "Neither do I. I much prefer causing pandemonium."

I laughed. "See? Problem solved. Now, where is everyone?"

"Patrice is with Miles and Shade, working on a fae infestation. We try to keep at least one person at home to protect the house, so here I am." She hoisted herself onto the counter and swung her legs. "I'm glad you got a picture of the sigils, but Chrys has the book and the skull. I'm surprised she hasn't summoned Mayhem yet."

"I will feel it when she does." Chaos stood and carried his bottle to the recycle bin. "But if we can find her first and summon him ourselves, he will be easier to control."

"And that's easier said than done," Ember said. "She's shrouded herself like she did to Shade. We tried scrying for her this morning and found nothing. Not even an inkling of where she might be."

"Did you visit her home and place of employment?" he asked.

She laughed dryly. "And every other place in Salem she frequents. She hasn't been to her job in more than a week. I tracked down her mom's phone number and called her. She said Chrys stopped talking to her years ago. There's no telling where she's hiding."

"I can scry with you," I said. "Chaos helped us find Shade, so I'm sure he can cut through her spell and help."

"I couldn't cast a spell to save my life tonight." She typed something on her phone and stood. "We battled three beasties and sealed two rifts this morning, in addition to the scrying. I'm spent, and the others will be too when they get back. We need to recharge."

"Can you scry alone, or does it require two witches?" Chaos asked.

I nodded. "Chaos and I can give it a try."

My sister crossed her arms. "Don't bother. I just tried it alone half an hour before you got here, and even if you did find her, we're all too weak to fight tonight. Tomorrow, she could be somewhere else. Save your vim, unless Chaos senses Mayhem."

We both looked at him, and he shook his head. "Nothing yet."

"I found out something else while we were in New Orleans." I drummed my fingers on the counter, hesitating to ask my question. If her answer was yes, I wasn't sure how I'd feel, but I had to know. "Were you aware that Mom bound my fire magic to keep me from fulfilling the curse?"

Her eyes widened, and she blinked in surprise. "No. Who told you that?"

"The High Priestess had some kind of inborn power to detect magic. She said I was blocked."

She wrinkled her nose like she'd whiffed a foul fart. "And you believe her? She's a dark witch. They lie."

I picked at the label on my half-drunk bottle. "Chrys didn't just tie me up and take my bag. She left me to die. Her roots were trying to bury me alive, and I burned my way out of it. For once in my life, my fire magic worked the way it's supposed to."

"You." She paced the kitchen again. "Why didn't you lead with this? How? What happened?"

"Chaos pissed me off so much, my fury got around the block." I couldn't fight my smile. "Ember, I set my *arms* on fire. My whole upper body. I burned through the roots, and when I got out, I called the fire back inside."

"She was incredible." Chaos stood behind me and squeezed my shoulders.

Ember's mouth hung open. "Holy crap, sis."

"Chrys underestimated Ash and didn't bother with fire-proofing." He grabbed another beer from the fridge and tipped it back. "She assumes Ash can only do spell work, which is why she keeps taking her bags. We can use this to our advantage. Ash can be our secret weapon."

"If we can figure out how to remove this block." I took a swig of beer and grimaced. It was already room temperature, so I pushed it away.

He took my bottle and dumped the contents into the sink before dropping it in the bin. What a good demon he was turning out to be. "You can call on your power around the magical block."

"Only if I'm royally pissed off."

"If Chrys doesn't do it for you, I'm sure I can." He winked, making my stomach flutter.

"No." Ember shook her head. "It's too risky. I won't take a chance that big. You have to figure out how to remove it."

I rested my elbow on the counter, cradling my chin in my hand. "It's on my miles-long to-do list."

"Move it to the top." She crossed her arms. "As in figure it out tonight. If Mom bound your magic, it must be in a grimoire in our library somewhere. Find it. Figure out how to reverse it. Tomorrow, we'll find Chrys and put an end to this shitshow."

She made it sound so simple. "You're not the slightest bit worried I'll screw up—this time epically because I'm at full power—and burn the entire town to the ground?"

She lifted one shoulder dismissively. "Not in the slightest."

"And you shouldn't be either." Chaos opened the door, waiting for me to get up.

I slid off my stool and shuffled toward him. "Excuse me for not having as much faith in myself as you do. I've been defective my entire life."

Ember threw her arms into the air. "Oh, for Hecate's sake, Ash. Get over yourself. You're a badass, you always have been, and if you can reverse Mom's spell, you'll be the baddest ass of us all. I'm going to bed. The others should be here in an hour. Yell if there's a problem you can't handle." She started toward the hall but stopped. "No one else needs to know about this. If you're going to be our secret weapon, we need to keep you a secret. Don't tell the others. Not even Patrice."

My bottom lip had started to poke out, so I drew it in as she walked away. "Okay. I guess we're looking for a spell book." I headed down the stairs.

Chaos followed. "Your sister is correct. I've told you from the beginning you're the most powerful witch I've ever seen. Your inborn location ability, your mastery of ink, and now your fire powers being unlocked… Few witches are blessed with so many gifts."

"Maybe." I stopped at my desk and rested my hands on the back of the chair. "Maybe you're right, but it took me summoning a Prince of Hell into my head to realize any of it."

He squeezed my shoulders. "Of course that's what it took. You were meant to summon me. Fate brought us together, Ash. You can't deny it."

I sighed and turned to face him. No, I couldn't deny it any longer. The way we fit together, the way we worked together, our powers contrasting and complementing each other… If fate wasn't to blame for this messy, effed-up relationship between a light witch and a demon, I didn't know what was. We were perfect together. Too perfect for it to have happened any other way.

"I can admit that now. You and I were supposed to happen, and I won't pretend we weren't. The problem is, when I find the spell my mom used to bind my magic, if I can reverse it, that's it. No more Ash the screw-up. No more excuses for staying in my little library alone."

He put his hands on my hips, and I rested mine against his chest. "And that's a bad thing?" he asked.

"Yes. I mean, no but yes at the same time. It's become a sort of crutch. When everyone's expectations of you are low to nil, you never let anyone down. Without any limitations, I…"

"You can grow into the witch you are meant to be. Think of the possibilities."

"I am, that's why I'm scared." I tucked my hair behind my

ear. "What if we fail? What if I unlock my magic, we go after Chrys, but we still fail?"

"You won't fail."

"But what if we do? With my magic bound, we could blame it on Ash the screw-up." I tugged on my bottom lip before worrying it between my teeth.

"Why would you want to hold on to that? You're too smart, too kind, and far too powerful to be the coven's scapegoat. It's time you came into your own, and I am looking forward to sharing the experience with you."

"Ugh." I tipped my head back to look at the ceiling. "It's just been this way for so long, I don't know how to be anything else."

"You're a fast learner. You'll figure it out quickly."

I looked into his eyes, a sense of resolve washing over me. "You're right. It's time I stopped hiding behind my weaknesses. I'm an effing Holland witch, and I need to act like one. I deserve respect."

"You should demand it." He shook his fist, rallying me even more.

"I should. I'm going to find that book and reverse this spell, and then Chrys isn't going to know what hit her. I'll be the Stealth Bomber. A ninja. A Jack-in-the-box that pops before it's supposed to and scares the crap out of anyone who plays with it." I marched toward the stacks.

"That's my girl. Silent but deadly."

I stopped short and spun around. "That's what my dad calls his farts, and I am not a puff of stinky wind."

"You are a hurricane."

"Damn right I am." I had to think. Binding magic was used way back when during the witch hunts to keep children from revealing their powers. Mothers would bind their magic when they were out in public and release it when they made it to the safety of home. I'd bet my left boob that's what my mom did to me.

"It'll be an old book, circa the sixteen hundreds."

"Don't think too hard. Let your magic guide you." He picked up a stack of books from the floor and set them on a shelf.

The excitement of my little speech had my heart racing, so I took a deep, cleansing breath and centered myself. "What spell did you use to bind me and where is the book?"

A tug in my chest led me to the back of the library, straight to the secret shelf where we'd found the aura-shrouding spell. A pale yellow book with a cloth cover leaned haphazardly against the end of the unit, and I grabbed it, flipping it open to the correct page.

My mother's elegant handwriting filled the margin. "'Spell must be rejuvenated every six months to keep fire subdued.'"

A lump formed in my throat, and I swallowed hard. "She's been casting the spell on me every six months for my entire life, and I didn't have a clue."

He rested his hand on my lower back and peered at the page. "How long have your parents been missing?"

"About six months." I carried the book to my desk and laid it open.

"That would explain why you could tap into your full power in New Orleans. The binding is losing its potency, and your fury helped you break through."

"Huh." Pressure built in the back of my eyes, and a sob threatened to escape my throat. "This is such a simple spell. I mean, I guess it had to be for parents to be able to cast it every day without depleting their vim. She just…"

Another sob rolled up from my chest, and I swallowed it too. "I know she did it for the greater good, but damn. Couldn't she have told me what was going on? If I'd known why my magic didn't work right… Did she not realize what it did to my self-esteem?"

He pulled me to his chest. "I'm sure she did what she thought was best."

Tears gathered on my lower lids. I blinked them away and pulled from his embrace. "It doesn't matter. I can break the spell. It's so effing simple." I scoffed at the ludicrousness of it all. My entire sense of self-worth had been determined by a spell used on kindergarteners in the sixteen hundreds. Sadly, that tracked for old Ash.

Not anymore.

"Let's go to the kitchen. I'll need a potion." I carried the book upstairs and set it on the counter before gathering my copper bowl and my mortar and pestle. Eucalyptus, hyssop, and sage combined with lemon oil would dissolve whatever was left of the binding, and I could…

"You're still afraid." Chaos's deep voice drew me from my thoughts.

I blinked and stared at the counter where I'd laid out everything I needed for the potion but hadn't mixed a thing. "Not scared, no. It's surreal to think about. If we had time to wait, my magic would come back on its own. I don't know. This is weird."

"Indeed." He opened two herb jars and slid them toward me. "But if you want to finish this before the others arrive, you should get started."

I crushed the eucalyptus and hyssop and mixed it with the powdered sage before adding three drops of lemon oil. It flashed and sizzled, and I dumped it into a half-glass of water and swirled it around. "Undo, unbind the magic I find. Set me free. So mote it be."

The liquid turned pale blue, and my heart hammered in my chest, excitement making my hands tremble. I took a deep breath, and then another, while Chaos watched me intently.

"Bottoms up." I pressed the cool glass to my lips and tipped it back, downing the contents in two gulps. My stomach burned and bubbled, a fizzy sensation rising to my chest before cascading down my arms and legs. A fist clenched in the core of my being, and an audible *pop* sounded from deep within, flooding my veins with heat.

I set the glass in the sink and looked at my hands. Was that it? Could my magic flow freely like it was supposed to now?

Chaos raised a brow. "And...?"

It felt rather anticlimactic for the thing that killed my self-esteem and made me feel like a failure my entire life to break that easily, but it was a simple spell. Simple, yet so effing powerful it had shaped the woman I had become.

And now...I was free.

I focused on my inborn power, feeling it churn in my chest before it surged down my arms. My fingers sparked, and I curled them inward, igniting a fireball in each palm. I held them up, even with my eyes, and watched the flames blaze.

"Call it inward," Chaos said.

Normally, if I summoned fire into my hands, I had to send it somewhere—into a sigil to activate it, the sink to extinguish it, the dry leaves in the cemetery to burn the place to the ground. This time, I focused on the source of the flames in the center of my being and opened it, allowing the fire to return to the place from which it came.

I closed my fists, and the fire just...went away like it was supposed to.

Sending the sparks back to my fingertips, I created two new fireballs in my palms. I closed my fists again, and it returned inside me.

A laugh rolled up from my chest, and I did it again, and a fourth time. "Do you see this?"

Chaos smiled. "Indeed, I do. Can you send the flames up your arms?"

I opened my hands, creating the fire, and focused on sending it upward. My arms ignited like Ember's sword, the flames licking up to my shoulders, my head spinning with giddy excitement. "Holy Hecate! Do you think I could do my whole body?"

"Are your clothes fireproof?"

My heart sank, and I extinguished the inferno. "No, dammit." I'd changed into my comfies when we got back home from New Orleans.

"Oh, I know what I can try. Ember can send out fire, and if it hits the wrong thing, it'll bounce back without charring anything." I rubbed my hands together and locked my gaze on the backsplash above the sink. Gathering a fireball in my right hand, I thought about my intent and hurled it, calling it back the moment it hit its target.

Only, it didn't come back.

The ball exploded, and flames licked up the backsplash, toward the window, setting the curtains ablaze.

"Crap!" I rushed to the sink, ready to douse it with water.

"Call it back," Chaos said. "You don't need water."

I looked at the faucet in my hand and the flames turning the curtains to smoke. "Yeah, okay." Focusing on the source, I opened up, allowing the flames to return inside me. The fire extinguished almost instantly, but not before it set off the smoke alarm.

A high-pitched squeal pierced the room, and I grabbed a dishtowel to wave in front of the offending device. Ember rushed into the kitchen, just as Patrice and the guys walked through the door.

"What the hell?" My sister raked a hand through her hair.

"Sorry. I uh..." I cut my gaze toward Miles and Shade. "It was an accident."

Shade shook his head and walked by without a word, and Miles followed. Patrice flashed a sympathetic look toward me before asking Chaos, "Still no Mayhem?"

"She has not summoned him yet."

"Good. I need some sleep." She shuffled through the living room and disappeared down the hall.

When everyone was out of earshot, Ember asked, "It didn't work?"

I flashed a ginormous smile and nodded.

"It did?"

"Yes!" I did a little excited jump and giggled. "No more blocks."

She cut her gaze to the charred curtains before giving me a look.

"She will need practice." Chaos wrapped an arm around my waist, tugging me to his side. "Her power is unique. It will take time for her to learn the nuances of what she can do."

"That's amazing." She yawned. "But don't practice out here. Those three don't have the best poker faces, and I want Chrys to underestimate you as much as possible."

I saluted her, my smile so big, my cheeks ached.

"Go to bed. We need to be operating at full capacity to take down Chrys." She turned and walked away.

"I'm too excited to go to sleep." I bounced on my toes.

Chaos laughed. "Come on, little witch. Let's get you to bed."

ASH

"I hate this." I sat on the edge of my bed and wrung my hands. "I'm not tired at all, Chrys has to be somewhere in Salem, and I feel like we should be looking for her."

Chaos sat next to me and stilled my hands. "I agree. How long will it take the others to recharge now that Chrys's hex has been broken?"

"A few hours, minimum."

"And if you scried for her, how long would you need to recover?"

I turned my head to meet his gaze. "It depends on how long it takes and how much of your energy I use, but you're not suggesting we go after her on our own, are you?"

He lifted his hands, palms up. "Your team is in no condition to fight, but you and I—"

I shook my head. "Let me stop you right there. She has

bested us twice already and nearly killed us both times. When we face her, it needs to be all six of us."

"But your fire..."

"Is supposed to be a secret. If we go after her now, and she gets away again, we lose the element of surprise. She thinks I'm dead. Let her keep thinking that." I stood and turned down the bed. His plan was tempting. I couldn't deny that, but we had to be logical about this, and logic was my jam.

"Just because this magic inside me has been unlocked, it doesn't change who I am. Ash Holland always has a plan. She's cautious and rational. She doesn't run off on tirades just because she can. Ember's the adrenaline junkie. I'm the librarian, and that's not going to change. I'm not going to abandon everything I stand for and join the leap-first-look-later crew. I'm always going to look, and I'm going to make damn certain the people I love do too."

He grinned, his gaze dancing over my face as he rose to his feet. "You are absolutely right. You are the librarian, the Ink Master, the logical, rational witch who has, against the laws of nature, found a home inside the heart of Chaos."

I crossed my arms, trying to ignore the warmth spreading through my chest at his words.

"You have kept your sister in check through all of this, your spells saving her life on multiple occasions. Can you see, now, how powerful you are? How powerful you have always been?" He rested his hands on my hips, pinning me with his emerald gaze. "Can you see yourself the way I see you?"

I laughed and clasped my fingers behind his neck. "My entire life, I've been *just*. Just a librarian. Just an apprentice. Just a screwup. Just…Ash." My chest tightened, not in a fist of dread, but of intense gratitude. "But I'm not *just* Ash."

"No, you are not."

"I'm Ash effing Holland, and I have you to thank for making me realize that."

He slid his arms behind my back, tugging me closer until our hips met. "I told you we were meant to be."

"And this couldn't have happened any other way." I rose onto my toes and pressed a kiss to my demon's lips. *My* demon. He planned to lift my curse, but he had already saved me.

An *mmm* rumbled from his throat, and he slid his hands down to grab my butt, pressing his hips harder against me. As if I couldn't already feel just how happy he was to hear me say that. Lucky for both of us, I had plenty of vim to cast a silencing spell on my room, no potion required.

I stepped out of his embrace, and his expression morphed into that of a predator. His eyes narrowed, his nostrils flaring as he inhaled my scent. "Don't back away from me, little witch."

Heat pooled below my navel, my lady bits throbbing between my legs. I couldn't tell you what it was, but every time he called me his little witch, I felt like I needed to change my panties. He prowled toward me, and I put my hand on his chest, stopping him.

"Two things first," I said. "Do you sense Mayhem in this realm?"

He closed his eyes and took three deep breaths, going utterly still. "No, but even if I did, I'd tell you he could wait."

A thousand butterflies danced in my stomach, flitting up to my chest. "Then give me a second to cast a silencing spell over the room, so I can have my way with you without the whole house hearing it."

He peeled off his shirt and tossed it onto the dresser before dropping his pants to the floor, and boy, oh boy, I almost forgot all about that spell I wanted to cast. Seriously, my gaze locked on his dick, and all thought drained from my brain, letting my hooha call the shots.

He chuckled. "Any day now."

I sucked in a breath, snapping out of my trance. "Right."

After reciting the incantation, I tugged my oversized t-shirt off and tossed it next to his. "Ready to be my bad demon?"

His pupils constricted, the green undulating like a stormy sea. The sigil on my arm heated in reaction to his arousal, and as he stalked toward me, I ran my fingers over the mark. He growled his approval.

"What does that feel like?" I asked.

"Like you are caressing every inch of me all at once. Pleasure in its purest form." He cradled my cheeks in his hands and lowered his mouth to mine. Our lips met, and, faster than I could blink, he swept an arm beneath my knees and carried me to the bed.

His kiss was urgent yet gentle as he lowered me onto the mattress, but when I wrapped my hand around his dick, he groaned into my mouth. I wiggled out of my sweatpants, tossing them aside and pulling him down on top of me.

Spreading my legs, I wrapped them around his waist and reached for his cock. He took it into his hand before I could, and rubbed the head between my folds, teasing me. I groaned and lifted my hips, all but begging him to fill me, and he pulled away, sitting up on his knees.

I rose to meet him and crushed my mouth to his. He held me tightly, wrapping his arms around me and drinking me in. "Take me," I whispered against his lips. "I'm yours."

He broke the kiss, his brow furrowing over passionate eyes. "Do you mean that?"

"Goddess, yes. I need you inside me right now." I reached for his dick, but he grabbed my wrist, stopping me. I tried with the other hand. He gripped that one too, and having both my wrists clutched in his strong grasp turned me on to no end. If I could growl like him, I would have. *Rawr.*

"You said you're mine." He slid off the end of the bed, pulling me toward him as he stood. "Are you mine?"

The intensity of his gaze nearly drew the breath from my lungs. He stepped back, tugging me off the bed until we stood face to face, my wrists still firmly in his grasp. My heart slammed against my ribs, my breaths growing shallow and more rapid as I gazed into his eyes.

Was I his? Could my heart belong to a creature from the Underworld? To a Prince of Hell? I sucked in a sharp breath as the realization sank in, and I swallowed the thickness from my throat. "You and I are meant to be."

"I belong to you, Ash, body and soul. Whether you bear my mark or not, I am yours for eternity, and I will find a way to be with you, whatever the cost." He lowered my arms, finally releasing his grip. "Do you belong to me?"

I rested my hands against his chest. "In every way possible."

He inhaled deeply, holding my gaze, and Ember's words passed through my mind. *What if he falls in love with you? What if you fall in love with him?* It seemed we were about to find out.

"I love you, Chaos."

He slid his fingers into my hair. "And I love you." He held my gaze for another beat or two before leaning in and brushing a gentle kiss to my lips. Pulling away just far enough to see my eyes, he smiled, an incredulous laugh rolling up from his chest. "You are…" He kissed my forehead. "You are everything."

I glided my hand down his stomach, and this time, he let me stroke him. He moaned and leaned his head to mine, trailing his hands over my shoulders, to cup my breasts. With a sudden grunt, he gripped my hips and pulled me toward him. His gaze turned feral, and a deep growl rumbled in his chest, penetrating to my soul.

He grabbed my butt, lifting me from the ground and pinning me against the wall. With one hand, he pulled my thigh up while using the other to guide his length to my slit. In one swift thrust, he filled me, electricity rocketing through my body as I gripped his shoulders and wrapped my legs around his waist.

Leaning into me, he thrust over and over, filling me completely and making every nerve in my body hum. With the wall behind my back and his rock-hard everything pressing into my front, I let out a moan that could have woken the undead in the middle of the day.

He grunted, his fingers gripping my thighs as he pounded his hips. The orgasm coiled in my core, spiraling through my body and releasing like a breaking dam. My nails dug into his shoulders, and I cried out, burying my face into his neck and breathing in his warm, spicy scent.

He thrust one more time, grinding into me and moaning the sexiest moan I had ever heard. Panting, our bodies slick with sweat, he held me there until our breathing slowed. Then, he lowered my legs to the floor and slipped out of me. He kissed my forehead, each cheek, and my mouth before scooping me into his arms and returning me to the bed.

I don't know how long I lay there, silently snuggled in his embrace, but I must've fallen asleep at some point because, when Chaos gasped and shot upright, my heart attempted to escape through my throat. His momentum knocked me off the bed, and I hit the hardwood with a *thwack*, sharp pain shooting through my shoulder, which took the brunt of my fall.

He scrambled to his feet, his eyes wild, every muscle in his body tense. "Mayhem."

I sat up, clutching my aching shoulder. "She summoned him?"

"I think..." He pressed the heels of his hands to his temples, his gaze bouncing all over the room, not focusing on anything until it landed on me. "Ash."

He raced to my side and kneeled next to me. "What happened? Are you injured?"

"You knocked me out of bed, but I'm okay." Clutching the edge of the mattress, I pulled myself to my feet. "Did Chrys summon your brother?"

"I'm so sorry." He rose and rubbed my shoulder. "Do you need Patrice?"

"I'm fine." I strode to my dresser for some fireproof clothes. Soft morning sunlight streamed in through the window, so snuggle time was over. "What's going on? Were you dreaming, or do you sense Mayhem?"

His brows slammed down over his eyes. "I'm not sure."

I tossed him some clothes. "Get dressed. Whether she summoned him or not, it's time to end this." I winced, a stabbing pain slicing through my heart. Why did I have to choose those words? Ending this meant sending the man I loved to another dimension and never seeing him again.

I couldn't think about that now. Stopping Chrys and saving the coven had to be my first priority.

He shoved his legs into his pants and pulled on a t-shirt. "I sensed him." Closing his eyes, he took three deep breaths. "But I don't anymore."

"Could it have been a dream?" I stepped into the bathroom and grabbed my hairbrush before raking through my tangled locks. "I've had dreams that were vivid enough to make me swear they were real."

Chaos joined me at the sink and squirted toothpaste on my toothbrush and then his. "It's possible. Or I could have felt him the moment he passed through the veil, and then her shroud concealed him. She is powerful enough to hide his aura from me." He jabbed the toothbrush into his mouth and scrubbed.

We spit and rinsed and made ourselves presentable before heading down the hall to the empty living room. I turned on the lights and strode to the kitchen for breakfast. Chaos stood in the center of the room, confusion tightening his features. If we weren't in crisis mode, I'd have said he looked adorable. But we were counting on his ability to sense his brother.

"Still nothing?" I grabbed a fresh carton of eggs and cracked them into a bowl.

He sucked in a breath. "No. Shall I wake the others?"

"Not yet. Let them recharge fully so we'll be in top shape for whatever's about to go down." I beat the eggs and set a large frying pan on the stove to heat. I couldn't find any bacon in the fridge, but Patrice had bought ham, so I added the thick slices to another pan to heat them up. They popped and sizzled, making the kitchen smell so savory good that my stomach growled.

"Can you start the coffee?" I dumped the scrambled eggs into the pan and stirred them around. "Ten scoops in the filter and a full pot of water."

He smiled softly, a small chuckle emanating from his throat as he poured in the grounds. "This domesticity is quite...quaint. I could get used to it."

"You'd get bored so quickly. Our lives aren't usually this fast-paced."

"I could never be bored with you by my side." He added the water to the machine and turned it on.

Ember strode into the room, dressed in her fighting yoga clothes, and settled onto a stool at the counter. "How's your vim?

"Completely full. You?" I took six plates from the cabinet and set them next to the stove before popping four slices of bread into the toaster.

"Good, because we're all going to need sigils before we go after Chrys." She locked her gaze with mine. "We need protection."

I blinked, my go-to response of *you know I don't do those* threatening to cross my lips. Old Ash would have blurted it out in a nanosecond, but I was new Ash now. "Protection, speed, and strength for everyone. I can do that."

She lifted her brows. "Five sets. You'll be okay?"

"I'm Ash effing Holland. Ink is in my blood." The coffee maker beeped, so I poured a cup and set it in front of her.

She cut her gaze between Chaos and me. "I like this newfound confidence."

I smiled. "Me too. Soup's on."

We filled our plates, and the others joined us in the kitchen. Coffee, eggs, ham, toast, my demon by my side... I could get used to this domestic life too. Patrice sat next to Ember at the counter, and the rest of us settled at the breakfast table and dug in.

"Do we have a plan?" Miles shoved a forkful of eggs into his mouth.

"Has she summoned Mayhem yet?" Shade asked.

We all looked at Chaos, who flattened his palms on the table. "I'm not sure. I sensed him this morning while I slept, but it only lasted a few seconds. She is either shrouding him, or I dreamed it."

"Did you get a sense of his location when you felt him?" Ember sipped her coffee, watching him over the rim of the mug.

"Sadly, no." Chaos cut a piece of ham and put it in his mouth, chewing and swallowing before he continued. "If she knows anything at all about summoning demons of our level, she will do it in a secluded place, not far from her home."

"We'll have to scry for her." I set my fork on my empty plate and folded my arms on the table.

"We already tried that," Miles said. "We can't cut through her shroud."

"Chaos can." I placed my hand on top of his. Their gazes flicked to where we touched, but nobody bristled at my suggestion. Yay for progress. "He's the reason we found Shade."

"We'll have to do it together," Ember said. "We share the vim so no one gets wiped out."

"So we'll share his magic too?" Patrice bit her lower lip, her forehead creasing.

"It's the only way." I stood and carried my plate to the sink. Chaos joined me, and the others sat silently for half a minute before Shade slapped his hand on the table.

"I'm in." He brought his plate to the sink. "Chrys manipulated me. All of us. I'll do whatever it takes to stop her." He caught my gaze and nodded. "Teamwork."

That was a word I never thought I'd hear Shade utter.

"I'm in too." Miles took the last gulp of his coffee and brought his dishes to the sink as well.

Patrice stacked Ember's plate on top of her own and slid off her stool. "This is crazy. You know that, right?"

"You probably won't even feel him," Ember said. "I didn't know he was helping Ash when we scried for Shade until I came out of the trance and saw his hand on her shoulder."

Patrice rubbed the back of her neck, her gaze bouncing to each of us before she nodded once. "Okay. Let's do this thing. I'll take care of the dishes while you and Ash set it up."

I grabbed the biggest copper bowl we had and filled it with water. "Here we go..."

CHAPTER 12
ASH

Our scrying bowl sat on the floor in the middle of the living room, and the five of us sat cross-legged in a circle around it, so close our knees touched. We'd tried putting everyone at the table, but we couldn't see into the water unless we stood. Sometimes witches passed out during a scrying session, and we couldn't take any chances.

With our luck...*my* luck...someone (me) would fall and smack their head so hard they'd be down for the count. We needed our entire team in top shape if we were going to succeed in our mission. We had twenty-something other coven members and the entire city of Salem counting on us, even though they didn't have a clue what was going on.

Chaos sat behind me, outside of our circle. Another chance we couldn't take was his magic driving someone mad in the process, so I'd absorb whatever he could give and keep it to myself.

Ember took my left hand, and Shade took my right, which was weird as all get out. I expected him to stay as far away from Chaos and me as possible, but with Patrice still wary of what we were about to do, he'd volunteered to hold my hand just in case Chaos's magic seeped through. Miles and Patrice completed the circle, and we centered ourselves, preparing for the biggest scry of our lives.

I looked each witch in the eyes and started my prayer. "We call on the goddess Hecate to watch over us and keep us safe from harm. Please aid us in finding Chrys and Mayhem so we may right what we've put wrong."

"As we will it, so mote it be," we all said in unison.

We stared into the water, letting our gazes soften. Relaxation washed over me as my vision lost focus, the water turning from clear to inky black. The hardness of the floor beneath me and the warmth of the hands holding mine slipped away, the hum of the furnace and the bustle of tourists outside silencing. The world became still, empty.

I focused on Chrys's energy, picturing her face in the blackness of my trance, searching for signs of her aura.

I felt nothing.

When we scried for Shade, we found him easily. The shroud had kept his location hidden, but his essence still registered in the abyss. With Chrys, it was like scrying for Cinder. Like she'd dropped off the face of the earth.

"Can anyone sense her?" Ember asked in our minds.

"No," Miles said. *"Not at all."*

Patrice and Shade confirmed. Chrys was nowhere.

"Do you think Mayhem took her through the veil?" I asked.

"Goddess, I hope not," Ember said. *"I'm pulling us out."*

My senses returned, jerking me out of my trance, and I inhaled sharply, opening my eyes and squinting against the living room light. Chaos's hand rested on my shoulder, and I placed mine over his. "It didn't work."

"I felt as much." He pulled his hand away.

I scooted back to sit next to him. "If she summoned him without a containment circle, would he have taken her to Hell?"

His expression darkened. "Without hesitation."

"Well, crap." I extended my legs, letting my boots thud on the floor. "What do we do now?"

"You're sure you don't sense him anywhere in this realm?" Ember grabbed the chair behind her and hauled herself into it. "Could he have killed her?"

Four seconds passed before he replied. "He would owe her a debt, but if her request was too high..." He clamped his mouth shut and screwed his lips to one side.

One second, two, four, seven. "Demons have a code, a set of rules we follow to keep the balance between worlds. When we are summoned, we can do a mortal's bidding in exchange for a price. Releasing him from prison would be enough compensation for nearly any request, but..."

We all stared at him, waiting for him to continue. When he didn't, I clutched his arm. "But what?"

He let out a slow breath. "Mayhem has never cared much

for rules. Lucifer has threatened to exile him on multiple occasions, and, quite frankly, I'm surprised he hasn't yet."

Ember stood, ready to pace, but Chaos and I sat in her path. I tugged him up, and we moved to the couch while the others took the chairs and loveseat.

"You're saying that even though he owed her a debt, he might have killed her anyway?" My sister took up her usual post, passing back and forth in front of the television. "And now he could be roaming free, wreaking havoc all over the place."

"I would sense him if he were in this realm." He clasped my hand.

"So Chrys is gone, and Mayhem is back in Hell." Crappity crap. There'd be no love lost over Chrys getting tortured for all eternity, but we needed Mayhem. We needed them all.

"Great." Shade clapped his hands together. "Problem solved. Send Chaos home, he can send Cinder back, and we're done with the demon infestation."

Ember clenched her jaw. "It's not that simple."

"Why not?" he asked.

"Uh, hello." I raised my hand. "I'll still be cursed to murder the entire coven, and killing me is *not* an option."

He held up his hands in a show of innocence. "I wasn't going to suggest that."

"There's one more possibility." Chaos scooted to the edge of the cushion and rested his elbows on his knees. "Perhaps Chrys simply hasn't summoned him yet. My sensing him before could have been nothing more than a dream."

"But all five of us joined to scry for *her*," Patrice said. "We would have sensed something with that many witches working together."

"Maybe not." Ember dropped into a chair. "Chrys is powerful beyond belief. She knows light and dark magic, and she could be in cahoots with Boston. Maybe five of us couldn't find her because she had help with her shroud."

"It makes sense." Pain etched lines on Miles's forehead. "It's too much of a coincidence for their people to show up here right when Ginger..." He sucked in a shaky breath. "They must be involved."

"She was able to control our guys." Ember shrugged. "Why not Boston witches too?"

I rubbed my forehead and squeezed my eyes shut, willing my brain not to explode. "We need to scry again." I looked at my sister. "We need to look for the skull this time. All six of us."

Shade snapped his head toward me, his lips scrunching like he was about to send me a giant eff you. Instead, he nodded once. "I agree. We can't sit here speculating all day. Let's search for the skull." He lowered to the floor and sat cross-legged in front of the bowl.

"No." Patrice shook her head. "I want to end this as much as you all do, but light witches shouldn't channel demon magic. There has to be another way."

"She's got a point," Miles said. "He's scrambled our brains before. If we invite him in, he might do permanent damage."

"That aspect of my power won't be utilized." Chaos squeezed my hand before sitting across from Shade. "I'll simply heighten the magic you're already using."

I moved to sit next to Chaos. "And I'll take most of it. My

magic counters his chaos power. I'm sure I can neutralize it if anything leaks through." I hoped I could at least, because we were out of options. Chrys was hell-bent on destroying our town, and we had to stop her...no bones about it.

Ember sat on the other side of Chaos. "I've channeled him before. It's not that bad." She rubbed her hands on her pants, no doubt remembering the electricity running through her when we set up the ward on the building.

Shade scooted around to my other side. "I've survived his brain scrambling multiple times. I'll chance it."

I gave him the side eye. Where was this sudden sense of comradery coming from? I didn't have a clue, but I wasn't about to question it. We needed to work like a team now more than ever.

Miles plopped down next to Ember and patted the space between him and Shade. "They're right. We're doing it for the greater good. Who's going to defeat the darkness if not us?"

Patrice swallowed hard, her gaze flicking to Ember. She opened her mouth on a big inhale, pausing and holding her breath. I pleaded with my eyes, begging her not to give us all the bird and walk out the door.

She looked at me. "You trust him?"

"With every fiber of my being." I slipped my hand into his.

She glanced at the others, who nodded their encouragement, and she let out a sigh before dropping to the floor. "I trust you, Ash. If you say this is okay, I believe it."

My shoulders slumped with my relief, and I took Ember's hand. "Remember, we're looking for Mayhem's skull. Don't focus on Chrys at all. She won't be far from the skull."

I said another prayer to the goddess, and we all fell into the scrying trance. My senses of sound, smell, and sight slipped into the abyss, taking touch with them, save for Chaos's hand in mine. His skin heated, a slight prickling sensation making my fingers tingle before a surge of energy washed through me.

"Whoa," Ember said in my mind.

I held onto the magic, letting it fill the core of my being as I focused on finding Mayhem's skull. Chrys's stellar shrouding skills kept it hidden, so I slowly let the magic go, sharing Chaos's power with Shade.

"Holy crap," he said as I let it trickle into him.

"Is everyone okay?" I asked.

"It's a rush," Miles said.

"I don't feel any different," Patrice said.

"Shade, let some go." Now was not the time for his ego to kick in.

"Oh," Patrice said.

"Okay. Everyone is channeling, and we're all connected. Let's find the skull." I sent out my feelers, picturing a skull in my mind and focusing on the vibrations in the abyss. Chaos sent another pulse of power into me, but I held onto this one, afraid to overwhelm the others.

"Chaos, do you sense him?" I asked, but he didn't reply. I searched the nothingness for his essence, but he wasn't in the trance with us. *"Looks like we're on our own."*

We sat silently, searching, feeling, sensing, until Ember drew us toward her. *"There. That has to be it."*

I focused on the space she guided us to, and a low vibration hummed faintly in the darkness. As I drew my consciousness nearer, it intensified until it penetrated to my bones. *"That's him."*

Chaos's hand tightened around mine, and I searched for him again. I felt Shade, Ember, Miles, and Patrice. Mayhem was unmistakable, but Chaos was nowhere to be found. He must've been reacting to my quickening pulse.

"Can anyone sense where he is?" Shade asked.

Another burst of magic surged through me, and this time, I shared it. An image of the skull came to my mind. Then the sensation of coarse fabric against my skin. *"It's in a bag. Do you feel it?"*

"Is it burlap?" Miles asked. *"It's scratchy."*

"It's softer than burlap." I allowed the sensation to wash over my entire body. *"I think it's wool."*

"Pull back," Ember said. *"It doesn't matter what kind of sack it's in if we can't see where it is."*

I let the coarseness of the fabric go and focused on the area around the bag. It sat on a slab of thick wood, worn smooth from decades...maybe centuries...of use. A wooden panel stood behind it, and another rose to its right. Was the skull in a bag, inside a box?

"It's a shelving unit," Ember said. *"Where are we?"*

I pulled back further in my mind to take in the scene. A massive antique wood table, a prayer bench, and a four-foot-tall crucifix made the location unmistakable.

"It's the basement of the big church," Miles said. *"I've been there before."*

"Gotcha," Ember said. *"Let's end the session."*

I focused on Chaos's hand holding mind, allowing my

physical senses to return. Patrice gasped, and I opened my eyes to find her panting, her hand pressed to her chest.

"Everyone okay?" Ember rubbed her palms together. "No one went crazy?"

"I'm good." Shade released my hand and rubbed his thighs.

"Me too." Miles shuddered and rolled his neck.

"That was...weird." Patrice rose to her feet and paced to the kitchen. "I'm going to make a restorative tea to return our psyches to their normal, nondemonic, states. It should help recharge our vim as well."

"Where is my brother?" Chaos stood, tugging me up with him.

"His skull is in a church basement." I went to the kitchen to help Patrice with the tea. "I guess what you felt this morning was a dream because, unless she made a decoy, his skull is still just a skull."

"It's not a decoy," he said. "I felt his vibration through our bond when you located him."

"Yeah, but you've 'felt' him before." Ember made air quotes. "She fooled you once."

"It won't happen again," Chaos said.

I crushed the herbs Patrice gave to me, and she added them to the metal diffuser before dropping it into a pot of hot water. Holding her hands above the mixture, she recited an incantation, and pink steam rose from the surface. Once it dissipated, she poured the brew into five mugs, and I passed them out.

"Do you need some?" I asked my demon.

He chuckled. "My normal state is fully demonic. I doubt a tea would change that."

I sipped Patrice's potion, and the citrusy flavors of lemongrass and orange zest contrasted the nutty, winter spice blend perfectly. "Does it taste this good without the spell? I could drink this every day."

She smiled. "It does. I'll have to write down the recipe for you."

"Drink up, folks." Ember set her empty mug in the sink. "Then we're heading downstairs for sigils and going after that skull."

CHAPTER 13

ASH

"Go to the studio. I need a minute to center myself." I sank into my squeaky chair and waited for the others to leave the library. Everyone filed out except Chaos, but that was fine. I might need a pep talk if I freaked myself out too much.

"You can do this." He massaged my shoulders, easing the tension that had them creeping toward my ears.

"I know." I patted his hand and stood before pacing toward the stacks and grabbing volume four of my sigil collection. I set it on my desk and ran my fingers over the embossed burgundy cover. Familiar magic tingled on my skin, and a sense of calm washed over me.

Real calm, not the fake kind Chaos could force onto me. Sigils were my jam. Ink was in my blood, and even with my fire magic unlocked, I knew *this* was what I was meant to do.

I flipped the book open to the protection symbol and traced the design with my fingertip.

"You aren't familiar with this one?" He tilted his head, examining the page. "Have you done it before?"

"I am, and I have. The last time I drew this one was the day Cinder went missing. I assumed I'd flubbed it, but now I'm not so sure." Because if she went across the veil with Discord willingly...that changed everything.

"What, exactly, does it provide protection against?"

I tapped the sigil. "Hexes, magical attacks, even physical trauma to an extent. It sort of creates a forcefield around the bearer."

His brow crept toward his hairline. "It makes you invincible?"

"I wish. Strong magic can still get through, but the sigil helps deflect the weaker stuff. Although, with enough persistence, the weak spells can too. This one wears off quickly with use."

"Your sister summoned a Prince of Hell. Even with the sigil working at full force, he could have easily overcome it."

I closed the book and returned it to the shelf. "Yeah, well, it sounds like she went across the veil with him by choice, so..."

"Another unnecessary hit to your self-esteem has been resolved."

"Exactly. Come on." I led the way into my studio, where Ember had already set up the tattoo machine.

My sister sat first and offered her forearm. I dipped the needle into the enchanted ink and drew the sigils for enhanced strength and speed in record time. Honestly, I probably could've done those two with my eyes closed.

With the first two complete, I added more ink to the needle and pictured the protection sigil in my mind. I drew a circle centered over two perpendicular lines with arrows at each end. A half-moon came next, then a swoosh down on the right side and the left, ending at a fine point.

"That looks absolutely perfect." Ember held up her arm, examining my work. "Next."

My sister got up, and Miles took the seat. He closed his eyes and went into his meditative state like he always did when he got ink. When I finished, I drew the same designs on Shade and Patrice. Then it was time for mine.

Chaos's mark occupied the space on my arm that was easiest to reach, so I had to flip to the opposite side and lay it on the table at an uncomfortable angle to find some free skin. My demon stood in front of me, watching intently, a smile curving his lips.

"What?" I glanced up at him before continuing my tattoos.

"I'm imagining how you must have looked when you drew my mark, so intent on using me to organize your library."

I laughed. "Not nearly this awkward, I promise."

My body tingled as I channeled the magic from the goddess and kept it inside rather than giving it away. The hum of the needle pulsing in and out of my skin filled my ears, and I inhaled deeply against the burning ache. Miles really did need to give a lecture on how to ignore the pain.

With my sigils finished, I let out a slow breath and returned the tattoo machine to its stand. "Ready to light these babies up?"

Shade examined his arm. "You're sure the protection will work? You swore you'd never try them again after Cinder."

Chaos tensed, ready to berate him for questioning my abilities, so I patted his arm. Thankfully, he took the hint because we *had* to operate like a team for this to work.

"Cinder crossed the veil willingly." I returned the ink well to its proper place. "Now that I know what really happened to her, I'm confident in my abilities."

He nodded. "You should be. You do good work."

Wait. What? Did Shade just compliment me? My face scrunched in confusion. "Thanks?"

"You first." Ember held up her finger, so I offered my arm. She shot a tiny, controlled flame onto my sigils, making them glow deep red before fading to cool blue.

My muscles tensed as the magic took hold, my stomach doing flip-flops while my pulse sprinted. Holy Hecate. I wasn't used to having my abilities enhanced. "How much stronger am I?"

I wrapped my arms around Chaos and strained to lift him three inches off the floor. I should have tried a before and after because he still felt heavy as hell.

"Don't waste it." Ember lit Shade's sigils before pointing her finger at Miles. "It lasts about six hours, but the more you use it, the less it works."

I rolled my eyes and laughed. "She says to the Ink Master."

She activated Patrice's sigils, and I clenched my jaw. That was my job. I could do it now. I didn't need the Zippo anymore, and it took all the willpower I could muster to not step in and take over. But Ember was right about their poker faces. We were counting on Chrys underestimating me, so it was best if everyone else did too.

Ember lit the sigils on her arm, and everyone pulled down their sleeves, hiding the protection marks. Chrys wouldn't be expecting those either.

We made our way to the library and gathered our supplies before heading to the back door. Ember grabbed the lever and held up a fist, telling us to wait. She slowly pulled it inward, peeking through the narrow opening, and I bounced on my toes.

These sigils made me feel like I was high on caffeine, and the anticipation of using my newly unlocked fire power had me itching to bust through the door and run to the church. Maybe this was why Ember always seemed so reckless.

No, she was reckless with or without the ink.

I needed to calm the eff down before I forgot who I was and started acting like my sister. I made a mental note to never enhance my speed and strength again and rose onto my toes to whisper in Chaos's ear.

"I can't calm down. Can you help?"

He arched a brow, questioning me, so I pulled up my sleeve and rubbed his mark. With a deep inhale, he closed his eyes, his lips curving upward, and sent a pulse of magic through our bond.

Calmness spread through my veins, warming me from the inside out, slowing my pulse, and relaxing the tension in my legs. I mouthed the words *thank you*, and we followed Ember out the door.

"Were you expecting an ambush?" Chaos asked as we paced toward the van.

"I'm expecting anything and everything she can throw at us." Ember scanned the alley in both directions before climbing into the driver's seat. Patrice took shotgun, and Miles went for the way back seat. I started to get in the back, but Shade cleared his throat.

"Hey, Ash?"

I stopped and turned toward him, and Chaos rested his hand on the small of my back, no doubt ready to defend me against whatever sourness Shade wanted to share.

He opened his mouth and closed it again before nodding. "I'm sorry for the way I've been treating you."

I flinched like he'd slapped me.

He gestured with his head at Chaos. "Does he know about our history?"

"He does..." Wariness lifted my voice.

Shade shrugged. "I don't handle rejection well, and I acted like a dick because of it. And then seeing you two together... I realized I never really got over you and that was fueling it too."

My mouth hung open, whatever words I should have said not even registering in my brain.

"Anyway, with the close calls we've had, I wanted to get that off my chest...just in case."

Chaos climbed into the van, giving us some perceived privacy, and my brain finally started working again. "Umm... Thanks for saying that, Shade. It means a lot, and..."

Now it was my turn to shrug awkwardly. "I'm sorry too. We've both behaved badly toward each other."

"Cool." He climbed inside without another word, so I did too.

I settled next to Chaos, and he took my hand, lacing our fingers together and giving me a squeeze. Ember started the engine and drove toward the church, where we'd either defeat the enemy and claim the demon or we'd die trying. Some of us might either way.

"Whatever happens, whatever she promises, don't trust her." I patted Chaos's leg. "I mean it. Even if she's got me strung up by the ankles over a pit of vipers, do not believe she'll let me go if you comply."

His jaw tightened, and he glanced at me out of the corner of his eye.

Patrice turned around in her seat. "That sounds like you're speaking from experience."

"We're both lucky to still be in this realm," I said. "When this is over, I'll tell you about it."

Ember's eyes narrowed in the rearview mirror, and she hung a right where she should have gone left. She glared even harder and hung another right before slamming on the brakes. The tires squealed, the van skidding to a stop in the middle of the road. "We're being followed. Arm yourselves."

She hit the gas, and we all turned around to see a dark brown delivery truck on our tail. "Now, Ash," she shouted.

"Move your feet." I reached down to open the floor compartment and passed out the weapons. Chaos held Ember's sword in his lap, and Miles and Shade strapped on even more knives than they already wore. I attached a dagger to each thigh and offered a sheathed hunting knife to Patrice.

She held up her hands, refusing it. "I don't think I could use that. I'll stick with spells."

"Take it," Ember said. "You might need to cut through some roots."

"Okay." She accepted the knife and strapped it to her right thigh.

Still flooring it, Ember ran through a stop sign and swerved around an old woman driving at granny speed. The woman, with silver hair and decades of wrinkles, gave us the bird, and, if my lip-reading skills were any good, she shouted a string of profanities as we whizzed by.

Our pursuers swerved around her as well, the top-heavy truck lifting onto two wheels for a second before it gently, unnaturally, returned upright. Fabulous. We had a telekinetic on our tails.

I turned to tell Ember what we were dealing with, but the words didn't have time to cross my lips before our wheels locked up and we skidded across the road. Ember hit the gas, revving the engine, and smoke billowed from the back axle.

"They've got a telekinetic." I opened my satchel and grabbed an undoing potion. I could usually break simple hexes without one, but this magic felt way too strong for just words. "I'll try to counter the spell."

After uncorking the same potion I'd used to unbind my fire magic, I dumped the contents onto the floorboard. "Undo, unbind the magic I find. Set us free. So mote it be."

Ember slammed on the gas again, and our tires screeched

on the pavement before lurching us forward once more. We peeled through an intersection as the light turned from yellow to red.

Horns blared behind us, followed by the sounds of metal crunching and glass shattering. I peered through the back window to see the delivery truck on its side in the crossroads and a blue Mazda smashed to bits.

"Please, goddess, don't let anyone die." We'd left enough carnage in our wake as it was.

"Did anyone get a look at the driver? Was it Chrys?" Ember flicked her gaze to the mirror.

"There was a glare on the glass," Miles said. "But I don't think it was her. She's not telekinetic, as far as I know."

"It had to be Boston witches," Shade said. "Either she's working for them or they're working for her."

"And they're trying to keep us away from the church," I said. "She's about to summon Mayhem."

"Then we better stop her." Ember hung a left, finally heading in the direction of our destination, and parked six blocks away. "We'll walk from here. Cloak us, Shade."

"On it." He held his palms toward each other, gathering gray fog between his hands before sending it outward to engulf us, desaturating the world around us.

"Do you want me to cast a silencing spell too?" I asked my sister.

Shade answered, "I can cloak sound too. I was saving my vim, but if you think we need it, I can."

I squelched the laugh that tried to bubble from my chest.

He might have apologized, but that ego of his wasn't going anywhere, was it?

"I don't think we need it yet." Ember slid out of the van and closed the door.

The rest of us filed out onto the sidewalk, and we hoofed it across the street, practically running the first three blocks toward the church. When we reached the fourth block, we really ran.

A tourist group stood outside a historical building, taking up most of the sidewalk, and parked cars lined the side of the road, making it nearly impossible to go around them without getting hit by traffic. We slowed to a walk and sidestepped the crowd, but a big, beefy guy decided to take a giant step backward, right into me.

His boot landed on top of my foot, and he lost his balance and careened backward, slamming me onto the hood of a car. I couldn't stop the yelp from escaping my throat or the *oof* as I rolled off the car and smacked the ground.

"What the hell?" He spun around, looking for whatever he smacked into and scratching his head when he found nothing there.

"Ash!" Chaos's deep voice boomed as he rushed toward me, and the entire crowd gasped.

I made a lip-zipping motion and reached for his hand when he offered it. He hauled me up, and I limped as I dragged him away.

"Salem is the most haunted city in America," the tour guide said to his patrons. "Did we just experience an angry ghost?"

With their attention returned to their tour, I stopped half a block away to loosen my laces before my foot swelled. I'd torn a hole in the knee of my fireproof leggings, but my skin wasn't marred in the slightest.

"Huh. I guess that protection sigil works after all." I wiggled my foot and took a tentative step. The pain was gone. "Nice."

"Almost there," Ember called. "You okay?"

"I'm fine." We caught up with the others and crossed the intersection at a fast clip.

"Shit." Miles stopped in his tracks and grabbed Ember's arm, pulling her back. "I recognize her. She's from BMS."

We peered through our shadow at the woman leaning against a stone fence. She crossed her legs at the ankles and looked down to type on her phone before letting out a sigh and looking right and then left. Her cheeks puffed as she blew out another breath, and she kicked at something on the ground, rubbing the sole of her shoe over the concrete.

"She must be a lookout," Ember said. "How do you know her?"

Miles cringed. "Her name is Wendy. She's the one I convinced to let me into their library. If I'd known she was working with Chrys, I…"

Shade clapped him on the shoulder. "There's a lot we'd all have done differently if we'd known what Chrys was up to."

"I'm sure there are others. We—" I clamped my mouth shut and stepped out of a woman's path, dragging my sister to the edge of the sidewalk. "It's time for a silencing spell if we want to make it in undetected."

She nodded. "Patrice, can you handle that?"

"I—" Shade started, but Ember held up her hand and said,

"We're sharing the vim, remember? You're cloaking us. Ash performed sigil magic and the undoing spell in the van. It's someone else's turn."

"Absolutely." Patrice sat in a patch of dead grass next to a fence and mixed a potion. We gathered around her as she recited the incantation, rendering us all soundless to the outside world.

Silent and invisible, we crossed the intersection and headed toward the church. When we reached Wendy, she pressed her phone to her ear. "Hey."

She rolled her eyes, listening to the caller.

"I know. Some High Priestess she'll be. It took her forever to find the damn skull. Then she didn't have the sigil to call on the guy, and once she found that, she had to get another book with summoning instructions. I can't deal with her right now."

We stopped to hear the rest of Wendy's conversation.

"I'm starting to think she's not as big and bad as she made herself out to be." She stuck her finger into her nose and flicked out a booger. Gross.

"Don't you dare report her… Because! We've been on the bottom rung of the ladder for years, and she promised us a seat at the table when she takes over."

"Keep moving." Ember jerked her head toward the church, and we continued up the walk.

"If Chrys wants to take over the coven, why recruit low-level witches?" Miles asked. "She'd have more power with stronger ones."

"The weak ones are easier to control," Chaos said before sucking in a sharp breath.

"What?" I clutched his arm. "What do you feel? Is it Mayhem?"

"Not yet, but she has begun the ceremony. The veil is tearing. We need to hurry." He took off in a jog, so I scurried behind him, making a mental note to seriously work on lengthening my strides.

The others followed, and as we reached the end of the last block, we smashed into an invisible wall of magic. The sensation of claws ripping across my skin made me scream. I pressed my hands to my face, expecting it to be covered in blood, but I didn't have a scratch.

The feeling subsided, and as I looked at my team and then at the church a few yards away, I realized what the ward had done. Our protection sigils had blocked most of the nastiness, but Shade's fog had rolled away, bringing the world into full color. Chrys had stripped us of our cloak, and six dark witches marched toward us.

CHAPTER 14
CHAOS

Chrys was a clever witch, setting up her ward far enough away that Ash wouldn't think to begin checking for magic. She'd posted guards outside our home, who had tried to run us off the road as we journeyed here, lookouts a few blocks away, and now more guards to keep us from approaching the building.

She was a clever witch indeed, but she was also a coward, and those souls were the favorites to torture in the Underworld. At least I had something to look forward to when I returned to Hell.

The witches approached from the churchyard, and Ember paced toward them. She did not draw her weapons and instead motioned for us to follow her toward the building. "Let's take this fight off the sidewalk."

"Come on." Ash took my hand. "We can't chance injuring an innocent."

I sent a wave of chaos magic toward our enemies, hoping to scramble their minds and end the confrontation before it began. Nothing happened, which meant Chrys had protected her warriors with whatever spell she'd concocted to block my power.

It didn't matter. Six against six was a fair fight, one I was certain we would win.

A shadow rolled around us, turning everything except our adversaries gray, and I looked at Shade, who shook his head. He didn't cloak us, so one of Chrys's minions had shadow power.

Ember clutched her sword, flames erupting on the blade, and Shade held knives in each hand. Patrice stood next to Ash, both holding potion bottles, and Miles strained, gathering energy between his palms like he had done when Chrys controlled him.

No one made a move.

I glanced at Ash, and she raised her brows, silently asking me to affect their minds. I shook my head, letting her know I'd tried.

Gathering fire in my hands, I eyed the six in front of us. These witches were not innocent, nor were they members of Ash's coven. My promise to cause no harm didn't apply, so I hurled hellfire at the woman closest to me.

She lifted her hand, drawing on the wind and extinguishing my flames before they reached her. An air witch. Interesting.

"Whatever Chrys has promised you, she's lying." Ash took a step toward them, clutching a potion bottle in each hand. "She's using you, and then she'll discard you when she gets what she wants."

The air witch scoffed. "This is coming from a light witch who summoned a demon." She raised her arms and motioned toward Ash, sending a gust of wind that, if she had been more powerful, would have knocked her off her feet. Instead, it merely blew her hair back.

"Standing tall or on your knees, in the name of the goddess, I force you to freeze." Ash hurled the powdered potion at them. The air witch squealed like a child afraid of a bug and swung her arm, her wind magic just strong enough to blow the spell away before it reached them.

"We don't have time for this." Ember marched toward a man with light hair and swung her extinguished sword, hitting the backs of his legs with the flat side and knocking him to the ground. With a knee on his chest, she pressed the tip of her blade to his throat. "I don't want to kill you, so don't make me."

Another man yelled and tackled Ember, freeing his friend, and chaos ensued.

For once, I wasn't the cause.

Our attempt to enter the church turned into a magical brawl. Miles threw his energy ball at a brunette. She tried to swat it away with her sword, but his power knocked her off her feet. She careened backward, landing on the ground with a thud, and a redhead screamed and barreled toward him.

I tossed a fireball at her, but her clothing absorbed the flames. Of course Chrys protected her flock against our greatest weapons. If I couldn't use hellfire or mind magic against our foes, I would have to fight like a mundane.

The redhead tackled Miles. I clutched the back of her neck and yanked her off him, letting her dangle in the air while he hit her with a binding spell. When she stopped flailing, I dropped her, and she crumpled onto the ground in a heap.

Ember wrestled with the man on top of her, rolling him to his back and landing a punch to the center of his face. "You're not supposed to kill people," she shouted at me before Patrice poured an orange liquid onto the man, rendering him unconscious.

"No one is dead yet," I replied, though I couldn't make any guarantees about the three remaining witches.

The air witch summoned wind again, blasting it at Ash and, this time, making her stumble. Ash fought back, running toward her and throwing another vial of orange liquid at her face. Again, she blocked the attack with a gust of wind.

I threw another ball of hellfire at her. She waved a hand, attempting to extinguish it, but her magic faltered. Her clothing absorbed most of the blaze. Her hair did not fare so well. Blonde locks went up in flames, and she screamed, calling on her wind to extinguish them. Her magic only made it worse.

"Call your fire back." Ash ran toward me and clutched my arm. "You're going to kill her."

"She is trying to kill us."

"Chaos!" She slapped my shoulder, and I sighed. Sometimes Ash took away all my fun.

"At least put a binding spell on her first." I called back most of the flames, leaving behind a small amount, which she could easily extinguish if she stopped running in circles.

"Patrice is mixing more. We're out."

"You don't need a potion. Simply say the incantation."

She nodded and held a hand toward the burning woman.

"Standing tall or on your knees, in the name of the goddess, I force you to freeze."

The woman stopped instantly, a look of sheer agony contorting her features as the small fire reached her scalp. If it were up to me, I would let her burn. Ash, on the other hand, wanted the woman alive, so I called back the fire, ending her suffering.

"Holy crap. It worked." Ash shook her head in disbelief.

Patrice poured the orange liquid onto the air witch's head and lowered her to the ground to sleep. "She needs healing."

"Not our problem." Ember swung her sword at a man. He blocked it with his own blade, the sound of metal hitting metal resonating in my jaw, making it ache.

With Ember taking care of him, only one adversary remained. The shadow witch standing off to the side, straining to keep the scene cloaked. Miles gathered another ball of energy between his palms and hurled it at the man. It hit his chest, and he gasped, his cloak rolling back into him, exposing us all.

"Shade!" Ash shouted as she kneeled by Patrice, helping her mix a spell.

"On it." He gathered his shadow magic and sent it outward, hiding us from view once again.

Patrice poured her sleeping potion on the shadow witch while Ember knocked the other man to the ground. She pinned his shoulders, and Patrice covered his head with the potion as well, neutralizing our final adversary in this battle.

But the war had only just begun.

A low vibration rolled outward from the church, making the

fine hairs of my arms stand on end. The energy around us shifted, the thickness indicating Chrys's summoning had nearly reached its apex.

"We must go." I stormed toward the church entrance, but before I reached the door, my brother's energy registered in my body and I froze. "Ash?"

She slung her restocked bag over her shoulder and rushed toward me. "What's wrong?"

"I sense Mayhem, but she has tricked me before. Is he here?"

She inhaled deeply and closed her eyes. "I think so, yes. Wait, maybe not."

I opened my senses to his vibration, expecting it to wash over me. Instead, it ceased. "Did she summon him only to vanquish him again?"

"I don't know." She snapped her head to the right. "Uh oh."

I followed her gaze to find a massive rift two yards away, where a swarm of fae poured through.

ASH

Hecate on a highwire. We did not have time to deal with the friggin' fae. Hundreds of the little buggers flowed through what had to be the biggest rift to date. I couldn't see the actual opening, but the sheer thickness of the swarm indicated a massive tear in the veil.

"I don't suppose you can control these guys like you did the imps?" I started toward the fray, but Chaos clutched my hand.

"I cannot. Ash, try again. Do you sense Mayhem?"

"We need to help the others." I attempted to tug from his grasp, but he tightened his grip.

"With a rift that big, she must have summoned him. I felt him for a moment. I know I did, and if he's in there, we must stop her. She'll use him to raze the entire town."

"I don't know." I looked from our team to him. "It's muffled. She's still cloaking."

"Go," Shade shouted as Miles hit a group of fae with a binding spell. "We'll take care of this."

"Ember?" I started for the door with Chaos.

"I'll be right behind you." She swung her sword, slicing two fae in half with one blow. "Remember, sis, you're at full power now."

Chaos tugged me through the door before I could remind her how much vim I'd already used throwing wasted spells at Chrys's second line of defense. I wasn't at full power. Honestly, the needle on my vim tank struggled to point to the halfway mark.

The sanctuary stood silent. A line of candles, half of them lit, sat on a shelf to the right, and rows of pews led to an ornate altar of carved wood with gold inlays.

We stopped halfway in, and Chaos took both my hands. "Where is he?"

Adrenaline battled with fatigue for control of my psyche. "You're lucky inborn powers like this don't deplete our vim."

"Focus." He squeezed my hands, and I half-expected him to send a pulse of magic through his mark. He stayed true to his promise and let me calm down on my own.

I closed my eyes on a deep inhale and searched for demonic vibrations. All I felt was the man in front of me, so I switched my focus to Chrys. "Her cloak is still in place, but I'm sure they're in the basement. She'll be as close to the earth as she can get inside a building."

"Which way?"

The tug in my body immediately showed me the path. I

pointed to the door to the right of the altar. "Through there. The stairs lead downward."

He nodded and turned, stalking toward the doorway like the predator he was. I followed behind, scanning the chapel for signs of another attack. If anyone lurked in the shadows, waiting for an ambush, they'd hidden themselves well. Did Chrys find another shadow witch to lure to the darker-than-dark side? It wouldn't have surprised me.

I spun in a circle, but no one jumped out, nor did Ember make it inside. Chaos reached the door in three more strides and grabbed the knob. I didn't even have time to shout, "Wait," before he shoved it open with his shoulder.

A massive blast of magic exploded from the door, knocking us both off our feet. I flew backward into a pew, smacking my back against the edge of the wood and tumbling to the floor. My head hit the ground with a *thwack*, and my vision swam, threatening to tunnel into darkness.

I could not let myself pass out. Clutching the sore spot on my scalp, I sat upright and shook my head. The pain faded in a matter of seconds, along with the protection sigil on my arm. Damn. Now that I knew I could make them work, I'd have to come up with a longer-lasting design.

Chaos groaned, and I scrambled to my feet to find him prone on the floor beneath a pew. Blood trickled from his forehead, and I reached to wipe it off before it got into his eye.

"Don't touch that." He knocked my hand away and lifted himself up, hitting his head on the underside of the bench. "Shit!"

He wiggled out from under the pew before sitting upright. "Demon blood can drive people insane."

I arched a brow. "And you're just now telling me this?"

"Come on." He stood and started for the open door.

"Chaos stop." I grabbed his hand. "Did you learn nothing from that explosion? Let me check for magic first."

He blew out a hard breath. "I can withstand—"

"I can't." I held up my arm and pointed to the empty space the sigil once occupied. "I'm out of protection. Whatever she hits us with, I will feel to my bones...and where is Ember?"

The floor rumbled beneath our feet, the vibration knocking an ornate cross off the altar. A painting of the Virgin Mary fell from the wall and landed face-down on the floor.

"We don't have time to wait for her." He gestured to the doorway.

I recited the magic-revealing spell, sending sparkles through the entry. A few clung loosely to the remnants of the ward Chaos had set off, but the rest dissipated. "Surely that wasn't her last line of defense."

"She probably didn't expect us to make it this far." He stepped into the hallway and descended the steps.

A crypt lay beneath the church, with four ornate caskets lining the left side. To the right, six more graves had been carved into the wall and covered with granite slabs. The air grew damp the deeper in we ventured, the room narrowing into another hallway before making a sharp right turn.

Chaos stopped at the corner. "Do you need to check for magic?"

"I do, thank you." Though every spell I cast taxed my vim

more and more, I recited the incantation. Nothing clung to the walls or floor, so we continued on our way.

The modern concrete floor gave way to worn wood as we approached another staircase. We followed it down into yet another corridor, and before we turned left, Chaos took my hand. "You can use my energy to cast your spell again."

"Actually…" I scrunched my nose as a thought formed in my mind. "I shouldn't need to use a spell. If I can sense people and objects, why not wards and hexes? I found the brooch in the antique shop by searching for magic, so why not?"

The ground rumbled again, and dirt rained from the cracks in the ceiling. Chaos gasped. "I sense him again. Do it quickly before she recharges her cloak."

I centered myself, breathing deeply and searching the basement for signs of magic. The low vibration of a demon other than mine registered in my psyche first. He stood in a room just around the corner. Sending out my feelers, I opened myself to dark magic, waiting for the tell-tale pull.

Everything I felt lay in the room around the corner and down the hall. "Unless her cloak is hiding a ward, I think we're clear."

He looked around the corner, his posture indicating he wanted to run. "Do you trust yourself, or do you want to try your spell to be sure?"

I started to consider his words, but the pull was unmistakable. "I'm sure. Mayhem is down there, and there's nothing magical to block our way."

"Very good." He turned the corner, tugging me along.

We crept down this part of the hallway, even the Prince of

Hell showing caution now. My palms slicked with sweat, and I wiped them on my pants. If my heart beat any harder, it might bust through my chest, so I took a deep breath to calm myself.

"What's the plan?" I whispered.

"I will deal with Mayhem. You can handle Chrys."

I laughed. "Can I?"

He stopped abruptly and turned to face me. "Do not doubt yourself, little witch."

"I haven't had time to practice my fire powers."

"You don't need to practice for this. Burn her alive if you have to. Take down the whole church if you must. You know how to call your fire back when you're through, and that is all you need to know." He pinned me with his gaze, the sincerity in his eyes giving me more confidence than I'd ever had before.

"You're right. If there was ever a time for me to start trusting myself, it would be right now." I nodded hard. "I'm ready."

"As am I." His brow slammed down over his eyes, and he flinched. "I no longer feel him. What is Chrys doing?"

"There's only one way to find out." I pointed at the last corner separating us from our final boss battle.

He straightened, curling his hands into fists, and strode into the hallway. The wooden floor ended abruptly, turning into dirt...because of course it did. It wouldn't be the final boss battle if the boss didn't have access to the source of her power.

The hall opened into a massive room with storage shelves lining the walls and a summoning circle taking up the center of the floor. Black candles, still burning, sat at each of the pentagram's five points, and... Was that Mayhem's skull resting in the center?

Chaos cocked his head and squinted at the skull. "What in Hell's name?"

"It's about damn time you got here." Chrys stepped out of the shadows, her eyes wild, her dark hair disheveled. She stopped by the circle, narrowing her eyes to glare at me. "Who helped you escape?"

My fire magic rose to simmer just below the surface, and I forced a neutral expression. "Does it matter?"

"I suppose not. Shame on me for acting like a Bond villain and running away without watching you die. I won't make that mistake twice."

Chaos couldn't tear his gaze away from his brother's skull. "What are you doing with Mayhem? Have you not summoned him?"

She strolled closer to us. "Oh, I've summoned him."

I took two steps back. "Did you vanquish him again?"

"Shut up. I know who he is." She clutched her head. "Yes, I know what he's capable of."

I glanced at Chaos, and his eyes widened in realization at the same time as mine. Did Chrys just do what I thought she did? Surely she was smarter than that.

"I said shut up! I don't care what you are!" She flung her arms to her sides and raised them, causing the ground to rumble and crack.

I grabbed Chaos's arm and tugged him toward the door, but the earth split between us, a fissure widening, separating us until I couldn't reach him. Chrys might not have been smart enough to summon a demon correctly, but she was still as powerful as all get out.

The building creaked above us, straining against the shift in the foundation. If we didn't stop her now, she'd bury us all beneath its weight.

Chaos threw hellfire at her. She waved her hand, and a thick root spiraled up, absorbing the flames. She stepped around it, patting the uncharred surface. "Do you know how much vim it takes to fireproof these? The sooner I get rid of you the better."

She pointed, and another root shot from the ground to snake toward Chaos. He stomped it before it could ensnare his leg and reached down to grab it, yanking it so hard, it snapped and shriveled away.

Jerking her head toward me, she sent out another root. Before it could grip my ankle, I darted right, yanked a dagger from my thigh holster, and stabbed the sucker, pinning it to the dirt. Yay for speed sigils.

Chrys clutched her head again, reminding me of the pounding headache Chaos had given me when he'd roared inside my mind. I'd learn my lesson about saying spells loud enough for her to hear them, so I called on what little vim I had left and whispered the binding spell.

"Standing tall or on your knees, by the—"

"Aarrgh!" Ember charged in with her sword ablaze, screaming like a banshee. She swung it like a baseball bat, hitting Chrys with the flat side, right in her stomach. My sister spun, this time aiming for her back, but with speed faster than any sigil could provide, Chrys turned and grabbed the flaming blade with both hands before yanking it out of her grasp.

Ember's sword was razor-sharp. It should have sliced right through Chrys's palms, but when she tossed it aside, her hands appeared unscathed.

Chaos hurled another fireball. This one hit her in the chest. Her fireproof shirt deflected it, and she rolled her neck before flashing a sinister smile. "Brother."

My demon's nostrils flared on his exhale. "Mayhem."

"Holy Hades." I cut my gaze between them. "It took you days to break through and take over my body, and he did it in a few minutes."

"That's because I was holding back." Chaos made a face at me, letting me know I wasn't helping, before scaling Chrys's fissure to stand in front of me.

"Why are you helping these witches?" Her eyes widened and narrowed like Chrys was fighting to take control away from Mayhem. "Kill them."

Chaos crossed his arms. "No. I must reason with you, brother."

Ember charged toward her, daggers drawn, but with Mayhem in control, she...they...dodged the attack, stepping aside and using my sister's momentum to throw her into a shelving unit. Books, bowls, and artifacts tumbled down with the impact, and a cast-iron pot smacked her on the head. Ember grunted and keeled over, her lids barely fluttering.

"Em!" I started toward her.

Chrys/Mayhem spun toward me, and a garbled yell ripped

from her throat. "Not that one! I need her alive." She'd clawed her way back to the surface.

"Standing tall—"

"No, Ash." She flicked her wrist, and dozens upon dozens of roots rose from the ground.

My speed sigil hadn't run out of juice, so I shot across the room as fast as The Flash. Sadly, the roots were faster. A thin one struck like a viper, slashing through my fireproof pants before encircling my ankle. I tumbled, smacking my shoulder on the dirt and grunting as a mess of the sorry suckers ensnared me, rolling me to my back and strapping me to the ground. Again.

I started to whisper the freezing spell, but she sent another root across my face, gagging me like she'd done before. I bit down, determined to chew through it, bitterness flooding my tongue.

And the rest of the dozens of roots penetrating the dirt? She'd trapped Chaos and built a cage over my unconscious sister in thirty seconds flat. I hoped to Hecate the rest of our team had dealt with the fae and were on their way.

Chrys clutched her head, her face pinching in agony. Chaos morphed into his demon form, and, with a guttural roar, he set his entire body ablaze. Heat from his hellfire blasted my cheeks, and I struggled against the roots, which only made them tighter.

He extinguished his flames, and the roots remained unscathed. Roaring again, he flexed, straining against his prison. It stretched with him, tightening again when he relaxed. "Mayhem, release me."

"I'm in control." Chrys shuffled toward me with an unsteady gait. Dark circles ringed her eyes, and she heaved in a breath. "If you can get this demon out of me, I promise to kill you quickly."

"Why ith he in oo?" I mumbled around my gag. "Oo had hith kull."

Chaos continued straining against his binding. Ember didn't move. I could imagine how depleted Chrys must've been. No doubt she used most of her vim on fire- and demon-proofing the roots holding him.

"I'm going to remove your gag, but so help me Hecate, if you try that damn freezing spell again, I will send the root through one cheek and out the other, taking half of your teeth with it."

Well, that sounded painful. I nodded my agreement, and the gag snaked away to rest two inches from my face, the sharp end pointed directly at me. "Why is he inside you?"

She shoved up her sleeve, showing me Mayhem's mark on her arm. "I wanted to control him like you control Chaos, so I did this."

How long had Chrys been learning sigil magic? "I don't control him. He helps me because he loves me."

"Lies." She tapped a finger to her temple. "He says that's not possible. Chaos would never be stupid enough to fall for a witch."

"It's true, brother." Chaos stopped straining. "Ash is mine. She has claimed me, so you will not harm her."

"Please, Chrys," I said. "You've got to perform an exorcism

or Mayhem will burn through your body and use your very essence to reform."

"Shut up! Let me think." She jabbed her fingers into her hair and pulled before whirling toward me. "Do it. Exorcise him. He's driving me crazy."

Chaos scoffed. "What did you think would happen when you invited a Prince of Hell called Mayhem into your mind?"

"You shut up too." She flicked her wrist, tightening the roots around him. "Help me get him out of my head, and I'll let you live."

"I can't." And even if I could, I didn't buy her lies for a single hot second.

"Yes, you can. You did it with that one." She jerked her thumb toward Chaos, who had resumed straining against the roots.

I couldn't imagine how much vim she put into creating them if he still couldn't bust through like he'd done at Shade's house. Yet she stayed on her feet, thanks to Mayhem no doubt.

She flicked her wrist at me, and the roots pulled away from the ground, jerking me upright. The pointy end of one pressed against my cheek, ready to rip my mouth apart if I tried to cast a spell.

It was time to take stock and figure out a plan. Most likely, she didn't fireproof my prison. I could burn through it right now and go after her, but with Chaos restrained and my sister out of commission, it would be me against Super Chrys, and there was no way I could defeat her/Mayhem on my own.

Sometimes knowing your limitations was a good thing.

"Do you have a grimoire with exorcisms?" I asked, trying to

keep a good poker face. "I can help you, but I need a book. I don't speak Latin, nor do I know the spell by heart."

She narrowed her eyes and backed toward the table, her gaze never straying from me. "Don't try anything."

"How could I?"

Chrys finally tore her gaze away from me to look at the grimoire in front of her. She flipped through the pages, muttering, "Shut up, shut up, shut up," as she searched for the spell. I could only imagine the things Mayhem was saying in her mind.

She turned the pages forward and back again, frustration making her movements jerky. "This is all about using demons to do your bidding. I don't see anything about exorcising them."

"Try the index." If I could convince her to free me, I wouldn't have to reveal my unlocked power. Then maybe I could exorcise Mayhem and lock him in a containment circle. With Chrys's depleted vim, I could defeat her easily if she didn't have a Prince of Hell coming in and out of control. Then Chaos could deal with his brother.

She flipped to the back of the book and ran her finger down the pages. "Nothing. There's nothing. If you can't help me, I might as well kill you now."

Ember groaned and pushed onto her elbow. Chaos had gone utterly still as if he were meditating, but at Chrys's words, his eyes flew open. She slammed the book shut and marched toward me as Shade, Miles, and Patrice darted into the room.

CHAPTER 16
ASH

"It's about damn time." I called on my magic, curling my fingers toward my palms and igniting fireballs in each hand. The flames licked up my arms and danced across my chest and down my legs, incinerating the roots holding me captive.

Chrys faltered, her eyes widening and her mouth falling open, which gave the others just enough time to start their attack.

"Holy shit, Ash," Shade said as he threw a dagger. Chrys dodged it easily, and it stuck into the dirt three feet from Ember's cage.

My sister reached through the roots, her fingers grazing the knife, but she couldn't grab it. Chaos strained again, roaring and setting his demonic form ablaze. The roots holding him groaned against his strength, a thin one splitting, hanging on only by a few fibers.

"Are these friends of yours too, brother?" Chrys smiled menacingly. "I will enjoy cracking their necks one by one."

"You will not harm them." He strained again, and the roots thinned even more.

Miles threw an energy ball, knocking her shoulder back. She snapped her gaze to him, and Patrice uncorked a potion. She managed two words of the spell when Chrys bent her fingers into claws. The ground rumbled, another fissure opening beneath our healer.

I lunged for Ember's discarded sword, grabbing it by the hilt and rolling twice. Patrice screamed, her speed sigil obviously depleted, and fell into the hole. Shade dove for her, reaching for her hand. Their fingers barely brushed before she disappeared entirely.

Scrambling to my feet, I hacked at my sister's cage. Her sword slashed through the enclosure, making a hole just big enough for her to wiggle through. "She's got Mayhem inside her," I said, and I grabbed Miles's dagger from the dirt. "Help me free Chaos."

We darted toward him, but with one final, guttural roar, he tore through his prison and stormed toward Chrys. He took three steps when a root jutted from the ground and pierced his chest. He stumbled and fell to his knees.

"No!" I screamed and rushed to my demon, clutching his shoulders, the rest of the fray fading into the background. Tears streamed down my cheeks, my stomach clenching, wrenching my heart down into it. I wasn't ready to let him go. "Please tell me you have multiple hearts that have to be pierced before you're vanquished."

Chaos groaned and pulled the root from his chest. "I have one, and he barely nicked it. That was a warning..." He snapped his head toward Chrys. "Which I will not heed."

"Have it your way," she said, and the ground exploded beneath Miles and Shade, sending them flying toward the outer wall. The moment their backs made impact, vines jutted out, wrapping around them and pinning them, their feet dangling four feet from the ground.

Ember rushed toward them, leaping over the fissure that had consumed Patrice. She hacked at the biggest root, splitting it apart. Three more grew in its place. "Damn hydras."

"This must stop, Mayhem." Chaos rose to his feet and stepped in front of me. "These witches are not the enemy."

"All witches are the enemy, and as soon as I'm finished enjoying this one's power, I will burn through her and kill her too." Chrys's eyes widened in alarm. She must've been scrambling to gain control, and for once, I wished she'd succeed.

"Standing tall or on your knees, in the name of the goddess, I force you to freeze!" I sent my magic out to Chrys, but effing Mayhem still had control. She flicked her wrist, and a wall of rocks jutted from the ground, stopping my spell in its tracks.

Ember pulled at the binds holding Shade and Miles, her hands engulfed in flames. Chrys snapped her fingers, and they tightened, squeezing the guys until they wheezed. I had no idea if Patrice was alive, but the way Shade's eyeballs bulged from their sockets said he wouldn't be much longer.

"Let them go!" Panic laced Ember's scream, turning it feral as she hacked and pulled, burned, and clawed at the roots killing our friends.

"Brother, stop." Chaos marched around the rock wall, his taloned fingers curled into fists, and I rushed to keep up.

"I warned you," Chrys said, and another root shot toward my demon's heart.

I swung the dagger with all my might, slicing through it before it reached its destination. Chaos knocked it aside and stood face-to-face with Chrys/Mayhem. I glanced at my arm. The speed and strength sigils faded away, leaving plain old *just* Ash behind.

And *just* Ash was all I needed. She always had been.

"Chrys, I know you're in there." I stepped in front of Chaos. "I can see it in your eyes. You have to find a way back to the surface. Take back control, and we can help you."

A sinister laugh erupted from her chest. "No witch can defeat Mayhem, Prince of Hell, destroyer—."

"Of armies and all who vex him. Yeah, I've heard that line before, and I'm not buying it." I crossed my arms. "Seems like the entire reason you're here is because a witch defeated you."

She growled and sent a root spiraling up my leg. I grabbed it with a burning hand, turning it to soot.

"Focus on your earth magic, Chrys. Cling to it, and let it propel you to the top. I had to do the same thing when Chaos took control of me."

Her eyes blinking rapidly, she let out a garbled groan. "This body...no longer belongs to the witch."

The ground trembled. The walls shook. The earth opened beneath my sister's feet. She clung to the vines that trapped Shade with one hand, swinging as the bottom dropped out from under her.

My head spun and my insides quivered as my heart took off in a sprint. "Come on, Chrys. You can do it. Take control."

"Give it to her, Mayhem," Chaos ordered, though I doubted his brother enjoyed being told what to do any more than he did.

"I won't." She clutched her head, her face scrunching in agony. Dragging her fingers down her cheeks, she thrashed from side to side. "This body is... This body is..."

I glanced at my sister. Her grip on the vine slipped, and she nearly let go.

"Drop your sword, Em," I shouted.

She held on by three fingers. Shade and Miles hung limp, their skin turning blue. Ember looked at her sword, her baby, and I swore to Hecate if she fell into oblivion because she refused to let it go, I would never forgive her.

"Aaahhh! This body is mine!" Chrys gasped, her eyes flying wide as she panted. "Shut up!" She spun and flailed, colliding with a shelf and sending a mess of two-by-fours clattering to the ground.

Ember huffed and released her sword, letting it fall into the abyss as she used both hands to drag herself up and get a foothold in the vines.

Chrys clutched the shelf, heaving breaths, fighting to maintain control. I searched in the core of my being for any vim I might have left and cast one last spell. "Standing tall or on your knees..." Ember joined me for the rest. "In the name of the goddess, we force you to freeze."

Our magic shot out, and, with Chrys finally in control, she wasn't fast enough to block it. She stilled, the look of panic in her eyes palpable. I remembered that feeling too well.

"How long will she remain bound?" Chaos placed his hand on my lower back, and I nearly jumped out of my skin. "Not long enough. Can you free them?" I shouted at my sister.

The roots and vines Chrys had summoned continued to squeeze the life out of the guys, as she had said would happen to me in New Orleans. Ember hauled a leg up to remove a knife from her boot, and she sawed through the one closest to Shade's throat. When it didn't multiply, she cut the one around his chest.

"One problem." She freed his arm. "There's no ground beneath us."

The crevice stretched seven feet wide and who knew how deep. She might have been able to crawl across the vines to the edge and make her escape, but the unconscious Miles and Shade wouldn't stand a chance.

"Can you reach Miles? Cut him some slack so he can breathe."

"I think so."

"What is your plan?" Chaos asked.

"First, we have to cast a containment ring around her in case Mayhem busts through the bind. Then, we're going to build a bridge."

My satchel lay abandoned a few yards away, so I grabbed it and pulled out my shaker of salt. Chrys's demonic grimoire held the incantation needed to trap a demon, and I opened right to the page. I pulled her away from the wall and poured a ring around her before scanning the words.

"Do you have enough vim for this?" Chaos asked.

"Sure don't. That's why I said *we* have to cast the circle." I slipped my hand into his.

"Demon magic can't be used to create a demon trap. My very nature will fight against it."

"And my very nature will counter yours. Have you forgotten we were meant to be together?"

"I could never forget. We are halves of the same whole." He squeezed my hand, sending a pulse of power into me.

My body electrified, my nerves hummed back to life with a blast of adrenaline that would keep a normal witch awake for days. I scanned the book one more time to be sure I had the words right, and I recited the Latin. Chaos's nature did try to fight back, but only for a moment. I channeled it into my being, turning it on its head and activating the circle like it was the easiest thing in the world. Honestly, it kind of was.

We broke contact, and I expected a wave of fatigue to crash into me like it had done in the past. But I felt fine when Chaos took back his magic. Even a bit energized. The bond I had with my demon kept growing and doing amazing things.

"Shade's not breathing," Ember shouted from across the room, spurring me into action.

"Grab those slats of wood." I pointed, and Chaos, still in demon form, scooped up twenty of them like they were toothpicks and carried them to the offending fissure.

Boy, oh boy, was that thing deep. I could see the bottom at least, but it must've gone twenty feet down. The guys would break their necks if we cut them free and let them fall.

"Patrice?" I yelled. "Are you still with us?"

"I'm here," her voice sounded tiny, but she was able to respond. Whew.

"How will you build a bridge with no nails or fasteners?" he asked.

"With physics." I began lining up the beams four across. I placed a perpendicular slat and then lay four more on top of it. Another perpendicular piece went across the center of those, and then four more. When I finished, I had an arched bridge that could easily stretch across the fissure...on one condition. "How far can you jump?"

Chaos chuckled and moved to one end of the bridge. We lifted it in unison, and I rushed forward as he leaped across with the grace of a panther. With the bridge in place, he tested its sturdiness. "You're quite clever."

"It happens when you read a lot."

He stood in the center of my creation, and Ember cut the rest of the vines holding Miles, dropping him into my demon's arms. He lay him on his back in the dirt before returning to the bridge to help down Shade.

My former nemesis's lips had gone white, the skin on his face pale blue. I checked for a pulse, but if he had one, it was too weak to detect. Tipping his head back, I pinched his nose and blew two deep breaths into his mouth. His chest rose and fell with my effort, but he didn't move.

"Come on. You can't make amends and then die on me." I clasped my hands over his chest and pumped his heart. When nothing happened, I gave him a few more breaths. Still nothing, so I pumped again. I breathed again, repeating the cycle three more times.

Miles moaned and rolled to his side. Ember found a rope in the mess Chrys had made of the space, and she and Chaos worked on retrieving Patrice.

Still, Shade didn't move. I checked for a pulse and again found nothing. My hand beneath his nose didn't pick up the slightest breath. "Listen to me, you goober. This can't be your final eff you. Wake. The. Hell. Up." I pumped his chest with each word and blew the biggest breath I could into his mouth.

He coughed. Then he sputtered and rolled to his side, gasping for air. A coughing fit racked his body, making him curl into the fetal position as he hacked and gasped, hacked and gasped.

I sat back on my butt in the dirt, my head spinning. When he could breathe normally again, he tried to sit up. I helped him get upright and rubbed his back.

"When I said I wasn't over you yet, I never dreamed it would make you kiss me." He smirked and laughed, which turned into another cough.

"Dream on." I slapped his shoulder and laughed before rising to my feet and dusting the dirt off my pants. "You okay, Miles?"

He took a deep breath and rubbed his chest. "I've been better, but I'll survive."

"We all will," Ember said, and I turned around to find Patrice sitting next to her on the ground.

I allowed myself to feel three seconds of relief before I gestured to Chrys. "She won't if we don't do something fast."

CHAPTER 17
ASH

"If your circle is as strong as the ones she cast, you can leave her be and let Mayhem take over her form." Chaos crossed his arms, eyeing the still-frozen Chrys in the circle. "She deserves worse."

"Nobody deserves to go through that, believe me." I patted his shoulder.

He jerked away, whirling toward me. "Have you forgotten everything she's done?"

I put my hands on my hips and raised my chin. No, I had not, but I wouldn't wish that on my greatest enemy, who, at the moment, happened to be the witch in question.

"We haven't forgotten." Ember paced around the circle. "Have you forgotten we're light witches? We don't kill people."

"On purpose," I added, which earned me an eye roll from my sister.

"Can you…" She gestured to his demonic junk hanging free since he'd torn through his clothes. "Ash might enjoy the view, but the rest of us do not."

"If I return to my human form, I will still be naked. Would you enjoy that view more?"

"Actually…" I opened my bag and pulled out the extra set of clothes I'd packed for him. "I had a feeling you might go full-demon."

He accepted the clothing, turned on his heel, and stormed away.

"Somebody's got his panties in a wad," Ember muttered.

"She has done some pretty bad things." I shrugged and zipped my bag.

"Whoa, Ash." She held up her hands. "Are you actually suggesting we do nothing and let Mayhem absorb her? Because, if so, we need to freeze you too. I won't let you turn dark."

Now it was my turn for an eye roll. "No, I'm not suggesting that. I just mean I can see where he's coming from. He's protective, and she hurt us all."

"We're performing an exorcism." Ember cocked a brow, challenging me to argue. "We need answers."

I crossed my arms. "Then we have to send someone home because we don't have the supplies to do it here. I didn't count on her possessing herself, or I would have brought the book with me."

Chaos returned to my side, in human form and fully clothed. "Thank you," he whispered, and I smiled.

"Can't we take her with us? It would be faster than a round trip." Patrice handed Shade the healing drink she'd been mixing.

I shook my head. "If we want her to survive, the exorcism has to happen in the place she was possessed."

"I can go get it," Miles said. "How long will the infantry be asleep outside?"

"At least another hour or two," Patrice said. "Are you sure you're up to it? You were unconscious for quite a while."

"I never stopped breathing." Miles clutched Shade's shoulder with brotherly affection, and Ember tossed him the keys. "Where's the book?"

"The cabinet in my studio," I said. "Bring the candles and salt with you too. It's all in there from..."

"Here." Patrice handed him a potion bottle. "Cast a shadow spell, just to be safe."

"Thanks." He turned and strode away.

"Are they all still lying in the churchyard?" I rummaged through my bag again and found two more binding potions.

"We dragged them around back and propped them against the building." Shade drained his cup and handed it back to Patrice. "Thanks for that."

She wiped it with a magic-neutralizing cloth. "It's what I do."

Ember nodded at the vials. "Are those the freezing potions? I've got enough vim for one more spell. Maybe two, but that would leave you on your own for the exorcism. We need Patrice to save her vim in case healing is required."

Shade lifted his hands in a WTF gesture. "She won't be alone. I'm still here."

Ember cut her gaze between us. "I'm not used to you two playing nicely together. Sure you're up to it?"

He stretched his neck and rolled his shoulders. "Good as new. Patrice is a goddess-send."

Our healer's cheeks flushed pink. "I'm glad I can help, but when this is through, I'd like to go back to the sanctity of my kitchen and stay there."

"Amen, sister." I gave her a high-five.

Chrys's fingers twitched, and Ember dumped a bottle of binding potion on her before reciting the incantation.

"If she's in a containment circle, why do you have to keep her frozen?" Shade asked.

"The spell freezes him inside her too," Chaos said. "It's the only thing that kept me from destroying Ash when our situation was dire."

Shade laughed dryly. "Damn."

"Indeed." My demon rested his hand on my back. "If you break the summoning circle, I will retrieve my brother's skull."

"I'll get it." Ember scooped up the skull and gasped. "I can feel his energy." She used her teeth to pull her sleeves over her hands, breaking the skin-to-skull contact. "He feels different than Chaos."

"He's a different demon," I said. "Do you think the rest of her minions gave up?"

"It sounded like they were already losing faith in her." Ember set the skull on the table and rubbed her palms on her pants. "They probably decided to cut their losses and pretend it never happened. That's what I'd do if I joined a failed coup."

Half an hour and one last binding spell later, Miles returned with my supplies and laid them out on the table.

Shade grabbed a candle and the exorcism book. "You didn't really have a stomach bug that day. This is what you had to clean up, isn't it?"

"Yep." I took the book and opened it to the containment spell. The one I'd cast around Chrys wouldn't be nearly strong enough once we released Mayhem. "Set the candles at the five points of the pentagram. We need to make this one stronger than we've ever done before."

I poured a second ring of salt around Chrys and sent a controlled flame to each candle.

Shade and Patrice looked at me in wonder. "How?" she asked.

I waved off her question. "My magic was bound. I'll tell you about it later."

"And you?" she asked Miles. "The energy balls you can create...that's new."

He lowered his gaze, his shoulders rising toward his ears. "Chrys drew it out of me. She made me swear not to tell anyone until I'd perfected it."

"That tracks." I shook my head. Our former friend was a master manipulator.

Chrys's hands curled and splayed. A moan emanated from her throat.

"She's coming to. Hurry." I grabbed Shade's and Chaos's

hands while Ember held the book out for us to read. Chaos sent a rush of demon magic into me, setting my nerves ablaze. I massaged it, softening it before opening up and sending some into Shade.

He gasped, shuddering before straightening his spine, and we read the incantation in unison, activating the stronger circle without a nanosecond to spare.

Chrys jolted upright, her eyes wild as she clutched her head. "You have to help me."

"We're trying to." I grabbed the skull, ready to toss it into the circle, but I paused. "Hold on."

"Release me!" Mayhem shouted through Chrys, scrambling to her feet. Her shoulder slammed against the invisible wall, making the magic shimmer.

"Not a chance." Ember clutched a dagger in each hand. "Put the skull in the circle, sis."

"I don't think I should." I returned it to the table.

Chaos jerked his head toward me, glowering. "If you exorcise him without it, he will not be able to reform. You'll have to vanquish him to his prison in Hell."

"You wouldn't dare," Chrys growled. "Brother, stop them."

Chaos looked at Chrys and then at me, his expression softening. "What is your plan?"

"He's not a happy camper, and whether we exorcise him with his skull or he burns through Chrys, he doesn't owe us a thing because we didn't free him." I drummed my fingers on top of the skull. "We need some kind of leverage."

My demon straightened his spine. "You have me."

"And he's listened to you fabulously so far." Ember

sheathed one dagger, clutching the other tightly. "Ash is right. I don't know what Chrys did to keep the mundane away from this church, but they'll be back eventually. If we let him reform here, we'll have to deal with transporting him back to the house."

"Chaos!" Chrys roared before her eyes widened and she clawed at her face. "Do it. Do whatever you have to do. Just get him out of my head."

He gazed into my eyes, and a full five seconds passed before he nodded. "Agreed." He turned to Chrys. "We will call you back, brother. Have patience."

"Patience?" Chrys's voice grew garbled. "What have these witches done to you? Kill them. Kill them and set me free." She slammed her fists against the circle, and the magic pulsed. The dark brown of her irises rippled with purple. Her nails broke the skin, drawing bloody claw marks down her cheeks.

"It's now or never." I grabbed my demon's hand. "Get ready to pull her out, Em."

Patrice rushed to the table to mix a healing potion while Shade held the book in front of me.

"What can I do?" Miles asked.

"How well can you pronounce Latin?" I held my hand toward him, and he took it.

"Don't let them do this! Yes. Yes, they have to!" Chrys alternated with Mayhem, her fists clenched, every muscle in her body straining.

Miles and I read the words.

"No!" she shouted. "I'll make you a deal."

"Don't take it," Chaos said.

"Didn't plan to." I squeezed Miles's hand, and we read the incantation again. On the third refrain, the walls shook. Chrys gasped and doubled over. A deafening pop resounded from somewhere inside her, and the tendons in her neck protruded until I thought they'd rip through her skin.

She stood upright, her mouth agape as she threw her head back and let out a blood-curdling scream. Purple smoke poured from her mouth and nose. She wheezed another breath, and more smoke rushed out with her exhale. Her third breath was clean, so Ember grabbed her arm and yanked her out of the circle.

The smoke billowed inside the ring, spiraling upward before crashing into the wall. The magic pulsed. Then it cracked.

Oh, shit. Crappity crap. "Why is he still here?"

"You must vanquish him," Chaos said matter-of-factly, as if that was a detail I should have already known. "If he breaks free, he will possess another person."

"You could have told me that ahead of time." I grabbed the book from Shade.

"I believe I did." Ever the helpful demon he was.

I took a deep breath and centered myself, willing my pulse and my breathing to slow before I passed out. Focusing my intention on a vanquishing spell, I flipped through the pages. "Here." I shoved the book into Shade's arms and took Chaos's and Miles's hands once more.

We recited the incantation. Nothing happened. Mayhem billowed, gathering his smoke into a ball and straining against the magic wall. Another crack.

We said the words three more times, and still nothing happened.

Chaos peered at the book. "I believe the third word is pronounced with a long E."

"Now you tell me."

Three more cracks formed in the magic. The biggest fissure began to split, a tiny stream of Mayhem smoke seeping through.

We tried the incantation again, hoping to Hecate we pronounced everything right this time. Mayhem continued seeping through the circle. The second recitation didn't help. Smoke spiraled upward, circling above Ember's head. She had no clue what was happening. She and Patrice continued attempting to revive Chrys, oblivious to the danger of our battle.

"Oh, hell no. Not my sister." I squeezed Chaos's hand, and he sent another ginormous pulse of magic into me. I shared it with Miles, and we recited the words a third time, giving it everything we had.

The smoke froze. Then it crackled. The once-billowy essence of Mayhem turned to thin shards of glass. A visible rift tore open inside the circle, sucking his rigid form through, but the part of him outside the wall slammed against the magic, unable to pass.

"Watch out." I raced to the containment ring and dropped to the ground, skidding across it like I was sliding into home base. My boot broke the circle, and the rest of Mayhem disappeared through the rift before it slammed shut, holding him on the other side.

"Holy Hecate." I flopped onto my back and panted. "Is he gone?"

Chaos stood over me. "He is, and he won't be happy when he returns. With any of us."

I waved off his words and dropped my arm on the floor. "That's a problem for tomorrow."

"Wake up," Ember said, and Chrys wheezed.

I rolled to my stomach to find everyone but Chaos kneeling around her. My demon offered his hand, and I let him tug me to my feet before I sagged in his arms. He helped me walk to the team and held me as I peered at our once-powerful adversary. Our once-friend.

Her lids fluttered, her head rolling from side to side. She opened her mouth, and a whisper crossed her lips.

"What did she say?" I wrapped my arms around Chaos, letting his warm, strong embrace envelope me.

"I can't hear her." Ember patted her cheek gently. "Chrys, what are you trying to say?"

"I..." Chrys squeezed her eyes shut as if speaking pained her. "I had...no choice."

Ember sat back on her heels. "Oh you definitely did, and you made the wrong one."

"No." Her voice was breathy, barely audible. "I had to." Her face relaxed, her body going limp.

Miles brought a hand to his lips. "Is she...?"

Patrice pressed two fingers to her neck and then her wrist. She held her hand beneath Chrys's nose and shook her head. "She's gone."

A collective sigh rushed out of us all, and we stood there,

saying nothing, doing nothing, for several minutes. We had neutralized the threat. We had the skull and the sigils, and we could finally move forward with our attempt to lift my curse. I had unlocked my magic and fallen in love. We had won.

So, why did it feel so much like we'd lost?

Chaos cleared his throat, breaking the silence. "We need to leave before the mundane come back. Shall I cremate her?"

"No." I wiped the mist from my eyes. "She was our friend. We'll give the body to her mom."

Ember sniffled. "That's the right thing to do. Gather your stuff, and let's head to the van. Cloak us, Shade."

Chaos cradled Chrys in his arms and carried her as we made our way through the labyrinth of tunnels to the ground floor. Mayhem's skull rested inside my satchel, and no one spoke on the fifteen-minute ride home.

We left her body in the basement—Patrice casting a preservation spell on her remains until her mother could retrieve her —and made our way upstairs. It would take time to process everything we'd won and all we had lost, but the energy in the house already felt lighter.

Ember opened the fridge and handed a beer to each of us. "To bittersweet endings. May Chrys finally find peace." We clinked our bottles in a toast, and I took a long pull from mine. The effervescent bubbles cooled me on their way down, reminding me that we were still very much alive, and our quest had barely begun.

"She said she had no choice." I laced my fingers with Chaos's. "What do you think she meant?"

"Rantings of a madwoman." Shade took a drink. "Mayhem nearly had her; I'm sure he scrambled her brain."

"Indeed," Chaos said. "He was moments away from overcoming her. Even if she had survived, she would not have been herself. I'm surprised she spoke at all."

"What do we do now?" Patrice asked.

"Now we rest," Ember said. "Recharge, recover, live to fight another day."

"I'll drink to that." Miles clinked his bottle to hers.

We finished our beer, and everyone headed to their respective bedrooms. I set my satchel on the dresser, but Chaos opened a drawer and slipped it inside.

"Don't want him watching us sleep?" I rose onto my toes and pressed a kiss to his lips.

"Not really." He slid his arms around me, holding me tightly. "I'd rather have one last night alone with my little witch."

I leaned back to look into his eyes. "This won't be our last night. We'll figure something out."

"We will try our best." He kissed my forehead, lingering there as he inhaled. "Right now…"

"Is all that matters." I angled my head up to brush his lips with mine.

He smiled, though it didn't reach his eyes. "I can't promise you the *happy ever after* you deserve."

I rested my hands on his shoulders, looking at him with all the sincerity I felt in every fiber of my being. "I'll settle for *happy for now.*"

He shook his head. "It's so much more than now. I will be by your side until the bitter end."

"Okay." I cupped his cheek in my hand, and he nuzzled into it. "How about *happy until the inevitable?*"

The corners of his eyes crinkled as he curved his lips. "*Happy until the inevitable.* That, I can promise."

The saga continues in Mayhem and Ember...

ALSO BY CARRIE PULKINEN

Fire Witches of Salem Series

Chaos and Ash

Commanding Chaos

Claiming Chaos

Mayhem and Ember

Mending Mayhem

Mastering Mayhem

New Orleans Nocturnes Series

License to Bite

Shift Happens

Life's a Witch

Santa Got Run Over by a Vampire

Finders Reapers

Swipe Right to Bite

Batshift Crazy

Collection One: Books 1-3

Collection Two: Books 4 - 7

Crescent City Wolf Pack Series

Werewolves Only

Beneath a Blue Moon

Bound by Blood

A Deal with Death

A Song to Remember

Shifting Fate

Collection One: Books 1-3

Collection Two: Books 4-6

Haunted Ever After Series

Love at First Haunt

Second Chance Spirit

Third Time's a Ghost

Love and Ghosts

Love and Omens

Love and Curses

Collection One: Books 1 - 3

Collection Two: Books 4 - 6

Stand Alone Books

Flipping the Bird

Sign Steal Deliver

Azrael

Lilith

The Rest of Forever

Soul Catchers

Bewitching the Vampire

About the Author

Carrie Pulkinen is a paranormal romance author who has always been fascinated with things that go bump in the night. Of course, when you grow up next door to a cemetery, the dead (and the undead) are hard to ignore. Pair that with her passion for writing and her love of a good happily-ever-after, and becoming a paranormal romance author seems like the only logical career choice.

Before she decided to turn her love of the written word into a career, Carrie spent the first part of her professional life as a high school journalism and yearbook teacher. She loves good chocolate and bad puns, and in her free time, she likes to read, drink wine, and travel with her family.

Connect with Carrie online:
CarriePulkinen.com